Though I Walk Sequel: From the Valley to the Mountaintop: Book Two of the Prescott Family Chronicles

Sheri Dean Parmelee
October 2024

ISBN: 979-8-218-53276-5

Cover design by Roger J. Rome
Inside design by Derecho Cat Media LLC. derechocatmedia.com

Special thanks

I would like to thank the following people for their assistance and expertise with the technical details of this manuscript: Nancy Dean, Sue Barbera, and Marti Skogebo for their support. Special thanks go out to Barbara Horstemeyer, my first editor. Additional special thanks to Alisa Jacinto, who also edited the manuscript. You ladies are the best!

This book is dedicated to adopted children who struggle to know who they are.

Prologue

"My mommy died two days ago." Ten-year-old Kurt Prescott stopped and wiped away a tear as he wrote in the journal his teacher had given him the day before. "Daddy and Mommy had been drinking and were fighting again after dinner. They always fight a lot. Sometimes Daddy hits Mommy. I ran upstairs to my bedroom and jumped into bed. I covered my head with my blankets, but I could still hear them. Then the kitchen door opened and slammed shut. I peaked outside, looking through the blinds on my bedroom window. I scrunched down reel small so that no one could see me watching. Mommy walked towards the creek. She was drunk and it was dark out- why would she go outside like that?

"I saw somebody big come up and talk to her. I think it was a man, but I'm not sure. The moon was pretty brite, but we don't have any outside lights, so I couldn't see very well. The man grabbed Mommy's arm. They might have been fighting, but I couldn't hear what they were saying. They walked around the bend, so I couldn't see them no more.

"I got real tired and felled asleep. Daddy pulled me out of bed in the midle of the night and told me to come downstairs with him. Peter and Candy were setting at the kitchen table, waiting for us. Nobody said nothing. My pajama bottoms were wet around the ankles and I didn't know why. I didn't want Peter to tease me, so I didn't tell anyone.

"Daddy said that Mommy was gone. That she had left. We weren't 'posed to tell nobody that they had been fighting that night. We weren't 'posed to say anything at all 'cept that our parents loved each other and we had all been home watching TV all evening. Daddy said that if we told anyone what had happened, we would be in big trouble and that he would bring out the strap. The big one.

"Peter, Candy, and me told him that we wouldn't say nothing he didn't want us to, but he kept us in the kitchen for a really long time. I think it was a couple of hours. I was so tired that I almost felled asleep a couple of times, but he yelled at me and woke me up. Finally, he let us go back to bed. I went upstairs and changed my pajama bottoms, but my bed was wet where my feet had been, so it was real nasty and hard to get back to sleep.

"The next morning, a couple of policemen ranged the doorbell. They said that Mommy's body had been found in the creek. She fell into the creek, hitted her head, and drownded. Daddy acted real surprised. Peter and Candy and I cried and told them what Daddy told us to say. I'm real sad. I'm ten years old and my mommy is dead. Her funeral is tomorrow. I guess she's never coming back."

Chapter 1

A whole year had passed since Susan Prescott's husband Kurt and his mistress Kelsey DeLuca had died in the mid-February, horrific car accident near BWI airport. It had also taken the lives of their two small daughters, Cassie and Christine. After all Kurt had put Susan through in their thirty-six years of marriage, it had been a total shock to learn that Kelsey, right before she died, had left Susan her entire estate, valued at five million dollars.

Susan had been living with her daughter Brooke for the past year. Previously, Kurt had sold the house she and Kurt owned, during Susan's six-month coma. The proceeds from the sale of their marital home west of Annapolis had gone to feather the nest he had built with Kelsey. Kurt had caused the car accident that plunged Susan into the coma. He had been chagrined when Susan regained consciousness. She had recuperated for several months in a nursing home. Yet, Kurt was dead, and had been for a year and a half.

Susan had spent six months in an imagined life as Princess Victoria Susan Anne. Susan thought of that fake life many times; it had been nice to be a much-loved, wealthy princess. She had quite a wake-up call when she came out of the coma and had to face her now-deceased husband's ire. He had wanted Susan dead, and he almost succeeded in fulfilling that desire. Instead, Kurt, Kelsey, and their two small daughters were gone. Susan shuddered, remembering how the couple's daughters, Cassie and Christine, had died in her arms. Such a waste.

      Since her recovery, Susan had cast around for the right job. She needed some source of income while she waited for the money she had inherited from Kelsey to become available. After looking around for several weeks, Susan took a job as a receptionist in a medical office. Being in her mid-50s, she couldn't see the point of going back to nursing school to update her skills. Happily, the full time job gave her spending money and medical insurance, relieving Brooke and her brothers Joshua and Christopher of a financial burden.

      Susan came home from work and went for a four-mile run. It was a lovely March afternoon; it had been a bit cool that morning. Things had cooled down some more, thanks to an early afternoon rainstorm. At least it hadn't been cold enough for snow. Things could be pretty iffy in the Annapolis area in early March. The run was quite pleasant. After a quick shower, she changed into casual but nice clothes, and took a critical look at her white hair. Even though her family had called her a Jaclyn Smith look-a-like for many years, the totally white hair Susan now had no longer made the resemblance quite so strong. That was fine with her. Now she looked like herself. She didn't have to depend on her resemblance to a famous actress to form her identity. She touched up her makeup, winked at her appearance, and headed downstairs to wait for her daughter Brooke.

      Susan fixed their dinner that beautiful evening, humming as she put a meatloaf and some veggies on to cook. Michael Bench, the nursing supervisor who was with Susan at the rehab center when she woke up from the coma was coming for dinner. He had become a very dear friend. Susan heard

Brooke's car pull into the garage.

"Hi Mom," Brooke said as she walked into her condo. "How was your day?"

"Just fine, sweetie. The standard colds and sports physicals. A couple of kids came in with temps. The usual. I hope you had a nice day, too." Susan hugged Brooke as she came around the kitchen island.

"Yep, we've got some interesting cases at the firm right now, and I'm getting pretty active in the research around them," Brooke, a paralegal at a major law firm in Annapolis, told her mom. Brooke picked up a carrot stick from the bowl Susan had placed on the island and took a bite. "Yummy."

"Good for you." Susan checked her watch. "What time will Michael be here?"

"I think he said six, which gives me enough time to head upstairs and put on something more casual than this black business pantsuit. I can't wait to get into my sneakers. These heels wear me out," Brooke told Susan.

"I'm glad I get to wear tennis shoes to work, even though they're white and not even remotely stylish!"

"Mom, we all know that these heels are why they pay me the big bucks, like you always say!" Brooke smiled, took another carrot stick, and gave her mom a quick kiss on the check on her way upstairs. "BRB."

"SYS," Susan replied. How in the world did conversation devolve into a bunch of initials? Surely "be right back" and "see you soon" weren't too hard for anyone to actually come right out and say! Goodness, gracious. The world today! Susan crunched on a carrot, as well.

Moments later, Brooke returned in casual jeans and a nice T-shirt, her long brown hair tied up in a ponytail. She looked like a teenager, her attire and hairstyle belying the fact that Brooke was in her mid-thirties.

"In my time, a young lady got dressed up when a young man came to call, Missy," Susan told Brooke.

Brooke's peaches and cream complexion reddened as she blushed. "Mom, Michael isn't coming to call..."

"Then I don't know what you'd call it; if he doesn't have intentions, it would be a huge surprise to me." Susan grinned. "He comes to dinner a couple of times a week, takes us both out for a lovely evening once a week, and stops by frequently just to chat. Right, Brooke, Michael has no intentions. Not!"

"Mom, we've been over that before. Michael and I are just really good friends."

"Brooke, my dear, you must be blind as a bat. We need to get you some glasses."

The ladies laughed, enjoying each other's company. Brooke went into the dining room to set the table while Susan finished cooking. Precisely at the stroke of six, the doorbell rang. Brooke ran to the door, followed closely by Susan. They welcomed the jeans-clad Michael inside. Susan smiled broadly as she noticed the huge bouquet of flowers the young African American man had in his hands.

"Evening, ladies," Michael said as he stepped into the foyer. He gave them each a peck on the cheek as he handed the bouquet to Susan. "Thank you, dear Susan, for giving birth to this lovely lady." He smiled at Brooke.

"Michael, you certainly know the way to a mother's heart," Susan told him as she accepted the gorgeous bouquet. She took the flowers into the kitchen to put them in a vase, giving the young people a little privacy. Susan heard Brooke's laughter and the deep rumble of Michael's voice as she prepared the flowers for display on the table. That Michael was a keeper!

They had a wonderful dinner, with some delightful and lively conversation. Then Michael grew quiet and signaled he had something to say.

"Dear Brooke, I have watched you show unconditional love to your mother through her times of great struggle. We've known each other for about two years now. I haven't wanted to rush you, but I wonder if you will do me the honor of allowing me to court you?" He bowed at Brooke, teasing her.

Brooke looked at Michael, then at Susan who was openly grinning, and back again at Michael. "Michael, I'm not given to speech making. Yes, I will allow you to court me." She bowed back, enjoying the fun. She turned to her mother. "You okay with that, Mom?"

Susan laughed and said, "It's about time!"

Chapter 2

Joshua Adam Prescott, Dr. Prescott that is, was sitting in his home office that Sunday night, looking over his schedule for the coming week. His thoughts drifted over the past year, since his adoptive father had died. Kurt had been a difficult man, not one given to warm hugs and happy conversations with his sons. Shoot, his father hadn't been a touchy-feely kinda guy to anyone. What he was good at was manipulating people. He totally screwed with my head. I was convinced that Mom was the bad guy in the family. Guess I was so eager to please Dad that I treated Mom pretty rotten, always believing everything he told me about her. Sheesh. He shook his head, combing back his slightly graying hair with his fingers. I'm glad she's forgiven me.

I wonder what my real dad, my birth father, was like. Guess he's not much better than Kurt. I mean the guy never showed up my entire life. Never contributed a dime to my support, from what Dad, I mean Kurt, told me more than once. Of course, Kurt wouldn't have exactly gotten out the welcome mat for the dude. I only asked Mom one time about my birth father and look what happened then. I buried it for so many years, but now I remember it like it was yesterday. Amazing how things flood back, now that Kurt's gone. Joshua let his mind drift back to that day in Connecticut.

I must have been about eight or nine at the time. Kurt had just adopted me the year before. Mom was in the kitchen getting dinner ready. I walked in after playing outside. I had been talking to that girl from down the block. What was her name? Angie, I think. She was talking about being adopted and how her birth parents had an open adoption. She didn't see her birth parents very often, maybe twice a year, but they sent her birthday presents and other stuff every once in a while. I told her that I was adopted and she asked me about my dad. I told her I didn't know anything about him. She said I ought to ask. Big mistake.

I came in from playing with Angie right before dinner, and asked Mom, "What was my birth father like?" and "Where does he live?" when Dad walked in from work. Boy, did he get mad.

Dad asked, "What's going on here?"

Mom answered," Oh, Kurt, dear. I didn't hear you come in. Joshua was just asking..."

"I heard him. How dare he ask about some guy who never gives him the time of day?" Dad's face turned beet red, He turned to me and said, "Get this straight. I pay for your food, clothing, and housing." He started punching me in the chest with his fist as he walked me backwards. "I'm the one who is here for you, day and night. That bum never contributed a dime to your support and doesn't give a wit for you. Got that? I'm your father. Don't you dare ever ask who your father is again. My name is on your birth certificate. I gave you my name. I am your father."

By this time, my back was against the kitchen counter, and I was being pressed into the countertop. Joshua cringed, even now, in the memory of what had come next. Dad picked up

7

a bar of soap and pushed it between my teeth. It tasted terrible. I gagged and almost threw up right then.

Dad yelled, "I'll wash those dirty words right out of your mouth. Don't you ever speak of that man again." He pulled the soap out of my mouth and said, "I hope you enjoyed the soap because that's the only dinner you'll get tonight." He looked at Mom. "Wash out his mouth, woman, and send him straight to his room." Kurt shrugged his shoulders. "Then get back in here pronto and get my dinner on the table. Your man is hungry." Kurt had swaggered out of the room.

Mom came over to me, crying. "I'm so sorry, sweetheart. I'm so very sorry." She hugged me. "Come on, honey, let's get you taken care of. I'm so very sorry."

At the thought of what came next, Joshua felt his stomach constrict as if it had been minutes, instead of years, ago. Sweat formed on his forehead as he sat in his home office. How could I have forgotten all this? He reflected for a moment. Then, the memories of that day returned in full force. What had happened next? Oh, yeah. I remember Mom took me to the bathroom and ran water in my mouth. I gagged a couple of times. I thought I was going to lose whatever was in my stomach, right then and there. After Mom got me rinsed out, I went into my bedroom and cried into my pillow. I had to be quiet or Kurt would hear and get madder. I never asked again, from that day to this. Joshua shook his head in disbelief of the memories that haunted him even now.

Joshua straightened up. Man, those memories were so bad. How did I keep them buried in the back of my mind so long? It was traumatic to even think about it now. But Kurt's gone and buried, or cremated, actually. He can't hurt me anymore. Joshua rubbed his chin, and then his face. Maybe she's ready to tell me. Maybe I'm ready to ask again. He hesitated for a minute. I'm relieved that there's no blood between Kurt Prescott and me. What a rotten person that man was. I always pictured my birth father as just the opposite- kind, strong, thoughtful. . . Hopefully, he's not a clone of Kurt. Joshua picked up the phone, took a deep breath, and called his mother.

Susan picked up on the second ring. "Hi, Joshua. What's up?"

"Hey Mom. Say, I was wondering if maybe we could get together sometime this week. What's your schedule like?" He drummed his fingers on his desk, waiting.

"Let me have a look-see at my calendar. Hum...How about tomorrow night? Thursday night would also work. I have the Widow's Life group on Tuesday night and choir on Wednesday," Susan told him.

"Umm... tomorrow night would work pretty well for me. Can I take you to dinner? Just you and me?" Joshua asked. He gulped, suddenly nervous. What if his birth father was a real jerk? Worse than Kurt?

"Sure thing, honey. Is something wrong or is this just a mom-and-son night out?" Susan was obviously curious.

"Uh... I've been thinking about some things lately and I just wanted to ask you about them. It's been a while since Dad died, and I . . . just had some questions to ask you that I couldn't ask while he was still around. I figure, now's as good a time as any. Is that okay?"

"Absolutely, honey. There have been too many secrets for too long. I'll be happy to answer anything you want to ask." She thought for a minute. "It's a good idea, Josh. It'll help us both heal. I'm glad you thought of it," Susan told him.

"Good. Okay, well, I'll see you tomorrow night at about

six. Does that time work for you?" He picked up his pen to mark his calendar. He'd have to tell Amanda he wouldn't be home for dinner, but she wouldn't mind. His wife had been encouraging him to get things out in the open for some time now. Maybe he could persuade Amanda to have a pizza night with the kids. Pizza was a family favorite.

Susan hesitated. "Yes, that's fine. But I wonder, instead of going out, could I just fix us something here? Brooke and Michael are going to a dinner for her law firm. I was just thinking, we could talk more freely here than in a restaurant."

"Sure, Mom, if you want. Maybe we could go out for ice cream after dinner."

"Sounds like a plan. I'll see you at six, with bells on."

"Mom, I've never understood how that expression got to be popular back in the day, but I'll see you at six tomorrow. Dressing up isn't necessary. Love you."

"Love you back, sweetie."

Joshua hung up and took a deep breath. Now if he only had the courage to ask the questions that had been on his mind for his entire life.

***

Susan hung up the phone and sunk deep into the cushions of Brooke's comfy living room couch. She knew in her heart that it was finally time to tell Joshua about his biological father. She was just guessing that the topic was what Joshua wanted to talk about. They'd never been able to talk about it since that horrible blowup by Kurt when Joshua had asked about his birth father as young boy. She sighed and went into the kitchen for some hot tea to calm her nerves. She perched on the stool next to the kitchen island and stirred the sugar into her cup. Yes, it was time. She would tell Joshua first, and then

10

call a family meeting so that everyone would hear it from her, firsthand. Joshua's two young sons didn't need to know yet, but they would be easily entertained by the computer games she bought especially for times like this when they needed to be with the family, but not necessarily in the same room. Joshua's two teenaged daughters might take her experience as a warning to guard their own hearts and bodies. She would clear the idea with Joshua first, but she felt pretty sure he would approve. Yes, it was time.

***

Joshua pulled up to Brooke's condo exactly at six the next evening. Deep breath, fella. Mom will make this easy, he felt certain. Well, maybe not easy, but easier, he knew. What if she refused to tell him? No, that would be out of character for Mom. His heart was racing. Calm down, Joshua. It's just your mother. He walked up the steps to the front door and rang the bell.

***

Susan was watching out the front window. She had arrived home from work a short time before and had made a hurried dinner. She opened the door to her oldest son's ring and welcomed him inside.

"Hi, Joshua." She hugged him.

"Hey, Mom." He returned the hug and then shifted on his feet.

She realized he was a bit nervous; she was, too. She was anxious about what she would have to confess. She knew why Joshua was here: Dan. That had to be the reason, so let's get right to the point. "I'm glad you're here, honey. We have about two hours before Brooke will be back. Do you want to nibble on some crackers and cheese and talk first, or have dinner and chat after?" Susan, slow down, girlfriend. Can't you see he's uneasy, too?

"Uh, well, I..." Joshua stammered.

"Dinner will hold, and I don't mind," Susan told him.

"I guess, talk first, then,'" Joshua told her. He swallowed hard.

"Come on into the living room and have a seat," Susan smiled at Joshua, trying to put him at ease. They sat on the couch, not on opposite ends, but comfortably close. She leaned towards him and took his hand.

***

Joshua wasn't sure how to start this. Come on, Josh. You're a grown man, a doctor for Pete's sake, and this is your mother. He took a deep breath and started in.

"Mom, you know how Dad, I mean Kurt was . . . difficult that one time when we lived in Connecticut, and I asked about . . . my biological father."

"Yes, honey. I've thought about that quite a bit since Kurt died." She stroked his hand gently. "It was one of the worst days of my life."

"I had buried it, Mom. I just realized in the last, oh, I don't know, maybe two weeks or so, that I never asked about my real father. It finally came back to me why that was."

"I had buried a lot of things myself, Joshua. It was easier, or maybe just safer, not to remember." She squeezed the hand she still held.

Joshua felt smaller than usual, somehow. "Mom, do you remember what happened that day?" He knew the look on his face was filled with the pain he felt at the memory.

A lump formed in Susan's throat. "With Kurt backing you into the sink and then putting the bar of soap in your mouth? Yes, I remember." Tears overflowed Susan's eyes. "I never kept soap there again, after that day. I always kept it under the counter. I told Kurt that the house looked neater that way, but I really wanted to keep it out of sight, to keep him from doing it again."

"Mom, why didn't we escape from him then? Why didn't you divorce him?" Joshua asked as Susan began to cry in earnest then, the tears streaming down her face. "Oh, I'm sorry, Mom. I didn't mean to upset you. That isn't even what I wanted to talk to you about." He moved towards her and took his mother in his arms. "Please don't cry."

***

Susan worked to regain her composure, wanting Joshua to be able to ask what was on his mind. She wanted the healing process to not be blocked by emotional issues. She wiped her tears and straightened up, while remaining in his embrace. "I'm sorry, honey. I felt trapped by my past and had no one except Kurt and you kids. Kurt had effectively isolated me from my family. I didn't have any friends. Everyone we knew were his friends, not mine. No one really knew me, except Kurt and my parents, and they lived far away. I didn't have any current job skills. I couldn't have supported the three of you. Staying and trying to keep the peace seemed like the only thing I could do."

***

Joshua looked at her. "I understand, Mom." Having kids himself, he understood the deep desire to make sure his children were provided for. "I'm sorry to have upset you, Mom.

13

I know now what a manipulative, controlling person Kurt was. That must have been really difficult for you." He hesitated. "Mom, what I really wanted to talk about is . . . who is my biological father? I mean, we avoided the subject when I was growing up, and I'd really like to know about him." He paused. "It's not that I have any inherited disease and need medical information," he said quickly. "It's just that I really want to know who he is."

"Yes, honey, I figured that when you called." She sighed deeply. "It's time, way past time, actually, for you to know the truth."

"Is he a deadbeat? He never called, never acknowledged me, as far as I know. What does he do for a living? Why has he stayed away?" Joshua paused, bearing the heavy weight of the next question pressing heavily on him, almost suffocating him. "Why did he give me up for adoption?" Joshua, calm down, fellow, just breathe. "Why didn't he want me?" Hold on, dude. Don't try to find out everything at once. You don't ask forty years of questions in two minutes.

Susan sobbed. "Joshua, honey, I'm sorry you had to carry these questions, unanswered, your entire life. You deserve to know the truth. Let me tell you my story."

***

Susan thought for a moment. Susan moved out of Joshua's arms, to think more clearly. Joshua was the spitting image of her first love, Daniel Walsh. She was embarrassed for what she would have to confess: That she had been barely seventeen when she delivered Joshua in secret. She sighed deeply.

Then, she shared with Joshua the story of the deepest

14

love of her life. While it had been one of the happiest times of her life, their breakup had been the most difficult thing she had ever had to do. It tore at her heart, just to think of what had happened. The notion that a 16-year-old had to go through what she had experienced still brought tears to her eyes.

"Joshua, your father and I were high school sweethearts. We had known each other since middle school, when his father had transferred from Ohio to Annapolis. Right before high school, his father was moved to another corporate office, this time in Florida. But in our junior year, his dad was moved back to Annapolis. I met up with Dan in the hallway on his first day at Annapolis High School. We had a couple of classes together and started dating."

Susan thought for a minute, trying to decide how to phrase what had happened next. "Dan and I spent a lot of time together and I became . . . pregnant. It was a time when 'nice girls' didn't do that kind of thing. I was only sixteen, just barely seventeen by the time you were born. My parents insisted that I break up with Dan, so that folks wouldn't talk. I loved him too much to ruin his reputation. His father was transferred again, before my pregnancy showed. Or was it a new job?" She sighed. "I can't remember." She hesitated. "I never told Dan about you. I never heard from Dan again." She considered her words. "I couldn't continue dating him or even think about marrying him, not to give him any kind of a future. He couldn't be saddled with a pregnant teenaged wife. He needed to go to college and have a real chance at life. I loved him too much to hold him back."

"So, you weren't married to him?" Joshua looked shocked.

"No, honey." Susan hung her head in shame. "I wasn't

15

married when I had you, in spite of the stories I told you when you were a little boy, before Kurt and I got married, that your father and I were divorced. By saying that I had been married, I was trying to protect both of us from gossip."

"So, all these years, you lied to me?" Joshua seemed stunned.

"Yes, Joshua. I didn't mean to tell you . . . something that was untruthful, but I didn't want you to think less of yourself . . . or for anyone to find out," Susan stammered. Her heart broke, having not realized how profoundly this would affect Joshua. Oh, if only she had realized that this would hurt him so badly. That was never her desire. "I'm so ashamed. I'm so sorry. This is the only thing I have ever lied to you about, Joshua." She hung her head.

"I'm . . . illegitimate? Fatherless?" Joshua shook his head, and then looked at her.

She looked back at Joshua, firm in her resolve. "You were a much-loved child. Your grandparents, my folks that is, loved you unconditionally. I loved you. I still do. I never regretted having you, even though I wish the circumstances had been different." Susan reclined back on the couch, and then leaned forward. "Honey, please forgive me. I never meant to hurt you. I love you dearly, and I loved your father, Dan that is."

Joshua sat, silent, for the moment.

Susan took his hand. "Your birth father, at least when I knew him, was an incredible man. He was kindhearted, intelligent, handsome . . . I can't even think of all the good things about him. He was . . . wonderful. He treated me like a princess. He loved me and I loved him. I have never forgotten him or our time together." She waited while Joshua absorbed the information.

Joshua sat there, quiet. Then, "Where is he now? Do you know?"

"No. The last time I saw him was across the school cafeteria a few weeks after I broke up with him. He had tried to talk to me right after it happened, but I refused to get back together."

Joshua sat back. "His name is Dan? Dan what?"

"Walsh. Daniel Jonathan Walsh." She smiled at the memory of her beloved Dan. She felt her face glow. "Six feet two inches tall, dark brown hair, bright blue eyes. He is the most handsome man I have ever seen." A Duchenne smile spread across her face at the thought of him.

"Do we," he hesitated, "look alike? Well, before my hair started going gray. I guess age, and having teenagers, will do that to you." He laughed, releasing the pent up tension of the conversation.

She laughed with him. "Yes, my dear Joshua. Both of those things will do it, I'm sure." She looked thoughtful, remembering. "Growing up, you were the spitting image of Dan. I don't know what he looks like now, but every time I saw you as a teenager and as a young man, I saw Dan."

"Did Dad . . . I mean, Kurt- . . . ever see Dan?" Joshua asked.

"No, thank God. If he knew what Dan looked like, he would have been even harder on you than he was." She shook her head. That would not have been good, for either of them.

"Have you ever tried to find him?"

Susan smiled sadly. She pulled at the hem of her dress, and then looked up. "No. He has a life, and it doesn't include me. I wouldn't want to do anything to disrupt that life."

Joshua smiled. "I understand, Mom." He sat back, with a

peculiar grin on his face. "So, my father is Daniel Jonathan Walsh." He took a deep breath. "That name sounds familiar . . . but I don't know why."

Chapter 3

Over the next few days, Joshua spent some time thinking over what his mother had told him about his birth father. The family meeting had gone fairly well, all things considered. Brooke had taken the news of his illegitimacy with kindness; Christopher seemed to smirk a bit. Typical for Christopher, I guess. Kurt was always pitting us against each other, so he'd probably have a field day with this information. That was one more reason Joshua was glad Kurt Prescott was not his birth father. On the other hand, the guy had tried, at least at first, to be a good father. Maybe he just didn't know how.

Something else was nagging at the back of his mind. Daniel Jonathan Walsh... Daniel Jonathan Walsh. . . Where in the world had he heard that name before? Every time he thought he remembered, it slipped from his mind. If only he could hold onto the thought for just a split second longer, it would come to him. But, no, it slid away.

He was torn about the knowledge he'd received. You'd think that a grown man in his 40s, and a medical doctor at that, would have more peace of mind. Sadly, he periodically felt like a little boy again, trying to find a man to call "Daddy," who would love him. I wonder if Mom felt pressured into marrying Kurt. By me. I remember being so excited when Kurt asked Mom to marry him. I jumped up and down, yelling "Say 'yes,' Mommy. Say 'yes.'" But, no, having false guilt wouldn't change how things had turned out. Mom wouldn't have been goaded by her five-year-old son into marrying someone she didn't love. Dump that thought, Joshua.

At least Joshua knew now that Dan had never known he was born. That relieved some of the pressure and some of the hurt he felt. It also answered the question of why Dan had given him up. He hadn't.

Something that was a huge issue in his mind was that his mother was a liar. If she'd lied about his birth for so many years, why wouldn't she lie about other things? But, no, he saw the struggle on her face when she gave him the news. This was her one lie, repeated many times. He had to forgive her and move on. Intellectually, he understood why she had done it. Emotionally, he was still unsure.

Susan had asked him over dinner on Monday if he was comfortable with sharing this information with the rest of the family. He asked her for a few days to process what he had learned, agreeing to let her know when he was ready. He told Amanda about it, during their quiet time when he got home that night. He was glad when the family meeting was over two days later. The Band-Aid was ripped off; the family knew. He could get on with his life. It was one less hurdle to jump over in his search for his father, for his roots. He wanted to know who he was, who his father was. Tonight, Thursday, he went into his home office and sat behind his desk.

Why did that name, Daniel Jonathan Walsh, sound so familiar? He couldn't get past the fact that he remembered hearing it before, though certainly not from his adoptive father Kurt. Time to check the dude out online. After all, just doing an online search wouldn't alert the guy that Joshua knew about him. He certainly wouldn't interfere with the guy's life. Joshua turned on his computer and entered "Daniel Jonathan Walsh."

Information popped up immediately. Joshua found

himself staring at a man whose eyes were identical to his own. Handsome face, if Joshua was any judge of men's looks. A business owner, though some time had passed since he owned the company. Daniel Walsh had sold his company, Walsh Consulting, to a larger firm two years ago. Joshua scrolled through the offerings online. Current address: Annapolis, Maryland! What?! He lives here? He scrolled down more excited now, if that was possible.

What's this? An obituary for Rebecca Smyth Walsh. She died of pancreatic cancer. Wait a minute! I know that name. Date of death: What? March 15th? It was almost a year ago. Eleven months ago, give or take a day. Place of death: Anne Arundel Medical Center. He sat back. My dear Lord in heaven, help me. He breathed slowly, trying to comprehend what he had just learned.

I know this woman because I treated her for an infection right before she died. I met her husband, my father, while I was treating her. Yes, it was about a year or so ago, from what he could remember, just like her obituary said. Wait a minute! The dude, I mean, Dan, gave me his business card. Where is it?

He pulled out his wallet and started going through it. Cards started flying in the air, as Joshua looked at and then rejected the cards. How many cards did he have in here? Then, there it was. He held it at arm's length. The business card of Daniel Jonathan Walsh. I can't believe it. I stuck it in my wallet and forgot it was there. He turned it over a few times, in shock that he had it. Dan must have known, or least suspected something. Joshua looked up in shock.

He asked me to call him sometime. It was right before his wife passed. People give me their cards all the time. I never call them. I just take their cards to be polite, to seem interested. I can give him a call now. It won't hurt Kurt because he's dead, and it won't hurt Dan because his wife is gone. He does have three sons, according to the Internet, but they're old enough to be on their own. He can tell them about me, if he wants. Or not. Joshua laughed out loud. I can get to know my birth father. Oh, yeah! His adrenalin started pumping on high.

Joshua jumped up and ran to the door of his office. "Amanda! Come quick! Amanda!" He stood in the doorway of his office, reading and re-reading the card.

Amanda came right away, her hands dripping from washing dishes, a dish towel in her hands. "Honey, what's the matter? Are you okay?"

"Amanda." He felt out of breath, like he'd just finished a marathon. "I met my birth father . . . last year. I took care of his wife right before she died." He caught his breath and tried to control his emotions. "He gave me this card and asked me to call him, but I never did. Amanda, he's here. In Annapolis." He laughed and cried at the same time. Amanda fell into his arms.

"Oh, honey, that's great that you found him." Amanda hugged him tightly. She pulled back and looked up at him. "What're you going to do?"

"I've gotta tell Mom. She's gotta know." He felt like time had suddenly sped up. "I've . . . I've gotta go tell her." He felt like he would jump out of his skin, he was so excited.

"On, honey, this is wonderful. I'll call your mom and tell her you're on your way over," Amanda said. She squeezed him tightly once more and then released him. She laughed, looking at his feet. "Go get your shoes on." She shooed him out of the room, punching in Susan's number as he left. "Mom, Josh is on his way over." She waited while Susan spoke. "Yes, everything is fine. Wonderful, actually. Josh will share his news with you when he gets there." Susan asked what was happening, but Amanda wouldn't tell her. "I'm going to let him tell you, but be prepared for some great news! Love you. Bye." Joshua gave Amanda a peck on the cheek and headed to his mother's house.

***

Susan wondered at Amanda's excitement as she hung up the phone. Her daughter-in-law sounded absolutely thrilled about something. Brooke and Michael came into the living room, where Susan had been reading. They had just finished bonding over washing the dishes.

Brooke perched on the arm of the couch and asked, "Mom, what's going on? Is everything okay?"

Susan answered, "Yes, Well, maybe. I don't know. Joshua will be here in a few minutes, and I guess we'll find out." She looked at her watch. "Guess I'll stay home from Widow's Life tonight. This sounds important."

Michael said, "I wonder what's up. Does Joshua usually come over, you know, just because?"

Susan said, "No, it's usually set up pretty well in advance. He's not really a spur of the moment kind of guy." She laughed as the trio chatted about Joshua and how predictable he was.

About fifteen minutes later, the doorbell rang. Sure enough, when Brooke went to the door, her brother was on the other side. Susan and Michael were close behind her.

Joshua came into the foyer, his face flushed with excitement, "Mom, Brooke, Michael, I found him!" He hugged them all; the pure joy in his face was evident.

Susan asked, "What? Where is he?"

Brooke and Michael asked in unison, "You found who?"

"My biological father," Joshua told the couple. He turned to Susan, "Mom, I treated his wife for an infection last year, about the same time as Kurt and Kelsey died. Dan's wife died a few weeks later. He gave me his business card, but I stuck it in my wallet and forgot about it, what with all the drama going on here with us."

Susan replied, "Oh, my. You treated his wife. Does that mean. . . Dan lives locally?" Tears of joy flowed freely down her face.

Joshua almost shouted, "Yes, Mom. He lives in Eastport, just across the bridge from downtown Annapolis. Before I found his card, I googled him." He hugged Susan again, squeezing her tightly.

Brooke explained to Michael, "Dan was Mom's high school sweetheart. Her first love." Then turning to Susan, Brooke said, "Hey, Mom, wait a minute."

"What honey? What's wrong?" Susan asked.

"Mom, Dan lives here and he's a widower. Maybe there's a chance that. . ." Brooke's voice trailed off.

Susan blushed, shocked at Brooke's comment. "Oh, no. Not at my age. What would people think if I . . . you know, got interested in him?" Susan gently popped Brooke on her shoulder. "Silly, romantic girl, Brooke!" She shook her head. "No, the important thing is for Joshua to get to know his birth father." Susan looked at Joshua. "Are you going to call him? See if you can meet up with him?"

Joshua looked at the three of them. "My whole life, I've wondered about him. Yes, I'm going to call him. In fact, I want

24

to do it right now."

"Yes, of course, sweetie. Do you want us to leave the room, so you can talk to him alone?" Susan wondered.

"No, Mom, I want you right here beside me. His story is your story, too." Josh grabbed her hand. He told Brooke and Michael, "You two can hang around too, if you want. I don't mind and it'll save a lot of time in explanations later!"

The trio agreed to stay. Joshua had something to say first, though, before he called his father.

"I want you all to know him, too. On the way over here tonight, I was remembering my time with Dan and his wife. Mom, you should have seen him. He was so tender towards her. I know that isn't a very masculine word, but he was so loving. She was in such bad shape, but he was there all day, every day watching over her." He thought for a moment. "I see a lot of patients and their families, but this man, he was something else. He fed her when she was too weak to feed herself. He wiped her mouth. He gently stroked her hand. When she ran a fever, he was there to bathe her forehead with a wet washcloth. Not with the hospital cloths. He brought her favorite washcloths from home, so that she could be comforted by them. He dressed her in nightgowns from home. No hospital gowns for her, not even at the end." He shook his head, almost in disbelief. "He provided the very best for his wife. He prayed for her, unashamed of who might listen in. Mom, I've never heard anyone pray like that. The total love and compassion he showed for her is something you don't see every day." Joshua hesitated. "I cared for his wife for only a couple of weeks before she passed, but the hospital records showed she was there for two months, solid. He ran his business from her bedside. He. . . he talked to her about decisions he was making, respecting her

25

opinion. If I'm this man's son, I'm proud of the fact. He's absolutely amazing." He blushed, sorry to run on, but the words just came out of his mouth and he couldn't stop talking. "Dad. . . Dad is a great man. He's not a bum. He's the real deal."

Susan smiled, "I'm not surprised that he acted that way. Maybe you can understand why I loved him so much, even as a teenager." Susan looked at the floor, and then spoke quietly. "I knew what I had, and what I was giving up."

Michael commented, "Dan had true agape love for his wife." He squeezed Brooke's shoulder in a side hug, as he told her, "It's what I want to show you for the rest of our lives." Michael kissed Brooke's cheek.

"So, I guess, I should call him now?" It was more of a question that a statement, Josh realized.

"Yes!" The three spoke enthusiastically and in unison.

Chapter 4

Joshua steadied himself as he sat on Brooke's couch. He was going to call his father, his real father, for the first time. What would Dan say when Joshua called him? His wife was dead, but what would his children think of a grown man, a father himself, calling their father and telling him who he was? Will he accept me? Will he tell me to get lost? Whew! This was gonna be harder than he thought when he first found Dan's business card. What if Dan has already moved on and wants nothing to do with me? Can I take his rejection? Can Mom? His thoughts and feelings were racing through his mind. Can I do this? But I want to, I really want to. I've never had the chance to know my biological father. He rubbed his sweaty palms on his pants.

He had only seen Mr. Walsh when he went into Mrs. Walsh's room to exam her as she lay dying. Now, he would face the man alone. Joshua felt nervous, concerned over what might happen. He looked over at Brooke and Michael who were on the couch opposite him; they shot him supportive smiles. He glanced at his mother, silently sitting on the couch next to him, waiting for him to make a move towards the phone. Deep, slow breaths. Steady as she goes, Joshua, old man. You have this.

Susan said, "It's time, honey. It's more than time. You can do this!"

Joshua nodded without speaking, took a huge breath, and punched in the phone number. Moments later, he heard the deep male voice answering.

"Hello. May I help you?"

"Yes. Mr. Walsh? I hope I haven't disturbed you. This is Dr. Joshua Prescott. I took care of Mrs. Walsh almost a year ago at Anne Arundel Medical Center." Joshua heard a deep gasp.

***

Dan Walsh heard the man on the other end of the phone line say he was Dr. Joshua Prescott. It was a voice from the past, albeit, only eleven months past. After a few weeks, Dan had given up the idea of ever hearing from the doctor. Of course, there was the death of his precious wife Rebecca, and then dealing with the will and other death-related activities. Still, he couldn't get the doctor out of his mind. Dr. Prescott was the spitting image of Dan's oldest son, Richard. They say everyone has a double, but this seemed to be too much of a coincidence.

Dan began to reason things out in his mind. *I mean, here we are in Annapolis, Maryland, where I grew up. At least, I grew up here partiallly, in between my dad moving our family all around the country. My high school girlfriend, Susan Thomas, and I did have sex without birth control. Susan broke up with me without any explanation. Dr. Prescott is the right age to be a child of mine, a fact confirmed after I googled him. Here I am, some 40 years later, with a doctor who looks exactly like my oldest son Richard and, truth be known, me at the same age. Dr. Joshua Prescott's gotta be my son. Who else could he be?*

***

Joshua waited and the older man hesitated. *He must be surprised to hear from me after all this time.*

"Yes, yes, Dr. Prescott. How are you?" Dan Walsh's voice carried over the phone so loudly that the trio waiting in Brooke's living room could hear him.

28

"Fine, sir. Thank you. Uh...How are you?" Joshua shrugged at his audience. He was uncertain how to move the conversation forward, having never been in this situation before. What do I say now? He looked at his mother, sister, and Michael. The group nodded their encouragement. "Go for it," they seemed to say. His heart was pounding in his ears. He swallowed.

"Fine, thank you, Dr. Prescott. Thank you for calling me." The voice on the other end of the phone hesitated. "There was something, a bit delicate I will admit, that I wanted to talk to you about."

"Please, sir, call me Joshua. I'm sorry about Mrs. Walsh's passing, sir. And I'm sorry that it's taken me almost a year to honor your request that I call you. My adoptive father died right about the same time as Mrs. Walsh, and things were very busy, as I'm sure you understand." Would his heart ever stop racing? Talk about stress.

"Yes, Joshua. I heard about Mr. Prescott's death and ... the situation there. As you know, it was in the news... I trust you and your family are doing better."

"Yes, sir. Thank you.'

"Please, call me Dan."

"Yes, thank you, sir....Dan. Actually, the reason for my call is . . . I'm not sure how to say this..." Joshua's face started blushing as he felt his blood pressure rising. Relax, Josh.

"Perhaps what we have to discuss is better done in person, Joshua," Dan said, not unkindly.

"Yes, I believe you're right, sir. Yes, that would be preferable, I think." Joshua was relieved, in a way, not needing to speak these new thoughts out loud yet to a man he barely knew. Whew!

29

"Yes, I think that might be just the thing. Perhaps we could have lunch sometime soon?" Dan asked.

"Yes, yes, I would like that. Perhaps some place close to work, so that I can be near the hospital, should the need arise for me to get back quickly?" Joshua's breathing was easier now. His blood pressure seemed more normal now. Yes, it was improving. He could feel it.

They compared schedules. Tomorrow was Friday. Noon would work for them both. The Nordstrom Café at the Annapolis Mall was decided upon, being close to the Lesly and Pat Sajak Pavilion where Josh's office was located and near the hospital.

"Oh, one more thing . . . Dan. I would like to bring someone with me."

Dan hesitated. "I had hoped that, because of the nature of our discussion, we could meet alone."

Joshua said, "I would like to bring my mother, Susan Thomas Prescott, if you're comfortable with that idea, Dan." He heard another sharp intake of breath.

"Yes, Joshua. I would like that very much. Tomorrow, then."

Chapter 5

Susan must have gotten up five times in the night, checking the time on her bedside clock, taking the time to go to the bathroom, and eating some crackers and milk in a desperate attempt to sleep. No such luck. Her thoughts tumbled about her. After more than forty years, today she would see her beloved Dan again. No, he wasn't her Dan anymore. He had been Rebecca's for many more years than he had ever been hers. Still...

She went out for a four-mile run early the next morning, trying to use up some of the pent-up energy she felt. It didn't work. After getting ready for her day, she tried on outfit after outfit, looking for the right dress to wear to the reunion with Dan. She was glad she had taken a personal day off from work. Oh, nothing seemed right. She settled on her favorite outfit, a purple A-line dress with long sleeves. She teamed it with some pearls, a gift from Brooke, who had tried to replace Susan's mother's necklace. The original necklace had been sold to a pawnshop by Kurt and Kelsey, to get money to feather their adulterous nest. Susan had no idea who was wearing them now. Pearl earrings that she had bought a few months ago and a matching pearl bracelet completed her ensemble. She slipped into her black heels and brought along a white sweater. She was always chilled at Nordstrom.

She had checked out Dan online, looking over pictures of the handsome older man she only remembered as a teen. Those blue eyes, that firm chin, the dimples that had so charmed her as a young girl were still there, topped off by snow white hair.

The pictures were only headshots, but there was no excessive weight on his face, so she assumed he was still in good shape. He had always worked out, even before it had become popular.

She looked at her watch for the hundredth time. Ten o'clock. Two hours to go. How would she last another hour and forty minutes before Joshua picked her up? They had agreed that he would drive them over together, for strength. She paced, sang a bit, and answered Brooke's frequent texts on how she was doing. Amanda chimed in a few times. There was nothing from Christopher, who was probably busy with classes at the Naval Academy.

Her mind drifted to her youngest child, Christopher. It was a nice relief from thinking about her upcoming meeting. Christopher was a hard nut to crack. While she had reconciled completely with Joshua, and Brooke's continuing support was unwavering, Christopher had not been very forthcoming. He held himself off from the family, as if he had no desire to build a relationship with her or either of his mutually-supportive siblings. How sad. I hope that one day, he'll come around. She glanced at her watch again. One hour left.

I wish I'd said I would meet them at the mall, so I could have put on my tennis shoes and mall walked. Of course, it wouldn't do to work up a sweat before meeting with Dan, but at least she could relieve some nervous tension. She picked up a book, putting it back down after reading the same paragraph numerous times and absorbing nothing. What to do to pass the time? Nothing came to mind.

Just then, her phone rang. It was Nancy Ferguson, her best friend. Thank God for Nancy. They had met while Susan was a rehab patient at the Chesapeake Center; Nancy had been her charge nurse. Susan had told her all about the recent events in a Readers' Digest Condensed Version. Nancy was very familiar with Susan's story of meeting Dan as a junior high school student and reuniting with him when his family returned to Maryland after a few years away. She remembered that they had dated for two years before IT happened: the Big P. and that Susan had never even told Dan that she was pregnant before Dan moved away. Susan sighed in relief, happy to hear from Nancy.

"Hey, girl, how you doing?" Nancy asked. "You hanging in there?"

"Oh, Nancy Beth. This waiting is so hard," Susan told her.

"Yeah, I bet it is. I've been thinking about you all morning," Nancy said.

"How are things at the Chesapeake Center?" Susan asked. Anything was better than focusing on waiting, even hearing about the number of diapers Nancy's co-workers had changed this morning, how many patients cried "help me, help me" in the corridor, or how many families never visited their elderly parent.

"You know, the usual. We've got a couple of live ones here right now," Nancy laughed.

"Oh, are Urinary Tract Infections leaving ladies and/or gentlemen a bit nuts?" Susan smiled, in spite of herself.

Nancy said, "Yep. I stopped one lady from tearing off her clothes in the game room. I had it figured out pretty fast that her problem was a UTI and got the doctor to sign off for an antibiotic, stat. It happens. Poor dear. If she was in her right mind, she never would have done a strip tease, but we got her fixed up pretty fast. She'll be fine, once those drugs kick in. Thank heavens her dementia means she'll never remember this.

She would be humiliated at the thought."

"You are the best, my friend. I remember how you took care of me for all those months I was recovering from my coma. If I haven't said it lately, thank you so much." Susan would never be able to thank Nancy enough. Being best friends now was a great start, though.

"Yes, dear Susan, but I was calling to check on you. How are you doing? It's almost time, isn't it?" Nancy asked.

Susan looked at her watch again. Twenty minutes till Joshua picked her up. Bless Nancy for distracting her. It was just what the doctor ordered. "Joshua will be here in twenty minutes. I'm a nervous wreck. It's been so long, Nancy. Dan moved on. I moved on. Do we want to go back in time to that relationship, or should we just part friends?"

"Now, girlfriend, you are trying to cross a bridge before you get to it. That doesn't work very well. Just relax and let what happens, happen. See how you both feel. Go from there. You never know . . . He might have body odor or bad breath or dentures that clack or endless belching or weird personal habits like singing off key or passing gas after every meal... or he could be the man of your dreams. You just don't know. Check him out. Scope out the situation. You're both single. Relax. Take it from there."

Susan had started laughing when Nancy got to her very vivid description of Dan's potential personal hygiene hang-ups. By the time Nancy got to the "man of your dreams" diatribe, Susan thought she was going to lose control completely. It was exactly what she needed.

"Oops, Joshua will be here in a few minutes. I need to go "powder my nose" as my mother would have said. Gotta run,"

Susan told Nancy.

"Oh, yes, women were much more discreet back in the day. Okay, I'll let you go for now, but don't forget I want a FULL description of the man and the hour when you get home, okay?" Nancy's smile could be felt through the phone line.

"Promise, cross my heart and hope . . . not to die anytime soon," Susan told her. She hung up the phone and took a deep breath. She chuckled over Nancy's wonderful sense of humor. She glanced at the clock. Bathroom time and then Joshua should be here. Then the rest of her life could commence.

Chapter 6

Joshua picked her up right on time. Susan was so nervous by then that she barely gave him time to stop the car before she ran outside and got in. She buckled up, after scarcely saying "hello." Joshua's face looked pale; she imagined her face did, as well. She pulled down the vanity mirror, as if to check her lipstick. Yep, her face was pretty drained of color, too. She smacked her lips as she pushed the vanity mirror back into place. Okay, here we go. She turned to Joshua.

Susan asked, "Are you ready for this? How are you feeling?"

Joshua answered, "Well, I have seen him before. I talked to him several times when I was treating his wife. It's not like this is my first time or anything..."

"No, but it is the first time you're meeting him as your father, honey," Susan said.

"Uh, yeah. Good point. Okay, I'm okay. A little nervous. Excited. Anticipating the unknown, that kind of thing. Amanda and I were talking about it." He hesitated as he drove the few miles to the Annapolis Mall. "It's different. I can't explain it, really." His voice petered out. "What if . . . he rejects me? Tells me to 'get lost' or something? Accuses me of ruining his life, this late in the game?"

Susan thought for a minute. "No, the Dan I knew would never do that. From what you have said about him, I don't think that will happen."

Joshua seemed to calm down a bit. "Yeah, well, I guess I

can hope."

"Joshua, you are loved by our family, no matter what happens." She thought for a moment. "Tell you what. Let me go talk to him first. Wait a few minutes, and then come into the restaurant. I'll ease the way a bit. How does that sound?" Susan asked.

Joshua said, "Yes, that might be a good idea. I don't know, Mom. What if he tells you 'to take a hike,' like you are fond of saying?" He appeared to be trying to joke around. It didn't work.

"Well, let's get on with it and see what happens," Susan said as they pulled into the parking garage underneath Nordstrom. She got out of the car before Joshua could move around to her side and open the door for her. Slow down, girlfriend. Relax. They went up two flights on the escalator, both looking at each other, nodding, and making an immediate right into the restrooms. Nerves had a tendency to do that to both of them. After their respective pit stops, she headed into the café. Joshua lingered behind, agreeing to give her a few minutes.

She walked in, noticing an attractive older man sitting at a table in the corner, facing the doorway. He was wearing what looked like an expensive suit, navy, with a light blue shirt and dark blue patterned tie. He smiled and stood, walking towards her. It was Dan. Her beloved.

Susan walked towards Dan, her eyes focused on him as if he were a light at the end of a long tunnel. "Dan." She stopped and stared, unable to say more.

Dan replied, "Susan." He embraced her in his arms.

Susan said, "Oh, Dan, I'm so sorry. Please forgive me for not telling you."

Dan soothed her, "It's all right, Susan. It's fine. It's okay now." He hugged her more tightly, and then released her. "I wasn't completely sure, even though Joshua is the spitting image of my son Richard. And, of course, me. I gave him my card, hoping he would call. I was conflicted. What would I say? But he didn't call. I thought maybe you had told him."

Susan said, "No. I just told him a short time ago. Please tell me you forgive me for not telling you I was pregnant, so many years ago? Joshua's your son, too. I'm so sorry." She hung her head.

Dan lifted her chin with his hand. He stroked her face. "Dear Susan. Of course I forgive you. There's nothing to forgive, really. You did what you thought was best at the time." Dan straightened, and smiled. "Please introduce me to your son . . . my son . . . our son."

Susan turned and motioned to Joshua, who was standing in the café entrance.

Joshua walked briskly to his parents. "Mr. Walsh, it's nice to see you again, sir." He held out his hand.

Dan looked at Joshua, smiling broadly. "Joshua, it's great to meet you...again. Please, call me Dan." They shook hands.

Dan patted Joshua on the shoulder.

Joshua said, "Yes, I'm sorry. Dan."

They all laughed, happy to be together, but most likely to relieve some stress.

Susan smiled, despite the tears that overflowed her eyes and ran down her cheeks. She couldn't take her eyes off him. Dan. It was really him. The man of her dreams for so long, right here, in the flesh. Dan. Then, "Dan, so, how have you been these last, what, forty-some years?"

"Good, good. Please, please have a seat. It's incredible to see you both," Dan told them. Dan looked back and forth between the two of them. None of them could stop smiling. They sat in Dan's booth by the window.

Susan grabbed a tissue out of her handbag and blotted her eyes, not wanting to frighten the nearby diners. She smiled and nodded at the nearby folks who were staring a bit, then looked back at Dan. "Dan, I've become someone who takes the bull by the horns these days, so I want you to know, just in case there is any doubt, I.... knew I was pregnant with Joshua when I broke up with you."

Dan nodded, but was silent.

Joshua added, "I just found out you were my biological father when I asked Mom about my birth a few days ago. My adoptive father, Kurt Prescott, was not in favor of my asking any questions, so I didn't say anything. But now, it's been more than a year since his death. After mom told me your name, I recognized it. It took a while to figure it out, but I remembered treating your wife before she passed. I recalled that you had given me a business card just before her death. I went through my wallet, and found it."

"And you called me." Dan was thoughtful. "I wondered

what had happened, why you didn't call, but I had heard about Kurt's accident on the news last year and figured something was up with that. The news reports mentioned your mom's full name, so I made the connection. I didn't try to contact you because I thought, well, maybe you had all the father you needed in him," Dan said.

The server came up. "Folks, do you need anything? I didn't see any meals put in for you. You need to order at the counter, you know."

Dan smiled at the server and thanked her. He turned to Susan and Joshua, "You know, this conversation is going to take a while, so how about if we go order and come back? It would be my pleasure to buy lunch for you both."

It was agreed that they needed to order, so they did so, with Dan picking up the tab for their lunches and iced tea. They returned to the table, eager to continue their conversation. Things were much more relaxed now, and Susan was able to share an abbreviated version of her story, with Dan filling in some blanks that Susan hadn't known about his father's transfer and his marriage to Rebecca.

Dan looked at Joshua, "So, medical school? Well done, Son, if I may call you that."

Joshua smiled, "Of course . . . uh . . . Dad, if I may call you that, as you say."

"Certainly, certainly, Joshua." Dan hesitated. "I told my kids about you, since you called the other day. I didn't mention you to them before then because I wasn't certain we would ever meet again." Dan waited, "Though I really hoped we would."

Joshua agreed, "I didn't know why you seemed so familiar, but Mom has shown me a couple of pictures of you from high school. I'm amazed by the resemblance between the two of us when we were teens."

Dan said, "The thing that I found incredible is that you are the spitting image of my son Richard. Kevin and Jim look like they're your brothers, which they are, but Richard, well, let me show you. A picture, as they say." Dan laughed. "I never realized how much I used that phrase until now. Forgive me." Dan handed over his phone, showing Joshua and Susan a few pictures of his other three sons.

Susan smiled as she watched the two of them chat. Easy conversation, all things considered. She admired the pictures of Richard, Kevin, and Jim, but found it difficult to take her eyes off of Dan. Her eyes studied his handsome face, noting that life had been kind to him, from an aging standpoint. Underneath the façade of the older man who sat across from her now, she could see the remnants of the young man she had loved so dearly. Adored so completely.

Over the next few hours, lunch turned to dessert, turning to a mall walk to "fluff their pillows." The Nordstrom chairs had gotten quite hard, as the hours rolled by. Joshua had to get back to work, so he left the couple somewhere during their second lap of the mall.

Susan and Dan talked so long that he invited her out to dinner. It was almost nine when he dropped Susan off at Brooke's condo, promising to meet her daughter and the rest of the family very soon. Susan smiled, looking forward to the bayside walk they had scheduled for the next afternoon after she got off work.

***

A few weeks later, Dan got a puzzling phone call from his son Richard.

"Dad, I need to drop by and talk to you a bit," Richard

41

told him.

"Sure thing, Rich. What's up? Is everything all right?" Dan asked his eldest son.

"Yep. Fine. Well, I actually wanted to give you something. From Mom," Richard replied.

"From...your mother? What could that be?" Dan asked.

"She gave me something for you and asked me to give it to you on the one year anniversary of her . . . death. That's today, so I wanted to see you."

"Absolutely. I was just thinking about how one year ago today she . . . left us. I know that Susan and I have been seeing a lot of each other, but, you know, I still miss your mom every day, Richard. I just wanted you to know that," Dan told him. Tears formed in his eyes. Would he ever get over losing Rebecca? He still thought of her daily. Or was it hourly? Even with Susan in his life, he still couldn't forget his wonderful wife. She was precious to him.

"Yeah, well, she gave me a letter she wrote and she wanted you to have it, so I'll drop it off. I haven't read it. It's to you, not me," Richard said. He arranged to bring it by on his way home from work. Later that day, Dan welcomed Richard inside the house, and then walked with his son into his comfortable and very masculine study.

"Have a seat, Son."

Richard handed him the letter. They sat, with Richard in the leather chair next to Dan's desk, and Dan behind the mammoth desk he had inherited from his grandfather.

Dan read silently:

"My beloved Dan. I am reaching the end of my time here on earth. I know that we have been trying to think positively about my treatment, and I've been a good soldier, but the truth is... I have known for some time that my time here is brief. I have come to great peace about it, knowing without a doubt where I'm going when I die. Death is not the end for me. I have every confidence in that.

"I know you will grieve, and I grieve that I won't be there to hold your hand, to hug you one more time. I will miss you and the boys, their wives . . . our grands. I would love to stay and be a part of their lives as they unfold, to see their graduations and weddings, but that isn't to be. If there's a window in heaven, I will be watching and rejoicing as you all celebrate.

"My dearest Dan, you have been a marvelous husband. No woman could ask for a better hubby. You are the very picture of kindness, love, and compassion. I remember the night we got engaged as if it was yesterday. The proposal just before we graduated from college came as a precious gift, when you took me to our favorite restaurant for my birthday and proposed in front of our families, telling them that I was the woman of your dreams. The birthday presents I got that evening were nothing in comparison to the incredible husband-to-be that I left with that night. You had kept the gorgeous ring you gave me a secret, but it was exactly my taste. You knew me so well. You still do. You are my best friend. I love you so dearly.

"I have treasured our time together, our walks in the evening after work, our making dinner together, and our holding hands while we watched endless re-runs of HGTV. And, over the past few months, our quiet times after my treatments in the hospital. Thank you for all those wonderful memories. You have been there through it all, praying, hoping, and begging for just a few more days together. Thank you for all you have done for me over the past 30+ years. I am truly grateful. I wish I could tell you more about what the years have meant to me, but I tire. I have asked Richard to deliver this letter on the one year anniversary of my passing, and he has assured me that he will. Let me close with one final message.

"Even now as I prepare to go home, I want to encourage you to be happy. I know that you love me and our family, but perhaps it is time for you to move on and love another. I want you to know that I do not begrudge you the gift of happiness. Rather, I want you to look for and find someone special to share your life with. Someone that you can laugh with, love with, grow old with. Yes, I wish those shoes were mine to fill, but they aren't. I'm so sorry. Move on, my beloved. I have been gone for one full year by the time you read this. Be happy again. I will rejoice, knowing that you have found someone to love.

Lovingly,

Rebecca"

Dan put the letter down. He took out his handkerchief and blew his nose. He wiped his eyes as he looked at Richard. His voice trembled as he said, "Your mother was an incredible woman. I loved her dearly. This letter reminds me of just how special she was." His mouth quivered. He was afraid the tears would fall again. So be it. He sobbed briefly, as Richard waited.

Richard nodded, also fighting tears. "Yes, she was something else . . . What . . . did she say?" he hesitated. "Do you want to tell me?"

Dan pushed the letter towards his oldest son, rubbing his face. "You can read it, if you want. Basically, she says that I am to move on." His voice broke. "Find love again."

Richard laughed, though his laugh choked back tears. He read the letter quickly, and then returned it to Dan. "That's

Mom for you." He cleared his throat. "So, your plans with Susan are . . . ?"

Dan said, "Susan was my first love, but that doesn't diminish the love I had for Rebecca all those years. Susan has come back to me, finally. I . . . plan on asking her to marry me."

"I figured. It's a bit soon, don't you think? Maybe you need to take a break from Susan." Richard looked uncomfortable. "I've talked about it with Kevin and Jim. We agree. Things are moving incredibly fast. We really want you to slow it down a bit. Make sure you're right for each other."

Dan stopped to think about it. He asked, "When did you all decide this was a good idea?" He hesitated. "I don't want you to think I'm mad about it. I understand where you're coming from, but it seems, I don't know, kind of unnecessary. Susan and I aren't getting any younger, like she says."

Richard said, "You've been back together for, what, a few weeks?"

"Three . . ." Dan's voice trailed off, as he thought about Richard's request.

"We just think that deciding so fast might not be the best course of action..."

Dan looked carefully at his son. "What are you asking, Richard?"

Richard hesitated. "We think you and Susan . . . Again, please don't think we're mad; we aren't. We just think that a break, maybe six months, would give things a chance to cool off. After that time, you could seriously think about the future with her, if your feelings are still the same or stronger. It's just that you are heading towards marriage at breakneck speed. This is not a 50-yard dash. It's a lifelong commitment. Make sure,

Dad. Don't rush into things just because you miss Mom."

Dan sat back and considered his son's comments. "I'll think about it, Richard. I'll talk it over with Susan, and see what she thinks. Fair enough?"

"Fair enough, Dad." Richard got up to leave, with Dan following him outside. They hugged. Richard got in the car and left, as Dan turned back to the house, with the burden of their conversation on his shoulders.

Chapter 7

Dan phoned Susan the next morning, a Saturday, so she was off work. "Susan, my kids have asked me to talk to you. It's pretty serious. Can we meet for lunch today?"

"Certainly, Dan. Is everything okay?" Susan was immediately concerned by the tone of his voice. She prayed that nothing was wrong.

"Yes, but I just need to discuss something with you. Can I pick you up at noon?"

"Absolutely. See you then." She hung up, wondering what had gotten him upset. She dressed quickly, having just finished showering after her morning run. She blew her hair dry and styled it. Things were looking up on the hair front, she noticed, almost absentmindedly as she wondered what was wrong with Dan. Ever since Kurt had shaved her head in the nursing home, her hair growth had slowed down considerably. In the past, her hair had grown about a half an inch per month, according to her hairdresser. Now, it seemed to finally be getting long enough to be stylish instead of making her look like a former chemo patient. She put on some dress slacks, a colorful multi-colored floral print blouse, her dark pumps, and some silver jewelry.

Dan was prompt. He looked . . . disheveled somehow. Not like his usual immaculate self. Almost like he hadn't slept all night. The tension from what he had to say was obviously bothering him. Rather than go outside to get in his car, she invited him in. Taking his hand, she led him into the living room and offered him a seat on the couch. "Dan, what's the matter?"

"My kids . . . have asked me to slow things down a bit. They feel things are happening way too fast." He let out a deep breath. "It was only a year ago that their mother passed and, well, you and I haven't been back together very long." He paused, looking straight at Susan, his eyes full of hope and uncertainty, all at the same time. "I told Richard last night that I want to marry you."

"Oh." She put her hands on her chest in surprise. Susan was startled by the news of his children's objections, but not shocked that he wanted to marry her. She loved Dan and knew she wanted to marry him; she had felt certain that Dan felt the same and that his intentions matched her own. Still, it felt wonderful to have him voice his love. But his children? They did have a point. This was quite sudden, to their thinking, she supposed. She gasped.

"They have asked me to wait six months, to make sure that it's the right decision. They don't want us to date during that time." His eyes welled up. "I understand how they feel. They're great young people. The thing is, I don't know if I can stand to be away from you for that long." He seemed to be in pain.

She felt faint. Was she to come this close to happiness with Dan, only to have it snatched away, even if it was only temporary, by people she had never met? She slumped against the back of the couch. She was unable to speak for a few moments.

"Susan? Are you all right?" He was instantly concerned.

That was so like Dan. He moved closer as she slowly told him, "I understand, Dan. They're hurting and afraid. I hope that our meeting didn't cause them pain, cause you pain . . ."

"My dearest Susan." He kissed her hand. "You've brought me nothing but joy since we were reunited." He spoke carefully. "I've learned that my decisions don't just affect me. My children as very important to me and, as much as it pains me, I want to respect their wishes." He thought a bit longer. "Give them the time they need to get comfortable with this. They're okay if we talk on the phone, email that kind of thing, just not meet in person."

"They feel you aren't ready for a relationship, or rather that they aren't ready for you to have a relationship." Susan felt like she was stating the obvious, but it was as much for her own benefit, as it was for his, that she had to voice the truth of the matter. Get things out in the open. Make sure they both understood. No hidden truths. She'd had enough of that in her life.

"Yes." He looked miserable. He said nothing else.

She sighed deeply and then spoke. "Then I think we should honor that, Dan. For now, though, I think that we shouldn't email or chat. Let the air clear a bit. See if we really care for one another or if this is just the infatuation of two old people. See if we're merely romanticizing the last forty years of our lives, remembering two teenagers who are no longer there, living lives that no longer exist." With great difficulty, Susan took his hand and pressed on. "Let's see if it's obvious that we should really be together. Time will tell. When you're ready, and after the six months have elapsed, and when your family is ready, then you can call me if you want to. Let's play it by ear." It took every ounce of courage she had to say those words, but they had to be said.

"Are you certain?" He looked absolutely miserable.

"About the complete separation? Yes, I think it's best for all concerned." She couldn't believe that she had told him to leave for six months, but she knew that it needed to happen. He had to be over Rebecca completely and she had to be over Kurt before they could begin their new life together. It hadn't occurred to her before, but she needed that time as much as he did. Even though their mourning would be different, it still had to be. She hadn't thought of it that way, but she knew it was true. And she told him this.

Dan left a short time later. She felt as if her heart was breaking all over again. She wandered about the condo for hours, unable to settle anywhere. She pulled herself together, finally, and said, "If this is the Lord's will for my life, then I can accept it. Whatever He wants is what I want." She got out her calendar and marked off six months. September seemed so far away. As Michael had often told her during her months of rehab from the accident Kurt caused when trying to kill her, she needed to live each day, trusting Jesus to lead, guide, and direct her path. Back then, it was the first time in her life when she started trusting Him to provide. Now, she needed to do it again. It wouldn't be easy, but she would get through this time of trial.

Chapter 8

Susan told Nancy about the situation, having called her early that afternoon. Her Hispanic friend rushed to her side immediately after her shift ended at the Chesapeake Center. Still dressed in her green scrubs, Nancy had to find out how Susan was feeling, what she could do to help her precious friend.

"Susan, what possessed them to make such a request of their father? How could they do that?" Nancy was practically dancing around the kitchen she was so disturbed by the news. All four feet, eleven inches of Nancy were involved in the dance. "I just don't understand why the two of you have to part. It seems so unfair."

"Nancy, I understand what they're thinking. I mean, I can imagine what Brooke and Joshua and Christopher would think and feel if the situation had been different with their father. What if we'd been deeply in love and he'd died after a short illness? I've had some time to think about Kurt's death. He died to me many years ago, yet I've still mourned this past year." Susan thought for a moment. "Dan just lost Rebecca a year ago. There's a world of difference in the two deaths. I miss who I thought Kurt was. That man has been dead for years. I miss the man he could have been. Dan misses Rebecca and truly grieves her passing because they were so happily married. I haven't experienced that kind of love or loss, but I do understand it. He has to have more time to grieve. His whole family does. Before he's ready to remarry."

"Susan, I don't know how you can put yourself in Dan's

children's shoes so completely. I guess you're just such a nurturing person." Nancy squeezed her hand. "You really are the best, you know."

"Nancy, don't build me up into some kind of saint with a halo and all . . ." She shook her head at the thought. A wimp, a doormat, maybe, but definitely not a saint with direct ties to heaven. Well, not more so than any other believer.

"No, Susan, it's time you know how other folks see you. You're sweet and loving, and you always see the good side of people." Nancy gave her a quick hug. "No wonder you're able to put yourself in those children's shoes so easily. You even gave Kurt the benefit of the doubt when he didn't deserve it."

"Well, I appreciate your kind words, Nancy, but I have a rusty halo, if ever there was one. If you'll recall, I wasn't thinking too highly of Kurt before he . . . went away forever."

"That's true but you had good reason to dislike him."

"And I did. Nancy, I think I actually hated him. You know, for years I never thought I would even consider re-marrying if something happened to Kurt. I was so terribly unhappy. I actually started hating marriage; I started seeing it as a prison with an unkind guard." Susan shook her head at the memory, especially of her attack on Kurt in the hotel that morning so many months before. Come to think of it, the sight of him slipping on the marbles she had thrown at his feet or the partially masticated leftover food she had tossed in his direction that splattered all over his hair and clothing would have been hysterical, if her life hadn't been hanging in the balance.

"Then you reunited with Dan. A good man makes all the difference, dear Susan." Nancy smiled. "Like my dear Patrick."

"Yes." Susan thought a moment. "You and Patrick are so

happy, but I couldn't see that, ever, for myself. The two of you are so loving, affectionate, you know, really good for one another. I never thought that would be possible for me. All that changed when Dan came back into my life."

Susan paused and switched gears, saying "You know, Nancy, this separation feels almost unbearable. But I want to be a blessing to Dan and his children, not a problem. If we are to be married, I want it to be with his children's approval, if that's possible."

"Well, Susan, we can pray that the separation is only temporary," Nancy told her.

"Yes. I can bear six months. I don't know if I could stand it if it was forever."

Brooke, who had spent the day with Michael, came in just as Nancy was departing. They had a hurried, whispered conversation that Susan couldn't hear, but was able to imagine. Brooke came into the kitchen and tried to comfort her, but Susan was still pretty delicate. Brooke called a family meeting for that night, which Susan thought was overdoing it a bit. She told her sons about the request and decision. They decided that the best thing was to keep her busy.

Over the next few months, she built on the new relationships with her sons that had begun over the past few months. They had only known their mother through the lens of their father's dislike and disgust. They talked about it often with her as they told her they had discovered a wonderful person in their mother that they had never known. It was a time of growth for them all. She learned new things and interests that her sons had that they had never shared with her before. She got to know Joshua's wife and children better.

Joshua and Amanda invited her over for dinner several

times a month. As the women worked together in the kitchen one evening a couple of months later, Amanda finally seemed convinced that her mother-in-law wasn't crazy. Amanda apologized for her unkindness to her through the years, telling her, "Kurt made you seem almost insane, and I listened to him. Please forgive me. I should've come directly to you, but he seemed so, I don't know, so right about everything."

"That was one of his many gifts, Amanda. The gift of appearing to be one thing while the reality was something different. And he was always right about everything, in his own mind. Still, I could have been more approachable, friendlier, you know, less standoffish. I thought you didn't like me, so I withdrew from you. That left room for Kurt's interpretation of reality. I was a different person back then, more passive. It's my own fault for not taking the lead with our relationship. Please forgive me for all those years we've lost. I hope we can become better acquainted, now that there's no one between us."

"Yes, Susan, I mean, "Mom." Is it alright for me to call you "Mom?" I'd like us to be friends." Amanda asked sheepishly.

Susan had been unaware that Amanda had dimples until that very moment. Her heart was filled with joy when Amanda called her "Mom." In the midst of pain, things were definitely looking up. Susan's heart was warmed by the new relationships that were forming. She wiped her hands on her apron and gave her daughter-in-law a squeeze. "Of course it's all right if you call me that. I'd be honored."

Still, the time did seem to go by so slowly, but she was making it through. She thought of Dan often, remembering his "God-frosted" white hair and handsome good looks. The sound of his laughter was delicious to her memory, but she knew this separation was right. They both needed the time.

Her loss of Kurt had taken place over years, not just the six months she was living through right then. There was a lengthy "goodbye" to her marriage. She likened it to Alzheimer's disease, where the person didn't die right away, but slowly. Her marriage hadn't disintegrated overnight. It was a long, slow process of death through Kurt's disinterest, on one hand, and her poor handling of the matter on the other. Susan began keeping a journal, writing down the various stages of her marriage's dissolution. The kitchen island in Brooke's condo was the perfect place to sip a cup of tea and add to her musings. She spent time thinking about their lives and trying to discern the beginning of the end. Yes, she even went through more grief, though it amazed her that she was saddened by Kurt's passing.

As she wrote, Susan analyzed how she could have responded differently, regretting that she'd never gone for help in handling Kurt's PTSD. She wondered how things might have worked out otherwise if she had reacted to his needs more fully. He wasn't perfect, but neither was she. The entire marriage disaster was not his fault alone, no matter how she wished that was so, and she needed to own up to that fact. She came to accept responsibility for her part in their marital problems. She learned to welcome the pain and allowed it to lead her into spending more time in God's Word and with His people.

The funds from Kelsey's will were beginning to come in, so Susan gave up her full time receptionist job. To keep her mind active, she considered applying for a part time job at Kilwin's Ice Cream store, then rejected the idea due to the high caloric counts attached to every product in the shop. She even resumed the long walks in downtown Annapolis that she had loved to take for so many years. She had avoided being in Annapolis, ever since the night she almost went for a unwanted Kurt-instigated mid-winter swim in the Bay. Instead of the ice cream option, she chose the healthier choice of walking around St. John's College and the Naval Academy. The former was a lovely campus while the latter was tinged with solemn memories of her times there with Kurt. For the most part, though, it was a wonderful time of reflection.

The days were counting down on her calendar. Faithful to her request, Dan had not contacted her at all. Would he remember to call her, or was their reunion just a flash in the pan? She prayed it was not so.

Dan had been in touch with Joshua, but Joshua didn't tell her what they discussed, just that they had met. According to her son, they saw each other once every other week, as Joshua's schedule at the hospital permitted. Occasionally, they included one or another of Dan's three sons, so Joshua could get to know his grown half-brothers. Susan hoped that they were becoming close, but she wasn't sure of that, since she never discussed Dan or his family with Joshua, following the break. Amanda told her that their children went out to lunch and to the playground with "Grandpa Dan" at least once a month, as well. They all loved this new man in their lives. Susan was glad they were getting back the years that the locusts had stolen. She missed Dan, but felt that so much good had come from this time. The question her heart pondered each day, every hour, remained: Would Dan come back to her?

Chapter 9

The mid-September day finally came when Dan sent word via Joshua that he would like to make a date for lunch, six months to the day since he had left her side. Susan "accepted with great pleasure your kind invitation," communicating through Joshua. She felt, and Dan apparently agreed, it would be too painful if one or the other had changed his or her mind, so letting Joshua be their conduit was the best for all concerned.

Wanting to look her best on their big reunion, she went out and bought a beautiful new dress: dark fuchsia lace, long flounce sleeves, and black shoes. Pink pearls complemented the outfit. She sat on the edge of her Amish rocking chair for a while, then went downstairs and paced the living room floor, waiting for him to arrive. Her nerves were so shaken that she practically wore out the carpet that morning, or so she would tell Brooke later when she described their reunion.

His car pulled up at noon on the dot. He strode up the steps to Brooke's condo, holding the largest bouquet of pink roses and baby's breath that she had ever seen. Heart overwhelmed with joy, she flung open the door before he even rang the bell. She knew the sparkle in his eyes matched the joy in her own eyes.

"Dan. It's so good to see you! Come in, come in!" Susan laughed the words.

"My cherished Susan." He entered the foyer joyfully. He tossed the flowers aside, throwing them onto the nearest chair in the living room. He chose hugging over holding the bouquet, engulfing her in the biggest but most tender hug she had ever experienced. "I've counted the days and the hours for the last six months. Praise God that the waiting is finally over." His bear hug delighted her. Laughing, he picked her up and swirled her around the room. She felt like a giggly schoolgirl as her head continued to spin, even after he stopped twirling her. What happiness! They both laughed. Typical of a man his age, he immediately grabbed his back. "Boy, I haven't done that in a long time. Not ever, in fact." He straightened up and took a deep breath. Sensing her concern, he said, "I'm fine." He reassured her, smiling. Recovering quickly, he picked up the gorgeous blossoms and bowed as he presented them to her. "My lady." More laughter. Unspeakable joy.

A few tears of happiness sneaked down her face. "Oh, Dan, you really had me going there, for a minute. I'm glad your back's okay." She breathed deeply. She nodded her head towards the kitchen. "Come on in. I need to put these flowers in some water." He followed her into the kitchen while she tended to the bouquet.

Dan leaned against the kitchen island. She felt his eyes upon her as she selected a vase, added water, and fluffed the flowers. She still felt a bit woozy- was it from the spinning or a result of the joy at their reunion? It was hard to tell. She sniffed the fragrance of the bouquet and thanked him again for the stunning combination of roses and mums.

"You're welcome, my dear. I adored buying them for you." He kissed her hand. He got very quiet for a moment, and then spoke. "Susan. There's something else that I need to give you. I actually gave it to you forty years ago, but you gave it back."

"What?" She couldn't imagine what he was talking

about.

He pulled out a little black box and opened it. The promise ring with the tiny diamond chip was inside. He knelt before her on one knee. "No other woman has ever worn this ring, Susan, but I ask you to take it back as a symbol of the promise I made back in high school. I want to have you as my wife someday. Will you accept it, again?"

It was all she could do to squeak out her reply. Her throat was constricted with emotion as she replied, "Yes, Dan. I will." She couldn't contain her joy as her eyes filled with tears of bliss. Dan slipped the ring on her finger, where it had been some forty years previously.

He stood to his feet, losing his balance for a moment, but she helped him stand as they both burst into laughter once more.

"I'm not as young as I once was!" He gave her a lovely kiss and a warm embrace. He kissed the top of her head as he held her in his arms. When he finally pulled back, he asked, "Are you ready for lunch? How does the Nordstrom Café sound?"

"Yes and yes." She grabbed a lightweight sweater and they headed out to his car.

They had a wonderful time talking about their lives for the past six months and making plans for their future. They met every day after that for lunch, which usually stretched into an afternoon walk and dinner. Wednesday morning Bible study became a joint activity, followed by the fellowship lunch. Family dinners with Joshua and his family, with Christopher, and with Brooke and Michael became a part of their routine. Nancy and Patrick joined the various couples at least once a week, having been completely adopted into the family during the months following Kurt's death and then the six month separation from Dan.

More importantly, Dan introduced Susan to his grown sons, their wives, and his grandchildren. They got along beautifully, though there was some initial hesitation on all their parts, based on their previous request that the couple separate for a half year. Susan addressed the elephant in the room that first evening and told them how grateful she was, in the end, for that six month waiting period. Dan assured them that he knew their advice, while painful, had been right. The family relaxed and enjoyed meeting Susan's extended family.

One late fall evening, Dan invited Brooke and Michael to go with them to the Chart House for dinner. Susan had changed into her favorite dress, an A-line swirl of purple, green, black, and white. She added a delicate silver necklace and threw a dark shrug over her dress to ward off the Chesapeake Bay night chill. Brooke almost skipped into Susan's room wearing her grey mini-dress with a white blazer and two long strands of intertwined white pearls, holding her shoes. Susan noticed how cheerful Brooke was but decided not to mention it, unless Brooke brought it up.

"I love that dress on you, Mom." Brooke was glowing with happiness.

"Thanks, Honey. That's one thing about having a whole new wardrobe. Everything is very up-to-date." They laughed, which was better than crying over the memory of how Kurt had sold or given away all of her clothing the previous year. What a sad man he turned out to be. Pathetic, to her way of thinking. She had learned so much about herself, and her deceased husband Kurt, during the six months she had been separated from Dan. Whenever memories of the numerous wrongs Kurt had committed against her came to mind, she felt nothing but pity for him. He had been a very troubled man, though she didn't understand why. Susan turned her attention to Brooke. "You look very chic tonight, Brooke."

"Thanks, Mom."

"Almost ready to go?"

"Yes, in a minute. Just have to put on my shoes." Brooke sat on Susan's bed. Susan sat down beside her. She noticed her daughter had something on her mind. She could wait until Brooke was ready to talk. It didn't take long. Brooke slipped into her shoes and then got right to the matter at hand.

Brooke approached the situation with care. "You know, Mom, Michael was a real tower for me when we were going through everything with Dad trying to kill you. Michael and I've become good friends, and, of course, we're courting."

Susan said, "I know, my dear daughter. I may have been recuperating, but I have seen looks between the two of you. I think it's a little more than 'good friends who are courting' don't you think?"

Brooke smiled and nodded. "What would you think of . . . I mean, what if our relationship was something more than friendship and casual courting . . . would you, I mean, would the family be okay with that?"

"Brooke, are you talking about something long-term and serious?"

"Yes."

Susan smiled. "My dear, I think we already know that there's something long-term and serious going on with Michael. We love him. It's as simple as that."

Brooke hesitated before speaking. "Well, you know that his parents have a racially mixed marriage. It wasn't easy for them."

"Yes, but they were married how many years ago? Don't you think things have changed since then, Brooke? I sure hope that people have become, I don't know, more kind about these things. More accepting?"

"Michael's told me that his folks went through quite a bit of hassle, with his mom being white and his dad being black. I talked to them about it, and they said that it made their marriage stronger because they were determined to prove the naysayers wrong."

"Yes, I've heard that from other folks who were in similar situations. They united with one another. Sometimes 'each other' was all they had." Susan reached out and pushed back a wayward strand of hair from Brooke's face. She took her daughter's hands in hers. "So, how do you feel about it, Honey? Are you willing to 'jump into the fray' as it might be called?"

"Yes, Mom, I am. I love him so much."

"Brooke, Michael is an outstanding young man. He's a devout Christian who led us to the Lord. He's a good, kind, tenderhearted person. You have my blessing to marry him."

"Thanks, Mom." Brooke gave her mom a hug. She looked shyly over at her mother. "Speaking of Dan, which we weren't but we are now, what's new with that? Any engagement news of your own that you think might be coming down the pike?"

"We've chatted about it. We haven't really mentioned a timeline. At this point, we're still getting to know each other better and rebuilding old bridges, I suppose you could say." She smiled tenderly. "I don't need to rush things, Brooke. I'm fine with taking it slowly."

"If you say so, Mom. Well, back to the topic at hand. If

Michael proposes, you think the family will be okay?"

"Yes, absolutely. Anyone who doesn't like it, well, they can put that in their pipe and smoke it, as far as I'm concerned." Susan laughed again, out of pure joy.

"Boy, I haven't heard you use that expression in years, Mom." Laughing, they hugged and headed downstairs.

Just then, the doorbell rang to admit Dan and Michael, both decked out in dark blue suits, Oxford blue shirts, and print ties. "Our mother dresses us alike," Dan quipped. They headed to the restaurant, where the foursome enjoyed a lovely romantic dinner overlooking the Chesapeake Bay. As they delighted in their dessert, Michael banged on his glass and asked for everyone's attention. They all listened carefully, as did some nearby diners who apparently thought the handsome young man had something important to say. He did.

"First, I just want to say 'thank you' to you all for how wonderful you've been to me. This family is precious to me and I love you . . ." He choked up a bit, swallowed, and then composed himself. "These past months while we've been courting have shown me what a superb woman you are, Brooke." Michael dropped to one knee and opened a little black box as he made his speech. "Brooke, I love and cherish you. I want to make you my wife. Will you marry me?" There was a stunning Masterpiece Radiant near-colorless diamond inside the box, a little over one carat.

Brooke gasped, and said, "Yes, Michael, I will." Brooke broke into a huge smile, joined in her happiness by the approval of her mother and Dan. The couple kissed.

Nearby diners, who had been listening in ever since Michael began speaking, broke into spontaneous applause and cheers. They all celebrated, toasting the new couple. Life was good.

Chapter 10

Susan and Brooke were getting ready for a family picnic on a lovely early spring day. It was another fellowship meal with Dan and his family. There had been many over the past few months, but this one seemed special, though she couldn't immediately say why. It just felt different. Susan almost sang as they prepared the food. Life was so wonderful these days. She tasted the baked beans. Perfection! Susan looked around the room. "Brooke, this is looking pretty good to me."

"Yep, Mom. I think we've outdone ourselves. If anyone leaves hungry . . ."

"It's their own fault!"

The hamburgers and hot dogs were ready for the grill, to be backed up by several types of salad and chips and dip. The baked beans were simmering on the stove and there was fruit salad in a hollowed-out watermelon rind. Several pies and cakes were on the counter, homemade butter pecan ice cream was chilling in the freezer, and pitchers of ice cold sweet tea were in the refrigerator. The tables were set with cheerful tablecloths out on the deck and were awaiting their guests.

Susan and Brooke were casually dressed in nice jeans and pretty blouses. She was wearing a bright pink shirt while Brooke was dressed in blue. As always, they were wearing feminine jewelry; this time, it was heart-shaped jewelry that complemented their outfits. Susan's hair had finally grown long enough to style quite fashionably, but it was still snow white. Blasted Kurt Prescott. Why had he felt the need to shave off her hair? Then again, it may have been why she came out of the six-month coma. Nothing else had awakened her. The electric razor he used sounded like a swarm of bees; she had never liked bees.

Brooke looked at her mother carefully as she washed the veggies for the veggie tray. "Mom, are you planning to start coloring your hair again? I mean, it looks really pretty, but you were always so careful to keep it brown."

Susan thought for a moment. She picked up her knife as she begin cutting up the watermelon. She said, "Brooke, I'm perfectly happy with my hair the way it is. I only colored it to make your father happy. I guess he thought he looked younger if I did. I like this new look and the new me."

"It is charming, Mom, and Dan seems to like it. I was just curious what you planned on doing about it?"

"Nothing." Susan nodded in agreement with herself. "Nothing at all. No more looking like an aging Jaclyn Smith for me. I just want to look like myself." Oops, she almost lost that piece of watermelon as it barely made it into the bowl. Be more careful, Susan Margaret.

Brooke said, "I know lots of folks said that's who you looked like. And that Dad favored Richard Gere." She arranged the veggies very decoratively around their serving platter.

Susan leaned against the counter, shaking her head. "I can't watch one of his movies without cringing inside, but it's not Richard Gere's fault."

They laughed. Susan thought for a minute as she pulled the ice tea out of the refrigerator. "Not to the change the subject, but I've been thinking. You and Michael are getting married and you'll need your own space. Have you decided where you'll live?"

"Michael and I've discussed it and decided to sell both of our condos and buy a house. We should be able to get enough from the double sales to buy a pretty nice four-bedroom house in Anne Arundel county somewhere. That way, when the kids come along, we'll have a place for them to play outside."

"I'd like to help you with the purchase. You know, my money from Kelsey's will has started coming in. I'm going to meet with some financial folks to work out some trusts and such. Who would have thought that my husband's girlfriend would leave me a wealthy woman? Go figure." Susan shrugged. "I'd like to make some initial gifts to you and the boys, so I can enjoy your enjoyment of the money while I'm still around. Maybe I could donate, say, $100,000 to your house fund? I'll give the same amount of money to both Joshua and Christopher."

"Mom, that's so generous of you. That would surely help, though Michael and I want to pay for the balance of the house on our own." Brooke hugged her mother.

"I understand. I'll also be establishing trusts for the college education of all the grandchildren. I'm hoping you and Michael and Christopher and his future wife will be adding to the four I already have. 'The more the merrier,' as they say. Joshua's girls are getting close to their college years, and his boys are right behind them. I don't need five million dollars to live well. I'd like to help you all." Since she had finished with the watermelon, she went over and stirred the baked beans.

"Mom, that's great! Have you talked to Joshua and Christopher about this yet?"

"No, Brooke, so please don't tell them about our chat. I want the time to be right." She banged beans off the spoon she had been using and put it on the spoon rest.

"I understand, Mom. No problem. It's really so kind of you to do this for us." Brooke gave her mom a quick side hug.

"You're the best."

"Certainly, dear. I just want to help you all get new starts, having lost your father and having had your opinions of him destroyed. Of course, you'll all inherit equally when my time comes, which hopefully won't be anytime soon!" They laughed.

Brooke looked thoughtfully at Susan. "Mom, Michael and I have talked about this a lot. We'd like you to consider living with us. What do you think?" Brooke asked.

"No, I've been imposing on your kindness much too long." She was quiet, and then said, "I saw a little cottage near the water on an internet real estate website yesterday. I was thinking about making an offer on that. It'd be nice to be near my children and grandchildren, yet still be able to enjoy the sunrises on the Chesapeake Bay. New beginnings each day, and all that. We'll see how things work out. Kurt and Kelsey's house sold two months ago, so I'll have those funds available after they make it through the legal gobbledygook. Since you're a paralegal, you know how things can be pretty complicated." Brooke nodded. "I do know that it's time to move on with our lives." She looked at her watch. "Oh, my. We need to get going. Everyone will be here soon and we need to get the food outside!"

"Thanks Mom." They hugged again and then got back to work.

"You're welcome, dear. Now, let's get a move on!" They pulled dishes out of the refrigerator and oven, preparing them for serving outside on the deck. Serving spoons were at the ready.

"What time will Dan and his family get here?" Brooke

busied herself with putting spoons in the dishes.

"They'll be here shortly. I look forward to everyone being together again. This should be quite a party!" Susan gathered up some bowls brimming with food. "Okay, let's get this stuff out on the deck."

Just then, Joshua and his family pulled up, with Christopher in tow and more food in hand. The gang piled into the house, giving hugs to their mother and sister. The children were full of delight, as they saw the food that Grandma P. and Auntie Brooke had prepared. Dan and his extended family arrived moments later with additional edibles, followed by Michael who was bearing sodas. As more cars pulled up, the early arrivals all headed outside. The families greeted each other happily on the front lawn, united by the love of their parents. Nancy and Patrick joined them with yet more food, excited to be a part of the festivities.

They all gathered on the back deck, ready to give thanks for their food, when Dan signaled that he had something to say.

"I'm so glad that everyone could come to the picnic today. We make quite a combined, extended family, don't you think? I know that this has happened in God's perfect timing, in spite of the trials we've all faced. Today's a new day, and we want to celebrate His love."

Everyone murmured their consent.

"Susan, my dearest one?"

"Yes, Dan?" Her heart began to flutter. She couldn't have stopped smiling if she had tried, which she didn't. Is the day I've been waiting for so long really going to happen? Her eyes widened and her mouth fell open, in a combination of utter joy and pure shock. Oh, my goodness, he's dropping down on one knee! Yes!!!!! She giggled like a school girl. Yes!

"Several months ago, you accepted a tiny diamond ring from me, one that I gave you forty years ago in promise that we would one day wed." Dan knelt down on one knee and opened the black box he had taken from his breast pocket. "I'd like to replace that ring with a new one, and I ask you this question: Susan, will you marry me?"

Susan said, "Yes, Dan, yes." She had never felt such incredible, unbelievable joy. He slipped the ring on her finger and gave her a huge hug. They kissed. Another hug ensued. Everyone offered their congratulations to the very happy couple. As hugs were shared all around, Susan took a look at the ring, which was a circle of large baguette diamonds. "It looks like business has been good, Dan!" They all laughed together.

"Yep, not bad," Dan replied.

"Took you forty years to finally ask me, didn't it?" Susan teased him with good nature.

"Well, Susan my dear, we've both been busy," Dan replied. Everyone laughed.

Chapter 11

Later that fall, Susan and Dan pledged their lives to one another. It was the wedding day she had waited 40 years for. As they sipped a cup of tea in Brooke's kitchen during the early planning days, Susan had tried to insist that the wedding be a small one, but Brooke wouldn't hear of it. Things had gotten a bit out of hand, with a final guest count of 150 people, but the early fall day had been lovely. She had to admit the day had been wonderful and a two-week European honeymoon had been the icing on the cake, in her opinion.

Susan looked across the breakfast table at her husband. Now possessing distinguished gray temples and the only-slightly-aging rugged good looks she had been so attracted to more than forty years ago, he was engaged with the morning newspaper at the moment and did not immediately sense her scrutiny. She studied his face, loving every inch of it. The laugh lines he possessed were etched by years of happiness and a life well lived. She took another sip of her tea and glanced outside at the new day dawning across the Chesapeake Bay. The huge white floor-to-ceiling windows gave her a stunning wide-angle view of the water. She had drawn the windows' light blue curtains back to welcome the day's arrival. She was looking forward to visiting downtown Annapolis and the Naval Academy this morning, followed by lunch at Nordstrom.

It might be a tad nippy this late fall morning, hence Susan's desire to wear her favorite gray wool slacks, burgundy turtleneck sweater, and warm, dark blue blazer. She set the outfit off with the pearl necklace and earrings that her daughter

Brooke had given her at their wedding two months before. Her handsome huggable hubby, as she was fond of calling him, was decked out for the day in a dark blue wool suit, white shirt, and burgundy necktie. They had color-coordinated their clothing without even trying, so finely attuned were they to one another. While some folks visited Annapolis looking like tourists, they always preferred to dress nicely.

She smiled at the memory of the last two months. Marriage to Dan was so unlike anything she had experienced with her now-deceased husband Kurt that she sometimes thought she was dreaming. Oh, no, wait. That was what she had done during her six-month coma.

She thought back over her life. Her first husband Kurt had been a wounded man, suffering from what was now known as PTSD, but it was an unnamed condition when it struck him. He had seen combat in Viet Nam as a young man, and had never gotten over it, though she was at a loss to understand why. He had never discussed the details with her, only that he had been in combat. End of discussion. They had raised three children together, but she never felt as if she had known him. There had been an impenetrable wall between them that had grown thicker with each day of the thirty-five years they had been married.

Susan and Dan enjoyed their morning at the Naval Academy, and then headed to lunch. During their meal, she finally told Dan more details about the plan she and her parents had made for her unexpected pregnancy with Joshua. She explained that she had agreed to break up with Dan pronto because, in her parents' eyes, there was no room for negotiation, no excuses. Although she cared very deeply for him, she and her parents couldn't take a chance that people would realize she was pregnant. Even though it broke her heart, she had agreed to break off all contact with him and she would not date anyone else. It was vital that there would be no hint that she was a "loose" girl.

Her excuse to everyone who asked about the breakup with Dan was that she was "focusing on her studies so she could get into a good college." The family had believed that people would buy into that idea, since "nice" girls did that all the time. She told Dan, "I was very sad at the time, heartbroken, but I see now that they had my best interests at heart. By doing what they asked, I was totally protected from the gossip that other girls in my situation faced. My folks did the right thing at the time. The world was different back then." She shrugged.

"Yes, but I would've been there for you, if I had known. We could've gotten married, Susan." He looked at her with pleading, but loving, eyes.

"Yes, but, if we had, I wouldn't have been a high school graduate. You might not have been either, if you had needed to drop out to get a job to support us. That wouldn't have been a good future for either of us. Remember my friend Marsha? She was pregnant and got married and had to leave school the next week when the principal found out. A few years after their son was born, her hubby did graduate from college, but he got bored with his 11th grade-educated wife and divorced her a short time later. She raised the child alone, while he started a new family with a college sweetheart. She and the child were forgotten. I loved you too much to steal your future."

"I guess that was the culture of the time, Suzy-Q. Still it must've been so hard for you, my beloved. I would've stayed with you, had I known." He reached across the table, squeezed her hand, and then lifted it to his lips.

The server checked their meal receipt, smiling at them as she left their table. "I'll be right back with your sweet tea and bread. Lunch will be out soon," the server told them.

"Thank you," they both said in unison.

"Jinx, you owe me a kiss," Dan said. He leaned over and gave her a kiss.

Susan giggled at his affection, feeling like a teenager and basking in the delight of the moment. She would never get tired of his kisses. Then, more serious, she spoke again. "My parents were there for me. My reputation was never questioned, at least not to my face. It turned out to be okay...though I did find our after-breakup chat very hard to handle."

"I got you to come out to the car with me..."

"Yes, after you confronted me at my locker. Dan, you can't imagine what went through my mind when I saw you standing on the other side of my locker after I closed it. I'd heard the other kids whispering and giggling, so I figured something was up."

"I had to talk to you, just one more time." His tender gaze spoke of the heartbreak that her rejection had caused him so many years before.

"It couldn't be. It broke my heart to turn you away." She squeezed his proffered hand.
"We're the product of our day and time, Dan."

He nodded. The server brought their lunch. "Enjoy," she said. He offered a brief prayer of thankfulness for their food. Susan took a sip of her soup, remarking how good it was, as he took a bite of his sandwich. Then, lightening his mood, he questioned her. "If you don't mind my asking, how did you hide your pregnancy so you could stay in school? There must have been some real logistics involved in that!"

"I stayed out of sight of Mr. Williams, the principal, for one thing." They laughed.

"Oh, yes, he would've made your life miserable if he'd known." Dan took a sip of his tea.

"The only thing was, a couple of times, he almost caught me." Susan shook her head.

"What happened, Suzy-Q?" He took a bite of his sandwich.

"It was, oh I guess, about seven months into my pregnancy. I was walking in from the senior parking lot. I'd been at the doctor's office and came to school late. Just as I passed that old storage shed. You know, where the landscape guys kept their mowers. I saw Mr. Williams walking into the parking lot. I jumped into the shed, but I guess I made some noise because he came running. I heard him outside as he nosed around the shed. I was shaking so hard! He was trying so hard to get the door open, while I was on the other side, trying to hold it shut. Just then, two rats ran over my feet and scurried underneath the door and out of the shed. Dan, I was so scared, but I held onto that door for dear life. Mr. Williams let out a yell and took off. I won't repeat what he said, but he didn't come back. I think the rats ran up his legs or something, based on some of the profane comments he made. A few minutes later, I peeked out through a window in the shed and saw him primping himself before he walked back into the school. Then I got the heck out of there, myself!"

"You've never been fond of rats or mice." Dan was laughing hard. So was she. "You said 'he almost caught you a couple of times.' What else happened?" He continued eating

74

his sandwich as she replied.

"Oh, my. Well, one day I was walking down the girls' staircase next to Mr. Williams's wife's class room. Do you remember where that was?"

He nodded. "I sure do. We had one of our first kisses just outside her classroom."

"Dan, you are such a romantic! I'm impressed that you remembered."

"Suzy-Q, it seems to me that you didn't." He nudged her gently in fun.

"I confess . . . I had forgotten, but you're missing the story." She took a sip of her soup. "Yummy."

"Sorry. Please do continue. What happened on the girls' staircase?" He straightened up and looked serious, which made her laugh.

"Well, I was a good eight months pregnant at the time, when I saw Mr. Williams headed my way. He called out 'young lady' and I took off. I headed down those stairs as fast as my little ol' pregnant body would go. When I got to the bottom, I ran into Mr. Lopez, one of the janitors, and his mop and bucket."

"Literally?'

"Yes. I hit that bucket so hard I thought we were both goners. Mr. Lopez grabbed my arm to keep me from falling. What a racket we made! Or, should I say, I made? Mr. Williams was starting to come through the doorway to the stairs when he got waylaid by Mrs. Williams, who had just come out of her classroom, wondering what the noise was."

"Saved by the wife, rather than the bell?'

"Not exactly, though it did slow him down a bit. Mr. Lopez whispered to me to give him my jacket, which he wrapped around his waist. You know, like guys do with jackets they take off and don't want to lay them down. And then he pushed me under the stairwell. I scrunched down as much as my very-pregnant body would let me and then Mr. Lopez began mopping the floor with great gusto. Mr. Williams saw him, but not me, and asked if Mr. Lopez had heard anything unusual. He said, "Oh, no, Mr. Williams. I am so sorry. I kicked my bucket when I came down the stairs too fast. I forgot it was here. I knocked it over and made a mess, but I'll clean it up right away, sir. So sorry. You best take the boys' stairway. This way, this floor is too wet."

"So he saved your skin."

"Yep, he sure did. I mean, he could tell I was pregnant, but Mr. Lopez was always so nice to me. He protected me. He told me he'd keep my jacket on for the rest of the day in case he ran into Mr. Williams again. In fact, he was going to make a point of being in Mr. Williams's line of sight during the afternoon, so that he wouldn't remember seeing a yellow jacket and a pregnant girl running down the stairs. Instead, he said that Mr. Williams would recall seeing a fat janitor with a yellow jacket around his waist and forget about me. The next day, he gave me my jacket back in a brown paper bag and suggested I not wear it to school again any time soon."

"That was really great of him to stick his neck out like that. He could've been fired for protecting you."

"Don't I know? I made him a big plate of chocolate chip cookies later that week and thanked him for taking care of me." She thought for a minute and sighed. "I haven't thought of those events in years. Mr. Williams almost got me twice, but I managed to stay out of his way for the rest of my pregnancy."

"What about the teachers at the school? Surely they

knew."

"I made sure my classes were with teachers who were sympathetic to girls in my situation. There were a few, you know, who thought the treatment of pregnant teens was horrid and that the boys got off scot-free while the girls suffered all the consequences. It was a pity that the day and age demanded pregnant girls be cast aside." She thoughtfully finished her soup and bread.

"Oh, Susan, I'm so sorry you had to go through this." He folded his napkin, finished with his meal. "I hope you didn't think I left town because I somehow knew you were pregnant and was afraid of what might happen to me . . . or to you." He looked at her so sweetly she almost cried.

"No. I knew you didn't know." She smiled sweetly at her hubby.

He leaned across the table and gave her a big kiss. "You always think of others, my dear little Suzy-Q. Even in the midst of your struggles, you always put others first. God bless you, Susan." He smiled at her, with his deep love evident. He reached up and brushed aside a lock of hair that had made its way onto her cheek. She so loved his touch.

"Oh, perhaps I should tell you the name of the father on Joshua's original birth certificate." She smiled as she got her trademark glint in her eye, knowing that he would never guess the name she'd used in a single moment of playfulness during that stressful time.

"Whose name did you put down?" He leaned forward, curious.

"Alan Jay Merrill." She couldn't control the laughter she felt at the memory.

"Who in the world is that? I never heard of him." He

looked perplexed. "But, somehow, that does sound familiar . . . I just can't place it." He shook his head.

"It's the names of three of the Osmond brothers." She grinned at Dan.

"What? You gotta be kidding me!" He laughed till tears rolled down his cheeks. When he regained some degree of self-control, he asked, "How in the world did you think of that?"

Sharing in the joy of the moment, she told him, "I was a big fan. I'd never met any of them, or even seen them in concert, so it seemed like a pretty safe choice. The nuns at Mercy Hospital might have suspected a false name if I used Donny or Marie in the name, so I stuck to the lesser-known, but equally-gifted, brothers."

"Susan Walsh, you are too much!" He kissed her once and then once more "for good measure," as he often told her. "Smart lady. I'm impressed." He smiled and kissed her hand.

"Thank you, sir." She bowed as she sat there, and grinned at her hubby. She felt so blessed to be with him now. He was a keeper!

"Yes, your parents really did the best for your little family. And, we're finally together again. That's what matters most." More smiles were shared at the lunch table. He glanced at his watch. "Time to hit the road. Shall we do a lap of the mall and then go to Dairy Queen as part of our walk?"

"Absolutely, kind sir," Susan replied.

Their rekindled relationship and subsequent marriage had been a difficult adjustment for Susan, in some ways. Dan was everything that Kurt had pretended to be but was not: caring, loving, gentle, kind. He was also a devout Christian. There had been some struggles for her as she made her way from an abusive marriage to one grounded in mutual love and respect. She was so used to the putdowns, the lies, and the adultery from her first marriage that she kept expecting those expressions of dislike from Dan. But they never came, which was both confusing and wonderful at the same time. It had the tendency to keep her slightly off-balance, not being sure of how to react, what to anticipate when they were together.

Susan knew from knowing her own personality so well that she would reflect on this numerous times in the coming months, but for now, here was the man she had adored so many years before, happy to be in her presence.

The two months since their marriage had been the happiest she had ever known. She was closer than ever to her beloved daughter Brooke and was getting closer to the sons Kurt had carefully trained to stay an arms-length distance from her. Dan's family was being integrated into hers, and she cherished the new children and grandchildren she was coming to know. Her life had become the Brady Bunch on steroids. She loved every minute of it.

Susan was glad her best friend, Nancy, was still an active part of her life. The petite Hispanic nurse Nancy and her massive Irish husband Patrick were delightful rays of sunshine from an otherwise dark time in her life.

There still seemed to be a cloud over her son Christopher as Susan embarked on her new life, but she assumed time and love would bridge the gap the years had worn away. He had been so close to Kurt, and here was a new man replacing his father. Though Christopher was a grown man, and a Ph.D. at that, he still occasionally reflected the attitudes instilled in him by Kurt. By his actions, he sometimes demonstrated a male chauvinist point of view, indicating by his comments that men were superior to women. There were other times when he spoke sharply and sarcastically to Brooke and Susan. She prayed that time would heal his emotional wounds sooner rather than later. Susan said to herself, "All he needs is a relationship with a strong man who will show him how to treat a woman. That, and a relationship with the Lord." She began at once praying towards those ends.

The days continued to fly by until they found themselves in early December. The days were getting shorter and cooler, so they got out their warm sweaters and lightweight jackets. Today, they were going to Grandparents' Day at the Mills-Parole Elementary School where Joshua's son Max attended. They'd made similar treks to Dan's grandchildren's schools earlier in the school year. They both embraced the opportunity to get close to each other's grands.

For now, they finished their breakfast and washed up their dishes. She was again surprised by Dan, who helped with straightening up the kitchen. Kurt would have never deigned to do that. Oh, I must stop comparing the two men. There really is no comparison. I have hit the jackpot with Dan! Wait, what's this? She found some house keys hooked on the top rack of the dishwasher. How in the world did they get there? Strange. She dropped them on the kitchen counter and completed her tasks. They hurried upstairs to brush their teeth and finish getting ready for the day. A few moments later, they scooped up the keys, headed to the car, and drove off to the school.

Chapter 12

Dan and Susan had enjoyed their time at Grandparents' Day, but about a week later, Dan noticed that Susan seemed to have something on her mind. His new wife had been quiet for most of the day, and still wasn't saying much that evening as she made the from-scratch cranberry cake with boiled frosting that had been her grandmother's claim to fame among family members.

"Suzy-Q, what's bugging you? You seem awfully quiet today." Dan walked up behind her as he spoke and wrapped his arms around her. He snuggled against her neck, showering her with kisses. "I do so love you, my dear wife. What's up?"

Susan turned and gave him a little peck on the cheek. "You have always known my moods, haven't you Dan?"

"Yes, my sweetness. So, what gives, as we used to say?" He waited by her side.

"I wanted to ask you about something, but I haven't been too sure how to approach it." Susan seemed to hesitate, then spoke again, "We haven't really talked that much about Rebecca." She hurried on. "I haven't wanted to cause you any pain. I know she hasn't been gone that long, but I am curious about her. What kind of woman she was. What your marriage was like. You know, those kinds of things."

His face sagged, though he hadn't meant for that to happen. He hadn't thought about Rebecca in at least a few days . . . four or five, anyway. How could he describe his wife of thirty plus years to his wife of a few months? "You want the whole story or a Readers' Digest Condensed Version?"

"How about something in between those two extremes? I've been wondering about my hubby's past life. You know, just in case you were an ax murderer or something!" Susan smiled, as if she was trying to lighten his mood.

He brought her hand to his lips and spoke, "Okay. I'll confess . . . I never was an ax murderer, but I was happily married to someone who was not you, Suzy-Q."

"Why don't we have a cup of tea while the cake bakes and just chat about Rebecca a bit? Would that be okay?" Susan gave his nose a kiss and stood back.

Dan said, "You should know our story." He looked serious. "The truth, the whole truth, and nothing but the truth, my lady." He bowed. "May I have some cookies with my tea?"

"Sure thing! You grab the cookie jar and some plates and I'll make the tea."

When they were comfortably settled on stools at the kitchen island, he began to share the story of how he met the second love of his life, Rebecca.

"We were both freshmen when we met the first time. It was Freshman English class, and we were both pretty green about college life. I was still sad about you, so I wasn't dating anyone. We talked a bit, but I didn't really connect with her. I saw her again two years later in Junior English and was settled enough to begin a relationship. We got put on the same team for a semester-long project. We started dating about halfway through the term." He paused, to see how she was taking his comments.

Susan said, "I've seen pictures of her at the boys' houses. What was she like, as a person, I mean?"

"Susan, she was a sweet woman, a tender person. She

loved me and our boys beyond belief. But, she did have one major flaw." He paused for effect, knowing Susan would eagerly await his confession.

"Dan, what in the world was that?" She leaned forward, her curiosity obvious.

"Well, you know how I love music." He waited, smiling at both the memory and her eagerness to hear his tale.

"Yes, Dan, you're a wonderful baritone. I love hearing you let loose in the shower every once in a while."

"Rebecca, my longtime wife, was completely tone deaf. She couldn't sing a note on pitch to save her soul, but she seemed completely oblivious to that fact." He laughed in memory of her flaw. "She bought these musical toys for the boys when they were young, and they were like nails on a chalkboard to me. They were sooo off-pitch and she LOVED to play them all the time for the kids and then the grandkids. Oh, she also began each day with a song or two from Annie."

Susan started laughing, "Poor Rebecca. To be married to someone like you. I sometimes think you have perfect pitch, Dan, and to have no gift for music . . . and to be totally unaware of your lack. That must've been murder for you, dear!" They laughed, not at Rebecca, but with her, if she had been there.

Dan chuckled with the memory and relaxed with the knowledge that this wouldn't be as hard as he'd feared. "She was a good woman, Susan, and I loved my life with her. But she couldn't sing a note. And, she loved to whistle. She . . . couldn't do that well, either." More laughter. He winced, remembering the tunes Rebecca had so totally mangled.

"I'm glad she made you so happy, Dan." Susan smiled sweetly at her hubby.

He took her hand and replied, "I was concerned that you

might feel, I don't know, a bit jealous. After all, you had so many miserable years with Kurt and the responsibility of raising your children fell totally on you, while I was so happy." He looked at her with the loving care he had always felt towards his bride. What a gift she was from God. I'm so glad He gave her to me.

"I don't begrudge you your happiness, Dan. I'm glad that the man I loved so long was happy. I'm glad Rebecca took good care of you and the boys." Susan smiled and patted his hand. "Tell me more."

He paused. What should he include in the story and what should he leave out? Not that there was anything bad, but Susan didn't need all the details, just the highlights. He thought for a moment. She remained silent, allowing him to speak at will. No rush. He knew she would wait.

"Well, we dated for about a year before I proposed. We planned on getting married right out of college and we did. We'd been active in a local church, but Rebecca wanted to get married in her home church in Florida, so I agreed. I mean, my friends and family didn't object to a quick trip to central Florida."

"Where in Florida did you go?" Susan asked.

"Merritt Island. It's on the space coast, near Cape Canaveral. There is a big Baptist church down there, and Rebecca had grown up in it. I was fine with the whole thing. They had this big sanctuary. It was beautiful. Even though we weren't going to be members there, everyone was very friendly. We had the reception in their fellowship hall. It was nothing fancy."

"Did you have a big dinner afterwards?" Susan was

curious about traditions in the South, having never lived there.

"No, no. Just cake, mints, and punch. Only rich people had dinners at receptions in those days. Remember we're talking about 1981 here. We were considered pretty well-off because we had mints and peanuts with the punch and cake. Non-alcoholic punch, at that. We had this big ol' fountain that one of the ladies at the church owned. The punch came through holes in the sides of the fountain. The only thing was that our wedding colors were mint green and yellow. Rebecca decided, I don't remember how, that she wanted yellow punch. As I looked at the punch bowl, I thought the yellow punch looked like . . . well, you know." He started grinning to beat the band.

Susan laughed, "Oh, my! I can't believe it! You've got to be kidding!"

He said, "No, my dear Susan. I kid you not. For about two hours, we were treated to the vision of yellow punch streaming out of that fountain. Folks started to get the giggles...We didn't have many takers on that punch, after a while." He shook his head in amusement.

"Poor Rebecca. How did she ever live that down?" She grinned at him.

"Well, people still reminded her through the years every time we went back to Florida for a visit, but it just became a family story for us. We were embarrassed at first, but time smoothed off the rough edges. We had some pretty good laughs about it."

She said, "I imagine so, Dan."

"There was one other thing...at our reception, I mean." He paused, for effect. "We got seventeen toasters as wedding gifts."

"Seventeen? You've gotta be kidding me!" she smiled at

his memory. "It must've been a good year for toasters."

"And for toast, apparently." He took a sip of his tea, draining the cup. "We gave away the ones we couldn't return. For every wedding we went to for a couple of years, they were our gift of choice!" He still chuckled when he thought about it.

"More tea, Dan?" She walked over to the microwave to heat up a little more water.

"Sure. Our story is a pretty long one, but I'll try to keep it short and sweet." He paused again, thinking. "So, we got married right out of college, then we started having the boys, one after the next. They came at about two year intervals. Richard was born two years after we got married, so that was 1983. Kevin came along in 1985, followed by Jim in 1987. We had a daughter on the way in 1989, but she didn't survive the pregnancy." Dan hesitated. This was the hard part. He spoke slowly. "Rebecca lost her when she was about six months along. That was very sad. We buried Katherine Elizabeth in a beautiful little dress that Rebecca had smocked. After that, we stopped getting pregnant. And Rebecca gave up smocking. She'd made a whole closet full of increasingly bigger sizes of smocked dresses in preparation for our little girl. She gave them all away when Katie Beth died. She –we- couldn't bear to look at them." He stopped to wipe away a tear. "Of course, now I have Brooke in my life, so she's a nice, full-grown replacement for my little Katie Beth."

"Brooke was born in 1983, so she would have been only six years older than Katie Beth. I hope you consider Brooke to be your daughter, since Katie Beth is waiting for you in heaven." Susan reached over and took his hand. "I'm so sorry for your loss, Dan, but we know that Rebecca and Katie Beth are

86

together and healthy." She poured him another cup of tea.

Dan smiled a slight smile and replied, "Yes, I know. That's such a comfort. You're such a comfort, Susan." He stopped to take a sip and grab a cookie. He took a bite, chewed, and swallowed. "So, the years went on. Rebecca had stopped working when the kids were born. She had been working in PR. I worked hard, building a business for someone else. I was doing quite well, but then decided to start my own company. The Lord was good. Business was great. Rebecca helped out some, a natural considering her background in public relations. A few years ago, I sold the business for a nice profit, and we moved back to Annapolis. We were really starting to enjoy the kids and grandkids. We went on vacations together and saw parts of the world we had never been to. We went on mission trips with the church. And that's when . . ." He broke down. The loss of Rebecca was still fresh in his mind.

Susan stood up, went to his side, and hugged him. "Maybe we need to stop for today."

Dan straightened up. "No. that's okay." He waited, to compose himself. "Rebecca was having trouble breathing one evening. I called 911. They came and found she had a collapsed lung. They insisted that she needed to go to the hospital. She had a lot of fluid in her chest, a couple of liters, they told us. The test results came back that there were cancer cells in the fluid. More tests were done. They discovered that she had stage four ovarian cancer. She'd been ignoring some symptoms that I didn't know anything about, until the night she couldn't catch her breath." He sipped his tea in an attempt to control his emotions.

"Then what?" She asked.

"We went through several rounds of different types of

chemo, thinking that each one would be the cure. A couple of times it looked like the tumors were getting smaller." Dan looked over at Susan. "She would've needed extensive surgery, even if the tumors had gone away. Life-changing surgery. So, even if the chemo had worked perfectly, she still would've needed a huge operation that would have knocked her for a loop for about a year or more, if she survived it. She might not have ever made it out of the hospital." He waited, to gather his strength. "But, instead, the tumors grew and multiplied. The cancer invaded her whole body. She was very weak, but not in a lot of pain, surprisingly. She lost a lot of weight, and she had been fairly thin to begin with. And then she got an infection. And we met Joshua. I didn't tell her who I thought he was." He stopped.

"You couldn't put her through the pain of knowing you had another son?" she asked.

"No, it wasn't that. I'd told her about you years before, but I didn't know about Joshua." He thought for a moment. "I just didn't want her to have any more concerns in her life. I don't think she suspected what I was pretty sure of – that Joshua was somehow my son- because she was in and out of consciousness quite a bit by then. I just focused on her. Then the infection was pretty much cured, but the cancer wasn't. She lost interest in food and stopped eating completely. She lingered a few more days, but it was over soon. She died almost six months to the day after her diagnosis." He sat silent in his chair, exhausted. Tears rolled down both of their cheeks.

"Let's call it a day, shall we?" Susan wiped her tears away, kissed his forehead, and gave him a quick hug as she removed the tea cups and plates. The cake came out of the oven right on schedule and she put it on the counter to cool.

He glanced at her and said, "Just a little while longer. Now we're getting into the happy part. You know the rest. I had met Joshua for the first time, reunited with you my beloved, and eventually married you. I love my life now. I loved it before, with Rebecca, but I feel like I've come full circle. There has been great happiness and great sorrow, but we're on the happiness part again." He seemed rejuvenated.

"Yes, my dear Dan. It's been a long while coming, but the happiness part is definitely here." With the cups and dishes safely in the dishwasher, Susan turned and he hugged her, having come up behind her. He then set out their breakfast dishes as was his custom. He liked to set the table in preparation for the new dawn, anticipating the day ahead like a little boy. It always made her smile, so he knew he would always do it.

Right before they headed upstairs for the night, Susan put the cookie jar away in their pantry. She turned to come out of the small room. He saw her hesitate.

"What's wrong, Susan?"

She asked him, "What are these slippers doing on the bottom shelf of the pantry, my love?"

Chapter 13

Brooke realized that the day was approaching when Michael would demand an answer to the question, "When are we getting married?" They'd been engaged since before Dan had popped the question to her mother, but Brooke had put him off and postponed for reasons even she had come to realize were pathetic. Tonight, as she got ready for their double date with her mother and Dan, she could feel her tension rising. She fretted through her shower, while she dressed, and as she put on her jewelry for the evening. She ran a brush through her long brown hair, fussing over a small tangle at the nape of her neck. She jerked the brush through, a bit too roughly, crying out as she felt the hair rebel against her tugs. A few strands of hair came out. At least the knot was gone. But, again . . . Why was she so nervous about committing to Michael? She loved him.

She'd known him in good times, like when he was very helpful to her mother at the rehab center as Susan was recovering from her coma. And in the bad times, like when they had flown to Vancouver, British Columbia to rescue her mother from the murderous intentions of her adulterous first husband Kurt, who was Brooke's father. They'd just made it in time to save her mom from Kurt and Kelsey's murderous plans.

So why was she so reticent to set a date and marry him? Michael Bench was an outstanding man and wonderful Christian who'd led many people to Christ. He was even the facilitator for the salvation of her mother and her...so why the hesitation? She sank down onto her bed.

The only thing Brooke could come up with was that she

didn't want their marriage to turn out like her parents' marriage had. Her parents' marriage generally and her father specifically were the examples of misery and pain that she didn't want to replicate under any circumstances. Yes, yes, she knew Michael wasn't like her father, but she cringed every time she thought he was responding as her father had. She found herself waiting for the other shoe to drop. But with Michael, it didn't.

Her dad- a man who seemed to be so nice and appeared to be the stereotypical wonderful husband- turned out to be a Dr. Jekyll and Mr. Hyde when he was at home. Brooke had watched her mother being mistreated for all the years she'd been growing up. No, she wasn't willing to take a chance that it would happen to her. No thanks.

But there was Michael. He'd been there for her, time and time again. She'd met his parents, who were living nearby in Eastport. She'd observed their interaction and saw that their marriage was built on a foundation of Christ and mutual love and respect. They hadn't always had it easy. They were an interracial couple, too. Mrs. Bench was white, while Mr. Bench was African-American, just as she had white skin to Michael's brown.

They'd talked to her numerous times about what it meant to marry outside your race. Mr. and Mrs. Bench had faced discrimination that, in today's more accepting society, she and Michael would not have to experience. Mrs. Bench had told her that the pain of the outside world had only worked to make them closer. For a time, their families had rejected them, but they came around when they saw the tremendous love that young couple shared. Michael's birth, and those of his sisters, had cemented the couple's relationship with both sets of parents.

But Brooke wouldn't face that. The Benches were devoted Christians, just like Michael, and they loved her unconditionally. Her father Kurt, who might have had something negative to say about her engagement to an African American, was dead. Her mother loved Michael like a son. Her brothers, Joshua and Christopher, wouldn't offer any resistance to the marriage. Joshua wouldn't because he didn't have a racist bone in his body and because he loved Michael like a brother. Christopher wouldn't cause issues because he chose to distance himself from the family, now that he knew the father he had so dearly respected hadn't deserved the pedestal Christopher had always put him on. So, what was her restraint in committing her life to Michael?

She and Michael were going out to dinner with her mother and Dan tonight. Based on hints Michael had been dropping for the past two weeks, she thought the time had come when he would simply ask her if she was willing to marry him or not. He would be over in a few minutes to get her. She was nervous and prayed that she would give the right answer when the time came to commit.

Brooke had dressed with care for the evening, as she always did when going out on the town with Michael. She had put on a red and white chevron short skirt with a black dress T-shirt, topping off the outfit with gold jewelry. It was quite chilly in the evening this early part of winter, so she would take a jacket with her, should she need it.

She glanced down at her ring finger. Her engagement ring still shone like the night he had slipped it on her finger at the Chart House. She thought back to that night. Michael had thanked everyone for being so accepting of him and commented on what a wonderful daughter she had been. He complimented the agape love she had for her mother and then dropped to one knee and asked her to be his wife. She remembered accepting his proposal immediately and joyfully, but things had reached a stalemate whenever he asked her to set a date.

They had set and reset the nuptials, but she had always moved it further away as it got too close. Sure, Brooke had offered plenty of excuses why it needed to be pushed off, but she even accepted that her reasons were flimsy. First, they needed to move the date because she didn't want to get married before her mom and Dan exchanged vows. "After all," she told Michael, "they've waited forty years to get married." He'd suggested a double wedding, but she wanted to give her mother the attention she thought a bride deserved on her special day and refused that idea. He accepted that excuse. It was, he had told her, logical and reasonable.

The next reason was that the photographer she wanted wasn't available for several months. Michael wasn't quite as happy to go along with that, since there were plenty photographers with excellent credentials in the Annapolis area. Then, she said that the flowers she wanted would be too expensive, since they were out of season or the caterer she preferred was already booked for the next few months or the venue was not exactly right or...or...or... Michael exclaimed that maybe they should just elope. "No," she told him, "that's what my dad and Kelsey kinda did in Hawaii. I'm not having any of that. We need to get married in front of our friends and family." He backed off. She didn't know how long she could continue putting him off, but things felt like they were coming to a crossroad. Brooke sighed and rose to her feet. Gotta get downstairs before they come. Before . . . who knows what will happen?

And she was right. Michael drove over to pick her up. Her mother and step-father arrived at the condo at the same time he did. The group came into her condo and said that they needed to have a little chat before heading out for dinner. She gulped, expecting that this was the turning point, and then offered them seats in her living room. Michael began the conversation.

"Brooke, my beloved," Michael started with a voice so soft that she had difficulty hearing him, "I think we need to decide something. We've been engaged for months and I just need to know: Are you going to marry me or not?"

"Why, Michael, yes, of course I am." Brooke hesitated, even as she spoke.

"When?" Michael looked at her with kindness, but he clearly wanted an answer.

"I'm . . . just . . . not sure when . . . exactly . . ." Silence reigned as the couple just looked at one another.

Susan and Dan shifted, obviously uncomfortable on the couch. Her mom was the first to break the quiet. "Brooke, you know how much we love the two of you. I think you're hesitating to marry because of what you saw with your father. Michael is not your father. He is nothing like Kurt was. I think you're afraid that Michael will turn out to be like Kurt. Is that what you fear?"

Brooke began to cry. "I'm so sorry, Michael. I just . . . don't think I can . . ." She shook her head, even as Michael looked on, openly crushed.

Her mother cut in, "Brooke. Do you love Michael?"

"Yes. I do." She was distraught.

"Do you trust God? He's the one who created Michael to

become the man he is today." Her mom's voice was quiet and gentle as she talked to the daughter she loved so dearly. Brooke knew how much her mother cared for her. They had been the best of friends for all those horrid years with her father.

"Yes, of course, Mom." She still continued to weep. "I just don't know if I can get over what I saw Dad doing to you."

"Brooke, I know that your upbringing was very hard on you, but look at me now." Her mom reached over and took Dan's hand, giving it a squeeze as she spoke. "I have Dan, the man of my dreams. Not all men are like your father was. Not all marriages are like the one I had with Kurt. I'm married to a very godly man who loves the Lord and who loves me. You're engaged to a man very much like Dan. Not like Kurt." Her mom put her arm around Brooke and pulled her close.

Dan spoke up in this intervention. His voice was the very heart of kindness. "Brooke, Michael and I have had several conversations about this topic. I told him that your hesitation wasn't his fault, and it isn't. Michael thought it might be a race issue . . ."

"No, it's nothing like that," Brooke told Dan in a hurry. She turned and said, "Michael, your race never, ever played into this." She wiped her hair from her eyes and begged him to understand.

Michael looked at his fiancée with tenderness, but then said, "Brooke, I've tried everything, from being patient to accepting every reason you gave me, no matter how ridiculous. I'm at a loss now. I don't know what else to do. I want to marry you, to make you the happiest woman in the world. I adore you, but I don't want to wait." Michael hesitated as she continued to dissolve in tears. "Brooke, we've already experienced things that most couples will never face in a hundred years. But I have

95

to know: Will you marry me? Or . . . not?"

***

Susan and Dan waited without speaking, praying that Brooke would make the decision that God wanted. They knew Michael was an outstanding choice for a husband, and they prayed that she would see it, too. They waited. Minutes passed as Brooke cried. Finally, Michael said, "I think we should be going." He was obviously a man defeated.

They had discussed this intervention with Michael beforehand, agreeing that they would leave if Brooke seemed unable to make a decision. It might be better for her to watch Michael walk out, to sleep on it. The trio left without a word, with Brooke still weeping.

Susan and Dan stood outside on the steps of Brooke's condo and tried to comfort Michael, but Susan knew that their efforts were in vain. She took him in her arms, "Michael, give her a chance to miss you. I believe that she'll realize what she's lost and come running back."

"Susan, I just don't know. I thought I could love her out of this, but maybe I can't." Michael looked like a broken man. He shrugged. "I think I'll take a few days off, maybe go on a short trip to think things through. I didn't want it to end this way, but I'm not going to force her."

Dan hugged Michael, slowly saying, "I would be proud to call you my son-in-law, Michael. I believe that God will bring Brooke to her senses, but it may take some time. She's witnessed years of abuse. It took Susan some time to work through her pain. I know what you're going through because Susan and I went through it. It's just taking Brooke longer than it did her mom. Hang in there, Michael. We'll pray you through this."

Michael tried to smile, hugged the couple once more, and headed to his own car.

***

Brooke picked herself up from the floor where she had slumped as the trio left her condo, and threw her body onto her couch. It felt like she'd been hit by a train. What was wrong with her? Why was she so frightened of marrying Michael? Of marrying anyone? She loved Michael without question, but when the idea of planning a wedding and going through with it passed through her mind, she freaked out.

Brooke understood that she was good at seeing attitudes in others, but not so great at examining her own motives and stirrings. She sat up all night. Forget dinner. She tried to make a list of pros and cons in marrying Michael, but the paper quickly became too waterlogged for her to write on it. She took the ring off her finger and placed it in the box he had presented to her that night at the Chart House. She had no right to wear it if she wasn't going to marry him.

Early the next morning, she decided to go out for a run, hoping the fresh, crisp air would help clear her mind of the cobwebs caused by stress and no sleep. It didn't work. Afterward, she saw her reflection in the bathroom mirror as she stepped into the steaming shower. Her hair looked scraggly; her face was pale; her eyes were swollen, puffy, and red. Not the best day for her, appearance-wise.

The phone was ringing as she stepped out of the shower. She picked it up on the third ring. Her mother was calling to see how she was.

"Mom, I just don't know what to do." Brooke began

97

crying again.

"Brooke, have you tried talking to Pastor? I know he's pretty young, only about your age, but he was a tremendous help when I was going through my time of doubt about marrying Dan." Her mother's calm voice was so comforting at times like this.

"Mom, I remember him from middle school and high school! He used to eat peanut butter and catsup sandwiches with salt on top! They were gross. I can't talk to him! He had zits the same time I did!"

In spite of herself, her mom laughed at her comment. "Yes, dear, I remember that, but keep in mind that Pastor has been through seminary and has had training in premarital counselling."

"I just don't think . . ." Her voice broke as she tried to answer.

"Brooke, wisdom isn't conferred through white hair. If not Pastor, then can you think of someone whose opinion you value? Can we find a Christian counselor who could walk you through this? There's got to be somebody you'd feel comfortable with. Michael is too good a man to lose." The stress in her mother's voice came through the phone.

Brooke remained silent. Then, "Mom, I need to get dressed. I need to go. Thanks for calling. I'll think about what you said, but I can't talk anymore."

"Honey, I'll be praying for you, that God will give you wisdom in knowing what the right path is through this."

"Okay, thanks. Bye." Brooke hung up, and then slowly got ready for her day. But what was that day going to be like? She and Michael had planned to go to the Eastern Shore, to visit St. Michael's before the town closed up for the winter. They loved visiting all the little shops, seeing the lighthouses, and taking boat tours. A romantic dinner at one of the waterfront restaurants would top off their evening before heading back to their homes. Now that was all off. Now, everything seemed off. She was off.

Brooke walked through downtown Annapolis instead. She visited the Naval Academy, hiked through St. John's College, and still she walked. She headed through the State House and Church Circle areas, past the Reynolds Tavern where she and her mother had had high tea on special occasions. There was the old hospital-turned-condo complex. She knew her mother still vaguely remembered when it'd been a hospital, since she mentioned it every time they walked past the building, but now its red brick façade was used to welcome home its permanent residents instead of the seriously ill.

She looped back to Duke of Gloucester and took Main Street down to the city dock. She was weary, but on edge. Hunger overtook her so she stopped by Charlie's Bar and Grill for a quick piece of pizza and a bottle of water. She walked some more, past the permanent home of the being-rebuilt Annapolis Yacht Club and then over the bridge to Eastport. The nearby beautiful and pricy homes weren't even on her mind as she walked through those neighborhoods. She turned around and headed back into downtown Annapolis.

She wondered what Michael was doing with his day. There'd been no contact. No email. No phone calls. No texting. Just silence. They always talked, every single day. They were together almost every day. Nothing. It was breaking her heart all over again to realize what she had given up. Finally, exhausted by her lack of sleep and her day of walking but never settling down, she headed home.

She called her mother. "Okay, Mom. Who do I need to talk to? I can't bear this."

Chapter 14

Joshua had been getting closer to his birthfather, Dan, for about a year. He'd also spent some time with his half-brothers, Dan's sons, both individually and as a group. Joshua enjoyed his time with Dan, but something kept nagging in the back of his mind. Take today, for example. The guys were all going to watch the Wizards play at the Verizon Center in Washington, D.C. Dan had been buying season tickets for years. How would his life have been different if Dan had raised him? That bugged the daylights out of him. What might have been? It wasn't fair that Richard, Kevin, and Jim had gotten Dan as their father. He was blood, too, but life had been so different for him. Okay, dude, stop with the pity party. What good does this kind of thinking do?

As he got ready for Dan and his sons to stop by and pick him up, Joshua put on the requisite red, white, and blue clothing that the Walsh men wore to show their support of the home team. He and Christopher had both been presented with the red and white shirt and blue slacks from Dan at the wedding reception, along with an open invitation to join them at future games. Christopher thanked Dan, but was uninterested in going; Joshua decided, "Why not?"

Joshua grabbed a quick bite to eat before they arrived. Amanda and the kids were off hanging out with his mom, so he was on his own. He threw together a turkey sandwich and a glass of milk. This ought to hold me over. As he ate, he considered his new family.

The sporting event comradery between Dan and his three

sons, that is, his three other sons, was something that he'd never had with his step-father Kurt. Sure, Kurt had taken him sailing when he was younger and they had played some basketball from time to time, but they had never once been to a professional sports event, no matter how hard he had begged Kurt. Kurt had turned him down flat. No negotiations. No chance.

Instead, he felt now that his adoptive father's whole reason for wanting to spend time with him had been to poke fun at his mother, Susan. He realized that most of their time together had been spent with Kurt engaged in some type of Machiavellian, negative comments about her cooking, cleaning, or managing of the household. What a manipulator that guy was! And I never saw it, never realized how he was pulling some invisible strings on how I felt about life, about Mom. Crud, dude, you were the pits. What? Where did that come from?

The milk he had been downing almost came out of his nose as he mis-swallowed. Dr. Prescott, that was language unbecoming a doctor. He choked for a moment, then continued thinking, but eating much more carefully. No gulping, thank you just the same, like Mom would say. He glanced at his watch. Dan and his family would be arriving soon. Better get my teeth brushed before they get here. He headed upstairs as he continued his thoughts on his life before Dan.

Joshua had noticed through the years that Kurt liked to set one brother against the other, almost as if Kurt wanted to keep his sons off-balance emotionally and feeling badly about themselves on purpose. Joshua had always excelled in school, especially math and science. Hence, he had studied to become a doctor. But Kurt had laughed at him whenever he didn't come in first in his class on a given test or assignment. Joshua could remember those types of conversations with Kurt like they were yesterday.

Kurt would come home from a trip, walk into the kitchen where Joshua was having a quick after-school snack at the kitchen table, take one look at Joshua's anatomy exam, for example, and say, "Gee, Joshua. How do you ever expect to get into medical school with a 98?"

"Dad, I had a migraine at the time." Joshua had tried to explain away the less-than-perfect grade, but Kurt had cut him off.

As his father reached into the refrigerator for a soda, he smirked at Joshua and said, "Well, your grades had better pick up soon, or you'll be wiping down tables at McDonald's for the rest of your life."

That comment had cut Joshua deeply, though he tried to hide it, saying, "Oh, come on Dad. I know it's important to do well. I promise. It won't happen again." He smiled at his father and hoped that the man would just go away. Kurt did, but not before he said more.

Kurt replied, "No son of mine makes a 98. Got it?"

"Yes, sir."

Kurt had turned on his heel, taken his bottle of soda, and locked himself in his office. Joshua heard him laughing a few minutes later. I wonder what he finds so funny. He just cut me, and now he's laughing.

At the time, he had shrugged it off as his father just wanting him to do his best and not accepting anything less. Now Joshua knew the kind of man he is. Oops, he meant was. Joshua sighed and wished his eyes had been opened to Kurt sooner. Then he would have been nicer to his Mom. Shoot, he thought, I was blind.

Then there was Kurt's other reaction to him: the cold shoulder. Kurt had snubbed him a lot, as if he wasn't quite good enough for Kurt's exalted taste. And, of course, Kurt's own flesh and blood son, Christopher, had chosen to attend the Naval Academy, following in his father's footsteps. No matter how well I did, Joshua ruminated, I was reminded over and over that I was an adopted son, while "my son" went to the Naval Academy.

Emerging from his thoughts, Joshua finished his preparations fairly quickly, brushing his teeth, and deciding to leave a love note for Amanda on her pillow. He was glad he'd started doing that again. She loved to get them and he realized just how much they meant to his wife and the mother of his four children. Why did I ever stop? He smiled. No sense in beating himself up, he would simply do it every time he thought of her. He pulled a notepad out of his bedroom side table. "My dearest wife: How I adore you. I'll miss you this evening but I hope you've had a lovely day with the kids and Mom. See you when I get home, though you don't need to wait up. Are we still on for our date tomorrow night? I'm looking forward to taking my beautiful wife out for dinner and a movie. You are more gorgeous with every passing year. Love, Josh"

Hearing Dan's car in the drive, Joshua went back downstairs, grabbed a jacket, and went outside. He smiled at the men waiting for him, greeting them enthusiastically. He realized later that night that he had been a bit quiet that afternoon and evening. He tried not to feel too badly about the great relationship that Dan had with Richard, Kevin, and Jim, but there were times, like this evening, when it was hard. He thought that, if things had been different, he wouldn't be as messed up as he felt now. If only his mom and Dan had gotten married when they were expecting him, instead of . . . No, it did no good whatsoever to even think about it.

As the days passed, he had to stop himself whenever he found his reactions to Amanda similar to the ones his father Kurt had expressed with his mother. He hadn't even realized he was doing it, at first. It was almost normal to be unkind, yet his beloved Amanda didn't deserve his mean temper. Joshua decided to undergo some anger management courses. He kept his studies online, so that his colleagues wouldn't be aware of his need. He followed those brief classes up with some counseling at Michael's church, but the pastor kept talking about a relationship with Christ and Joshua wasn't ready for that. Not just yet. Things were getting better, he had to admit that, and Amanda seemed a lot happier.

He had Dan and his sons to thank for their positive influence in his life. He knew that they were all "religious nuts," as he had called Christians in the past. As he drew closer to them, and as they demonstrated their unconditional love for him, Joshua was able to come to terms with his negative upbringing and be a better husband and father. His four kids had been invited to something called "Awana" at Michael's church, which Michael said was "kinda like a Boy Scouts or Girl Scouts program for Christians." The kids had really gotten excited about going and had met many new friends. Even his daughter Madison had agreed to go, in spite of being in high school.

The kids wanted to memorize Bible verses for the Awana program, so that they could win prizes. He and Amanda helped the kids each week, and spent some time learning the Scripture as well. It wasn't long before they felt the need to commit their lives to Christ, even though they had always tried to live good lives. They realized it wasn't enough. He and Amanda made the commitment first, and, one at a time, their children came to saving faith as well. A short time later, they were baptized as a family. It was a good decision, he knew.

At a family dinner, he had the chance to talk to his half-brothers. Richard was just getting his plate filled up when Joshua came up behind him. While filling his own plate, Joshua hesitated for a moment and then asked, "Hey, Richard, can I ask you something?"

"Sure, Josh, What's up?" The tall, black haired man grabbed some silverware from the serving table. He turned toward Joshua. "Private or public?"

Joshua said, "Well, kinda private, if you don't mind."

"With my brothers or without?" Richard hesitated, "Oh, man, I'm sorry. I meant with our brothers or without." Richard slapped him on the shoulder, quite embarrassed.

"I understand. We're all still getting used to this family thing, me included. No problem." Joshua finished filling his plate and said, "Do you think the family will miss us, if we all four duck out for a minute or two?"

Richard looked around and said, "Nope. The ladies are busy with the kids and Dad is helping Susan, so we should be okay." He turned to Kevin and Jim. "Hey guys grab a plateful and come join Josh and me on the deck for a couple of minutes, okay?"

Joshua said, "Thanks, Richard." He turned to Kevin and Jim. "I just wanted to talk to you guys about something that's been a bit puzzling to me."

After the men had gotten settled, Joshua asked, "So this thing with having Mom and Dan separated for six months. What was your reasoning behind that? It wasn't because you didn't like her, was it?" Joshua rubbed his face, nervous for their answer, but he had to hear it straight from them. Of course, he had talked to his mother about the forced separation right after they had reunited. His natural reaction had been to be angry at his half-brothers for putting her through more emotional turmoil.

Susan had patiently explained their reasoning many months before and told him that it had been for the best. After all, the couple had been brought back together less than one year after Rebecca's funeral and Dan began talking about marrying Susan almost immediately. This was too sudden for Dan's children. Conversely, Joshua was surprised by their request and was eager for his mother to begin anew with Dan. Joshua thought, boy, I didn't miss Dad as much as I thought I would. I mean, I don't miss Kurt. My dad is still alive.

Richard took a bite and thought for a moment. "Well, Josh, we didn't want Dad to rush into anything. I mean, he hadn't seen Susan for what, forty years? We didn't realize how great your mom is at the time, but we still wanted them to slow things down a bit."

Kevin said, "Yeah, Josh, please don't think it was because of Susan herself. We had just lost Mom less than a year before. Dad was still grieving Mom when they got back together. You know, I heard of a pastor who remarried one month after his wife died. That was so tacky, in my opinion."

Jim spoke up, "Yeah, man, that reeks of 'another woman,' at least in the eyes of people who knew him." He hurried on to explain. "We aren't saying Susan was the 'other woman'! No way. Of course she wasn't. But we didn't want things to look bad." Jim hesitated. "Man, I just put my foot

directly into my mouth, brothers. I did not explain that well."
He took a bite of food. Silence, except for chewing.

Joshua said, "Okay guys, I understand. It was nothing against my mother. You would have reacted the same way with any woman who seemed to be replacing – well, who actually, when you come right down to it – was replacing your mother, fairly close to her death."

Heads nodded all around. Richard said, "Again, Josh, it was absolutely nothing against your mom. We needed time to grieve, and so did your family. The good news, well, the great news, is that things have worked out…What does Madison call that? Superbly well."

They laughed and headed back into the house. It was a bit too chilly to stay outside for very long.

***

Joshua and Amanda were getting ready to take the kids to a family-friendly movie at the Annapolis Mall one Saturday afternoon, when he got a panicked call from Richard.

"Hello?" He recognized Richard's number and picked up on the first ring.

"Hey, Joshua?" Richard's voice cracked with stress.

"Yes, Richard . . . Hey, man, what's wrong?" He could hear sobbing on the other end of the line. Richard's wife Lauren was talking in the background. Joshua realized that she was the one crying.

"Our little Sadie . . ." Richard seemed unable to continue. Joshua heard Richard coughing, almost choking.

"Richard, take it easy, buddy. Where are you?" Joshua's doctoring livelihood came to the forefront as he whispered to Amanda, "There's something wrong with Sadie, but I can't find

108

out what's happening from Richard."

"We're at the hospital, Josh. Sadie woke up this morning with nausea and vomiting. We thought it was the flu or something. Then she got this terrible pain. Really, really bad, Josh. Her face was absolutely white. We called her pediatrician, and he told us to bring her here." His voice broke again. "They operated a little while ago, but her appendix burst right before the operation. She's in pretty bad shape."

"I'm on my way over, Richard. Where are Lauren and Zachary?"

"Lauren is with me. Kevin and Samantha picked up Zachary a little while ago. He wanted to make sure his twin sister was okay, so he came with us, but she's not. We thought it would be best for him to go home with Kevin and Samantha while...things get sorted out. Sadie's only nine years old, Joshua." His half-brother was pleading with him, somehow, as if being nine should guard her against serious illness.

"I'm heading over there. Where exactly are you right now?" Joshua got the floor number from Richard, then he looked over at Amanda, "Sorry, but I need to be there." He hung up with his brother and headed for the door. As he left, he heard Amanda talking to the children.

Amanda sent her love with him and then told the kids, "I'm going to see if you can hang out at Grandma and Grandpa Walsh's house and then I'm going to see Uncle Richard and Aunt Lauren. Your cousin Sadie is very sick, and Dad has to go see her in the hospital instead of our all going to the movies. We need to pray for Sadie."

Joshua heard the kids respond. They knew what it was like being the children of a doctor so, though they were disappointed, he knew for a fact that they understood. Since it was one of their little cousins who was ill, they said it was even more important that he go. They were all still getting to know Dan's children and grandchildren, but they loved the sweet-spirited Sadie and her twin brother Zachary. They were a couple of cute kids.

Joshua hopped into his BMW and headed to the hospital as fast as possible. He knew that Amanda would be a comfort to Lauren, and was pleased that she would be coming, as well. He drove down Riva Road, thankful that he lived so close to the Anne Arundel Medical Center. He pulled into the parking garage, and went into the hospital at a trot.

His half-brother and his wife were waiting and pacing as Joshua hurried up to them.

Richard grabbed his arm. "Joshua thanks so much for coming. The doctors are with Sadie right now. I asked them to call you." Richard was frantic. Lauren was silent and wide-eyed.

"Richard, my team doesn't work with pediatrics, and I haven't been called in to consult on Sadie's case. If you give permission, her doctors will talk to me about the situation, and I'll explain what's happening to the two of you, in laymen's terms." Joshua thought it best to get things right out in the open.

"Sure, Josh, we understand. That's what they told us. I told them it was okay to talk to you. We just want someone in the know to tell us what's going on," Richard said, breaking down. Lauren stood by, not speaking, but nodding.

Joshua hugged them both. His cellphone rang. It was, indeed, the team that was working on Sadie, inviting him to stop by. He told them he was already at the hospital, and would be in Sadie's room in just a moment. He hung up and turned to the distraught couple.

Joshua squeezed their arms and said, "Amanda will be here in a few minutes. Let me go have a look-see, and I'll come back and tell you what I know, when I know something."

Richard said, "Thank you, brother."

Joshua realized as he walked into Sadie's room that it was the first time Richard had called him by that moniker.

Joshua came out a few hours later. He found Amanda with her arm around Lauren. Richard and Lauren looked exhausted. Their pastor had arrived, along with some folks from their Sunday school class. Joshua was very concerned about how they would take his news.

"Sadie has had a few rough hours there, and tests confirm that she is septic." He said as he looked at his family. "That means that the infection from the rupture has spread bacteria throughout her body. They're getting ready to transport her to Children's Hospital." Richard and Lauren sucked in air and grabbed each other's arms. Joshua tried to reassure them. "This is pretty serious, but they're used to working with smaller people at Children's. We really aren't equipped to handle this at Anne Arundel. I believe taking her to Children's Hospital is our best course of action to get Sadie well again."

"When are they going?" Lauren asked, now able to speak for the first time.

"They'll leave as soon as the helicopter gets here." Joshua turned to Amanda. "Sweetie, I'm going to drive Richard and Lauren over in their car. Would you please meet us at the hospital, so I can get back home?"

"Sure thing, honey." Amanda turned to Lauren, "Do you need anything from your house before I come to the hospital?

Maybe a change of clothes or something? I don't know how long you'll be there, and it might be nice to freshen up."

Lauren gave her a quick list of things she would like to have for an overnight stay, a spare key to their house, and the alarm code. Amanda headed out. Joshua thought it was a good idea for his wife to start on her way to their house, so that they could arrive at Children's Hospital at about the same time. Zachary could stay where he was and just use some of his cousins' clothing, since he, Tyler, and Tristan were about the same size. The pastor and church friends said goodbye for the time being but assured them that they would continue to pray.

Over the next few days, Sadie continued to make headway against her illness. She was pretty tired by the time she was released from the hospital, but everyone thought she would bounce back pretty fast. Joshua told Amanda over dinner one evening, "Poor kid. This sure isn't the way I would chose to spend my Christmas break. At least she didn't miss any school."

Richard and Lauren were very grateful for Joshua's help in their time of distress. "I couldn't do much, since she wasn't my patient, but I'm glad I could be there for you all," Joshua told the couple at the New Year's Eve celebration at Susan and Dan's home.

"I guess having a brother who's a doctor comes in really handy!" Richard smiled at him.

Joshua grinned. "I'll call you, Richard, when I need some engineering stuff done."

"I'm your man, Joshua, you just say the word!" Everyone laughed out of sheer relief for Sadie's recovery.

Richard and Lauren hugged him again as they said good night later that evening, thanking him yet again for being there. After the couple had departed, Joshua turned to Amanda and told her, "I wouldn't have wished this on anyone, but Sadie's illness has changed the way Richard and I relate to each other."

Amanda replied, "That's a hard way to bond with your brother and his wife, but they were talking nonstop about how thankful they were for you while Sadie was sick."

Joshua told her, "Then something very good has come from something that could have had an unhappy ending." He smiled, grateful that his relationship with Richard had forever been changed.

Chapter 15

Susan and Dan were having breakfast at the kitchen island the morning after their New Year's Eve party. They had combined their efforts in preparing the meal, with Dan helping her by making the toast while she made the softly scrambled eggs her family had always loved. Bacon was sizzling in the pan. Moments later, they sat together, reading their Bibles and eating.

"You know, Dan, this could have ended very tragically." She took another bite of her eggs as she glanced over at Dan.

"Yes, I know. They kept Sadie in a medically-induced coma during the early days of her illness, didn't they?" Dan buttered his toast and took a bite.

"Actually, I don't think her meds were quite that strong. Comas are induced because of brain swelling, like I had from the accident. I was out for a couple of days because of the meds they gave me in the ER, but then I didn't wake up on my own. Sedation is different. Mostly, I think they just kept her asleep so she wouldn't be in pain from the sepsis. Joshua explained the difference between the two types of sleep to me a couple of years ago, after I woke up from my coma." Susan finished her breakfast, and headed for the sink with her dishes.

"Speaking of waking up, I know you thought you were royalty during your coma. That's pretty nifty- I'm married to a former princess and all. But you didn't really talk that much about who you saw and that kind of thing. What happened to you during those six months?" Dan brought his empty dish and mug to the sink, and leaned forward, curious.

Susan rinsed the china off and put them in the dishwasher. "Let's go out for our walk, and I'll tell you all about it. It's too pretty a day to be cooped up inside." She smiled at her hubby, who nodded his agreement.

"Good idea. Who knows how many nice days we'll have, before winter makes another attempt to keep us inside? It's been known to snow in Annapolis quite a bit in January. It's unusually warm today. It must be all of 70 degrees already. And look at those gorgeous white, puffy clouds. Let's go!" Dan exclaimed. They grabbed their lightweight jackets, in case the breeze turned cold, and they were out the door.

As they walked down the street, Susan asked, "Okay, what do you want to know?"

"Well, I know you said that you were the third child of this royal couple, but there must've been other folks around. It's my understanding that people in a coma can dream, but that your dreams are restricted to what you know, consciously or sub-consciously." Dan held her hand, swinging it as they walked.

"Yes, that's what I heard...and what I looked up on Google." They laughed. Susan told him, "There were other people around, other than just the royals. Of course, I was familiar with them, due to their very extensive press coverage."

"My, aren't we formal," Dan laughed.

"Oh, yes, my beloved. Formality reigned with those folks, you might say." She dropped a slight curtsy, and chuckled as she continued. "I felt like I was in a scene from The Wizard of Oz. You remember how Dorothy saw people over the rainbow who she knew from the farm? Well, it was the same way with me."

"You saw people from The Wizard of Oz?" Dan asked.

"No, no, silly" she laughed her answer. "I saw people I knew from before, when I was alive here in Maryland."

"Did you know them as the people in Maryland, or just as the people in Britain?" Dan asked. "That's something I'm really wondering about."

"Well, I knew I knew them, but I wasn't sure why. I was very comfortable with them in their new roles. Dan, I had the understanding of an adult, but the body of a child. I know it's kind of hard to wrap your mind around that. I spent a lot of time thinking about it, especially before I was able to talk or write. I thought 'there's something really strange going on here,' but I was at a complete loss to understand it. Of course, I understand it now, but back then it was one huge mystery." They walked in silence for a few minutes. She tilted her head back to enjoy the sun on her face.

"Who did you see?" he asked, interrupting her thoughts. "Anybody I know?"

"Y-e-s" she said. "Do you remember our really bizarre Spanish teacher from high school?"

"Yes, of course. Who could forget that weird old lady? Mrs. Adams, as I recall." Dan paused. "Hey, she was always talking about living previous lives. She seemed to think she was royalty or something strange like that in a past life. Did you really see her?"

"Yes. But she had a major demotion, I'm afraid. She was...my Nanny Marian." Susan laughed. How incongruous!

"So, she was attached to royalty, but she wasn't royalty herself?" Dan asked. "That must have been a major comeuppance for her."

"Yes, but don't tell her, if she's even still alive. She was little better than an underpaid servant in my world as Princess Victoria Susan Anne," she told her husband.

"Boy, she wouldn't have liked that." He chuckled. "Who else was there? Was I there?" Dan inquired.

"Maybe you were and maybe you weren't, but let me keep you waiting on that answer." She teased him. Then, "Brooke was there."

"As what?" Dan didn't seem to mind being put off, but that was typical of his low-key temperament.

"Brooke was my lady-in-waiting, Mrs. Patricia Minghella." Susan curtseyed. "That's really very much like Brooke. She was always in my court with Kurt, and she took good care of me as my lady-in-waiting when I was with the royal family." She stopped to pick up a bit of trash that had fallen out of her neighbor's recycle bin when the garbage men came by. She placed it back in the receptacle and said, "They really ought to be more careful when they put stuff out for re-cycling. It falls all over the place if they don't take care with their recycle container's lid."

Dan stopped and looked at her, "Stop begging the question and tell me who else you saw."

"Well . . . Your father was there." She looked at Dan, feeling shy, and wondering what he thought of that revelation.

"My dad? Really? But you hadn't seen him in years. He's been dead, what, twenty years now?" Dan looked very surprised. "He had a major heart attack and left us before Rebecca and I even had any grandkids for him to enjoy."

"Yes, I did indeed see him. Dan, your father was my tutor, Mr. Matthew. He was a very nice man who taught me all about philosophy and Socrates and all those fellows from so many years ago." She chortled. "Remember how I used to roll my eyes when your dad would start off on one of his tangents about existence and stuff? I wasn't ready for it as a teen, but apparently what he said stayed with me because I was debating it with him as Victoria Susan."

"Are you serious? That's amazing!" Dan looked shocked at her news. "I'm surprised you could remember that stuff. I couldn't . . . Was there anyone else in your dreams?"

"I had a couple of newspaper reporters who looked amazingly like Joshua and Christopher, but there was only one other person I knew who I spent much time with." She hesitated.

"Who was that?"

"You." She twisted around to face him. "It was a younger version of you than what I see looking back at me now. Of course, I was going with the mental picture I had of a young man named Dan Walsh, since we hadn't reunited at that point in time. You were Corporal Ainsworth, the double-amputee who I visited in the rehab center . . . Shocked?"

"Yes. What did you do with my legs?" He said this, half-joking and half-serious. "In your dream, you amputated my legs? What were you thinking, my dearest love?"

She smiled, and then told him, "It's my understanding that our sub-conscious minds sometimes mimic what we feel in real life, but don't always express." She laughed and twisted her body as she teased him. "No, by the way, I did not amputate your legs. You were in that condition when we met, but I've been thinking about this quite a bit since it happened." She hesitated. "I think that your one missing leg represented my breaking up with you, and the other leg was when I took Joshua away from you by not telling you he existed." She turned forward again and continued walking down the street.

"Well, that's kinda gruesome, don't you think?" Dan said as he caught up with her.

Susan twirled back towards him again, feeling quite girlish. "Yes, in a way it is, but think about it. You didn't have any legs so you couldn't chase after me, just like you didn't chase after me in real life. The Corporal got his fake legs and could've outrun me, but he never did. I think that shows me the kind of man I've always known you to be: kind, tenderhearted, thoughtful, and considerate. Corporal Ainsworth was all those things."

"Hey, I'm starting to really like this guy." He leaned towards her and kissed her cheek.

"And he married while I was in my coma. I supported that marriage and actually arranged for him to have a very nice ceremony, thanks to our incredible wealth. I think I knew somehow that you would have gotten married to someone and I wanted you to be happy, even if it wasn't with me." She smiled. "They got married at Windsor Castle with Princess Victoria Susan Anne as one of their bridesmaids. There aren't too many commoners who can say that! None, in fact, especially since she never existed except in my mind." She shook her head in remembrance.

"Suzy-Q that is so like you. Always looking out for the happiness of others. And always getting involved." He smiled at his bride.

"The Corporal was a wonderful man. Like you, my handsome huggable hubby." She leaned over towards him and gave him a great big kiss.

"Watch out! The neighbors will think we're newlyweds or

something!"

They laughed as they continued walking down the street.

Chapter 16

Christopher stretched his arms and legs in preparation for getting out of bed for that early February day. Augh . . . He rubbed his temples and ran his fingers through his hair. Oh, man, what a headache. Well, a little more booze should calm things down a bit. "The tail of the dog that bit you," as they say. He stretched once more, and then jumped as he noticed the sleeping brunette woman lying next to him. What? Where did she come from? Worse yet, what was her name? Man, better think of it quickly or there would be trouble with a capital "T!" Dames got really mad really fast when they thought you didn't remember who they were.

Christopher put his hand to his face and rubbed it hard as he tried to force himself to remember the previous night. A hint would come in handy. Handy? Candy? Sandy? Mandy? No...yeah, wait! Was that it? No, something a bit longer...like, oh yeah... He leaned towards her, and nudged her gently awake. He smiled, kissed her left cheek, and said, "Miranda, how are you this morning? Hey, Babe, thanks for a great night..."

The thirty-something woman turned over and glared back. She said, "No, Christopher, my friend's name is Miranda. My name is Shannon. Better luck with names next time. Loser." She got out of bed, threw her clothes on, and headed for the bedroom door. She slammed it as she departed without a backward glance at him.

"Oh, Babe, I'm so sorry. I just . . ." She was gone. Man, he was gonna hafta work on his name recognition a bit better. Can't let the word get out that ol' Chris beds them without even knowing who they were. "Shannon who?" he spoke to the closed door. Moments later, he heard the front door slam and a car drive away.

Okay, so what day is this? He gripped his throbbing forehead in both hands. Think! Saturday? Yeah. Good. No Naval Academy classes to teach. Man, I hope she wasn't a midshipman! That could be big trouble. No, wait, I remember now. She teaches at one of those private Christian schools near Annapolis. Nope, I'm good. She can't complain or even talk about me, lest her principal find out that one of his teachers is a young woman of "loose moral character." I'm safe. He breathed a sigh of relief.

Christopher headed for the bathroom, his mind a lot clearer having faced the dilemma of Shannon and her rapid departure. She seemed like a nice gal, from what he could remember. Shoot, they all seemed nice, after a few drinks on a Friday night. He brushed his teeth and splashed some water on his face. He remembered then that the maid wouldn't be there till Monday, so he cleaned up the water that had made its way onto the countertop and floor. He pulled on his winter jogging pants and long-sleeved T-shirt, planning to run a few miles before breakfast. He grabbed his Navy running jacket on the way out of the house.

The brisk winter air cleared his head. He was looking forward to the upcoming spring days, instead of another blast of winter. It's sure cold today. So, what's on tap for today? Oh, yeah, tonight he was on deck for a family gathering. Mom and Dan were having a Family Night, which he could very easily do without. There would be a lot of people, what with the Prescott/Walsh extended families and their kids, and, of course those annoying Fergusons. Why did he have to hang around with all those boring, non-drinkers? And most of them were Christians! He had better things to do, but there was nothing to be done about it. Nope, he would have to show up and pretend like he enjoyed their company. He groaned at the thought.

Of course, he could turn on the charm at will. "Like father, like son," he thought with a smile. Well, maybe not totally like Dad. Dad had been committed, at least at first, to his mother. But he got tired of her and divorce would have been very expensive. Attempted murder was not the path Christopher would have chosen, but he understood why his dad tried it. His dad had wanted to protect the family assets, so why shouldn't he have tried to stage an accident or two? It did seem kinda cold-blooded, but Dad had told him once when they were alone why he needed to have Mom out of the way. Christopher appreciated his father's concern to save the family money for his children, but had gotten royally ticked off at the man he called "Dad" when he realized that his father was saving money for his children by Kelsey, not for him. What was he? Chopped liver? Christopher learned fast that he needed to lookout for Numero Ono.

Christopher had his own way of looking at marriage. "If you don't commit, you can't be guilty of cheating," was his mantra. So, he simply refused to commit to one woman. Why buy the cow when he was getting milk for free? He had plenty of one-night stands, and that was fine with him. He had started getting serious with a certain someone when he was in California, but then there was the big mess with his folks, what with Dad trying to kill Mom after taking up with Kelsey. Christopher dropped the girl fast. Nope, that was too big a potential mess if he got tired of her. Better to be on his own, alone, than with an unhappy entanglement like his folks had experienced! He shivered. Man, it's cold out here this morning. Better pick up the pace.

But back to the family gathering he had been roped into attending. This new family group was the Brady Bunch gone wild, in his mind. The good news was that the party wouldn't last long. All of them went to church on Sunday mornings, so the evening would be short by default. He could still hit some bars in downtown Annapolis and maybe he could get lucky. Though not with Shannon again, obviously.

He headed back home halfway through his ten-mile run. When he got back inside his warm house, into the shower he went, drying himself and throwing on some jeans and a shirt before he took a quick look in the refrigerator for breakfast. Apples and beer? Milk! That's good. But how long had that been here? He took a quick sniff. Oh, yuck! Nope, that was really sour! After pouring it down the drain, he continued to peer into the refrigerator, as if something would change if he looked long and hard enough. Seriously? This was all he had? Well, at least apples were healthy. He grabbed one and took a huge bite. He really needed to go to the grocery. Maybe he should get something to bring tonight...No, scratch that. Bring it once, and they would expect it every time. He could still play his "single, unattached, non-cooking man" card and eat for free.

Maybe his mom would even give him some food to take home. Likewise, Amanda and Brooke had been known to give him the rest of whatever dish they had made. Since it was wintertime, maybe Mom had made her wonderful chili or fabulous lasagna. She couldn't make much else, from what his dad had always said, but those two dishes were superb. Yep, there would be some good eating this coming week! Free home-cooked food fixed by good cooks, at that! The denuded apple core was tossed for a free shot point into the garbage can. Score!

The family didn't know that he was, in fact, a very good cook. He had learned from one of his many girlfriends while he lived in California, and could throw together some awesome Tex-Mex stuff, along with some healthier cuisine, should the spirit move. He didn't cook that much these days, though, just a quick breakfast at home, lunch at the Naval Academy between classes, and dinner at one of the many bar/restaurants that lined the main drags in Annapolis. He couldn't see the point of going to a great deal of trouble to cook for one, though every once in a while he cooked up a lot of food and then froze it in individual serving sizes. When the spirit moved, that is, but it didn't move that often.

A short while later, Christopher ran into his local food store and bought the few items he needed for this weekend's lunches and some good breakfasts for the coming week. When he got home, he straightened up the house a bit, just in case he did get an evening visitor. He changed the sheets on the bed and threw out some trash, including the pizza box he had stuck in the oven to hide it two nights ago. As long as the place looked good on the surface, the girl he might bring home wouldn't notice. The maid would clean things up better when she came to the house on Monday.

Okay, so Christopher still had some time before the command performance, so he decided to check his email. He dispatched a few quick answers to a couple of students, and then checked on his personal email. Oh. It seemed he had mentioned his personal email address to Miranda-who-was-actually-Shannon at some point in time. He had a not-so-nice missive from her, which made some strong suggestions regarding his personality. Clearly, she was still unhappy with him. He sighed. Win some, lose some. Delete.

He took a quick stroll around his house. He was pretty pleased with himself. He had just finished his Ph.D. when the Navy brought him back to Annapolis to teach at the Naval Academy. He'd gone out with a real estate agent one afternoon to look at the homes in Severna Park he had previewed on line. He walked into this house and knew it was perfect. With four bedrooms and two and a half baths, it was an older, natural stone home on a wooded lot in a nice neighborhood. He had worn his uniform that day and had totally charmed the elderly homeowner, who had just been widowed. He made a below-market offer and was accepted pronto. The widow loved servicemen, having been the daughter of a World War II veteran of the Navy and the mother of an Army vet.

Yep, he had been pretty savvy that day, and it paid off. He had immediate equity in the property and loved the Southern cottage style house. The previous owner left some furniture behind that he was able to use to furnish his new pad. A few thousand bucks later, he had decorated the place in an eclectic traditional/contemporary fashion he felt at home in. The yard was pretty easy to keep in line, since there was thick grass only in the front yard. Of course, this time of year he didn't have to do anything to the outside. The once-a-week maid fit into his budget and kept him from doing tasks he felt were better suited for a woman.

Christopher dressed for the evening, wearing a pair of dress pants and Oxford blue shirt. Shiny shoes completed his look. Nice but understated, that was his plan. He went to the coat closet and pulled out a heavy coat that still managed to be "cool." He glanced at himself in the foyer mirror. "Looking good, Christopher, my man!" He double-checked his uniform for work on Monday while he still had a few minutes and then headed out, planning to arrive precisely on time. No use hanging around the family any longer than need be. "Okay, I just need to get through the next couple of hours and then it's off to Annapolis!"

He made it through the torture of his family, having smiled at and been charming to one and all. It paid off in spades: he had enough left over lasagna, salad, and dessert to last for several days. He wouldn't even need to stop by his house to refrigerate it on the way to the bars, since the winter temperatures would keep the food cool enough in his trunk for the next few hours. "Ladies, Kurt . . . I mean Christopher Prescott is on his way to you!" He parked in the Noah Hillman Garage and hit the town.

A few drinks later, he realized that his stomach was "being persnickety" as his mom would say and decided against bringing home a companion. He said his farewells and returned home, making it just inside the door before he lost his dinner. Probably just ate too much. He looked for his mother's remedy for an upset stomach: ginger ale and crackers. The ginger ale he found in a cupboard was expired. The crackers were stale and stuck in his throat. Not a good evening. He hit the rack early, hoping to sleep off his distress.

By Monday morning, Christopher was feeling back to his old self and headed out to work. He ate a regular breakfast and lunch, hoping that the tummy troubles were a thing of the past. Sure enough, by the time going-home traffic had piled up outside the Naval Academy gates and all the way up Route 2 past Severna Park, he was firmly ensconced in his new favorite watering hole. No rush hour traffic for him! He would wait it out in a bar, as was his habit. He changed bars often enough to not appear a drunkard, and to look for new talent among the ladies.

He had walked into the Federal House Bar and Grill, selecting a table that was near the windows. He enjoyed the wood, brass, and stone décor, though he didn't make a big deal about it. It appealed to his masculinity and, of course, the place had a Navy blue front door. He had already ordered his Shrimp and Grits and was beginning to chow down on his salad when he spotted her. He led her on, playing with flirting and trying to decide if he wanted to buy her dinner or if she could be had for less than the cost of an entrée. He overheard someone address her as "Ruby Mae." How appropriate.

Ruby Mae had been eyeing him from the bar for about a half an hour when she seemed to think it was time to make a move. Her slinky, short dress marked her as the skank she was. It had been inching its way up her thighs for some time. She made no effort to pull it down to a more acceptable length. Her low cut neckline plugged well below the limits of respectability. Christopher could tell that she was available to any comer. For the price of a few drinks, she could be his, for a few hours anyway. She walked over to his table and said, very predictably to his mind, "Feeling lonely, sailor?"

He stood to greet her, and invited her to join him for dinner. She proceeded to chat while downing drink after drink. She ordered the same Shrimp and Grits he had, apparently too uncreative to order something else. Fine. Still, her idle chatter was somewhat irritating to him. It wasn't something he could nail down, but she seemed conversationally limited, and she just didn't strike him as very bright. Her table manners bugged him, as well. She spoke with food in her mouth. The sight of her partially masticated food gagged him. Her conversational drivel was, to be honest, boring.

She kept sending signals that she was his for the asking, giggling and touching his hand and rubbing his thighs, but he questioned if he wanted to take her up on what she was offering. Nope, not tonight. Maybe tomorrow night, but maybe not even then.

After finishing his dinner, he announced, "Well, I need to make it an early night." He paid the bill and told her, "It was nice meeting you, Ruby Mae." He handed the check and some cash off to the server and said good night.

He could tell she was shocked that he hadn't wanted her to accompany him, but she shrugged it off with a "See ya, Chris. Thanks for the dinner."

By the time he had reached the door, he turned around and noticed she was already walking over to another solitary diner. What a boring woman. Gorgeous, and an obvious tramp, but boring. A real bimbo, actually. What's wrong with me? I used to like that type. Very nonthreatening and sometimes a lot of fun. Am I getting too old for this? That's scary!

He drove home, throwing on winter-weight sweatpants and a T-shirt and hunkering down in front of the television with a beer. He watched Jeopardy and Wheel of Fortune before he realized what he was doing. Have I completely lost it? Old people do this kind of thing, not me! Hence, there were seemingly-endless commercials for denture adhesive and constipation remedies made by companies that sponsored these shows.

Christopher watched television so rarely that he had never gotten cable installed. His choices were pretty limited. Man, what's wrong with me? He clicked off the set, disgusted.

He pulled himself off of the couch and went into his home office. He paid some bills, checked his email, and went to bed. Tomorrow would be another day.

He went into work and was summoned by his Commanding officer. "Chris, I'd like you to meet Lieutenant Audrey Johns. She is on TDY from Norfolk. She's rotating in, to team teach your classes with you. She'll be working with us for the upcoming term, and I'd like you to show her around. Of course, she's a graduate of the Naval Academy, so she doesn't need the grand tour, but please introduce her to folks and make her feel welcome, okay?"

"Yes, sir. I would be happy to do so." He turned towards the woman and couldn't believe his eyes.

The woman was a stunning brunette, about 5'6" tall, and 125 pounds. She wore the Navy uniform as if it had been custom-made clothing, designed with her in mind. Her gorgeous legs revealed that she was a runner. Her sparkling brown eyes demonstrated intelligence and no nonsense. He smiled and she returned the smile without a trace of flirtation.

After a few minutes of conversation, they were dismissed. They walked out of the CO's office and started back towards Christopher's office. "So, Lieutenant, where do you hail from, originally?" Christopher decided that the open, friendly approach might work best on her. He was already thinking how much he would like to take her home. What a knockout!

"Florida. If I may, do you mind if I call you Christopher?" She asked, smiling.

"Oh, yes, please feel free to do that. Of course!" He stumbled over his words. What's wrong with me? I don't usually react like this. I'm Cool as a Cucumber Chris!

They walked into his office, and she closed the door.

Audrey turned and faced him. There was no trace of a smile remaining on her face. "Okay, here's the skinny, Christopher, if you will. When I found out I was coming here to work with you, I checked you out. You have quite a reputation, if you don't mind my saying so. 'Womanizer' is the most frequent description I've heard. There were other comments, but they were not nearly as flattering. You may think you have the world on a string, but I'm not interested in anything you're selling. I've looked into your background, which is actually quite interesting, but I believe you are unscrupulous and I think you need to 'shape up or ship out,' as we say. Our relationship is now and always will remain completely professional. Do I make myself clear? Keep your hands to yourself and don't plan on bedding this sailor." Her gaze changed from stern and frank to a much softer one. She smiled again and asked, "Now, where were we?"

Christopher was speechless. No woman had ever talked to him like that! He had a reputation? Well, maybe, but he hoped it was as a stud, not a . . . what was that she called him? A womanizer? He thought for a few moments, too stunned to even respond.

By the time he had thought of anything to say, Audrey had walked back out into the main office and had started looking through some documents. So, she would be team teaching some classes with him as part of the Navy's normal rotation. He was used to that happening. They better get along, or it wouldn't be good for either of their careers.

A group of instructors was going out to lunch that day. Everyone wanted to learn more about Audrey, so she was kept pretty busy answering questions about her service since her graduation from the Academy. He laid pretty low at the luncheon, listening for information that he hoped to use towards furthering their relationship. For now, that relationship was on very rocky ground, given her earlier speech to him. But he didn't want it to stay that way.

He realized fast that she was a unique woman. She was not only gorgeous, but she was accomplished, talented, and fantastic. The more she spoke, the more entranced he was by her. By the time the meal was over, he wished he was a different man. He felt, for the first time as an adult, that perhaps she was better than he deserved. It was quite a revelation.

Over the next few weeks, they spent a lot of time in each other's company, due to their joint efforts with the Oceanography major. He stopped frequenting bars and spent a lot of time at work. She was keeping him on his toes. For every lecture he had prepared, she had two already up and running. His Power Points were good; hers were outstanding. For every source he planned on citing as he spoke, she had two at the ready.

He realized that her exceptional work performance was not the only thing that was different about Audrey. He knew that many Navy females were hard-drinking, swearing, slap-around gals who were trying to keep up with their male counterparts. Not Audrey. She didn't need to keep up with anyone. They had to keep up, in the professional world, with her. All Navy officers at the Naval Academy were outstanding in their field. She put them to shame. For the first time in a very long time, he had to scramble to keep up with someone.

Christopher's sure-thing charm was lost on her. Completely. She was not buying into anything he was selling.

What gives with this gal? She's stunning and single. I'm not bad looking, if I say so myself, and I'm single. No baggage. Why can't I get her? He tried asking her out one evening as they were getting ready to leave for the day.

"Audrey, it's getting a little on the late side. What say we stop by the Federal House and get a bite to eat? It's nearby and the food's excellent." He didn't offer to pay for her dinner, since he didn't want to scare her away by suggesting it was a date.

Audrey said, "I see something in you, Christopher, that could be fascinating, but you are too messed up to know it right now. I'm not interested in you until you clean yourself up, major league."

She was always surprising him. "What are you talking about, Audrey? Messed up how?" He hadn't gotten in bed with anyone for weeks- not since that Shannon woman had left in such a huff. That was very unlike him, but he only had eyes for Audrey since the day they met.

"I googled you and your family. What a disaster, Chris! I did some in-depth checking and I'm really glad I did. Your dad was in the Navy, an Academy graduate who served three tours in Nam. He flew for American Airlines and was working for them at the time of his death. I read about the car crashes- both of them. Your father was a difficult man, from what I've learned. And I think that, beneath that boyish charm of yours, you are seriously fouled up. I'm not getting involved with you unless there is some major work done in your life."

"What? How dare you check me out?" Christopher was fuming. He was . . . livid . . . He was, he realized, responding just like his father would have. Frantic, he said, "I'm sorry, Audrey. I have to go." He bolted out the door, eager to get away from those eyes that seemed to see who he really was.

Who in the world was she? He decided then and there to do some checking on his own. He jumped into his car and became frustrated by the bumper-to-bumper traffic that he was soon sitting in. He had forgotten about the usual traffic jams, in his eagerness to get away from Audrey and her all-knowing eyes. He hit the steering wheel in frustration. Blast this traffic!

Where to begin as he investigated her? Well, she said she was from Florida and he had picked up on all of the other information she had chatted about that first day at lunch. He'd also made mental notes about her every time they talked, which was every day. Okay, that gave him something to go on. Finally, after endless traffic jams, he arrived home.

He almost ran into his house, decided to skip dinner, and sat down at his computer. A few hours later, he knew quite a bit about her. She was born in Rockledge, Florida, at Wuestoff Memorial Hospital on July 29, 1987. That made her two years younger than he was. Her father was listed on the birth certificate as Jeffrey Michael Johns; her mother was Marlene Stuart Johns. She was the eldest of five children, according to the U.S. Census Bureau.

Her high school yearbook showed that she graduated from Rockledge High School in 2004, having been vice-president of the Drama Club, Homecoming Queen, and president of the National Honor Society. She was her class valedictorian. Christopher looked for newspaper articles that would indicate family problems, but she appeared to have led a normal, happy life.

There were a few pictures of her in various stage productions throughout her growing up years, but there was nothing scandalous in her past. None of her siblings had gotten into trouble, either. There were a few newspaper pictures of Audrey and her siblings performing at the local Baptist church; they had a family band. She played the keyboards and sang, based on the photos he saw.

Christopher already knew that she graduated with honors from the Naval Academy in 2008, and had gotten a master's degree from the Naval Postgraduate School in Monterey, California after serving overseas for five years. She had told him she was considering pursuing her Ph.D. in the next year or so.

He couldn't find anything else on her. She had never been arrested, never been married, never even been engaged, which he guessed from the lack of an engagement announcement in her local paper. He couldn't even find a parking ticket on her. Nope, she was clean as a whistle. He was even more entranced by the thought of her.

Christopher realized that he was famished, and then checked the clock. Nine o'clock? He had been so engrossed by his investigation that he had forgotten to stop long enough to eat dinner. He checked out the refrigerator- well, the lasagna was long gone, but he did have some breakfast food, so he made breakfast for dinner before calling it a night. As he shoveled the food into his mouth, something occurred to him: She was playing keyboards at a Baptist church. Could she possibly be . . . a Christian? Boy, he sure hoped not.

Chapter 17

Susan got a phone call from Brooke, who suggested they get together. Brooke had been going to counseling for a few months and seemed to be making progress on her feelings towards marrying Michael. Susan prayed that her daughter's visit would result in good news, but it was hard, for once, to read what Brooke was calling about. Dan had taken all of his sons to a men's conference at church, so Susan was home alone.

Brooke showed up a short while later, carrying a large cardboard box. She was not immediately forthcoming about what it contained, so Susan took Brooke's lead and ignored the container for the moment. She offered her daughter a cup of her favorite Starbucks' brew and some oatmeal raisin cookies. They took their snacks into the dining room, where Brooke had placed the box when she arrived.

Susan smiled at her daughter with love, wondering if the box had anything to do with Michael. Susan would not, however, be the first to bring up the delicate topic of Michael. Typical of Susan's own curiosity, however, she did broach the topic of the box. "Brooke, honey, I feel like there's an elephant in the room. What in the world do you have in the box?"

Brooke took a big sip of her coffee. "Mom, you know how my counselor has been telling me to get in touch with my feelings about Dad?"

"Sure, honey. That's a huge part of helping you recover." Susan was grateful that Brooke had agreed to go to counseling in the first place and was proud that she had stayed with it.

"Well, Joshua, Christopher, and I went over to the storage unit where we moved Dad's stuff when we cleaned out the house he and Kelsey lived in. You know, after it sold, we had to do something with his belongings, so we sold some of the furniture and then just got a storage unit to hold his junk till we had time to go through it."

"I know. I didn't want to take a chance of finding some of Kelsey's mementos, so I've deliberately stayed out of it. Does this box have something to do with his memories? I'm not sure..." Susan hesitated to open that door. It was obvious Brooke had felt that the items were worth bringing over, so maybe it would help her to talk about what they'd found.

"Mom, did you know that Dad kept a journal? Journals, I should say. He started keeping them as a young boy."

Susan was shocked. "No, I had no idea. What . . . how many were there?"

"About ten. He started using spiral notebooks as an elementary school kid. He moved into black leather journals as a young man. He kept them while he was in Vietnam through to his relationship with Kelsey, so you're included in the books. We...also found some pictures of his siblings."

"Siblings? I thought he was an only child!" Susan's mouth hung open in disbelief. How could her husband of thirty-five years have hidden the fact that he had brothers and sisters? Impossible! She put her hand on her chest in shock.

"No, Mom. He was the second youngest of seven. There were four boys and three girls in the family." Brooke shook her head. "Amazing, isn't it?"

Susan was dumbfounded. She likewise shook her head as her hand fell back in her lap. "He never mentioned them, not once." She felt utter disbelief. "How could he have not told me?" She caught her breath. "I guess he had more secrets than we thought."

Brooke asked, "Would you like to see some pictures? He has a cigar box full of them."

"Sure...yes, I guess so." She didn't know what else to say. This was so strange! She shook her head to clear it. See the pictures of people she didn't know existed? "Of course, dear."

Brooke pulled a cigar box out and removed a handful of photos, yellowed and curled with age. They were marked for identity. Brooke handed a pile over to her.

Kurt's parents' pictures were there; each one was labeled by a feminine hand. "William Charles Prescott" was born January 1, 1918. His wife, "Mary Ruth Taylor," was born September 12, 1919. Their marriage license, dated October 6, 1939, was also tucked into the box. Their children arrived in quick succession, following their marriage, except for the final two children.

The first child was William 'Will' Charles Prescott Junior, born October 31, 1940. The next picture read "Margaret 'Maggie' Frances Prescott, born May 18, 1942." The next was of a boy named John 'Johnny' Kenneth Prescott, born July 3, 1944; the next was a boy named Peter Russell Prescott, born March 27, 1946. The next picture was Candace 'Candy' Geraldine Prescott, born August 14, 1948; the next photo was Kurt Stephen Prescott, born February 9, 1954. The final child, a girl, was Ella Cassandra Prescott, born February 9, 1960.

There were some other group family photos, but not many. No one was smiling. Each individual was an island into him or herself. They were a disconnected family. Even when pictured together, they stood mutely apart, not touching. There was an invisible wall between them all. The father had a stern look of disapproval on his face, while the mother looked beaten down.

Susan almost cried, "What a sad family. Is this really Kurt's family? No wonder he had...problems. They weren't only related to Vietnam, from what this shows." Susan continued to sort through this pictorial testimony of an unhappy family. Miserable.

Brooke told her, "That's not the worst of it. The journals are . . . unbelievably sad."

"Can you give me the Readers' Digest Condensed Version, or have you read them all?"

"Well, I could tell you about them Mom, but I really think you should read through them yourself. You knew Dad better than anyone . . ."

"Not as well as I thought, as these pictures show." Susan shook her head, incredulous.

"He was a complicated man, Mom. I have read through some of them, just enough to get the gist of things. Before I went any further, you had to know about them. Technically, as Dad's widow, they're yours."

"Did your brothers read them?" She searched Brooke's face for a clue.

"Some, not all. We agreed that you needed to look through them first. We all read the first one. It was pretty heart-breaking." Brooke wiped a tear away.

"Wow. I really don't know... Kurt kept them secret for thirty-five years. Should we really disturb his memory by reading something he obviously wanted kept hidden? Do we have the right? It's kind of like, I don't know, peering into his soul." Susan was not entirely convinced that she wanted to read them. Her wounds from Kurt were deep and had been around for years. Did she really want the upheaval they were bound to create in her heart?

"Mom, from what we've read already, I think it would help us understand who he was and why he was the man he was. It isn't very pretty, but I think we all need to do it." Brooke forced a smile. "You need to go through the collection first, Mom, since you knew him the longest."

"Oh, thanks, honey. You are so thoughtful." Susan tried to smile back, but she was still flabbergasted by the whole thing. It was surreal to her. Kurt had siblings? His parents were dead- he had told her that before they got married- but what about the other six people he had never mentioned, not even once, in more than thirty-five years? Incredible.

"To make things a bit easier, we already put the journals in order by their date, with the oldest one on top. We also numbered them. One of them has some pages ripped out, but I'm not sure why. Maybe you'll be able to tell, based on what

139

the rest of that one says."

"Okay, well, it looks like I have some deep reading ahead." Susan pulled the box to her side of the table.

"Yes, you do. Mom, do you want me to stay here while you're reading, or at very least, while you get started? It's gonna take several days."

"I imagine that it'll be very emotional and it'll take some time, so, no, you need not stay." She looked at her watch. "Dan will be home soon, and he can sit with me, if I need him to."

The women hugged, and Brooke got ready to leave. "Mom, Joshua, Christopher, and I are all behind you on this. You can call any or all of us to be here, if you want."

"Thanks, Sweetie. I'll let you know."

Brooke left. Susan decided to tell Dan immediately about the find. When he got home, he said "hello, Honey" on his way into his home office. She waited for a few minutes, trying to compose her thoughts.

Susan went into Dan's office, where he had started working on financial spreadsheets, and told him what she would be doing for a few days. He gave her a quick hug and said, "Are you sure you want to do this?"

"Yes, dear. I think it's the only way to bury the dead, once and for all."

"Call me if you need me." He gave her another squeeze.

"Will do."

Susan took a cup of tea into the family room. She brought the box in and started a fire in the fireplace. She settled into the couch and she turned to her late husband's journals.

Journal One: Dated April 15, 1960, when Kurt was six years old. The handwriting was that of a child- it was scrawled across the first page.

"My name is Kurt Stephen Prescott. I am in the second grade. I have three brothers and three sisters. My basketball coach gave me this notebook so that I would have someone to talk to about my family. I don't know why he wants me to do this, but okay, Mr. Harris, here goes."

"I don't have any friends. That's because my parents are drunks and I don't want to invite nobody over to play. I go to school, I go to my basketball and baseball practices, and I come home. People think I'm mean. They laugh at me and poke fun. That's okay by me- that way, they don't make fun of me because of my mom and dad. I am mean sometimes. I don't like cats, so I tie things to their tails and watch them get mad. It's so funny! I used to have a boy cat but Daddy killed it when it got up on our table and he threw it through the window. Daddy said, 'Serves him right.' Then I got a dog for a while. I really likked the dog but it was sick and it died. I couldn't take it to the vet because I didn't have any money, but it was just a stray anyways. Daddy hated that dog. I don't care that it died. 'Good riddence,' my daddy says." The spelling was pretty bad, but she was impressed that he could write so much at such a young age. Then again, Kurt was a very smart man, so he was demonstrating that intelligence, even as a little boy.

She read about Kurt's oldest brother Will leaving home at the age of eighteen. Will had just graduated from high school. He had left while Kurt was four years old. Kurt didn't say much about this brother; he apparently just wrote what he heard his siblings saying, based on the vocabulary. Will had walked away from an abusive home life. The older siblings said that they would never see him again because the young man told his brothers and sisters that he would never come back. He didn't. "I have to look at the pictures in my mother's cigar box to remember his name and what he looked like. William 'Will' Charles Prescott Jr. was his name." another entry read, "Daddy got mad and tored up Mommy's photo albums last week, so this is all she has left. He is so mean. Mommy cried and cried."

Kurt justified the abandonment, saying he guessed Will just never fit in. A couple of years later, his oldest sister Maggie headed out the door for what turned out to be the last time, saying she was going to the library. She never said "goodbye" to Kurt, but his siblings said she planned it that way to save herself some grief from their father. He'd found a note she'd written some years before and stuck in her dresser, saying that was her plan for escape. He remembered what it was like, even two years later, so he wrote about his feelings when she left, though he was quite young at the time of her departure. He had felt close to her, like a little brother does with a big sister he looks up to, so this was the first time he felt sadness on this scale. The pages of the journal were creased with tears shed long ago. Susan turned the page.

"Maggie walked out the door after dinner. She looked fat. Fatter than usual. Johnny told me later that it was because she had bunches of clothes on so she could take them out of the house without Daddy knowing about it. Daddy and Mommy were already drunk, so they didn't notice. They didn't see her leave, but I did. Some guy in a red sports car picked her up. She had her books with her and said she was going to the library. But when I woke up the next morning, she still wasn't home. She never even said goodbye to me! Where did she go? Will she ever come back?"

"My Mommy was suspecting a baby for a long time. She had my sister Ella a couple of months ago. Ella is really cute. I don't know why my parents wanted "another mouth to feed" like my Daddy says all the time. Neither of them seems happy about it. Peter doesn't care what they do. Candy says it's nice to have a baby around again, but she hopes she doesn't have to babysit too much."

Kurt's mother had gone to the hospital one day while he was at school, and she didn't come home for a couple of days. His father was upset about the extra work he had to do, but some neighbor women came in and helped out. When his mother came back, she was carrying a little pink blanket with his baby sister Ella Cassandra inside, according to the verbal picture Kurt painted in his journal. There were some childish drawings in the book, as well.

Kurt reported the first time he saw his sister. "There she was, looking right at me. She was so small! Mommy said that she was a good size for a girl, but she looked so little to me. I was standing there, when she grabbed my finger and held on. And then she smiled at me. She's so cute! I love her!"

In the days and months following, the journal reported that he hurried home from school to spend time with her. He didn't do "gross things" like change her diaper, but he fed her a bottle in the afternoons and loved it when she smiled. She seemed "to like me a whole lot better than anybody else." She became his pride and joy. He was there when she took her first steps. He played with her as she became a toddler, which his father mocked as being "unmanly" and "ridiculous." Kurt didn't care what his father thought. His mother seemed happy for the break his love for "Ella my Bella" gave her. The days moved on.

Kurt was now eight and he had already figured out that his next brother, Johnny, would be leaving soon. The boy had played football and basketball with Kurt. Kurt wrote that Johnny had served as a "surrograte father" for Kurt when their own father was too drunk to come to his games, according to what Kurt had overheard the other fathers say when they talked about him. Sure enough, Johnny left, also right after high school. "Why did he leave me? I thought he would always be around. I feel so sad. Please come back, Johnny. I miss you so much," Kurt wrote.

There were a few more entries on the missing Johnny. His departure had left a big hole in Kurt's life. It was a gap not filled by his parents, but by his next brother who stepped in to take Johnny's place. Peter was a different kind of fellow, based on what Kurt had written. He stole money from his mother's purse, justifying it by saying that he needed a bigger allowance or that she owed him money from last week. He taught Kurt that it was okay to fib and steal your way through life, showing him how to take money without being caught.

Kurt wrote that Peter had told him to make it seem like his mother's fault for not keeping better track of her money. Peter had called their mother "stupid" and a "doormmat" on more than one occasion, according to the journal. As Susan read what Kurt had written, she mused that he had learned his lessons well, especially with regard to blaming others for his problems. Peter must have been a master at making women feel inferior, based on the words Kurt attributed to him.

Kurt adored his little sister; that was certain. She had been born on his birthday. Instead of resenting her for stealing his birthday, he took it was a sign that they were to be best buddies forever. She was a blue-eyed blonde, as shown in her photograph, and he doted on her. She followed him around as she grew older, he reported, but that was okay by him. He played with her every day when he got home from school. By the time she was four, she used to sit and look out the picture window in the living room, till he got off the school bus. She would run out to greet him.

Kurt's journal was filled with happiness whenever he wrote about her. It was as if she was the only island of joy in his otherwise sorrow-filled life. And then came the day that he would never forget. The journal pages were crumpled with tears and words struck out. Some pages were missing completely, having been violently ripped from their rightful spot. The force of the pages being torn out was obvious from the twisted wreck of the journal.

The best Susan could make out was that her late husband's beloved little sister had been kidnapped. The story of how it happened was gone. The rest of that journal was empty, though it was obvious from the binding that many pages had been taken out. The next journal began with the story of Kurt's mother's death.

It was shortly before Peter departed that their mother had died under mysterious circumstances. The journal indicated that it was in September 1964, one month to the day after Kurt's last journal entry about Ella. When he fell asleep at night, he told his journal, he dreamt he was walking to the creek, following his mother. Someone big and scary jumped out of the bushes and grabbed her arm. Kurt guessed he was a man because of how big the person was. He talked "mean stuff" to

Mommy and then pushed her onto the rocks and ran away. Kurt went to her side and tried to lift his mother's head up, but dropped it each time he tried, until it made a big "splashing noise." He heard his father coming through the grass and ran away. He hid in his bedroom until...he woke up. He reported having the same dream over and over for months.

According to Kurt's journal, the police didn't pursue the case, since Mrs. Prescott was known to be an alcoholic. He guessed that drunks didn't matter to the world. This one had mattered to him, but no one else seemed as sad as he did.

Kurt tried to write about the "autoppsee" but couldn't seem to decide how to spell it. His father hadn't told Peter, Candy, or Kurt about the medical procedure, but Kurt saw Peter sneaking into their parents' bedroom, and then looking at the results that their father had received in the mail. Peter had seen his father hide a paper in his special metal box when it arrived. Peter had waited until their father had passed out that evening, to snatch it and bring it into Candy's bedroom. Candy had picked the lock with one of her hairpins and was holding the document, when Kurt snuck into her bedroom.

"What's that, Candy?"

"It's an official paper that explains what happened to Mom."

Candy read it to him, explaining that their mother had died from what Kurt wrote in his journal was "drownding do too bunt forced trama" or something like that. She had hit her head on the rocks in the creek. If someone had pulled her out, Candy explained, she might have lived, but no one did and she was dead. Peter stuck the paper back in the box and put it where Daddy kept it. Daddy never knew they had seen it or he would have beaten them all. No one ever mentioned it again. Mommy was forty-one years old when she died. Kurt didn't talk to his siblings about what he had seen that night. He didn't talk to anyone about the darkness that hounded his dreams, or so he wrote.

Like his older siblings, Peter departed a few months

later, but not before instilling a "Look out for number one" attitude in Kurt. Also like his brothers and sister, Peter never returned. He did say "goodbye" to Kurt, taking him to lunch at the local diner and preaching to the little boy about always making sure you came out on top of every situation. Peter's attitude was one of giving others a raw deal before they gave one to you. He dropped Kurt off at home, and walked out of his life for good.

Susan's heart was breaking as she read this story of abandonment. No wonder Kurt was so messed up. He was in bad shape before he even landed on the shores of Vietnam. Susan had to put the journal down and walk away more than once. How could anyone live through such sadness?

She went for a long walk with Dan, telling him about her discovery. When they returned, he joined her in the family room, a silent companion in her journey as she turned the next pages.

Sister Candace was the only sibling left at home with Kurt by this time. Four years older than he, she had taken over role of mother almost a year before from their always-inebriated and now-deceased mom. Kurt wrote about how she would make his school lunches, giving him an occasional treat from her babysitting income so he could buy his lunch instead of carrying it every day. She, he wrote over the next few months, was good at bandaging scrapes and defending him against bullies. She made sure he ate dinner, got his homework done, and took a bath almost every night. Daddy just drank, from the minute he came home at night, till the early hours of the morning. He traveled out of town on business once a month, leaving the children home alone.

Kurt wrote about trying to talk to her about the night their mother died, but Candy hushed him up every time he said something. Why wouldn't she talk about it? He was family. She was family. As long as they kept the secret between the two of them, why not talk? She'd told him that someone might overhear and that it would make things bad. He took that to mean their father, but he always made sure Daddy wasn't home when he talked about Mommy. No, Candace refused and started singing to quiet him. She wasn't good at singing.

His father was a mostly absentee parent by that time, leaving the preteen on his own. It was good that Candace was there to guide him, although Kurt wrote that she was getting pretty weary of trying to stay out of her father's way when he was drunk.

One night, Kurt wrote, she wasn't so fortunate. "Daddy came home from work really drunk and really mean. He did some mean things to me while he screamed about Mommy's death and then started picking on Candy. I ran upstairs to get away from him. I was hiding in my room, but I could hear Dad yelling and hitting her. She came upstairs to my room and said that she couldn't take it anymore. She was going to leave soon, but that I shouldn't say anything to anyone. I cried myself to sleep- don't tell the other kids at school- who will take care of me if she leaves?"

The next day, a Saturday, had been very difficult for Kurt as he tried to get some information out of Candy. She didn't say much, but Kurt saw the bruises on her arms. She packed a bag when their dad left for a liquid lunch. There was little food in the house, but Daddy's focus was on more important things, like his next drink. Candy made Kurt a peanut butter sandwich, hugged him, and told him to take care of himself. She walked out the door. Kurt was almost thirteen years old, based on the date of that entry.

When his father came home that evening, late, he was very noisy in his comments about the departed Candy. Kurt remained in his room, hiding in his closet until his father went to bed. The next day, it was as if Candy had never existed. Pictures of her had been smashed and thrown in the garbage can. Kurt grabbed a single photo of his sister out of the trashcan before it was hauled away on Monday. She was never mentioned by his father again. Flipping through the next pages, Susan noticed that Candy, like the others, had vanished.

As Susan turned the pages, she learned that Kurt's father had some "stomach" problems. Kurt had overheard his father talking on the phone with the doctor, who was telling the very-drunk Mr. Prescott that he had to stop drinking or he would die. His father insisted that he barely drank at all, and started shouting at the physician. Mr. Prescott hung up the phone in anger, and then muttered to himself "I'll just have another." As the man stumbled for his next drink, Kurt wrote that he glared at his son and muttered something about "are you going to kill me, too?" Kurt wrote that he was confused by his father's comment. "Why would Dad say that?"

Kurt's father continued to decline, but he never gave up the bottle. Even though he was pretty young, Kurt had figured out that it was the booze that was killing his father and begged him to stop. Finally, the stomach pains got so intense that the man had no choice but to quit drinking, at least temporarily. As soon as the symptoms subsided, the bottles came out of the cupboard again.

The next few years, Kurt became a father to his dad, nursing the man through his times of alcohol-induced illness. There also came along a series of pseudo mothers, women who his father picked up on his nights out on the town. The women hung around for a while, but seemed to get their fill of Mr. Prescott and his teenaged boy pretty quickly.

There were nights when Kurt didn't get dinner. He wrote that he was tired of being hungry, so he started befriending the other boys in his school, in the hopes that their mothers would invite him over for dinner when he stuck around late in the afternoon. The sympathetic women did, so at least he had figured out a successful way to "take care of number one."

Kurt started keeping track of the ways he flattered the mothers of his friends, and wrote notes on what nights he could expect a dinner from this one or that one. As she read, Susan watched him grow through his teen years. She became aware of how experienced he became at manipulating the emotions of others. For the first time, however, she saw it as a way for him to survive, not because of an inherent mean streak. Kurt did what he did as a first strike against the unfairness of life. Susan sat back, amazed at what she had learned about the man she thought she had known. She shared this information with Dan, who agreed with her that she should tell her grown children what she had learned thus far.

Susan asked the boys and Brooke to come over for dinner, inviting Joshua's wife Amanda to come along, though she didn't want their four children to attend the family meeting, so they stayed home with a sitter. After a somewhat subdued meal, Susan invited everyone into the living room so that she could share what she now knew about her late husband. Dan, as always, was by her side to encourage and uplift her at this very stressful time.

As Susan told the family about Kurt's early days, Brooke and Amanda began to weep. Brooke exclaimed, "This explains so much about his attitudes towards our family and towards women. He was pretty screwed up by his abusive father, doormat mother, and weird disappearing siblings."

Amanda added, "Mom, how did you live for thirty-five years with a man whose background made him so...I don't know, psycho? He might have killed...oh, how silly of me. He tried to kill you three times!"

Joshua said, "No offense, people, but I'm very glad there's no blood between Kurt and me!"

Amanda said, slapping his arm, "Joshua! Hush, now! They can't help it!"

Susan said, "We are one family, no matter how strange, okay?" She looked at her eldest son with an impish grin. "Don't rub it in, Joshua!"

Susan's sudden defense of Brooke and Christopher made the room erupt in laughter. It was just what was needed to break the tension. Susan told them, "I think this gives us a new perspective on Kurt. He learned at an early age that if he was going to survive, even to the next meal, he had to manipulate and play people. He had this issue with abandonment, as well. I mean, look at the disappearance of every single one of his siblings, especially the little sister Ella. How could a little boy cope with that? His mother died when he was a preteen under really strange circumstances that he doesn't explain fully. The night of her death is just so mysterious. Who was that man – or woman- out at the creek with her? Kurt doesn't say, at least so far. Maybe he never knew for sure who it was. His father became his son at an age when Kurt was still growing up. Add that to the time he served in Vietnam, and you have a recipe for a seriously messed up man. I'm surprised he coped as well as he did!"

Joshua asked, "Do you think it was Grandpa Prescott who killed her? He seems to have known something about her death. I mean, he pulled Kurt out of bed and held a family meeting in the middle of the night . . ."

Dan asked, "What about the brother Peter? He left shortly after she died. Do you think he did it and then took off?"

Susan said, "I don't know. Candace had good reasons to keep her alive because her mother was a buffer between Candy and her dad, so I don't imagine she did it, but I don't know about Peter."

Dan asked, "What about Kurt's wet feet? Why would he have wet feet and pajama bottoms in bed? Feet and clothes that were wet enough to dampen his sheets? Susan, you said that he wrote that his father suggested later that he might have done it, that Kurt might kill him, as well. And those dreams Kurt had. They say 'guilty as charged' like nothing else."

Amanda spoke up, "What if one of the departed siblings came back for the evening? There were three of them. Maybe one of them stopped by for an unplanned visit, and snuck in to see his or her mom."

Susan said, "You all have really good ideas. Basically, there are six siblings and a drunken father, all of whom might have done it, except for Ella who wasn't living there anymore. We have seven people who were related to Mrs. Prescott, but there's also the possibility that someone from the town did it or perhaps a stranger came by. And we have Ella's kidnappers, who might have been trying to make a deal to return the little girl. We have a forty-eight-year-old crime here. And, yes, I do think it was a crime that was never fully investigated. The police obviously thought Mrs. Prescott was really drunk, slipped on the rocks by the edge of the creek, and fell in the water where she drowned. Kurt saw something, but we don't know what, at least not yet."

Brooke asked her, "So where do we go from here?"

"I'm going to keep reading. Maybe we can get some hints about what happened. I've only gotten through the first three journals, but I think that the journals will help us understand ourselves better, whether the mystery is solved in the journals or not. Each of you might want to look through them, as well, especially you, Brooke. I think it's colored how all of us see marriage and with your relationship ending with Michael . . ."

"Mom, I think this talk has really helped me figure out where I went wrong with Michael. Because of Dad's treatment of you, I didn't want to ever get married. But I see now that it was Dad who was so afraid of abandonment. Michael had a wonderful home life growing up. He isn't anything like Dad was, so he won't react the same way. Michael is a different man. I miss him so much. I . . . might . . . just give him a call." Then, speaking fast, "Do you think that would be all right with him? I haven't heard from him at all since we broke up that night."

Brooke looked so sad that Susan had to confess. "Brooke, Michael and I talk every day. He asked me not to tell you, unless I felt there was some hope for your relationship. I know he wants to hear from you."

Brooke beamed at this news. "I'll call him right after work tomorrow. Maybe I could ask him out for dinner? Or is that too bold?"

"Well, I wouldn't invite him to the Chart House just yet," Susan said, referencing the place where Michael had proposed, "but I know he would be open to an invitation. Perhaps you might even . . . phone him tonight."

"Yes, yes, I will." Brooke looked ready to run out the door that very moment.

Dan said, "I'm happy for you Brooke, that these journals have helped you see the reality of your relationship with Michael. We all miss him." Everyone nodded. "Please bring him back to the family." Dan gave her a quick hug.

Joshua asked, "So, Mom, I guess we'll meet again when you have read some more journals, and we've had the chance to learn about Kurt ourselves?"

"Yes, I think that's a good idea. Let's split up the three journals I've finished then, so you can look at them and see if there's something I missed about his mom's death. We can chat again in the next week or so, to see what we uncover. Is everyone okay with that?"

They all nodded and got ready to leave. It was not until the door had closed on the last person that Susan realized that Christopher had not spoken all evening.

Chapter 18

Susan read the next few journals as time permitted, sipping a cup of tea as she sat on their comfortable living room couch or in her favorite chair in Dan's study, while he silently did paperwork to keep their financial well-being intact. Dan was an anchor that blessed her heart as she read about the storms that troubled Kurt's childhood.

These next journals covered the years that Kurt became a young man. His father had made a vain attempt at re-marriage, but that didn't last long. The newly-wed woman got a full measure of the man behind the charming façade within months and had exited. Rumor had it that she resumed her maiden name, only too glad to jettison the drunk who had swept her off her feet when they first met at an AA meeting. His attempt at sobriety was a perfunctory action designed to keep the Child Protective Agency folks from removing Kurt from his home.

One of the neighbors had finally reported Mr. Prescott when she saw him berating his son in the back yard. They had been standing next to the creek where Mrs. Prescott had died. Mr. Prescott had been screaming about darkness and identity or something such as that, while he struck Kurt with a belt. Kurt didn't go into details of the reprimand but did say that he wished the police knew what had really happened.

Kurt told his journals that his father had found AA a convenient way to make contact with women of a similar addictive personality. His father had found it very flattering to have the attention of so many women in need of comfort as they battled alcohol abuse. His father had bragged to Kurt about how many women he bedded during his time with AA. "Addictive personalities are addictive personalities," the teenaged Kurt opined.

Kurt wrote about the revolving door on his father's bedroom, which Susan realized was further destruction to the young Kurt's sense of right and wrong in relationships. Some of the women came on to Kurt, but he took off for his friends' houses, not interested in aging drunks who were old enough to be his mother, no matter what they were offering. He was not going to live The Graduate, Mrs. Robinson-type of life. Kurt was in his mid-teens by then and well aware of his father's self-destructive actions.

The next journal was written when Kurt was in his senior year of high school; the draft for the Viet Nam Conflict was in full swing. When the draft numbers were pulled, his birthdate made his being drafted a sure thing. He didn't want to go into the Army, so he signed up for the Navy on a delayed enrollment deal. He would finish high school and then be sent to Navy boot camp. Kurt wrote that it would be a relief to finally escape his father's house, and that he understood why his siblings had left. The nightmares that had plagued him since his sister's kidnapping and his mother's death were finally retreating a bit, but he still woke up occasionally, calling for Ella to come back from a car where she was sitting or shouting his mother's name as she lay face down in the creek.

Once in boot camp, Kurt wrote about his unsuccessful attempts to manipulate the drill sergeants into going easy on him. He finally recorded that they were used to working with young men like him – they were not taking any of his garbage. He kept his head down and just got through it.

Viet Nam was heartbreaking for him. He was befriended

by an older man who represented the very best of marriage. His friend Joe Barham was a devout Christian who adored his wife, was faithful to her in spite of being a half a world away, and loved his children. Joe wanted to serve his nation so he had volunteered for service, in spite of having a wife and three very good reasons to not have to go.

Joe took Kurt under his wing. Kurt admitted to being in awe of the man. One day they were flying a mission over enemy territory when their plane was shot down. Everyone was injured, though their injuries varied based on where they were on the plane. Kurt had a broken arm, but still tried to pull his friends from the downed plane before it burst into flames. Some of them stumbled out under his guidance before collapsing nearby. He managed to get Joe out of the plane and a short distance from the aircraft, but Joe had too many injuries to sustain life. Joe died in Kurt's arms. In the end, Kurt was the only survivor that day. In order to save his own life, he had been forced to abandon Joe's body and the other helpless and dying men. He knew enough about medicine to realize they wouldn't last longer than a few hours.

Kurt grabbed Joe's dog tags and wallet, and then took off before the enemy could capture him. He made it safely back to his own regiment's camp but wrote that it had killed him to abandon his men. Kurt was placed in a MASH unit and then airlifted out of Nam. He ended up in physical therapy and didn't return to the battlefield. The rest of the journal dealt with his feelings about life, God, and the loss of Joe. It was not a pleasant read.

Kurt was just shy of his twenty-second birthday when he returned stateside, after serving three tours in Nam. His father died of cirrhosis of the liver a few months later. The man had become more and more dependent on booze, having given up the pretense of sincerity with regard to AA after Kurt left home. Kurt understood that his father still frequented the AA meetings for available women, but that he drank like a fish swims when not in attendance. His bulbous red nose covered in broken blood vessels and pale yellow skin were a silent testimony to his father's continued reliance on booze, Kurt wrote.

Kurt had spent the next two years following his return cruising around town in his sports car, trying to figure out what he wanted to do with his life. He had a small inheritance from his father. He made a point of going back to the creek and saying "goodbye" to his mother's memory before he sold the family home. He wrote about trying to remember that long ago night, the darkness of the memory, and faces that were still so blurred to him.

"Why can't I remember more about that night? Maybe if I write about it... I was ten years old. My parents had been fighting, as usual, I heard Ella's name a few times. Daddy was blaming Mommy for Ella's disappearance, saying that if she hadn't left Ella in the car while she went into the bar for a drink, no one would have taken her. Why didn't they try harder to find Ella? I don't think they cared about her at all! I did! Why didn't they go look for her? Where is my sister? I want to know, and I want them to go bring her home. This was all Mommy's fault!

"I walked into the kitchen where they were drinking and talking about children. When they saw me come in, they started talking about Will and wondering where he was...Nam was going strong...did they think he was there? I don't know. Why would they talk about him? He had been gone for so many years . . . Why talk about him now? He left home before Ella my

Bella was born."

Kurt had tried to remember something, anything, about his brother Will, but he had left when Kurt was so young. Will was a pretty good-sized fellow. Kurt knew that from looking at his picture. But, no, there were too many years between Will's departure and Kurt's memories. He wouldn't know Will if he saw him on the street.

A piece of paper! That's it! His mom had been holding a scrap of paper in her hand that night when he had come into the kitchen. Was it a letter? No, I don't think so. It was too small for that. Maybe it was folded, though. A note of some kind? Maybe. Let me think about this some more.

He must have gotten distracted, though, because there was nothing else written about that night in that journal. Kurt wrote later that, after several months of searching for something to do with his life, a friend had told him about the free education he could get from the military, so he applied for acceptance at the Naval Academy. As a decorated war hero, he would have a good chance of acceptance. He would just make it under the wire, having been accepted and starting his studies at the ripe old age of twenty-four. The deadline of graduation by the age of twenty-eight would be met, so Kurt began his work as a freshman. He made a note that he would be storing his journals, along with some other personal stuff, in a friend's garage while he was away from home. He would collect his belongings when he got assigned to a permanent duty station.

Susan realized that now he was getting into the years when she knew him, having met him the fall of his senior year at the USNA. She took a break from the journals, feeling that she was violating his thoughts by reading about herself. She had been passing the journals along to first Joshua, then

Brooke, and finally to Christopher as she read each one. Her emotions had been drained by them, so she decided to take a week or so off to vacation with Dan. It was a lovely time of year, May, so the weather had not gotten too hot to enjoy the beautiful outdoors.

Chapter 19

Susan and Dan decided to head to Williamsburg, Virginia. She loved history and enjoyed seeing the old houses and shops that had been so lovingly restored. Dan made an excellent traveling companion. He was supportive of her appreciation of history, even if it was not his first choice for vacations. They stayed at the Williamsburg Lodge and ate a meal at King's Arms Tavern. They attended a recital while there, enjoying the old fashioned music. It was a great way for her to decompress after the stress of reading Kurt's journals.

Joshua and his family joined them at the end of the trip; they all went to Busch Gardens and several water parks for a few days. As a surprise, Brooke and Michael also came, having reunited in March. She was happy to see that Christopher had come along, albeit at Brooke's request.

"Mom and Dan?" Brooke beamed at her mother and step-father. "Michael and I have some news for everyone!"

Susan looked at her daughter, guessing what the news was, but wanting Brooke to say it for herself. "What's that, dear?" She smiled a huge smile.

"We're getting married in October!"

Everyone expressed their great joy at the news. There were hugs and handshakes followed by more hugs for all. Michael's face could not contain his happiness; Brooke's eyes overflowed with tears of exultation.

Brooke told them, "I have an appointment you need to keep with me, Mom and Amanda. I'm trying on wedding dresses next week at Wren Bridal. It'll be a pretty fast turnaround for the gown, but they have assured me they can do it. Will you both come?"

"Of course!" "I wouldn't miss this for the world!" "Absolutely, my dear Brooke!" The news made their vacation complete.

***

Christopher examined his new family's dynamics while on vacation with them in Williamsburg. As he sauntered down the dusty streets, he kept a close eye on how they treated each other. Loving. Kind. Joking. Happy to be with one another. Maybe these people weren't as weird as he'd been led to believe by his father. Christopher had been reading the journals along with his mother and siblings. His dad had experienced such a horrible childhood. Christopher was beginning to understand why Audrey, his beloved Audrey, thought he was such a mess. He was.

Christopher wasn't in favor of counseling, but Brooke seemed so much happier than ever before, even with reading what kind of man their father really was. These folks were also devout Christians...well, maybe not Joshua and Amanda . . . maybe. He was having trouble telling exactly where they stood. Joshua was, after all, a man of science. Doctors shouldn't believe in God, should they? Isn't that kinda against everything that medical science says? A creator of the world? Well, maybe Intelligent Design. Christopher might go for that himself, but a single creator and a literal seven days of creation seemed like a real stretch.

Christopher went back to work after the family trip, where he had been talking to Audrey and getting to know her better. He no longer attempted to make any moves on her. She had seen right through him and wasn't buying any of it. She didn't back down. She held her ground with him, which was something no woman had ever done to him, ever. They had been working together for months, and it appeared that the Navy was going to leave her in Annapolis for the time being. That was fine with him. That was more than fine!

Christopher started dreaming about Audrey. He dreamt about her walking down the aisle of a church in a beautiful white wedding gown. He was waiting at the altar for her, with a smile of contentment unlike anything he had ever experienced on his face. The place was packed with people. Just as he imagined what it was going to be like to be married to her, different women stood up and began to talk. There was Shannon . . . and Ruby Mae, among many others. They all shared what it was like to be with him. Although he had slept with many of them, others like Ruby Mae had just spent the evening with him. They warned Audrey not to do it, to walk away and jilt him at the altar. He found himself screaming, "No, don't tell her that. I'm not that man anymore." He always woke up with a start, never sure if Audrey would take their advice or not.

Christopher trembled at the thought of never seeing Audrey again, sure that she would leave him standing at the altar alone. The testimony of many witnesses was against him. She would never marry him now, not with what they told her. Not with what she now knew.

One night, he had a dream unlike any of the others. He entered the candle-lit church. No lights were on, only flickering candles offered any source of illumination. Golden candelabras stood on the altar, platform, and in the empty choir loft. The floral arrangements he expected to see had been replaced by bare sticks protruding from oversized red and black vases.

161

Where were the flowers?

The organ music swelled, to signal the entry of the bridal party. It was not any song he had ever heard. The cacophony made his ears hurt. He glanced at the congregation and noticed the people were so dimly lit that he could not discern any features on their faces. They were all dressed in black.

He was waiting at the altar and saw Audrey's maid of honor walking into the church in a black bridesmaid dress and carrying a bouquet of black, dead roses. A few moments passed. The doors at the back of the sanctuary swung closed and then reopened to reveal his bride. Audrey was standing there, dressed in a low-cut, solid black lace gown that revealed her womanly charms. A long black veil flowed over her head and arms, trailing behind her on the floor. She had massive, brightly-colored tattoos on both arms and she held a bouquet of knives.

Audrey began her slow walk down the aisle, grinning as if she were a mad woman. Christopher pulled back, repulsed by the lady he saw coming. He heard a familiar laugh behind him. He turned and looked into the eyes of his deceased father.

"Hello, Christopher. Looks like you got a live one here. She should be fun," his father told him, poking him in the ribs. Kurt laughed again.

"Dad, what are you doing here? You can't be here. You're…" He felt horrified, but wasn't sure what bothered him more: his dead father or his walking dead bride-to-be.

"Dead? Yes, Christopher, dead and buried, as they say. Cremated, actually. Come on now, let's have a wedding here." Kurt snickered once more and leered at Audrey.

Audrey had arrived. As Christopher looked at her, her face morphed into that of Ruby Mae, the girl from the restaurant.

Christopher turned to the officiant, and saw he was looking into the eyes of a clown. The clown laughed, and pulled off his mask. It was his father.

"Dearly beloved, we are gathered here . . ." Kurt began.

"NO, no, this can't be happening!" he screamed at his father. He looked back at the bride. "You aren't my Audrey . . ." he yelled at anyone who would hear him.

Audrey/Ruby Mae spoke for the first time. "What, you don't like my black dress, Christopher? It matches your black heart and soul. Or maybe it matches mine. Someone has a life that is not pure. You want me to marry you. What kind of deal is that for me?" Her laughter spooked him.

He seemed paralyzed. He couldn't move away from this wretched mess. How had he not seen who Audrey/Ruby Mae was? He screamed out . . . and woke up, clenching his sheets in his sweat-soaked hands. He sat on the bed, his head in his hands. How could this be? When would these dreams stop?

Christopher dreamt on another night that he told Audrey all about himself, all the wretched details of his immorality. He was not proud of what he felt obligated to confess, but she didn't seem to judge him. At the same time, she didn't appear eager to marry him. Sometimes he would dream that he had tricked her into marriage, and that she was yelling and screaming as he dragged her down the aisle.

A short while later, the day came when he knew he had to talk to someone. He called Brooke for the name of her counselor.

"Hey, Brooke." How was he going to tell her what he wanted? This was so unlike him.

"Hey, Christopher. What's up?" Brooke sounded

surprised to hear from him, since she was the one who usually called him.

"Uh . . . yeah . . . You know how Dad's journals make him seem so screwed up?"

"Yeah. He was, Chris."

"Yeah, I know that now . . ." He was unable to continue. Maybe he could ease his way into this. "So, how are things going?"

Brooke hesitated. "Fine, why do you ask?"

"Uh . . ."

"Christopher, what is it? Are you okay?" Brooke's voice sounded strained at the mystery of his phone call.

"Yes . . . uh, no, not really . . ."

"Christopher, you're starting to worry me. What's happening?"

He sighed. "Well, I just . . . I was wondering if maybe you could . . . give me the name and number of that guy you have been talking to...some things aren't going like I hoped . . . you seem so happy these days, in spite of reading Dad's journals and I thought maybe . . ." He couldn't go on. His father, who he had adored for so many years, was not the man Christopher thought, and it had profoundly affected him. He knew it. He had to do something about it.

"Oh, I see . . . sure thing . . . he's my pastor, Christopher. Are you okay with that?"

"Talking to him seems to have made such a huge difference in your life, Brooke. I don't know what it is, but you're so happy and I don't think it is all Michael's doing . . . well, maybe it is."

"Because I talked to Pastor, I was able to get my heart right with God, and now I can be happy with Michael. Are you ready for that? I mean, I'm happy that you want to talk to Pastor, but I just want to make sure you know that he will talk to you about Jesus and about becoming a Christian."

"Yeah, I figured that. Can you give me his number, please?" He hoped he wasn't opening a can of worms with this whole idea, but it was better than continuing to have bad dreams about the woman he adored and, yes, wanted to marry. She wouldn't have him in his present state, not that he blamed her a bit. If this was what it took to get Audrey to even go out with him, so be it.

Chapter 20

"Audrey thanks so much for lending a hand with Vacation Bible School!" The over-worked music director smiled her gratitude as Audrey picked up the children's trash from the front pews and straightened the hymnals in the pew racks. "I'm amazed at your ability to sight read the piano music after the CD player broke on the very first day of VBS! I don't know how I would have managed without you!"

Audrey was only too happy to help out. She missed working with the children now that she was TDY in Annapolis. She had been actively involved with her Baptist church in Norfolk, and this June activity was a great opportunity to work on a temporary project while she was in the area.

"You're most certainly welcome, Stephanie! It's been fun." Audrey smiled at the harried 40-something woman who was putting closing program bulletins together. She wondered why VBS music directors always waited until the 11th hour to complete such a task. She always had the programs finished by the end of the first day of VBS, when she was in charge of things. "Today's the big day!"

"Yep, only a couple of hours to go before the program kicks off. Do you have those invitations and directions to the Walsh's house ready to hand out?" Stephanie looked ready to collapse, but she was scurrying around as she spoke, marking the places the children should stand for the program on the carpet with masking tape, stuffing bulletins, and tidying the orchestra pit. Audrey noticed Stephanie had a bit of lint on her sweater, so she picked it off.

"Yes. That was so nice of that couple to invite us all over to their place for the party tomorrow. It's right on the Bay, isn't it?" Audrey asked.

"Yepper." Stephanie said. "We'll have to ask the parents to keep a close eye on their kids, but it should be really nice."

"How many children do you think will come?" Audrey was concerned about overwhelming the kindness of the couple.

"Well, it's only the middle school kids. The Walsh family has a bunch of middle school grandchildren, so I guess that's why they asked us over. I think there will be about fifty kids, plus their parents and siblings, so maybe there will be about . . . shoot, over a hundred and twenty-five people if they all come. But I doubt that many will come because it's the middle of the day on a Saturday and all. The good news is that they live on the west side of the Bay, so we don't have to go over the bridge. That traffic is horrid on a pretty day in summer." Stephanie thought for a moment. "They could still have a pretty big crowd . . . with our workers there and all."

Stephanie had a habit of scrunching up her face when making calculations, whether it was where to block the children in the final program or figuring out a guest count. It wasn't very attractive, but she was otherwise a very nice person. Well, perhaps a little flighty, Audrey thought, as many creative people are.

"What all do they have planned?" Audrey was curious about the length of the party and what they would have to eat.

"Oh, you know, a bar-b-que followed by various games for the kiddos. We'll have to be part babysitters and part game coordinators, most likely. It goes from eleven to three, so it won't be too long . . . I'm glad I have the night to rest up, before hitting the deck running on Sunday. Also, I'm looking forward to seeing the Walsh's house."

"Will they give us the grand tour, do you think?" Audrey loved looking at decorating and getting ideas for the house she hoped to have, once she settled down.

Stephanie laughed. "The kids have to use the bathrooms near the pool, but adults are invited to use the facilities in the house, for which I am eternally grateful. I plan on looking around a bit, if I need to go inside."

"You're such a character, Stephanie! But I know what you mean. Maybe things will work out just right . . ." Audrey smiled at her newfound friend.

The closing program went on without any challenges, a short time later. The children remembered all of their songs and lines. Audrey played the piano without error. She was glad it turned out so well. She'd been a bit rusty on her piano playing, but her twelve years of lessons and hours of practicing over the past week had paid off. The parents were appreciative and offered numerous compliments to her as they thanked the workers for their dedication.

Saturday morning was glorious. The sky was blue with only wisps of clouds. The temperature and humidity were pleasant, considering it was a Washington area summer. The breeze off the Bay made it quite comfortable, as Audrey crossed the lawn towards the picnic tables that were set up bayside.

Audrey wore a fashionable but conservative pair of white shorts, a blue and white striped T-shirt, and white sandals. Her long brown hair was pulled back in a ponytail that whipped from side to side as she walked. She carried some cookies from the local food store in her hands, having figured that they would be popular with the kiddies.

"Audrey, it's good to see you!" Stephanie yelled as she approached. "Come meet Mr. and Mrs. Walsh."

Introductions were made. It became "Susan" and "Dan" very quickly. Audrey accompanied Susan back into the house for a few last-minute condiment pickups. They joined the others on the back lawn as Dan offered thanks for their time of fellowship and food. The hundred-plus visitors had a great time, but the afternoon party was over faster than Audrey could have imagined.

The guests helped put things right with the yard before leaving, though Susan and Dan explained that they would be having a family gathering for their whole clan that evening, so not much needed to be put away.

Before Audrey left, she asked Susan if she could use the bathroom. Susan said "sure thing" and accompanied her into the house, offering a grand tour afterwards.

"I'd love to see your place, Susan. Thanks so much for asking. I've always loved decorating – I'm constantly getting tips for when I get my own house."

The ladies walked through the residence after Audrey was finished in the necessary room. Everything was stunning. They finished the tour with a visit to the family room. A baby grand piano stood along one wall.

"Oh, Susan, do you play?"

"No, no, my dear Audrey. Dan and his children play, but I don't. We have a family band when his kids come over, but my children weren't interested in music when they were growing up. They were more into sports."

Susan paused by the nearby bookshelf. "These are my children and grandchildren from my first marriage. And these are Dan and Rebecca's children and grands from his first time down the aisle."

Audrey couldn't believe her eyes. Staring at her from among the photos was a picture, in dress uniform, of Christopher Prescott. Her mouth felt dry, her hands were clammy. Her heart was beating- could Susan hear it? – so loudly. That horrid man Christopher had been birthed by this wonderful, warm woman? How could that be?

"Susan, thank you so much for the tour, but I really mustn't take any more of your time, especially if you're expecting more company." She wanted to beat feet before Christopher showed up, assuming he would be attending the family gathering.

"Audrey, you're certainly welcome. Are you sure you wouldn't like to stay for the evening? We have plenty of food and definitely have room for one more!"

"No, but thank you. Perhaps another time." What could she say to get away fast? What time had Susan said the clan was coming over? Four? Five? Rats, she couldn't remember for sure. It was almost 3:45 now and if he was the type to show up early...

No, wait . . . Audrey had heard Christopher saying to one of the other officers more than once over the past several months that he had a "Command Performance" this weekend or that at his folks' house. He made no bones about his dislike of any time spent with his family. There was no way he would be there ahead of time. Whew. She was safe. She could make a gracious exit and not draw any suspicion on herself and how eager she was to depart. She calmed down, took a deep breath that she hoped was not obvious, and continued to chatter with

Susan as she walked towards the kitchen door.

Just as they got there, the door swung open. There stood Christopher Prescott. Early.

Chapter 21

Audrey was face to face with the one man she didn't want to see. Drat the luck! She thought she was getting away fast enough to avoid Chris. She hadn't wanted to be rude to Susan, who was so nice, so she had chatted while moving towards the back door at the same time.

She knew for a fact that Chris hated going to his parents' house. He had been so vocal about it in the office. Why in the world would he show up early?

Chris also seemed startled. "Audrey. What are you doing here?"

"I . . . ugh . . ." Her voice wasn't working so well.

Susan said, "I didn't know you two knew each other. How did you meet?"

Audrey recovered pretty fast. "Oh, Susan, we work together at the Naval Academy. I'm here on TDY from Norfolk, team teaching the Oceanography major with Christopher." To Chris, she said, "I was here with the children from VBS. The party's over, and I was just getting the grand tour from your mother."

Christopher said, "We're having a family gathering tonight. I hope you'll stay."

Audrey replied, "Oh, no. I've imposed on your family's hospitality long enough." To Susan, "I really need to get going." She gave Susan a quick hug, and then continued walking towards the door.

Susan looked from Audrey to Christopher and back. She seemed confused by their strained and stilted conversation. She didn't say anything.

Christopher said, "Audrey, I understand if you have to leave, but could we just chat for a few minutes? Please?" He smiled at her, tall, dark, and handsome in his navy blue shorts and red shirt.

The guy was a hunk, no doubt about it, but he was an unhinged hunk in her humble opinion. Audrey didn't see a way out of the situation. Susan had been so gracious that Audrey didn't see how she could turn him down in front of her. So be it. "Okay, Chris."

"Let's go out to the dock, okay?" Then to Susan, "Mom, I'll be back in a few minutes." He gave Susan a quick peck on the cheek and turned to Audrey. "Ready?"

Audrey smiled what she hoped looked like a sincere smile at Susan, and thanked her again for the afternoon. She walked with Chris to the dock in silence.

He gestured that he wanted her to come out to the bench at the end of the dock, so she complied, unwilling but unable to think of a single satisfactory reason to turn him down. Nothing came to mind. Well, at least it was a beautiful view. After they sat down, Chris began to talk.

"Audrey, I didn't know you were going to be here, but I'm really happy that you are. I know we didn't get off to a very good start when we first met, especially since you told me how messed up you think I am." He smiled, but she noticed the smile didn't make it all the way to his eyes.

"Chris, where is this going? Because . . ." Audrey stumbled through her words. What was going on here? This was uncomfortable. Awkward!

"Please hear me out. I might not get the courage to say this again. Audrey, you were right. I was . . . maybe still am . . .

173

messed up. We found some journals my father kept that explained what was wrong in his life. He was abandoned by everyone who loved him, when he was just a little kid. I'm not using his problems to explain mine, at least not totally, but I learned a lot about myself by reading what he had written."

"Chris, I'm sorry you had a rough childhood because of your dad, but your mom seems like a very nice person. I can't believe that she was . . . less than supportive of you and your siblings." She looked at him with questions in her eyes.

"No, Audrey, Mom was great, but I didn't know it. She's exactly the person you think she is- a loving wife and mother."

"Where's this going, Chris?" She was getting her craw full of this guy really fast. Why is he acting so weird? Nice, almost. For him, creepy. She leaned away from him on the bench, wanting to put as much distance between the two of them as possible.

"I realized that Brooke was so happy all the time, at least nowadays. So is Mom. Dan's a great guy, but that didn't explain their true happiness, their joy. Even my brother Joshua seems happier than he ever was before, and he was always a nice guy." He leaned towards her.

"Okay. So they're happy." Big deal, buddy. That doesn't excuse who I know you are. She shifted on the bench once again, trying to put as much distance as possible between the two of them.

"Audrey, they're happy because they're going to church and they got some counselling. I couldn't explain it. I'm probably not explaining it very well now, but a little over a month ago, I asked Brooke about going to her counselor for advice about dealing with my past. Please don't tell anyone in the office- it could torch my career, but I needed to find out

174

why I was- like you said- so messed up."

Audrey was surprised, shocked that he would tell her this. She couldn't even speak.

"Audrey, I was living a life that wasn't good. Sure, I looked successful at work, but I was – you called me a "womanizer"- and you were right. I didn't treat women very well. Not well at all, actually. I used them. I threw them away. I was wrong. Very wrong. I've been talking to Brooke's pastor on a regular basis, and he's showing me the way that I should be around women. He's also teaching me about the relationship I need to have with God. He's really guiding me, and being the father I always needed, but didn't have."

Audrey squirmed on the bench, not sure what to say.

"Audrey, I'd like to ask for your forgiveness. I investigated you when I got mad that night when you told me I was messed up."

"Investigated me? How?" What in the world? How dare he? Then again, it matched his creepy personality.

"I looked up information about you on google. I was looking for some kind of dirt to use against you. But, of course, there was nothing there. I wasn't acting manly. I was acting like a spoiled little boy, which is what I was. Will you forgive me?" Christopher reached about and almost touched her hand, but then backed off.

"Uh, yes, Chris, I will. I mean, I kinda investigated you, too, so if you'll forgive me, I can most certainly forgive you." Okay, this is getting more awkward by the minute.

"Thanks, Audrey. That means a lot to me. I . . . uh . . . did have something else to say, if you have time."

"Okay, Chris. What is it?" Maybe he does have something

worthwhile to say. I'll give him a chance here.

"I'm guessing that you are really into God. Is that right?"

"Yes, Chris. I'm a Christian. I got saved when I was a little girl, and have served Him ever since. That's why I'm here today. I took off work this week so that I could be involved in the Vacation Bible School program at my church. I worked in the music department." She hesitated, and then decided to plunge ahead. "Why do you ask? No offense, but you don't seem like a churchy kinda guy to me."

"I'm still checking this God thing out." Christopher put up his hands to wave off her offense. "I mean no disrespect, Audrey. I know this is important to you, but I'm still looking for answers. My family never put any emphasis on the Christian faith, at least, not until Mom was in the rehab center and Michael Bench told them about God. Brooke and Mom have told me that they "got saved," became Christians, like you just mentioned. Dan and his family are all devout Christians. I don't know about Joshua, but he and his family seem to be getting closer to God these days."

"Yes, Susan was telling me about that when she was giving me the tour." Audrey couldn't fathom where this was leading, but at least it seemed to be headed in the right direction.

"Look, Audrey, I have to be completely honest with you. I don't know if I'm going to become a Christian anytime soon or not. I do know that I feel better about life and myself since I started talking to Pastor. But, whatever happens, I just want you to know that I'm not the man you met a few months ago. I just wanted you to know that." He smiled for a moment. "I'm being redundant, aren't I?"

"Yes, quite." She smiled back. "Thanks for your honesty,

Chris. I get the impression that you aren't usually this forthcoming with women. Or with anyone, for that matter."

"Yeah, I'm not. I . . . uh . . . I care for you Audrey. I'm not asking you for anything except the chance to show you that I've changed." Christopher looked out at the Bay. He sighed, then said, "I'm not going to try to get you to go out with me right now, Audrey. But I hope that you'll consider it in the future."

"Chris, I cannot and will not be unequally yoked. You probably don't know what that means but, next time you talk with Pastor, ask him about it, okay?"

"Sure thing. Thanks for letting me talk to you, Audrey." He hesitated. "May I walk you back to your car? I mean, I would love for you to stay, but I understand that you might want to hit the road."

"Thanks, Chris. Yes, you may walk me to my car. I have plenty of things to think about, and it's already been a long day." Audrey smiled again. Okay, maybe he isn't so bad after all.

"No problem. Shall we?" He stood and then held out his arm, to guide her off the dock. She reached over and took Christopher's arm. His sharp intake of breath told her that he hadn't expected it. As they walked back up the dock and then across the grass to her car, she felt a still small voice telling her, "This is the man I have for you."

Her head jerked up in surprise. She stumbled into her car after saying goodbye to Chris. "Him, Lord? What are You thinking?" She drove away, waving to Susan and Dan, who had come outside to prepare for the family party. Tears formed in her eyes. How could this be?

She headed home, driving as if in a fog. She shook her head, certain she had misunderstood. The voice spoke to her heart again, "He is not who he will become. Wait upon Me, and

I will show you great and mighty things that you don't know about."

Audrey prayed as she drove, "Lord, how can he be the man for me? You know the man he was . . . maybe still is."

"Wait, my child. I will tell you when the time is right. Be patient and pray for Chris. He is the one for you, but not yet."

"Yes, Lord. Yes." Tears streamed down her cheeks, knowing that the Lord's will was always perfect. She began to pray for Chris's salvation and his walk with God. What a shock! She was going to marry Chris Prescott? She would have never guessed that!

Chapter 22

Brooke called a Prescott family meeting for that lovely July day, asking everyone to come. They met, as usual, at Susan and Dan's home, since it was the largest of the clan's residences. They settled into the family room, sitting on couches with some sweet iced tea and sugar cookies that Susan had made that afternoon.

Brooke said, "Thanks for coming, everyone. I know you probably think that this is a pre-wedding meeting, but it isn't. Michael and I . . ."

Everyone gasped. They murmured. Was the wedding being called off?

Susan asked, "Honey, is everything okay?" Susan looked back and forth between the couple, but everything seemed fine.

Brooke assured them, "Yes, we're good, nothing's wrong. Everything's fine. Really good. I just talked to Michael about something, and he's okay with the idea." She took a deep breath. Slowly..."I would like to know what you think about our looking for Dad's family- his brothers and sisters."

The family just stared at her.

Joshua asked, "Why would you want to do that?" He hesitated a moment. "I mean, I wouldn't do it if it was me, but it's your blood relatives." He shrugged and then looked embarrassed.

Christopher said, "You found your dad so this isn't important to you, but we might just like to find our aunts and uncles." He sent a scowl in Joshua's direction.

Joshua said, "I'm sorry Chris, Brooke. I didn't mean to come across that way. What I'm trying to say is that we have such a great family now. What if we find something we don't like?"

Christopher's face relaxed, and he replied, "No offense taken, Josh. Please forgive me. I'm sorry I mouthed off like

179

that. It was very bad of me. I'm sorry. Everyone, please forgive me." He turned to Brooke. "But are you really interested in opening that can of worms?"

Brooke said, "I'm just curious about these people we've been reading about. Are they still alive? What happened to them after they left home? Did they know about their mother's death? Did one of them kill her? Did they see who did kill her? What about Ella? Did anyone ever look for her?" She looked around the room with curiosity. "Don't you think that could be intriguing?"

When everyone had a chance to say something, the votes were pretty much split. The women- Brooke, Susan, and Amanda- thought it could be fun. Solving a years-old murder and kidnapping could be interesting, exciting even. The men- Michael, Dan, Joshua, and Christopher- weren't too sure that they wanted to get pulled into this. What if the murderer was still alive and didn't want to be found? What if they found Ella's body in the middle of a forest or found out that she had been tortured? That didn't make for nice bedtime reading.

Dan asked, "Brooke, honey, don't you have enough to do to get ready for the wedding without digging around to find people that you never met?"

Brooke answered, "Sure, we have plenty to do, but I still think it's worthwhile."

Michael spoke up, "It's kinda like Alex Haley and Roots. Looking into the past to understand the future, that kind of stuff."

Christopher said, "If you want to do it, it's fine by me. I'm really not interested personally, but go ahead if you want and see what you come up with. Be discrete. We don't want to fish you out of the Chesapeake Bay."

Joshua agreed, "Yes, Brooke, go ahead if this is something you really want to do. But do me a favor, and don't talk about me with these people, if you find them. I don't need any crazies coming after me at the hospital. As a doctor, I have enough contact with strange people, without going out and looking for them." He grinned, but seemed perfectly serious.

Brooke said, "That works for me. Michael, can you bring in the white board, please?"

"Sure thing, Brooke." Michael went into the downstairs bedroom and brought back a white board that she had already started writing on.

Joshua said, "Gee, Brooke, you're organized. I'm impressed."

Brooke grinned and said, "Okay, here's what we know so far. Kurt's mom died when he was a preteen. She died as a result of falling into the creek, after banging her head on the rocks. We don't know how she got there, but it does seem like someone must have hurt her. She could've slipped on the rocks and fallen in on her own, but it's unlikely, especially since we have the unknown piece of paper that Kurt remembered seeing and his comments about Will. We don't know what the fight was about on the night of her death."

Susan said, "Oh, and remember that Kurt's dad died several years later, after Kurt got back from Nam. His dad's death was related to his drinking a lot. I think the cause of death was probably 'excessive alcohol consumption.'"

"Do you think his father had any more kids after his wife died?" Joshua was curious.

Brooke said, "Dad's journals don't say anything about his father fathering more children, though I suppose that's a possibility. He might have also had more kids when she was still alive, if the note was from a mistress he impregnated. Mommy found out about Daddy's fling and had a fit. That kind of thing." She waved her white board marker around as she spoke.

Christopher said, "I don't think we can rule that out, or in. I mean, you never know about someone."

Susan spoke up. "Yes, the family wasn't exactly the forthcoming type, I mean, look at my marriage to Kurt. I had no idea he had siblings." She turned to Brooke. "Brooke, you might want to make a note about Mr. Prescott fathering more children for further reference, though I suppose we can let it go for now

181

and just focus on the people we know about."

"Good idea, Mom." Brooke wrote on the board. William Charles Prescott and Mary Ruth Taylor, married October 6, 1939, were given the notation "deceased." Then, "Possible other children by William? Unknown for now."

"Now then, William 'Will' Charles Prescott, Junior was born October 31, 1940. That means that he is about seventy-eight years old now, if he's still alive." Brooke added his current age to the board.

"Next, we have Margaret 'Maggie' Frances Prescott, born May 18, 1942. That makes her about seventy-six. She could very well be alive." Her age went up next to her name.

"Then, we have John 'Johnny' Kenneth Prescott, born July 3, 1944. At seventy-four, there's a good chance he's still living." Another board entry was made.

"The next child is Peter Russell Prescott, born March 27. 1946. He's going to be a seventy-two year old man. Probably alive." Brooke marked the board again.

"After that, we have Candace "Candy" Geraldine Prescott, born August 14, 1948. She's only seventy so she might be alive." A smiley face accompanied that information.

"Then we have Kurt Stephen Prescott, born February 9, 1954. We know he's dead." His death had already been recorded on the board.

Susan remarked, "Oh, yes, I have it on good authority that he is definitely deceased."

The laughter was refreshing, given the nature of their conversation.

"Finally, we have Ella Cassandra Prescott, born February 9, 1960. She was kidnapped when she was about four, according to the dates in Dad's journals, but there's a lot of information missing." Brooke entered the information next to Ella's name.

Joshua said, "She could be alive or long-time dead. Who knows?" He looked at his sister.

Dan nodded and asked, "So, Brooke, what's the plan?"

Brooke told him, "I'm going to start with google and

maybe join one of those ancestor search groups and see what I find out. When I learn something substantive, I'll call another meeting."

Amanda said, "I'd like to help you, Brooke, if you want."

"Absolutely, Amanda. Thanks for offering. Anybody else want to join in the fray?"

Christopher spoke, "Yeah, you know, I think I might just give it a shot after all, Brooke. Who would you like me to check on? Maybe if we split things up a bit, it'll go faster."

Joshua said, "My schedule is always kinda hectic, but I'll hang out with Amanda and give her a hand."

Susan told them, "I'm still working my way through the journals, but let me do this: I'll give you a hand once I finish the reading. I'll let you know if I come across anything that might help find them. How does that sound?"

Brooke was happy that the family had decided to get involved, especially the formerly uninterested menfolk. Brooke said, "You know, maybe we can get started on this right now. It might not be as fast, but how about if we work together on this? Family bonding and all. Dan, can we use your laptop?"

Dan answered, "Sure thing. Let's get this show on the road!" He grabbed his computer from the study and brought it into the family room. "Give me a minute to get this baby running." Then, "Here you go, Brooke. Have at it."

Brooke typed in the name "William 'Will' Charles Prescott, Jr." There were some half dozen obituaries for a Willy, Charlie, and Bill that appeared on the screen. The one that showed a match for William's year of birth was a man who died May 18, 2000.

"Hey, I think we found him!" She clicked on the entry and read, "Sergeant Major William 'Will' Charles Prescott, Jr. aged sixty, died May 18, 2000 in the Philadelphia VA Medical Center. Prescott served in Vietnam from 1958-1962 as a member of the United States Army. He retired from active duty service in 1978. He was preceded in death by his wife, Louisa Crowley Prescott. Interment will be in the Philadelphia

National Cemetery on Monday, May 22nd at ten am. In lieu of flowers, donations may be made to the American Cancer Society."

"Is there a picture?" Susan asked.

"Yes. Here's one of him in uniform." Brooke pulled it up on the computer. Everyone gathered around to see this man. The stranger staring back at them had Kurt's eyes. The man, who appeared to be in his early forties at the time of the photo, was not smiling and there was something haunting about his countenance.

Susan said, "He looks like his father, William Senior, don't you think? That picture that Kurt had in his cigar box of photos . . . this could be the same person. And those eyes- I've seen that look in Kurt's eyes, I can't count how many times."

Christopher said, "So that's my Uncle Will. Doesn't look like a particularly nice man, but you never know."

Joshua said, "He died of cancer. I wonder if it was related to his service in Vietnam. A lot of vets have had a horrible time with various types of cancer since they got back." Then, "any sign of children, Brooke?"

Brooke said, "Nope. Not that they list in the obituary. I wonder if he was sterile or if they just didn't want kids."

Christopher commented, "Maybe he avoided children because he was afraid of becoming like his father."

Brooke said, "Maybe, Chris. We all know that I've had commitment issues because of who our father was."

Michael hugged her and said, "I'm glad those issues have been worked out, Brooke."

Brooke smiled and said, "Me, too!" They kissed.

"Who's going to update the board?" Dan asked.

"How about you?" Brooke smiled at her step-father and handed him the erasable marker.

Dan entered Will's wife and date of his death on the board, with a notation that there were no known children. Reason for death: cancer at age 60. He also noted that Will was a Nam vet whose tours had been completed two years before his mother's death. PTSD? Could he have returned home unexpectedly and murdered her?

Susan said, "Who's next? Shall we give this another try?"

Brooke said, "Okay, Maggie's next." She typed in Margaret Frances Prescott. "There isn't much here for her. Sadly, we don't know if she was married or not."

Christopher said, "Hey, Brooke. One thing I just thought of is: what if she took her mother's maiden name when she left home? Maybe she didn't want to be found."

She replied, "Good idea, Chris. So then her name would have been Margaret Frances Taylor. Taylor seems like a pretty common name, but let's see what we come up with."

Brooke typed in the name and, sure enough, several obituaries came up. The huge surprise was that the one which seemed to match the closest was for Sister Margaret Frances of the Sisters of St. Francis in Sylvania, Ohio. The write up said that she had come to the convent in 1963, having led, her own words, "a life of sin" before that time. She made her vows and continued to serve the Lord through the ministries of the convent for the next forty-nine years until her peaceful death at the age of seventy on April 3, 2012. She had died in her sleep after a brief illness. There was a picture of her seated and smiling with her fellow black-clad fellow nuns in the newspaper. The accompanying column said that she was greatly mourned by the community. Interment was on the grounds of the stone chapel.

Dan wrote on the board "Nun. No known husband or children. Died April 3, 2012, at Sisters of St. Francis, Sylvania, Ohio. Age: seventy years old." He put down the erasable marker.

Brooke said, "She looked really happy."

Susan said, "Yes, Brooke. She seemed at peace and quite content. She served God for so many years."

Brooke asked, "Do nuns get time off for good behavior or something? She would have been in the convent for about a year at the time of her mother's death. Do you think she came back home one dark night and murdered her mother?"

Michael said, "I don't think she could have had that sense of peace about her if she was hiding something so serious."

Everyone agreed that she probably didn't do it, and that she looked very friendly.

Joshua said, "You know, we might not want to discount the idea of her having children. She left home at eighteen and lived a "life of sin," as she said. She might have given birth a couple of times or more."

Brooke asked, "What about the kids?"

Susan said, "Adoption. That would be my guess." Susan turned to him. "Okay, Dan, let's leave the door open on Sister Margaret Frances's offspring."

Dan marked Sister Margaret Frances' information on the board, along with the question "children?" and "Presumed innocent of the murder of her mother."

Michael said, "Look, I know we aren't Catholic, but we serve the same God. Can I pray for Sister Margaret Frances? Would that be all right?"

Susan said, "I think that would be very nice, Michael. Please do."

Michael said, "Lord, we thank you for the life and ministry of Sister Margaret Frances. We didn't know her, but You did and You still do. We praise You for this wonderful woman, and pray for comfort for those who did know her. We thank you for the blessing that she became to others. We don't know what went on in her life during those dark years of sinful living, but we thank You that she is forgiven and living with You now. We pray that you will guide us to her offspring, if she had any children, that You may be glorified. In Jesus' name, Amen."

Brooke said, "Well, we missed meeting her by about six years."

Susan said, "That's a pity. I would have liked to know her, I think." She smiled at the family members gathered. "We all might have enjoyed knowing her."

Dan gave Susan a little hug, like he did when agreeing with her. Brooke had noticed that several times and rejoiced at seeing the couple so happy. How refreshing. But, on to other things.

Joshua said, "Yes, Brooke, our batting average doesn't look too good right now, but maybe we'll have more luck with Johnny. Are you up to trying another sibling?"

She asked, "What do you think, folks? Shall we try another one for the road?"

Christopher said, "Sure. I'm game."

Susan and Dan nodded their assent, and Amanda agreed.

"Okay. Better luck with Johnny. So, let's see what google says about him." She typed in his name and date of birth. A mug shot appeared. "Oh, no! He's a crook!"

John Kenneth Prescott was wanted for embezzlement. It turned out that he'd made a habit of stealing people's bank statements from rural mailboxes, taking down their banking information, and copying their signatures. After gathering the needed information, he would re-seal the statements and drop the envelopes in a mail box, where the statements would be re-routed to their rightful owners, according to the newspaper story. He used these documents to order checks, which he then used to empty out their bank accounts. He was also guilty of setting up automatic withdrawals from some of the accounts, which he used to pay rent at a variety of apartment complexes. When he was found out at one complex, he moved on to another. He also used the account information to pay credit card bills that he had run up.

John was currently wanted in Virginia, North Carolina, and Tennessee. He had served time briefly in 2005, which was the date of the latest mug shot. He was released due to a clerical error, after serving ten months of a ten-year sentence and was still at large. There were several newspaper stories about his mistaken release that warned people to keep track of their bank accounts carefully, since he was on the loose. The article mentioned he had a rap sheet as long as a man's arm.

Susan commented, "I guess he's still looking out for Number One. I vote that we don't look for him, based on my desire to keep my checkbook intact."

Dan read, "This says he is 'Not armed and not considered dangerous.' I guess the only danger is to people's finances. I'm with Susan. This is a "don't go looking for trouble, which he definitely is" vote."

Everyone agreed that Johnny could stay lost. Hopefully, he wouldn't turn out to be the murderer. They all agreed; if the evidence was not strong enough against another member of the family, Johnny would win the title of" killer" by default. Goodbye to Johnny. Good riddance. Brooke clicked out of the screen and shut down Dan's computer, closing the lid firmly.

Brooke shivered and said, "I guess, on this happy note, we should call it quits for tonight."

The family agreed it was time to head home, but decided to get back together soon, saying that it was a lot of fun to search together. They would meet again one week later. Brooke was glad they'd found a common interest in their hunt for their missing relatives. This could be a really great way to bond, especially after all they'd been through.

They were all incredibly busy that week, especially Joshua, who had an extra load of patients due to the illness of one of his partners. Brooke was working on a very complicated case that took up extra time, while Michael pulled a couple of double shifts at the Chesapeake Center. Christopher was prepping for some new classes and was working late. No one had the time to dig into the family mystery on their own, but they all showed up at their folks' house the next weekend, ready to work. They retired to the family room once again, plopping onto couches and chairs that Susan and Dan had arranged in front of the white board and computer.

Brooke said, "Okay, let's get started."

"Brooke," Christopher said, "you sound like a college

professor."

Brooke was so glad that he'd become more involved with the new family that she beamed at him. "I'll take that as a compliment."

"Peter Russell Prescott is next, Brooke," Dan told her.

Google was once again invoked. Dead. Peter had been an Air Force test co-pilot. He was killed in a training accident on June 18, 1980, at the age of thirty-four. The accident occurred over the Gulf of Mexico. He had been stationed at Eglin Air Force Base in Florida. He was survived by his wife, Glenda Jo Lawrence Prescott and three daughters: Kimberly Michelle Prescott, aged fourteen; Lisa Marie Prescott, aged twelve; and Natalie Leanne Prescott, aged ten.

Brooke said, "Hey, we might be able to find them. This is the first rabbit trail where we might get lucky."

Joshua said, "Okay, so the girls would be, roughly fifty-two, fifty, and forty-eight today. Their mom was probably about the same age as Peter- this is just a guess, so she would be seventy-two. We don't know if she re-married or not. Shall we keep looking?"

The general consensus was that, yes, they would continue looking for the widow and her daughters, after they found information on Kurt's sister Candy. Brooke typed in the name. Candace was indeed still alive. Everyone was shocked. Candy had become a college professor.

Susan said, "Look at this everyone. According to the university website, Candy is a 'tenured full professor at the University of Texas at Austin, where she teaches American and British literature. She got a Ph.D. from Cornell in 1980. She has published several textbooks on American and British literature, and is an active contributor to numerous scholarly journals.' That's really impressive."

Michael said, "Yeah. Let's contact her first. She looks like a real winner."

Dan said, "That sounds good, but let's slow up here a bit. Keep in mind that she knows where she's from, but hasn't made any attempts, that we know of, to find her lost family. Maybe she wants to stay hidden."

Michael said, "She could be our killer. We know she was there the night her mother died, and that she took off a while later."

Susan added, "That's a good point. She's what- about seventy now? She's had all these years to contact Kurt, but I don't see anything in his journals about her showing up or anything. I certainly never met her, as far as I know. I haven't finished reading the journals, but we might need to respect her privacy."

Dan said, "And keep a possible Mama killer at bay." They laughed.

Joshua said, "How about if I reach out to her as a medical professional? I'm not sure what tack I can take, though. Any suggestions?"

Amanda said, "Honey, I think that maybe you ought to talk about possible chronic illnesses that might be common to the family. The only thing is you don't have any Prescott blood. And I don't see that any of the folks in this room have a serious illness." The family tittered.

Joshua looked around the room and asked, "So how are you all feeling?" They laughed loudly. "Yep, you all look pretty healthy to me. Okay, so maybe that wasn't a good idea, after all."

Christopher spoke up. "I'll email her. I have the clout of the Naval Academy behind me, if I use my USNA email account. She might be impressed enough that I'm not an ax murderer or a policeman, so she might respond. What do you all think? Brooke?"

Brooke said, "I think that's a great idea, Chris. Go for it."

Christopher said, "Okay, then. If everyone agrees, I'll email her tomorrow. Her university email address is right here, so maybe I can read her most current article and send her a question or two about her comments."

Susan said, "That's outstanding, Christopher. Thanks for

offering."

"Sure thing. Okay, we found one sibling for sure and she doesn't appear to be a lunatic, so how do we look for Peter's widow and daughters?" Christopher asked.

Brooke answered, "Google hasn't let us down yet. Okay, who's first? Mom?"

Susan said, "Let's start with his widow. Google 'Glenda Jo Lawrence Prescott' and see what comes up, Brooke."

"Humm . . . Here's a wedding announcement in the Northwest Florida Daily News for Glenda Jo Prescott and Stephen James Henry dated July 25, 1985. She apparently decided to remarry five years after Peter was killed. The girls would have been between fifteen and nineteen, so she may have decided they needed a father figure."

Joshua said, "I think you're right about that Brooke. Kimberly would've been finished with high school, Lisa Marie-oh, I just got it- they were Elvis fans- would've been a junior, and Natalie would've been a sophomore. Those're very challenging days for girls who haven't had a man in their life for five years."

Susan said, "I hope they're happily married, Glenda and Stephen."

Christopher asked, "Brooke, do you see any death notices for either Glenda or Stephen?"

"Nope. They might both still be alive. Let me google Glenda Prescott Henry." Brooke typed in the name. Good news appeared in the form of an anniversary announcement dated July 25, 2015. She read it to everyone.

"'Mr. Stephen and Mrs. Glenda Jo Prescott Henry celebrated their thirtieth wedding anniversary this past weekend by renewing their vows at Oakland Baptist Church in Ft. Walton Beach. Their three daughters Kimberly, Lisa, and Natalie were bridesmaids and sang in the service. Their husbands were groomsmen. Following the ceremony, the guests were treated to a dinner reception in the church hall.' Oh, look at this picture- they look so happy. There's a whole photo

191

spread here. The girls are so pretty. Kinda old, though."

Dan said, "It's nice to see some good news on the Prescott home front. The family is happy and actively involved in a church. And, Brooke, none of them look like ax murderers!"

Everyone laughed.

Susan asked, "So how do we go about contacting them?"

"Mom, we google it, for sure!" She teased her mother. Sure enough, the address was easy to locate.

Susan said, "We should make contact with Glenda Jo, rather than the daughters, since the girls are married. Does the article list the names of the daughters' hubbies, Brooke?"

"Yes, Mom, but it is kinda unclear who is married to whom. I think you're right about getting in touch with Glenda Jo first."

Susan said, "If no one minds, I'd like to be the one to contact Glenda Jo. Our husbands were brothers, they were pilots or co-pilots, they were both in the service, they're both dead, and we have both re-married. Happily, I might add. I have a lot in common with her." Susan smiled at Dan and gave his hand a squeeze.

Everyone agreed that it was a great idea.

"How will you contact her, Mom?" Amanda asked.

Susan replied, "I am going to write her a letter. Hand-written, at that."

"Okay, now we have one more sibling to check out. I'm guessing that newspaper articles will tell us what happened to little Ella. Shall we give it a try?"

Everyone looked very somber, but agreed that it needed to be done. Brooke googled the local newspaper for any mention of Ella Cassandra Prescott. A bunch of stories came up.

The first one talked about how Mr. and Mrs. Prescott reported their daughter missing on August 12, 1964. Mrs. Prescott initially said that she had gone on errands and returned home, noting that her daughter was asleep in the back seat of the family car. Rather than disturb her, Mrs. Prescott said that she had rolled the car windows down and left the child in the car in their driveway. When she returned a short time later to check on Ella, the child was gone.

The newspaper reported on August 14th that some eyewitnesses claimed that Mrs. Prescott had been at a saloon on West Street, having parked her car in front of the establishment and gone inside. After some time (witness accounts of how long she was inside varied), Mrs. Prescott had gotten into her car and driven off, apparently without looking into the back seat.

On August 17th, the newspaper reported that the police had determined that Mrs. Prescott had left her daughter in the car to visit the saloon, where she remained for about thirty minutes. She then drove home, where the neighbors reported she had gone into her house without the child. It was about an hour later when they reported her standing at the side of her car, screaming that her child was gone.

There were a few more newspaper accounts of the missing child, who had vanished without a trace. There were a few more updates and then, one month later to the day after Ella's disappearance, the report of Mrs. Prescott's death by drowning.

Susan asked, "Where could the poor child have gone? How could Mrs. Prescott have turned her back on a four-year-old child? I just don't understand what kind of person would have done that."

Dan touched her hand and said, "That's because you aren't anything like her, Suzy-Q."

Amanda dropped her head to her hands. "I can't imagine going into a store for even a minute and leaving one of the kids alone in the car. I dragged sleeping children with me for years, and never once did what Mrs. Prescott did. I wonder just how long Ella was alone in the car?"

Joshua squeezed Amanda's hand. "One thing we need to keep in mind is that we don't know if Ella disappeared at the saloon or at home. Mrs. Prescott might not have noticed that her daughter was missing at first. Heck, she might have been so drunk that she forgot the kid was in her car. She went home, drank some more, and then realized she hadn't seen Ella lately. She went out to the car, saw the child was missing, and started crying."

"It's not a good scenario, any way you look at it," Brooke said.

"Brooke, are there any more stories about Ella?" Susan asked.

"Just a few short stories that say no suspects have been found. There were some rumors that a small man or a large woman was seen looking into the car at the saloon, but nothing ever came of it."

Joshua said, "It's a very cold case, that's for sure. I don't know how we can possibly find Ella, but maybe Glenda Jo will remember hearing Peter talk about his sister, or maybe Candace will have some information about her."

Brooke said, "I guess we'll have to wait and see."

Dan wrote on the white board. "Okay, folks, here's what we have so far. Christopher will contact Candy, Susan will write Glenda Jo, and we will all avoid Johnny like the plague. We still need to find out if Sister Margaret Frances had any kids. How can we do that?"

"Michael and I will visit the Sisters of St. Francis on the way home from our honeymoon."

"What? Why would you want to do that?" Christopher almost yelled. "Sorry." He paused and shrugged. "It's just, well, that seems like a crazy way to end your honeymoon."

Michael smiled, "We plan on taking a driving trip. First, to Philadelphia, where we'll pay our respects at William's grave, then we'll go to Mackinac Island for a week. On the way home, we'll stop by Sylvania, Ohio to see the Sisters. We'll be gone about two weeks."

Joshua spoke up. "Would you mind if I take the Philadelphia trip instead? I could pay the family's respects, and take the kids to see the sights in Philly."

Brooke realized that Joshua was feeling left out. "Sure thing, Josh. No problem. Philly is actually out of our way, so that'll save us some driving. Thanks for thinking of it. That'll work, right Michael?" She turned to her hubby-to-be and winked. Michael's eye contact and returned wink told her he understood.

Michael replied, "Wow, that would be great, Joshua." He turned to Brooke. "We can fly to Michigan and drive to Ohio from there, instead of driving the whole way."

"Sure honey. We can work the details out later, but that sounds good."

Dan marked the new information down. "Okay, so, we have Joshua and his family with William, Christopher with Candy, Susan with Glenda Jo, and Brooke and Michael with Sister Margaret. We'll all keep our eyes open for information on Ella. That about does it, I would think. Do you agree, Brooke?"

"Yes. After we make contact, we'll have to see what turns up!" Brooke said.

Chapter 23

Mrs. Mary Ruth Taylor Prescott had gotten a letter that September day from the person who had her daughter Ella. Of that she was absolutely certain. She held the note tightly in her hand as she begged her alcoholic husband to listen to reason. She had even put on his favorite floral dress and touched up her makeup before he got home from work that evening, hoping that her improved appearance would garner his support of her meeting the stranger. She had had her share of booze that night, but it was only to calm her nerves. My baby is gone, but maybe I can get her back. Anything to get her baby back home.

"William, please listen to me! This person says he wants to meet with me. I have to go."

William sneered at her and said, "You're chasing pipe dreams, Mary. Ella is dead and there's nothing you or I or anyone can do to bring her back. He's trying to get money out of you, that's all." He took another swig from his iced tea glass of whiskey. "You're a fool if you go to the creek tonight. I'm not going, that's for sure. Nobody is roping me into believing he has our..." his voice broke..."little girl."

Mary took a long drink from her tall glass. The Bacardi and Coke she favored wasn't doing its best to help her that evening. She felt such angst at the disappearance of her little Ella. "Well, I'm going, and you can't stop me." One more sip, then another, and she was out the door, umbrella in hand. The kids were upstairs and wouldn't hear her go, and William certainly wasn't in any shape to stop her. Not that he would do anything to help her, even if he wasn't drunk. That wasn't his style.

Rain! Heavenly days, would this deluge ever stop? She was grateful for her big umbrella, but the wind threatened to whip it out of her hands. Hold on, Mary! Oh! She almost slipped on that last step. Better slow down. Whoops! She slid a few inches in the grass, but caught herself before she fell flat on her butt. She rose, albeit with great difficulty. Mary, watch your step on this slippery mess. Her heels caught in the long grass. Her shoes almost fell off that time. Oops! Blast it all! Then the right shoe came off and the left one was close behind. I should've worn flats, but this dress looks better with heels. "Vanity, thy name is woman," as William always says. She stumbled for a moment, but caught herself and got the recalcitrant shoes back on without falling. Her missteps propelled her forward, faster than she might have wanted. A few steps later, she managed to get herself slowed down a bit. One step at a time, Mary girl. Easy does it. There you go. She stumbled slightly again. Bother!

Drat it, she wouldn't have had such a rough time walking normally, but the grass needed mowing again. She would have to mow the lawn again tomorrow, if it dried out enough. William would never do it. She slipped and slid her way down the rest of the yard. She caught herself on the gate and straightened up. At least she wasn't falling forward anymore. The wind was trying to turn her umbrella wrong-side out, when it suddenly died down. The rain slowed, and then stopped. It was eerie, like calm in the midst of a storm.

Oh, the blasted latch was sticking on the picket fence. Again. Come on, you darn latch. Let me outta here. She collapsed the umbrella and set it aside to deal with this new problem. She jiggled the latch one way and then the other. This is so frustrating. I should've gone out the front door. Finally! It opened at last. I better fix this stupid latch tomorrow while I'm mowing. William would never bother. William was so lazy these days. She picked up the umbrella as an insurance policy against more rain, and continued on to the creek.

Mary couldn't see her watch. She thought she was here about the right time- 8 pm, but it was too dark to see what time it was. She thought she'd walked out the door about five minutes before the hour, but wasn't too sure at the moment. Oh, rats, her watch was probably ruined by the rain. I should have left it inside the house. It was no good here, anyway.

Okay, here's the spot. The note didn't say exactly where to meet him, but this was the straightest line from the house. It was private, but not hidden behind those bushes over there. She leaned the umbrella against a tree and waited. She rested against the tree, her hands behind her back to protect her dress as she stood thinking. This was actually her favorite place in the summertime. Cool, refreshing, peaceful. But not tonight. This mid-September night was too cool for her taste. It would be nice to be back inside with her baby. Four years old and oh, so bright. She loved Ella and knew that Kurt doted on her. Mary wished she had brought her drink with her. Calm herself down while she waited, don't you know. She moved forward, thinking she heard something. Nope. Oh, why had she gotten so near the tree? Now she had wet globs of bark on the back of her dress. She tried in vain to pull some of the bark off, but it was really stuck. She gave up trying to redeem her appearance. Well, I guess the guy that's coming won't be picky...

She heard footsteps. She turned and looked up at the man who approached her. He was dressed in black, she assumed to hide better in the night. She stepped towards him, but not too close.

"Who are you?" She was angry at how her voice shook. How can I be scared? This man has my little Ella. I want her back, and I want her back now. Stand up to him, Mary! She crossed her arms. She dug her heels into the grass in an attempt to look more intimidating. "Give me back my daughter!" Oops! Her digging in almost caused her to fall backwards. Her blasted heels were sunk into the muddy grass. Gross! Focus on this guy, Mary. Don't worry about your heels.

"Who I am doesn't matter. I was coming to see about bringing your daughter home, but I've been checking you and your husband out. I think she's better off with my family. I just wanted you to know that she's fine and has adjusted to being with us. We're keeping her. I am just doing the decent thing and telling you she's fine."

"The decent thing would be to bring my baby back!" Mary stepped forward a bit and shoved him. He grabbed her left hand, reaching around with the other hand to grab at her right hand and ripping in two the note she held, as he tried to retrieve it from her grip. They wrestled momentarily. She started to lose her balance and lunged closer towards him.

"Don't touch me, you drunk. You stink of cheap liquor. You couldn't even stay sober long enough to meet with me. Do you really think your daughter is better off with a couple of drunks taking care of her? You'll never get her back." The man's voice rasped at her, condemnation in every syllable.

He pushed her away from him, turned, and walked away. She tried to follow him, but her feet were stuck in the mud. Just then, the rain started up again and began pelting her body as the wind picked up once more. The sky opened up directly above her, or so it seemed.

"Oh, bother, more rain." Mary pulled her feet out of the gook. She took some steps backwards as she stumbled slightly over the umbrella that had fallen. "Gotta get that guy." Just as she spoke the words, her body twisted violently and she lost her balance. She fell and hit her head on the rocks next to the creek. Her face plunged below the surface. Her body slid into the water. Cold! It was like falling into a bathtub of ice cubes.

Mary pulled herself up on the rocks, sopping wet and shivering like the time she tried to stop drinking a few months back. Good thing the water is only a few feet deep here. She tossed her mop of hair back as she ran her hands through the mess that had previously been her nice hairdo. How awful she must look, with her hair all askew and her clothes clinging to her body. Even worse, the smelly old creek water was repulsive. I'm freezing, stinking, and sopping. How disgusting! She tried to make some semblance of order to her appearance, in case the stranger came back. Just as quickly as the rain had started, it stopped once more.

She got herself into a kneeling position so she could turn

around and head back toward the shore when she noticed that it was daylight. Huh? Daylight? But it's after eight o'clock at night. It was dark just a second ago. How can that be? She looked around, trying to get her bearings. What in the world is happening to me?

A man was sitting on a rock nearby, dressed in a radiant white outfit. He was a Pat Boone lookalike, if she ever saw one. Even his shoes were white. Impressive on such a rainy night.

"Hello Mary." His voice was as pleasant as the smile on his face. He seemed to know her.

"Uh, hello yourself. Ugh, my head. I must've hit it when I fell. It hurts." She rubbed her temples as she looked over at him. "Are you the man who has my baby? No, wait. You can't be him. He had black on. Did you see him? He was here a minute ago." She looked around towards the street. "He went that way." She pointed in the direction she thought he had gone.

She looked back at the new stranger, and then up and down. White on white on white. Nice clothes, in fact. Fresh out of the laundry, unless she missed her guess. Short grey hair or maybe blond. It was hard to tell for sure, with her head aching like this. Handsome. An accomplice of the other guy? He didn't look like the kinda guy who kidnaps children, but you never know. Oh, man my sinuses are screaming. She continued to hold her head in her hands, even as they chatted.

"No, I don't have Ella, but I know that she's fine. I'm not here for Ella. I'm here for you, Mary. My name is Allen."

"What do you mean you're here for me? I don't understand." She tried to make herself look a little more presentable. After all, he looked so nice. Here she was, sopping wet from her fall, hair a total mess, shoes long gone, and bark probably still sticking to the back of her dress. Not her best glamour day, for sure.

Allen was standing in front of her now, and pulled her to her feet. "Let's get you more comfortable, Mary. Kneeling on the rocks can't be very pleasant. Have a seat. Let's chat."

Well, he doesn't seem like a weirdo. Okay, so I'll sit. She

tried sitting on the rocks with her feet pulled up in front of her, but her feet kept slipping into the water. She looked around. Her shoes were nowhere to be seen. She must have slipped out of them on the bank. Oh! The creek felt so refreshing! She gave up trying to move her feet and just let them stay submerged. The high tide almost tickled. Very nice, no longer freezing.

"How do you know my name? I've never met you before."

"Like I said, my name is Allen and no, you don't know me. But I know you. I've been asked to come see you. Life hasn't been easy for you." He didn't go on, so she picked up the conversation.

"You can say that again. My little girl was kidnapped last month. That's why I'm out here now. The man who has her told me he isn't going to give her back." Mary sobbed for a moment and then continued. "That's not the half of it. My older children moved out as soon as they turned eighteen so they could escape from my husband. . ."

"And from you, I would guess." Again with the smile. Not unkind, not spooky, but the kind of smile that can see right into you. Into your heart.

"Uh, yes, well, I suppose so. I'm not perfect." How dare he say that? What kind of nerve does he have, approaching a total stranger like me and going on as if I were a bad person?

"It's the alcohol, Mary. It's very hard on children to see their parents ...what do you call it? 'Three sheets to the wind' every night."

"I enjoy my drinking, Allen, if that's your real name."

"Yes, it's my real name, Mary." He waited, then, "You didn't always drink."

"No, my husband talked me into having an after-dinner drink with him when we first got married. I didn't drink at all at the time, but he got mad when I turned him down, so I stopped turning him down. I found out pretty fast that he had a bad temper, and I was afraid of setting him off. Anything could make him mad and if my drinking made him nicer, so much the better. So I started drinking and found out after a while that I liked it. It took the edge off my days."

"What happened then?" Allen looked at her kindly.

"I guess the drinking kinda got out of control. I mean, we had one drink a night, and then we had some nights when we had another and another. It came to be a habit." Mary was surprised at her willingness to talk so freely with this Allen man.

"How often?"

"Every night. When I was pregnant with the kids, I could put him off. Tell him I didn't want to hurt the baby, and he accepted that. I still had a glass of wine with him. I figured that was okay, but no hard booze." She nodded.

"Like I said, Mary, I know your life has been difficult. You have a daughter whose life didn't turn out like you expected." Allen smiled, encouraging her to talk.

"You mean Maggie. She became a nun. I don't know how that happened, but she's been writing to me. I sneak the letters out of the mailbox before my husband gets home. William would be really upset if he knew what she's up to. He doesn't believe in having crutches, which is what religion is to him."

"People who are lame need crutches." Allen smiled sweetly at her.

"I'm not lame." What was he saying? He wasn't making any sense. What a goofy smile the guy had. Almost like...he loved her or something. Fat chance of that.

"In some ways, you are, Mary. All humans are lame in one way or another."

Mary looked at him like he was crazy, which is exactly what she was thinking. "How so?" This guy, this conversation, is getting weirder by the moment. I wonder if I can just leave. He doesn't seem to be a muscle man. Maybe I can just move my feet and scram . . . Hey, what gives? I can't move my feet. They're stuck in the creek and I can't get them out. She started panicking.

"Mary, we need to chat a bit more. I don't want you to

leave just yet." He smiled again.

She tried to splash him with creek water. A lot of good that did. I know I hit him, but he's not wet. She tried again. Nope, he's dry, even though I know the water hit him right on the face. What gives?

"Mary, you're going to tire long before you dampen me or my clothes. Just sit tight for a minute or two and talk to me."

She kept splashing, harder than before, but all it did was wear her out. Okay, so be it. She threw down her hands. Talk to Allen. Her shoulders slumped, like when William was being mean to her. Except that Allen wasn't mean, for all that. He just wanted her to stay. She gave up the fight. "What do you want?"

"You wonder what happened to Maggie. She left home, like the others, right after she turned eighteen. That way, she couldn't be arrested for running away from home. She took up with a man who was not kind to her. After some struggles of her own, she came to realize that real peace comes from knowing God and His Son Jesus."

"Yeah, she sent me a Bible and told me to read it." Is that what this was all about? Maggie? I don't understand.

"And you did. Good for you, Mary." He waited. "But I don't see the peace that Maggie has in you."

"William came home early one day and saw me reading it. When he couldn't tear it up, he threw it into the fire. He said he'd . . . kill me if he ever saw me with a Bible again. I haven't had one since. And I told Maggie not to write so often because he might find out."

"So you gave up?" Allen asked.

"Of course I did. I didn't want to die. He's a lot bigger than me, and I know he's stronger. He's broken more than one of my bones. Things don't go so well for me when I cross him, so I don't. Keep the peace, that's what it's all about these days." Just keep the peace at all costs. Her shoulders sagged even more at the thoughts going through her mind.

"How about now, Mary? He's nowhere to be seen. Do you want to know the peace that Maggie has?" He reached out and touched her shoulder. "It can be yours, Mary."

She ignored his last comment, which she heard but not well. She began talking again, more to herself than to Allen.

"It felt good to be reading the Bible. I liked what it said about God being our heavenly father. Both my parents died right after William and I got married, so I couldn't tell them what he was really like. He was really mean. He wouldn't let me have friends. He said they distracted me from him. He was to be the only focus in my life. It was a woman's job to live her life for her man, he said. He wasn't like I thought he was when I married him. He seemed really nice before we got engaged, but he had a malicious streak. I found out after we got married. He insisted that I not work. He gave me a small allowance, but it didn't go very far."

"He beat you too, didn't he?" Allen looked at her as if she was a small child. "Not at first, but later."

"Yeah. He beat me with his words early on, and then later with his fists." She shook her head, trying to remove the memory. "He's a brutal man who only appears to be nice when other people are around. I hate him." She scowled. Men are animals. William is a beast.

"Mary, you can forget all that and have everlasting peace, if you want it."

"Will I ever get away from him?" Everlasting peace sounded good, real good. If only she could escape William. Okay, she knew she'd still have some problems. She was a mess, truth be known. Like right now. She was a wreck on the outside, but not much better on the inside. Maybe the years of abuse had finally gotten to her. Creeping crud. What's this? Time to examine herself? Well, maybe that's not such a bad idea. She tried to shrug it off, but didn't do so well. Finally, she realized, I am a total disaster. She slumped in complete surrender.

"Yes, Mary. William will not be a part of your life very soon." Allen took her hand. He held it tenderly. She was shocked at his caress and straightened up. No man had ever touched her like that before, loving her but not seeking anything from her.

"God loves you and Jesus Christ died for you. He can give you strength, comfort, and love. Do you want that?"

"Yeah, Allen, I do." Mary sat straighter still, waiting to hear what came next. Wanting to hear, thirsty and parched.

"Then pray with me." He led her in a simple prayer, so simple she didn't see how it could do much good. But it did. She instantly felt full of the love of God. Amazing! Glorious!

"Mary, you have one more thing to do in this life and then you can come with me."

"What's that?" She couldn't imagine what . . .

"Finish what has begun. It will be over quickly, and then I will take you to meet God."

Before she could respond, she was back in the creek, face down in the rushing water. She started to get up, but felt someone or something holding her head down in the water. She struggled against the force, but couldn't overcome it. She began fighting for her life, even as the breath came out of her. The person was stronger than she was. She scratched, clawed, to no avail. Finally, she began breathing water. Even as she struggled to not choke on the water, it was taking her life. Cold. Dark. Gone.

Mary opened her eyes and stood. Allen was back. He held out his hand to her, and pulled her out of the creek. She looked around at the beautiful daylight streaming all around them. She caught a glimpse of her reflection in the water. What a gorgeous, white gown she was wearing. She looked years younger. Stunning, actually.

Allen said, "Let's go, dear sister." They headed into the light coming down from heaven. Mary was whole, happy, forgiven.

Chapter 24

Susan took some time to visit with Kurt's journals later that week. She'd avoided them for some time, not wanting to read his thoughts on their marriage but, at the same time, wanting to know if he hated it as much at the beginning as he seemed to at the end. What she found as she sat outside on the deck enjoying the cooler temperatures of late summer and the calm breeze of the Bay surprised her. Yes, he had been suspicious and, yes, he had hired a private investigator before they married, but he had loved her.

His journals were filled with the insecure ramblings of a man who seemed to have everything together but who, in reality, was a frightened little boy in need of reassurance. Susan realized that her actions had sometimes fed his fears, especially whenever she expressed unhappiness about anything. How could she have been so blind not to see how he felt? She couldn't accept all the blame, however, since she hadn't known anything about his childhood. But why hadn't she at least asked? Her feelings teetered between anger at herself and irritation with him. Why couldn't we just talk to each other?

It seemed that, every time she gave birth, he was concerned she might die. Really, really afraid he would lose her. And then came the day that she was the same age as his mother had been when she passed, forty-one years old. His writing showed how terrified he was that she would die at precisely the same age. That's so weird- I don't even drink and his mother drank every day and night. We weren't in the same shape

206

physically or mentally, but there it was, in black and white.

We also didn't live on the water. We enjoyed going to the city docks in Annapolis after eating dinner sometimes, but our house wasn't located anywhere near a creek. Kurt wrote that he was happy that none of their children were big enough to kill her. Well, that's good news. Like my own kids would have wanted to do me in? He was convinced that she would die just like his mother, and that he would be stuck with three little children to raise alone. When she made it one day past his mother's age at her death, his journal seemed to sigh in relief. Susan asked the question, "So who did kill his mother?" She wished he would do a little more remembering about his mom in the journals.

Kurt wrote about looking for a replacement wife, for "just in case." Which one of their friends could fill in the gap left if she died? He actually rated the women they knew, based on looks, physical fitness, cooking skills, housekeeping abilities, and care of children. Comparing his rating of her to them, which he had been considerate enough to include in the journal, she was happy to be well ahead of all the competition. What a shock! He actually approved of her and the way she did things, though he seemed loath to tell her. But then Kurt wrote that he "would have to look outside their circle of friends for a replacement." Well, I guess he did. And her name was Kelsey.

Susan shut the journal with mixed feelings. It was nice to see that he had loved her, in his own twisted way. It was nice to know that he knew she wasn't going to be easy to replace, should the need arise. But the fact that he had already started looking when their kids were young was both a compliment and a slam. Maybe she just didn't realize how men thought. Maybe she should ask Dan about it. In any case, that was enough for now. Back to the wedding preparations for Brooke and Michael, albeit with the journals offering more food for thought about her late husband. Susan took the journal inside the house and returned it to the box where the next journals waited to be read.

Chapter 25

Christopher had been in contact with Candy since the end of July, meaning that they had been exchanging emails for . . . about two months now. He tried to ease his way into getting to know her by discussing one of her most recent articles, but she commented on their same last name in the first email they exchanged. He admitted to her in early August that he was her nephew by Kurt. He had decided not to mention the murder until he knew her better.

He didn't hear back from her for a few weeks, until one Saturday afternoon in September, when he sat down at his home computer to check his email.

Her email read,

"Dear Christopher:

"I apologize for not contacting you for several weeks, but I was shocked to hear the name 'Kurt Prescott' again. I left home when he was still quite young, no more than twelve as I recall, and my life has been so isolated for such a long time that I did not know how to respond.

"I am no longer a young woman and many of the scars left by my disastrous upbringing have been buried for decades. I have my books and my articles and my colleagues to keep me company. But I do realize that they are not the comfort they once were, especially as my friends and I age. Some of them have already died off. My own turn will come before I know it.

"May I assume that you contacted me with the idea that we would one day meet? After much reflection, I have decided that I would be open to such an event. Please let me know what

209

you have in mind and I will check my schedule to see if that can be accommodated.

Sincerely,

Candace Geraldine Prescott, Ph.D."

Christopher leaned back in his chair and thought, so she is really for real. My aunt. He rubbed his face with both hands. Whew! He put her email in "keep as new" after he printed it off to show the family. He would wait to respond, still in shock at the confirmation of her existence. He was glad that a family meeting had been scheduled for that evening, and he brought it up right as soon as he arrived at his mother's and step-father's home. He told the family about her email as he waved it for all to see, and asked, "Where do we go from here? Should I meet her on my own or do you all want to come along? Should I go there or should I bring her back here?"

Susan and the others gathered around to read it. Susan looked up from the brief missive and said, "We all want to meet her, Chris. Perhaps we could arrange to fly her here, if she is in good enough shape to make the trip."

"Mom, she's only seventy and still active in teaching. I would think that she could make the trip," Christopher told her. "I googled her some this afternoon. She runs marathons and seems pretty active at her university."

Dan waved his hands and spoke up, "Whoa, whoa, Chris. We do need to keep in mind that she is the only sibling that we know of who was present for her mother's death. Are we inviting a murderer into our family?"

Christopher answered, "We don't know for sure. The little evidence we have about her shows that she was very considerate to Kurt. He doesn't report any suspicion of her being the murderer, and he says that their father beat her right before she took off. Apparently, that happened a lot."

Susan said, "Let's take a chance on her. Maybe she can tell us something that we don't know about Ella's disappearance and her mother's death. And she is seventy, after all. The men in the family should be able to subdue her pretty easily, I would think." She smiled at each of the men in turn.

Brooke said, "Well, the wedding's coming up in less than a month. We're all really busy right now, so what would you think of inviting her for Thanksgiving? It's a huge travel weekend, but she'll be out of school."

Joshua suggested that they offer to fly her to Maryland for Thanksgiving, but also proposed they bring her east right after the holiday, so that she had options. "Bringing her here for Christmas might be pressing our luck because she obviously has things she normally does for the holidays, but coming in between the two holidays might work, at least for a weekend visit before final exams."

Susan said, "Or she might like having a family Thanksgiving or Christmas. She said that her friends are dying off...I think the key is to invite her for the wedding, but explain that we have a very busy time ahead and wouldn't be able to focus on getting to know her."

Dan said, "We also don't want to invite a potential murderer to Brooke's wedding. That would be really problematic." Everyone laughed, but it was a good point.

Christopher told them, "I just checked the University of Texas at Austin's fall schedule. Their graduation is December 23rd and she'll have to attend, as a full time faculty member. If she comes in December, and can't make it for a weekend, then she couldn't make it till Christmas Eve, which might be a little much for a woman her age. If she comes right after the New Year, she could possibly stay a while because her classes don't start back till January 22nd, but she would probably have to report back by the first or second week in January. Also, the weather might be 'iffy'."

Brooke said, "Just talk to her about it." She hesitated. "Without treating her like she's so fragile she might break. You don't want to insult her, if she's as healthy as she seems. Just find out: What would she like to do?"

Dan said, "Yes. Leave it up to her and we'll make it happen. I'm not blood, but I'd like to meet her, too."

Susan agreed, and said, "In spite of her being a possible mother murderer?" Everyone chuckled. "Okay, everyone, let's say grace and eat. I think the natives are restless and by that I mean the kids!"

Sure enough, the kids, who had been running about in the back yard, had their faces pressed against the family room's window panes, looking at their parents and grandparents with expressions of great hunger. Melodrama reigned supreme in the back yard. Message sent and received.

Chris added, "And me, too. I haven't eaten since breakfast, but you know how bachelors are." He tapped his head, "Oh, I almost forgot- I made an awesome taco salad, which I left in the car. It's in a cooler in my back seat. Let me go out real quick and get it. I hope you all like it."

As he ran out the door, he heard Brooke say, "Chris cooks?"

Chapter 26

Brooke could smell the coffee and bacon as she woke up. In fact, that was probably what awoke her. She stretched in bed before her feet hit the floor. She'd stayed over at her mom's and Dan's house so that she could have some company on the big day. Her mom had asked her to just make up the bed that October morning because there wouldn't be enough time to wash the sheets before heading to the hair dresser's salon. Brooke complied and then threw on her fuchsia running clothes before heading downstairs.

"Hey, Mom, Dan. How's it going?" She grabbed a slice of toast and a piece of bacon as she hugged them both. "All ready for my big day?"

Susan said, "Sure thing, Brooke. Headed out for a quick run?"

"Yep. I figure it will calm me down a bit. What time do you want to leave for the beauty shop?"

Susan glanced at her watch. "Let's say . . . ninety minutes? We have to be there by ten. The wedding's at one. Will that work for you?"

"Sure thing. I can run for about an hour, head back here for a shower, and then grab a quick bite to eat." She kissed them both and then ran out the door, putting the toast in her mouth.

As Brooke ran, thoughts of the preceding year passed through her mind. She still couldn't believe it. Her wedding day, where she would become Mrs. Michael Bench, had arrived at last.

Michael was a wonderful Christian man. He'd been there through all the trouble with Dad and Kelsey, steadfast in his love and support. She must have been nuts to ever doubt that she should marry him. No, scratch that. She wasn't nuts; she was the daughter of an abusive man. There was a huge difference.

So, the wedding would take place in about - she looked at her watch - four and a half hours. Her strapless white lace ball gown with the sweetheart neckline was hanging in the guest bedroom at her mom's house. She would wear her white pearls, which consisted of a necklace, earrings, and bracelet that her mom had bought her just for the occasion. Amanda would be her matron of honor. Her bridesmaids – Michael's sisters Nichelle and Kameelah, and Dan's daughters-in-law, Lauren, Samantha, and Whitney, would attend her. Because there were six little girls between her new extended family and Michael's, they had decided against flower girls and ring bearers. Their attendants' dresses were a jewel tone of deep blue; she loved the color. They had picked a variety of styles for the bridesmaids' dresses, wanting each woman to look her best in her floor-length gown.

Michael would have Joshua and Christopher standing with him, as well as Nichelle's and Kameelah's husbands. As it happened, Michael was very good friends with Patrick Ferguson, so Patrick would join the men's side. Michael's best friend in college, Cori Douglas, would be his best man. The men would wear black tuxedos with deep blue bow ties. Brooke had asked Dan to give her away. She already felt closer to him than she had ever felt to her own father.

Okay, so was everything done? She ran through a mental checklist as she ran through the neighborhood. Flowers were already made. They had decided on the permanence of polysilk flowers, so they made the bouquets, boutonnieres, and other assorted corsages last month. The cake would be delivered to the church hall later that morning. Though they could have afforded a fancier reception, they chose to have a catered mid-afternoon brunch at the church, rather than run folks all over town just to eat. That way, they could have more folks attend the wedding and reception, since their location kept the price down. Instead of "extravagant," the cost was only "excessive," at least compared to Joshua's wedding some twenty years before.

The caterer was well-known for outstanding food. They had verified the business' reputation through several well-planned visits. Delicious visits, at that. They would have a variety of sandwiches, fresh fruit trays, veggie trays, and cookies. A non-alcoholic punch, tea, and coffee would also be served. And, of course, wedding cake.

Okay, there's the big tree at the end of the neighborhood. Time to turn around. Yep, thirty minutes out, thirty minutes back to the Walsh house. She headed back. She glanced at her watch again. Four hours till the wedding.

The family had decorated the church sanctuary yesterday afternoon. It was awash in tulle, candelabra, and flowers. They had real cut flowers in huge vases that would be a nice balance to the size of the one thousand seat auditorium. Dan's family would provide the music for the wedding, since all of his children were musically gifted. Joshua's daughters, Madison and Abigail, would keep the guest book. His son Liam would try to keep his younger brother Max out of trouble.

Christopher was the surprise of surprises. He had asked if he could read the love chapter of Corinthians as a part of the service. She had been so shocked that she said "yes" before she even asked Michael. She was glad that Michael had agreed; Michael had asked Joshua to read from the book of Ruth.

After the reception, she and Michael would stop by to change at Dan and Susan's house, where their wedding finery would be either sent to the cleaners or returned to the tux shop. They would then head out for a wedding night on the eastern shore and then drive to BWI, fly to Detroit, and then drive to Mackinaw Island the next day.

Brooke was back at the house, right on time. She checked the mailbox out of habit, even though it was early. Oh, the mailman had already brought the mail for today. Let me grab it and then hit the shower.

"Hey, Dan. Here's the mail. Gotta scoot upstairs." Brooke

handed him the missives.

"Thanks, Brooke." He took it from her as she exited the room.

At ten, she and Susan drove to the hairdressers. Susan told her, "I really thought that the mail would bring the special gift I have for you, but I guess it didn't come yet. I'm sorry honey, but I guess I might as well tell you. I got you a sapphire pin that's identical to the one my grandmother, mother, and I wore on our wedding days. The pins we wore were…disposed of by Kurt, but I ordered one special for you. It should have arrived by today."

"Oh, Mom, that is so sweet. I would have loved to have worn it . . . oh, well."

All the ladies of the wedding party were at the salon. Their hair was curled and teased into place while their makeup was done by professional stylists that they had field tested over the past few months. That finished, they went back to Susan's house to dress. Susan had planned for them to have a little snack before dressing, so she pre-heated the oven. Something smelled bad. Susan opened the door and found her mail and the remnant of a plastic jug of half and half. "What in the world? How did this stuff get in here?"

"Mom, I gave today's mail to Dan when I came in from running. I just remembered that. Do you suppose he put it in there?" Brooke looked concerned.

"Oh, my. There has been some weird stuff going on, Brooke. Things are being misplaced all the time these days. I'm at a loss to explain it, but I thought it was just me," Susan told her.

"No, Mom, I don't think it's you." Brooke shrugged and headed upstairs to finish her preparations. "See you soon."

One hour before the wedding. Hair and makeup done. Check. The photographer was due to arrive any minute. Brooke was so excited, she couldn't stand still. Her mom had retrieved the pin from the somewhat charred envelope and presented it to her. It would be a lovely accent to wear on the bodice of her gown. She was the only one not completely dressed at the minute. Everyone decided to pitch in and help. She thought she was in a big enough whirlwind without having too many cooks in the kitchen, as they say...

"Brooke, dear, I have your shoes." "Here's your pantyhose." "Your garter is over here." "Brooke, where's your brassiere? You can't wear the usual one. Not with that gown."

Brooke shot a look of horror at her Mom, who quickly suggested everyone go downstairs for a quick snack. A few minutes later, everyone had retreated, leaving the two of them alone.

Susan said, "Honey, how can I help?" She laughed. "Things were getting a bit hectic there."

Brooke answered, "Thanks for clearing the place out, Mom. It was crazy!"

Susan helped her into the gorgeous white gown. Her pearls were in place and she slipped into her shoes. Perfect.

Just then, the doorbell rang. They rushed downstairs to see who it was. A floral delivery man greeted them, carrying a huge arrangement of pink roses for Susan. Everyone gathered around to see who it was from. Susan smiled as she read the card. "Thank you for giving birth to my lovely bride, Brooke. I'm excited about our future together, and promise to always love her as Christ loved the church and gave Himself for it. Love, Michael."

Susan choked back the tears and told Brooke, "He's a keeper!"

"Oh, yeah!" Brooke hugged her mother and then said, "We'd better get a move on!"

The dressing was complete, so they got into the stretch limo that Dan had arranged for as part of their wedding gift. All the ladies broke out into song, in spite of the Prescott gals not having much of a gift for singing. They launched into "Going to the Chapel" and other oldies related to love and marriage. The driver appeared very relieved to arrive at the church, in spite of his not complaining.

Brooke was at a loss to explain all the whirl of activities that had happened, when she thought about the day later. Her mother and Mrs. Bench, Gayle that is, or Mom, entered the church, proceeding to the altar to light the candles she and Michael had left for them. Brooke heard a familiar wedding song beginning as she stood in the hallway. Her attendants entered one by one. The doors to the sanctuary closed as she and Dan got into position. The Wedding March began. The doors were opened, and she got her first glimpse of Michael waiting for her at the altar. Handsome. Smiling. There were blurred faces on each side as she walked down the aisle; she could only see him.

Pastor was waiting with Michael, but he and the groomsmen were a haze of black tuxedos compared to her beloved Michael. Why had she waited so long? Her fears were replaced with joy and excitement. Her eyes shone with love and tears as she walked closer to him. She saw there were tears in his eyes, as well.

"Dearly beloved," Pastor began. When it was time, Dan gave her away, kissing her on the cheek, offering a quick hug, placing her hand in Michael's, and taking his place next to her mother on the second pew, left hand side. Songs were sung in beautiful harmony by Dan's children. Christopher read the love chapter from Corinthians. Joshua followed that with a reading from Ruth. Michael's sisters sang a duet. Brooke heard a lot of sniffling when they were finished. The song they sang was gorgeous.

They took up the candles their mothers had lit before she and Michael had entered the service and combined their flames with the unity candle. They kept their individual candles lit and returned them to the candle holders. Pastor explained their candles were not extinguished because they were still individuals, though united in the bonds of love and marriage. He spoke of their mutual love and affection, and their willingness to remain pure during their engagement. He talked about Christ's love for the church. He talked about challenges they might face, and how their love could survive. Then it was time for the rings and the vows.

"I, Michael Joseph Bench, take you Brooke Eliza Prescott, to be my wedded wife, to have and to hold, from this day forward, for better, for worse, for richer, for poorer, in sickness and in health, to love and to cherish, till death do us part, according to God's holy ordinance; and thereto I pledge thee my faith." Michael smiled, though some tears threatened to overflow.

"I, Brooke Eliza Prescott, take you Michael Joseph Bench, to be my wedded husband, to have and to hold, from this day forward, for better, for worse, for richer, for poorer, in sickness and in health, to love and to cherish, till death do us part, according to God's holy ordinance; and thereto I pledge thee my faith." Brooke sniffled, though some tears did manage to run down her face.

Pastor said, "Let us pray. Dear Father in Heaven, we do commit these two people to you and to one another. We thank you for their salvation and pray that any children they are blessed with will come to know You at a young age." The prayer went on for a few more minutes, but all Brooke could think about at that very moment was that she was committed to Michael for the rest of their days. She felt so blessed. "Amen."

"As much as Michael and Brooke have exchanged their vows before God and this company, have pledged their commitment each to the other, and have declared the same by joining hands and by exchanging rings, and by the authority invested in me by the state of Maryland, I do now pronounce them husband and wife. Those who God has joined together let no one put asunder. Michael, you may kiss your bride."

They kissed, like Pastor had instructed them, "long enough to be sincere but not so long as to become embarrassing." Amanda returned Brooke's bouquet, and they headed down the aisle as husband and wife. After the requisite number of photos, they went into the reception, and then headed out for their honeymoon.

Brooke had asked Michael if they could spend their wedding night at a bayside hotel for a specific reason. As they unpacked, she took a small baggie out of her luggage.

"Brooke, honey, what is that?" Michael asked. He was hanging tomorrow's clothes in the closet. "What is that stuff? It looks like rocks and sand."

"It's a little something left over from . . . well, it's my dad." Brooke smiled shyly, quite embarrassed about the humble container for her father. She hadn't wanted something bigger that would take up too much space in her luggage, so she had settled for . . . a baggie. Not a very fitting end for Kurt, who would have been upset that he finished his earthly walk encased in a plastic bag. Tough stuff for him. No, I must not think unkindly towards the dead.

"It's what?" Michael looked completely shocked.

"Dad. When he was cremated, I asked Joshua and Christopher if I could have some of Dad's ashes. They wondered why and I admit I planned on doing something really mean with them. But then we found out about his journals and I learned why he was the man he was and..."

"You couldn't bear to do the 'something mean' anymore. That... and you were walking with the Lord more closely by then." Michael walked over and hugged her.

"Yes, you could say that," she said. She giggled slightly, joined by Michael, who shook his head in amazement. She looked up and kissed his cheek.

"I just did, my beloved wife. My precious, unpredictable, slightly nutty wife. Okay, so what do we do with dear ol' Dad now? I mean, he isn't really going on our honeymoon with us, is he?" Michael seemed to be half kidding and half serious.

"No, Michael, he's not going with us. I'd like to dump his ashes in the bay tonight. Right now, actually. It'll signal my desire to get rid of the unpleasantness in my life and replace it totally with joy." She smiled at Michael, hoping he would understand.

Michael thought for a moment and then asked, "Would you like me to go with you or is this something you'd prefer to do alone?"

"I would like you to go with me, please." She walked over to the closet and pulled out lightweight jackets for them both. She handed his jacket to Michael. "In case there's a breeze."

"Brooke, I don't want to upset your plans, but is it legal to dump him out at the beach?"

Brooke never thought that disposing of a baggie of ashes might be illegal but, when they quickly looked it up online, they found that they had to be four miles from the coast or they would break the law. Sitting next to him at their room's computer desk, she looked over at Michael, baggie in hand. "What now?'

"Brooke, I hate to start our marriage by breaking the law. How about taking a boat ride tomorrow morning, before we head to the airport?" Michael shut the laptop and began putting it away for safekeeping.

"That seems like a lot of bother . . ." She thought for a few minutes. "Let's put him in the trash." She stood to her feet. "Yep, that's the very thing to do."

"What?"

"I mean, he was so mean to Mom and to me for so many years. I don't see any sign that he was ever sorry for the pain he caused us, so let's just put him in the hotel dumpster and let him end up in a landfill or something."

"Brooke!" He sat back in amazement. "You can't be serious."

"Michael, let's think about this a minute. I've seen the pictures of Dad marrying, and I use that term loosely, Kelsey on the beach. I was thinking about burying the past, releasing Dad into the Bay, that kind of thing. But maybe the fact that it's illegal makes me think that maybe that's not the way to go . . ." She headed for the door.

"Take the high road here, Brooke. That's not the high

road. I'm not even sure that's on a road . . . bury the past." He jumped to his feet and caught up to her, her hand on the door knob.

"Michael, this is burying the past. You don't get more buried than in a landfill."

Brooke had her way. Dear old Dad ended up thrown over the side of the dumpster out back of their hotel. The charming words she had prearranged to say as she...disposed of... his remains escaped her mind when the time came. She had planned to talk about their challenging relationship, but how she understood why he was the way he had turned out. Instead, the only comment she made was "Bye, Dad. I hope you're happier where you are now than when you were with us as a family." She turned to Michael and said, "Let's get going. I'm done holding on to the past and wishing it could have been better."

Michael kissed her and said, "Let's go make our future."

***

Christopher was checking his email after work one evening when he noticed another message from Candace. He'd asked her about meeting the family that fall or in the winter time, but was startled at her request. Her email read:

"Dear Christopher:

"As I previously stated, I am willing to meet you, as the eldest surviving representative of the Prescott family. I would prefer if the meeting could be between just the two of us, for now. I have been alone most of my life and have not had a family to depend on, or even to chat with. I feel that meeting everyone at the same time might be a bit overwhelming. I realize that my solitary life has been by my own choice, having made no effort to find any of my siblings or their offspring, even with the advent of the Internet.

"Since you are, like me, unmarried, I wonder if you would be free to join me in Austin for Thanksgiving. I will understand completely if you wish to spend the holiday with your family in

Maryland. If that is the case, perhaps we could meet the first of the year, before our classes resume. Please let me know your decision.

Sincerely,

Candace Geraldine Prescott, Ph.D."

This was the first year he had actually been looking forward to spending the holiday with his family. He no longer saw their presence as a burden to be borne with a stiff upper lip, while possessing a wild desire to escape to the bars of downtown Annapolis. He was hoping that Audrey might be convinced to come to the gathering with him. He had, after all, almost a month and a half to work on her. He hadn't heard yet if she was headed to Florida to be with her family, or if they might be coming north. He was faced with the dilemma of what to do.

Against type, he decided to ask the family at their next meeting how they would like him to handle it. Aunt Candace wasn't getting any younger, for sure. Boy, this sure isn't like the old me! I wouldn't have cared a whit what the family thought about anything. Am I getting wishy washy? I can make my own decisions. But, no, Pastor mentioned taking the feelings of others into consideration. Christopher would ask them how they felt. If he did decide to go to Texas, he would have to act fast on the airline tickets. Prices wouldn't be dropping, for sure.

Chapter 27

Brooke and Michael headed out from the lovely bed and breakfast where they had spent their wedding night. It had been everything she had ever hoped for and then some. She hugged herself with the knowledge that he was hers. Yes! Michael was the man of her dreams and she couldn't wait to spend the rest of her life with her precious hubby.

They would be going to BWI and taking a plane to Detroit, Michigan. They would take a rental car for the five-hour drive to Mackinaw Island. After a week there, they would return to Detroit, fly into Cleveland, Ohio and drive to the Sisters of St. Francis in Sylvania, Ohio. They would return home using the rental car and stop at BWI to pick up their vehicle. Yep, that was the plan. It was a lot of driving, but they had plenty to talk about.

They had a wonderful time as they walked all about the island and spent some quality romantic time together. Marriage was truly wonderful! Their honeymoon destination fit them both to a T. They loved the historic feeling of the whole island, but were ready for some serious sleuthing when they went on to Sylvania. They landed in Cleveland while it was still daylight, hopped into a dark blue Toyota Avalon, and headed for Sylvania. It was another long drive made easier by the company they enjoyed.

Early the next day, they pulled up outside the Sisters of St. Francis Motherhouse. They saw a lot of older women walking around the grounds, but none of them were wearing a habit and very few had the traditional veil on. Brooke and Michael had done some pre-visit research on the convent and grounds, surprised to learn that the stone buildings they were looking at were just over 100 years old.

They had made an appointment with the Reverend Mother and were ushered into her dark paneled office. The late-middle-aged spiritual head of the convent was dressed in a simple, solid-colored dress and had a massive cross on a chain around her neck. Her silver gray hair was cropped short. Brooke was glad she and Michael had chosen Sunday best clothing for their visit.

The Reverend Mother said, "Please be seated," as she waved them towards the chairs near her desk.

Brooke and Michael sat in the burgundy leather chairs, though Brooke noticed that, like her, Michael perched on the edge of his seat. I guess we're both a little nervous. She said, "Reverend Mother, thank you for seeing us."

"You are certainly welcome, my children. Your email didn't specify how I could be of assistance. What can I do for you, as they say?" The nun leaned comfortably back in her own chair, perhaps to make them more relaxed, and touched her pen to her lips.

"I am Brooke Prescott Bench- that Bench was added just last weekend" she smiled at the elderly woman. "My father was Kurt Prescott, and he had an older sister, Margaret Frances Taylor, who joined your convent in 1963. She had assumed her mother's maiden name, which is why our last names are different. She was known here as Sister Margaret Frances."

"Yes, I knew Sister Margaret Frances well. She was a devout, wonderful Christian woman. She had been here more than twenty years when I arrived." The Reverend Mother's eyes twinkled in remembrance. "It was a blessing to know her."

"Yes, Ma'am. Well, we just found out about her by reading some journals that belonged to my late father. We didn't even know she existed until just a short time ago. We googled her and traced her here. They had a very difficult childhood, and she left home when my father was a very young boy. We'd hoped to get to know her, but can't because she's dead. I wonder if you could tell us about her, since you knew her and we never did."

"Yes, I can tell you. Would you care for a cup of tea? The

story is long and may take a little while to share."

"That would be lovely. Thank you, Reverend Mother." Brooke smiled.

The nun rang a bell, and made her request to the nun who answered. One of the Sisters brought in a pot of tea and some cookies, which they enjoyed while the Reverend Mother shared what she knew with Brooke and Michael. The couple settled back into their chairs, to hear the story of Sister Margaret Frances.

"She told me her family called her 'Maggie,' so I will tell you about her using that name. It's faster than saying Sister Margaret Frances, to be sure!"

They laughed, enjoying the lady's sense of humor.

"Maggie arrived here before my time. The only nun who knew her when she first showed up is long since deceased. Maggie told me herself that she had left home at eighteen, and "lived a sinful life" before coming to the Sisters. She never went into specifics with me, but I did know that she had a tattoo of a heart on her right shoulder. Back then, women did not get tattoos unless they were pretty wild, which I guess Maggie was."

Michael asked, "Were there any words with the tattoo?"

"The names 'Ralph' and 'Robin' were in the center of the heart, from what I understand. She never told me anything about the meaning behind the tattoo, just that she had it. Due to our sense of propriety, she never actually showed it to me, you understand."

Brooke was taking notes on everything the Reverend Mother said, but the nun was so friendly and the story so interesting that she relaxed some more into her seat. She noted that Michael did the same. "That's strange. They aren't the names of any of our relatives. Why would she pick those names?"

"I can't tell you, my dear, but she had them, that's for certain. Anyway, she came to us in 1963, and stayed for the rest of her life. She was a godly woman who served the Lord and the community. She loved the little ones and always worked in Sunday school classes."

"Did she leave anything behind, Ma'am?" Michael was polite but curious.

"Yes, she left a letter, saying that if any of her family ever came here, we should give it to them. She left a few small trinkets, as well, most of which she asked us to give to the children in her classes. We did as she requested, but there are a few things that we kept aside for her family, should they ever show up."

"Oh!" Brooke was shocked. She hadn't planned on a letter from beyond the grave, as it was, but maybe she shouldn't be surprised, given her father's journals.

The Reverend Mother went across the room, reached into a filing cabinet drawer, and pulled out a manila envelope. "It's a bit lumpy because of the rosary beads, but Maggie had sealed the envelope shut, to protect her letter. Would you like to read it here or later?"

Brooke looked at Michael, and then told Reverend Mother, "Perhaps I could read it now, so that I can ask you questions, should I need to."

"Of course, my child. I will step out of the office so you and Michael can have some privacy. Just ring this bell when you are ready for me to return. I won't be far away." The older woman smiled as she left the room.

She looked at Michael and asked, "Are you ready to meet my Aunt Maggie?"

"Go for it, Brooke." He leaned in towards her, peeking over Brooke's shoulder at the letter.

Brooke opened the envelope gingerly, not wanting to muss the contents in her enthusiasm. Immediately inside the manila envelope were the promised rosary beads and some letters from Maggie's mother. Brooke pulled the legal-sized envelope out next, and unsealed the letter written by Maggie. It read:

"To my nearest living relative:

"Hello from Margaret Frances Prescott, also known as Margaret Frances Taylor and Sister Margaret Frances. I am the eldest daughter of William Charles Prescott Senior and his wife Mary Ruth Taylor Prescott. I was born May 18, 1942, and left home at the age of eighteen in 1960. I have not met with any of my relatives since that time, by my choice. If you are reading this now, I am dead and buried and you missed meeting me.

"I am surprised you were able to locate me. I have been here at the Sisters of St. Francis since 1963, where I found true peace and happiness serving God. In the three years between my leaving home and coming here, I did some things that dishonored God. I will tell you about them now, since I know that God has forgiven a sinner like me and saved my soul.

"When I walked out of our family home for the last time, I went into the arms of my boyfriend, a man I had met just a few weeks before. It was the era of free love and sex without consequences, but I quickly discovered that there were indeed penalties to flaunting God's law. Ten months later, I gave birth to my son Ralph Vincent Taylor on March 11, 1961. (I had assumed my mother's maiden name in order to protect myself from my father's wrath.) I worked as a waitress at a greasy spoon restaurant in southern New Jersey, which is as far away from home as I got, at first. On July 29, 1962, I gave birth to my daughter, Robin Melissa Taylor. My boyfriend left me while I was in the hospital giving birth to Robin. He asked our neighbor to watch Ralph for him while he went out for cigarettes and beer. He never came back.

"I got out of the hospital two days later and found my neighbor angry at both of us. She shoved a very unhappy Ralph into my arms and went home. I tried to manage with two children, but I was only twenty years old, alone, and unemployed. I gave both children up for adoption a few months later, and have never seen them again. The adoption was through Catholic Services and was a closed adoption by my choice. I have regretted that decision many times since then, because I would like to know where my children are and how they are doing.

"I spent six months traveling through the Midwest, seeing the sights and working low-paying jobs. I got a tattoo on my right shoulder of a heart and the first names of my children, hoping that they knew how much I loved them, but knowing that I couldn't take care of them. I was an unfit mother.

"I came to the Sisters of St. Francis in March of 1963, when I was weary of being a wanderer. I had happened upon the chapel one Sunday morning and realized that I was in desperate need of God. I saw the joy and contentment the Sisters had and wanted it for myself. I was tired of running away from God and away from my family. I knew that my parents would never accept the woman I had become without God, and that my father would mock me if he knew that I was a Christian now.

"I made no attempt to contact either one of them initially, except for a brief visit home that the Reverend Mother insisted on in September 1964. She wanted me to make sure I was willing to give up my previous life before taking my final vows to the Church. I walked through the downtown of my childhood. A funeral was going on, and I found out from the locals that my mother had died three nights before, on the 12th. I did not attend her service, though I did stop by the cemetery the next day to place flowers on her grave. I saw a young boy, who I believe to have been my brother Kurt, standing by her grave crying, but he did not recognize me in my nun's habit.

"I also found out that my baby sister Ella had been kidnapped in August 1964. She had been born about six months before I left home, so I did not know her well. My brother Kurt was devoted to her, from what everyone in town said. I am certain that he was greatly traumatized by her disappearance that summer. My companion and I ate dinner at one of the local diners, where we overheard a lot of rumors about my family, from speculation about my sister's kidnapping to gossip about the death of my mother one month later. People can be very cruel when they don't know who is listening. I left the area that evening and have never been back since that time.

"I made my final vows later that year and have had a blessed life since that time. My children, if they are still alive, are grown. They have lived a life without their biological mother and not knowing who their father was. His name is Dale Spencer. I did not list him on the birth certificates. I just wrote "father unknown" because I didn't want him to come back and bother me, if he decided to take the children from me at a later date.

"If you are given this letter in time to meet my children, please tell them that I loved them dearly, but knew that they would have a better life without me. They would most definitely have a better life without their maternal grandparents. I don't know anything about their father or his parents, since we were together such a short time. Perhaps a year or so sounds like a long time to live with someone and not know him, but Dale, or Spencer as he preferred to be called, did not talk about his family or his life before he knew me. He was very much centered on the here and now. He was a product of the flower-power culture and was a staunch liberal.

"I know that my time on earth is short now, which is why I wrote this letter. I would like to think that maybe someone somewhere cared enough for me to come looking. Thank you from the bottom of my heart. I know that God cares for me beyond measure, but it is a comfort to know that you care, as well. I wish there was something more to leave you than just this letter, my beloved Rosary beads, and a few letters I received from my mother after I told her where I was. But there isn't, so that is that. I pray that you know the peace of God like I did and that you are His child.

In His Grip,
Sister Margaret Frances"

"Michael, she was in town the week her mother died." Brooke felt her face turn red in shock. Could this nun, who was so highly thought of, have killed her mother?

"Yes, Brooke, but she says she arrived after the fact. Why would she lie about being at her family's home?" Michael's voice betrayed the concern he felt.

"I don't know that she would have. Her faith seems very devout. Her letter doesn't talk about her mother's death, except to say that she didn't attend the funeral. Why wouldn't she have gone? She was right there." Brooke searched the letter again. Perhaps there was something there she hadn't seen. No. She dropped her hands to her lap, the letter still firmly grasped.

"Why don't we ask Reverend Mother?" He reached out to comfort Brooke, but it was a futile effort. She felt distraught.

"Good idea. Let me invite her back in." She rang the bell. Sure enough, the woman was a person of her word; she was quickly with them once more.

"Did the letter help clarify anything for you?" The Reverent Mother sat as she asked the question.

"Yes, thank you Reverend Mother. I'm wondering, though, about something maybe you can help us with. My aunt returned home in time for her mother's funeral, but she didn't go. Do you have any idea why she would have stayed away?"

The nun leaned back in her chair, her hand to her chin and thought for several moments. "People sometimes talk freely when nuns are around because they think we can't hear or, in the very least, that we won't tell anyone what they said. Maggie told me a few years back that she had heard the townspeople harping on what drunks her parents were and how the community couldn't be sure if it was suicide, an accident, or murder that killed her mother. Some folks said that they thought the parents murdered their little girl and then hid the body. Yes, Maggie overheard some very unpleasant things about her family in the couple of days she spent in the area. No one recognized her, she was certain, but she was afraid they would know who she was if she went to the funeral. Maggie, and the Sister who accompanied her, stayed at a local hotel but made the decision to leave almost immediately after Maggie spotted a young boy who she thought was her brother Kurt in the cemetery, the day after the funeral. She didn't want to breeze in and out of his life for fear of making things worse."

"Yes, it might have been worse for Kurt to get her back, only to lose her again. And who knows how my grandfather might have reacted to her . . . new wardrobe and way of life."

"I got the impression from Maggie that he was a very difficult and unkind man whose character was made worse by his drinking."

Michael said, "That's a very nice way of describing him, Reverend Mother."

Brooke asked the Mother, "Which Sister accompanied my aunt on her trip?"

The Reverend Mother said, "I don't know right off hand, but let's have a look at our log. We keep records of the Sisters' comings and goings. They rarely leave on trips, so it shouldn't be too hard to find." She led them into an office where the ledger was kept. She flipped back to the year 1964, and looked over the September entries. "She left with Sister Mary Catherine on September 9th and drove to her hometown in Maryland." The Mother ran her hand over the entries. "She reported that it was a two day journey. They returned to the convent at six pm on September 15th ."

Brooke said, "It was a two-day journey that they started on the 9th?" She glanced at Michael. "What time did they leave on the 9th?"

The Mother said, "The records show the Sisters left at nine am. That would have been after morning prayers and breakfast. Why do you ask?"

"Oh, there seems to be a little discrepancy over when they arrived in Maryland. Perhaps Maggie got confused."

"Yes, that's entirely possible. She was a young woman when she entered the information in the log, but some thirty-nine years had passed when she wrote the letter. It would have been easy to forget exact dates." The nun smiled at them.

Michael said, "Yes, that's completely likely. Is Sister

Mary Catherine still alive?"

"No, Michael. She was a diabetic. She died shortly after they got back from the trip. Went to bed one night and didn't wake up in the morning. Apparently, she took too much insulin. She was in a coma for a few days and then passed. She was such a nice woman, too, from what I have been told."

"I'm sorry for your loss, Reverend Mother." Brooke was trying not to be too obvious. Maggie might have killed her mother and then covered up the other nun's suspicions by killing her, as well! Or, it could have simply been a coincidence. Get a grip, Brooke!

The nun smiled and asked, "If you don't mind my asking, how is the family doing?"

Brooke gave the older woman a quick run-down on Maggie's siblings and then talked about this generation of Prescotts.

The Reverend Mother shook her head and said, "I'm glad things are finally working out well for your family, Brooke. I will be praying for you all. Michael, it was nice to meet you. Congratulations on your marriage. May God bless you with many years of happiness and many children." They all stood to leave.

"Thank you, Reverend Mother. I appreciate all the time you gave us today and for the letters." Brooke reached out to shake hands, but the nun embraced her warmly. Michael got a hug, as well.

"You're welcome, my dear children. I've enjoyed chatting with you. If you have any additional questions you think I can help with, please send me an email." The nun walked them out to their car and wished them Godspeed.

They climbed back into their rented Avalon and left the convent. Michael asked, "When are we going to read Mama's letters to Maggie?"

"I thought it would be a nice way to keep you awake on the way home. I'll put them in order based on their postmark, and we'll see what Mama had to say to her formerly wayward and now Christian daughter."

"Sounds good to me, my dear sweet Brooke." Michael grabbed her hand and kissed it.

Chapter 28

Brooke got things sorted out with the letters, checking the postmarks to determine where each one fit into the larger picture of Maggie, the nun with an apparent poor sense of dates. She got the handful of letters organized and opened one to read.

"Okay, Michael, here goes. The first letter is dated April 5, 1964." She read:

"My precious Maggie,

"It was such a joy to hear that you are alive and well. I've been worried about you ever since I realized that you were never coming back home. I miss you every day. Your father is the same, as usual. I will try to check the mail every day before he comes home, so that I can get any letters from you before he sees them. It would not do for him to catch me in correspondence with you. I know you understand why.

"I was surprised to hear that you have become a nun. We aren't even Catholic and didn't raise you in a so-called Christian home. Still, if you are content, that is fine with me. I haven't heard from your brother Will at all, so it is nice to hear from a child who has left home for good. I really think that Will was drafted, though I do not know for sure. He got some mail that he wouldn't let me see right before he left, so who knows? He was always a bit of a sneak.

"Johnny left home last year right after graduation. I haven't heard from him, but let me know if you know where he is. Peter, Candy, Kurt, and Ella are still around. They keep me busy with all of their needs, especially Ella, but it's much easier with only four children. I don't know how I handled seven of you. I was a younger woman, ha, ha.

"Thank you again for writing.

Love,

Your Devoted Mother"

Michael said, "Wow, that's not a very loving letter, when you think about it. She says she misses her but then drops the subject and moves on."

"Yes, Michael, but maybe she wanted to get the letter written before her hubby came home. She seems concerned that he not be made aware that they were writing, or even where her daughter was." Brooke flipped through the letter again, but it was what it was. She didn't think she would have appreciated the letter if she had received it, either.

Michael said, "I'm sorry, Brooke, but this family was just plain weird. I mean, the kids left home without a word, and then when Mama hears from one of her kids, she keeps it a secret from her hubby. That's not the kind of marriage I want us to have."

"Honey pie, sugar plum? I agree completely." She leaned over and gave his cheek a kiss. "So, you want to hear the next letter?"

"Sure, Brooke. I'm a captive audience." He glanced in the rear view mirror, and then looked back at her, silently awaiting the next missive.

"Okie dokie. This one is dated June 13, 1964."

"My dearest Maggie,

"I'm glad you're happy now. Your father is still the same. He comes home like a roaring lion and stays that way all evening long, until he's been 'sipping' long enough to become sleepy. I still drink, though not as much. I pretend to have several drinks with him, but I give him enough liquor fast enough to get him three sheets to the wind before he realizes that I stopped at one drink.

"When he questions my consumption, I just tell him that I've had almost as many as he has had and I act tipsy. I've also been pouring my drinks into the potted plants next to the living room couch, which makes my drinks disappear faster. It doesn't seem to bother the plants, especially since they're plastic. I'm just tired of that life. The booze doesn't speak to me like it once did. I don't find satisfaction in it any more. Why does he love it so much?

"I've been thinking about the stuff you have been telling me about God. Thank you for the Bible. I can't read it in front of your father, and I keep it hidden most of the time under my side of our mattress. He never, ever changes the sheets or makes the bed because that's woman's work, so I'm not worried that he will find it. I've gotten pretty good at getting to the mail before he gets home, so I can retrieve your letters before he finds out about them. I leave the rest of the mail in the mailbox for him to bring in, which is what he demands, as always.

"Thank you again for your concern about my soul.

Love,

Your Devoted Mother"

Brooke shut the letter. "Wow." She folded the letter back into its envelope.

"Yeah. Maggie doesn't sound like a mother-killer to me."

"So why did she lie about the dates?" That made no sense to her.

"Brooke, maybe the Reverend Mother was right. She got confused about when she was there. It had been a very long time since she went home on leave."

"Let's read the next one." She pulled it from its envelope, shaking her head. The family was totally dysfunctional in her mind, but they did seem to manage, somehow.

"Please do, Brooke."

"Okay. This one is dated July 30, 1964. The writing is very wobbly, almost like a kid wrote it. "

"Dear Maggie,

"I'm sorry I haven't written lately. Your father found my Bible. I'd been reading it in the living room when he came home unexpectedly. He was in the room before I'd even heard him come in. I stuck it down in the couch pillows as fast as I could, but he came barreling into the room and snatched it up like it was a dirty magazine. He tried to rip it into pieces, but he couldn't tear it so he threw it into the fireplace.

"He grabbed my arm . . . and broke it. My shoulder was dislocated at the same time. It hurts so badly. He fixed my shoulder by yanking on it, but wouldn't let me go to the doctor for my broken arm until he'd sobered up the next day. Please don't send me another Bible or things will be worse. You know how he is. I better go for now. I don't know if you can read my writing, but it is better than it was.

Love,

Your Devoted Mother"

"Man." Michael seemed unable to get any more words out. They drove in silence for a few miles.

"Why don't we take a break?" Brooke massaged his arm as he drove. It was hard to comprehend such a difficult man as her grandfather. It made her father seem like a saint.

"How many letters are left?"

"Only one. She died in September, you know."

"Yeah, Brooke, let's talk about something else, for sure."
They talked about the future and their plans to sell both of their
condos and buy a house. Susan's gift of $100,000 had come
through and, now that they were married, they were ready to
find their own home. They would be staying between the two
condos for now, living part time in her condo and part time in
Michael's. Since they wanted children, they decided a house
with a nice backyard in a good school district would be right for
them. They wanted to stay near the family, so that meant the
Annapolis area.

Brooke would probably go part time in her job as a
paralegal when the children arrived. She could do some of her
work via telecommuting, so she could be a stay-at-home mom.
Their mothers would both want to be involved with the grands,
so things could work out really nicely. They'd already planned
on starting their family as soon as God decided it was time,
since they were in their mid-thirties and her biological clock
was ticking. They chatted about that, happy at the thought of
children gracing their home.

They pulled over for dinner and spent the night in
Lancaster, Pennsylvania, at a cute B and B. They got on the road
after a leisurely breakfast the next morning and headed back to
Maryland. The whole family was expecting them for dinner.
They would make it to her mother's and Dan's house in plenty
of time, so they would stop by her condo to freshen up from the
long trip and throw in a load of laundry. Brooke got behind the
wheel, since Michael had driven most of the trip.

"Do you want to read me the last letter while you drive,

Brooke, or would you prefer to wait?" Michael asked.

"Let's wait until the family is together for one of our pow-pows. Let's not end our honeymoon on a sour note." Brooke smiled in his direction.

"Very good point, my lovely bride. So, what's on the agenda for the next couple of days?' Michael picked up her hand and kissed it.

"The folks' house tonight for a family dinner, church in the morning, and back to work for both of us on Monday. We need to get our condos in good shape, and then put them on the market. Let's get 'em sold, Mr. Bench, and get ourselves a house!" She leaned over carefully and kissed his check.

Chapter 29

Susan had contacted Glenda Jo Henry a few months before, congratulating her on her thirtieth anniversary to Stephen and asking about her first husband, Peter. Glenda hadn't known about Peter's siblings and was shocked to hear about the family background. Peter had been as tight-lipped about his brothers and sisters as Kurt had been. Glenda wanted to know more and felt that her daughters needed to know about the history of the Prescott clan, as well.

It had taken a few weeks to hear back from Glenda Jo at first, but they had been in regular contact since then, via email. They agreed that it was much faster than snail mail, though not quite as charming. Glenda Jo turned out to be a delightful woman who had many fond memories of her young husband. Yes, there had been some trials along the way, but she had loved him dearly. He was a good father and a strict teetotaler, which Glenda Jo had agreed with most whole-heartedly, as a devout Baptist. His sudden and unexpected death had been a tragedy for them all. After a few weeks of emailing, they decided to talk on the phone.

Susan called Glenda Jo one November afternoon, sharing a long distance cup of tea with the gal as Susan sat in her dining room.

"Hello, Glenda Jo. It's nice to finally meet you, at least on the phone."

"Yes, Susan, I'm so glad to hear your voice. How was the wedding?"

"Delightful. It was a very special day," Susan said.

"Thanks for the photos. We enjoyed seeing them. They were certainly more fun to look at than the pictures of the Prescott family!" Glenda Jo hesitated. "I mean, I'm thankful that you sent copies of them to me, but . . ."

Susan laughed and said, "No need to apologize. I know

what you mean. I positively wept when I saw the pictures of Kurt's siblings and parents for the first time. I'm glad that someone's still alive who can tell us about Peter. All we have of him is a few journal entries of Kurt's, from the standpoint of a little brother, who felt deserted by yet another sibling. I was wondering what you can tell me about Peter." Susan settled into her chair at the dining room table, ready to take notes on everything Glenda Jo said.

"Sure thing. Ask away."

"So how did you meet Peter, Glenda Jo?"

"Peter was in the service, the Air Force. He was so young. He must have enlisted right out of high school."

Susan said, "Yes, that seems logical, since the journals say he was barely eighteen when he left home."

"Well, Peter came into the Blue Collar Café in Fort Walton Beach for breakfast with some of his friends. I was working there as a cashier, and he was so handsome, he swept me right off my feet! He started going to church with me and my family. He got saved a few months later, and started doing a Bible study with some of the men at church. As soon as I graduated from high school, we got married."

"Glenda Jo, that sounds like a whirlwind courtship."

"It was. We'd known each other for less than a year. We both had some growing up to do, that's for sure, but I positively adored him and he was so good to me."

"Did he have any anger issues?" Susan had hesitated to ask, but the truth needed to be known.

"Yes, at first. I was so shocked because it didn't fit in with the man I thought he was. After we got married, he would blow up at the slightest thing. Go off on a tirade, you know. Then he would get very quiet. He always apologized and then said that it wouldn't happen again. One time he got really upset about something. You know, I'm not even sure what set him off. He said he was going to go off for a few days on his own. He took a few days of leave and said he needed to be alone. When he got back, he went to talk to the men who had been mentoring him at church. They got him through it, and he never yelled again. They showed him the Christian way to deal with disappointment." Glenda Jo paused.

"That's great that the men at your church were able to help him. Did he say where he went on his trip?" Susan wondered if perhaps the trip was to see his family.

"I think he went to see his father, to deal with some issue or something. He told me later that it was the anniversary of his mother's death. He'd been there when she died, but he didn't go into a lot of details. He didn't talk to me about his childhood, not much anyway, but just said that he had grown up in a home where his parents quarreled and drank all the time. He said he wasn't putting me or our future children through that."

"I guess he went back to heal old wounds. When did he go?" Susan scribbled fast and furiously on her notepad. The family would be very interested in her insight into Peter's personality.

"Perhaps. I do know he wasn't happy with himself when he went. Let's see, when did he go? Was it . . . August 1965? No, that doesn't sound right. Let me see. We got married in June of 1965, and he was struggling with his anger issues for a couple of months. So, June, July, August . . . I think he went in September. Yes, it was right around payday . . . you know, I think it was right before payday because we were strapped for cash, and he took some money out of our savings account to pay for his trip. I don't remember the exact dates, but it was before payday in mid-September. Maybe the tenth or so? He was gone about a week."

"How was he when he got back?" Susan asked.

"He seemed to have put some things to rest. He became the man I always knew he was, after that season."

"Did he ever talk about his sister Ella?" Susan asked.

"No. I never knew she existed until you sent me her picture. He didn't talk about his other siblings, either. I was shocked to learn about them. I thought our relationship was one where we could talk about almost anything, but I guess not." Glenda took a sip of her tea. It was apparently rather hot, as she sputtered a bit.

"We're trying to piece together what happened to Ella, but nothing's turning up, so far." Susan tried to calm things down, not wanting to upset Glenda Jo.

"I'm so sorry. I wish I could help you. He never mentioned her, not once."

"What about his relationship with your daughters?" Susan was curious how things were with Peter's family.

"They came along at pretty regular intervals. Natalie was first- she was born in 1966. Lisa Marie was born in 1968 and, yes, we were Elvis fans! Kimberly was born in 1970. The girls loved their Daddy. He could do no wrong. He took them to father-daughter activities at the church, helped them with their homework, and things like that. He wasn't the disciplinarian- I had to do that. I think he was afraid of losing control, so I was the bad cop and he was the good cop. They knew I loved them, even though I was the one who punished them. There was no 'wait till your father comes home' at our household. When they got older, I told them why he always had me do the punishing. They understood."

"And then there was the crash . . ."

"Yes, my beloved Peter went to work one day, and he never came back." Glenda Jo's voice cracked, and then she moved on. "They were on a training mission. The pilot lost control or something. I never really understood what happened. The plane disintegrated on impact. Peter and the entire flight crew were all killed. He was so young. We were devastated but, you know, Peter will be forever young to me. He was only thirty-four years old when he died, so that's how old he will be forever. I'll see him again one day. He's in heaven. We know that, the girls and I."

"I didn't mean to open old wounds, Glenda Jo." Susan heard sniffling in the background.

"No, Susan, that's okay. A few years after Peter died I met a wonderful man, Stephen James Henry, at church. He'd just been transferred by his company to the Ft. Walton Beach area. We got to know each other and got married five years after Peter's death. The girls were in their teens and really needed a father figure. I was still a young woman in my late thirties and wanted to re-marry. Stephen is a good man. We've been very happy together. I struck pay dirt with both of my husbands. Life is good."

"I would love to meet you and your family sometime, Glenda Jo."

"Do you ever get down to Florida?" Glenda Jo asked.

"Dan and I might be able to arrange that. Let me see what I can do."

"You bet! I'd love to show you around our hometown and have you meet the girls. I guess you're their Aunt Susan. They ought to meet their Aunt Susan, don't you think?"

***

Brooke and Michael were comfortably home from their honeymoon later that afternoon. The next family meeting about the Prescott family was called for that evening. The family greeted the returning honeymooners happily and ate some homemade treats. The young couple read them the letters from Mrs. Prescott to her daughter Sister Margaret Frances. Brooke pulled out the final letter Mrs. Prescott had written.

"We didn't read this last letter because we wanted to learn what it said at the same time you did. It's dated right after Ella was kidnapped," Brooke told the family.

"August 17, 1964

"Dear Maggie,

"I cannot believe this has happened. My precious little Ella has disappeared. I went into a store in downtown Annapolis. I was just in there for a minute. Ella had fallen asleep on the back seat of the car and I didn't want to disturb her, so I rolled the car windows down to make sure she had some air and went inside to pick something up. I wasn't gone

245

for more than five minutes.

"I came back outside. Things are very hazy . . . Did I look at her in the back seat when I got back in the car or did I just see the blankets and drive home? I don't know. I can't remember. When I got home, I thought she was still asleep in the back, so I rolled the windows down in the front seat, as well, and went inside for a while. I figured she would be waking up soon, so I went outside to check on her after about thirty minutes and she was gone!

"I started screaming and the neighbors called the police. The cops didn't seem to do much good. They haven't found Ella yet. Kurt is beside himself with grief, like we all are. We searched our yard and the creek, but she wasn't there. Where is my baby? Why doesn't she come home? I walk the floors at night, wondering if I will ever see her again.

"The neighbors were very nice, at first, but now everywhere I go, I hear people murmuring about me and how I left my child alone. She was asleep! The town gossips are in full action. They think I can't hear them talking about how I killed my child and how I'm covering it up. They're wrong! I want my little Ella back, for Kurt's sake if nothing else.

"The police brought me into headquarters and talked to me for hours. Your father hired an attorney to represent me. He thinks the cops are building a case against me . . . William said the other night that I might rot in jail. You know how your father is. If I'm down, he kicks me hard to keep me there.

"I don't know how much more I can take. I'm back drinking again, but it's the one thing that keeps me sane. I know you disapprove. It gets me through the nights. I'll let you know if we hear anything. Please pray that we will find her alive and well.

Love,
Your Devoted Mother"

The family was silent for several minutes.

"Wow! That's some letter, Brooke," Amanda said.

"I can't imagine what Mrs. Prescott was going through.

You can hear the torture in her voice as she writes," Susan said.

Dan said, "But she lied. We know the "store" she went into was a bar. We know that she'd been drinking, if the newspaper reports are anywhere near accurate."

Joshua added, "Why would she lie to Maggie? The woman was a nun, for Pete's sake. Isn't she bound by nun-parishioner confidentiality or something?"

Christopher commented, "Maybe she was afraid that Maggie would think less of her, though she does say that she's been drinking again. Do you think she ever really stopped, like the earlier letters claim?"

Michael said, "We don't know, but the newspaper accounts seem to suggest that the neighbors knew she was hitting the bottle. Of course, maybe folks weren't talking about her, but she thought they were."

Brooke replied, "Honey, you always look at the bright side of things. People are mean, especially when a little child goes missing. I think Mrs. Prescott was probably right about the town folk talking about her. It would be pretty hard not to, given the circumstances."

Amanda said, "Brooke has a good point. Mommy is out drinking in mid-afternoon, she leaves her child alone in the car, someone bad comes and takes her, and the parents never see the child again. It's sad, but quite plausible."

Susan said, "How very, very heartbreaking. Mrs. Prescott had to live with the guilt for the rest of her life."

Brooke remarked, "Which wasn't very long, Mom. She died one month to the day after her daughter vanished."

"That pulls us back to – who took Ella and who killed her mother? I don't see anything that says it is the same person, except for the note," Dan said.

Christopher said, "Then we'll just have to ask the one person who is still alive who might know- Aunt Candace."

***

Christopher had talked things over with the family, and

they had jointly decided to honor Aunt Candace's request that she meet him alone. So here he was- on a Southwest flight to Austin, Texas out of BWI. He had taken the day off on Wednesday and headed to the airport for a mid-afternoon flight. His flight would get in pretty late that evening, so he would meet his Aunt Candace for Thanksgiving lunch the next day.

He understood that there were several grocery stores in that area, so he could buy her a bouquet as a gift to say 'hello' for the first time. It would have to come in a vase so that the flowers wouldn't wilt by the time he delivered them on Thanksgiving.

He'd be staying at the Hampton Inn. It was reliable, clean, his kind of place. In the past, he might've gone in for something a bit more exciting, but his new lifestyle was considerably more sedate. Tame, actually. And the hotel was close to the University of Texas. He'd learned that his Aunt Candace lived within walking distance of the campus, so that made things convenient.

Christopher arrived on time and picked up his rental car; it was a silver Toyota Avalon. He noticed a Whole Foods Market on his way to the hotel, so he stopped by and bought a lovely bouquet of fall flowers. Personally, he didn't know a mum from an orchid, but the lady behind the counter assured him that the arrangement she picked out for him would be super for his aunt's table.

The next day, he pulled into Aunt Candace's neighborhood. She lived in a small stone cottage with a big yard. He loved the house at first sight. It reminded him of his own house in Severna Park. He was guessing that, judging from the age of the neighborhood, the house had been built in about the 1940s. It was meticulously maintained. He was willing to bet she had a landscape company look after it, though perhaps she was into gardening. Time would tell.

As he got out of his car, a slender elderly woman came out of the front door. She had short grey hair and a bit of a limp as she came towards him. She smiled and said, "Christopher Prescott? I am your Aunt Candace. Welcome!"

After they exchanged a quick hug, he presented her with the bouquet and followed her into the house. The door opened into the fragrant Thanksgiving smells he loved. Turkey, stuffing, and pumpkin pie were all present and accounted for. They had a delicious meal, taking the time to get to know one another. He helped her clean up, and then they went into the living room for coffee.

And that's when he noticed her stuffed animals. Real stuffed animals: Dogs, cats, birds. They were all over the living room. Deer heads hung on all four walls, draped with seasonal artificial flowers. Okay, this is a little strange.

"So, Aunt Candace. I see you're into taxidermy. How long have you been doing that?" Christopher tried to sound nonchalant but wasn't sure he was carrying it off too well. It really felt spooky, weird. A drop of sweat made its way down his spine.

"I see you have spotted my . . . collection, Christopher. I loved these animals, but they died. I didn't want to lose them, so I learned taxidermy in order that they would always be around."

Okay, time to leave. How to make his exit? She had seemed pretty normal, until now. "That's very sweet." What else could he say? The old dame was crackers.

"Yes, let me introduce you. This cocker spaniel is Daisy. She died in 1980, so I have had her for a long time. Such a sweet dog." Moving to another animal, "This is Petunia Blossom, my little Sheltie. She passed in 1995. She was so smart. You know, I would say 'time to go to bed' and she would go into my bedroom and turn down the covers for me. If I didn't show up in a few minutes, she would walk back into the living room and tilt her head as if to say, 'I thought you said we were going to bed.' I love having her nearby."

"That's wonderful, Aunt Candace." She didn't seem to

hear him.

"The birds are Rose, Lilly, and Marigold. The cats are Aster, Bluebell, and Buttercup. The deer are Dahlia, Violet, Rosemary, and Pansy." She turned to him. "I like flower names."

"Yes, Ma'am, I noticed."

"Do you know how to do taxidermy, Christopher? After something is dead, you skin it." Aunt Candace smiled and moved towards him. He moved back.

Hers was kind of an uncomfortable smile that made him shiver, in spite of himself. He didn't feel very well, all of a sudden. Have I eaten too much? No, I don't think it's that. It's her.

"Aunt Candace, I hate to make it such an early evening, but it's been a long journey and a busy weekend. I really need to be going. Thank you so much for your warm hospitality." He turned and started for the door. He jiggled the door handle. Locked.

***

"Excuse me, sir, but your seatbelt is not on, and you need to return your tray table to its full, upright, and locked position before we land." The flight attendant beamed at him.

"What? Huh?" Oh . . . sure thing." Christopher was greatly relieved to see that he had not yet visited his Aunt Candace, though he was going to ask for a house tour before dinner, just to make sure there weren't any stuffed animals in the living room. Or stuffed relatives.

He got off the plane, picked up his car, and, once again if you count his dream trip, tried to head towards the hotel. Boy, am I glad that was another one of my crazy dreams. I also hope it wasn't a sign that Aunt Candace is a candidate for the looney bin!

The next day, he arrived at Aunt Candace's house, bouquet in hand. The home was exactly as he pictured it, since he had gotten on the Internet and checked out the address. Just as in his dream, a slender, elderly blonde came out, sans the limp, and greeted him with great happiness. There the comparison ended. Aunt Candace was kind, though rather formal in her demeanor, but not as stilted as her emails suggested. She took him on a tour of the house right away. There were no stuffed anything awaited him, to his great relief. He was amazed by how nice her house was. They had a delightful dinner, and then she suggested they have coffee in the living room.

It was once he was seated that he noticed the pictures of Aunt Candace with various celebrities scattered about on the bookshelves, end tables, and every horizontal surface.

"Aunt Candace, I have to ask, where did you meet all those famous people?"

"Well, Christopher, I have had a very interesting life. Settle back and I'll tell you my story."

Christopher made himself more comfortable on her sofa and he told his hostess, "Please do tell- I am all ears, as my mother always says."

Aunt Candace began one of the most fascinating tales he had ever heard about someone's life. She told him she had left home at about eighteen years of age. She had been very eager to get as far away from Maryland and her father as she could. She'd been saving her babysitting and chore money for years, hoping that one day she could escape from the life she had growing up. One day, a friend and her family were headed to Oregon, so she got a ride.

They made it across country in about a week, visiting various tourist locations along the way. Her friend's parents had paid Candace's way into the attractions since they didn't want to exhaust her resources by the time they arrived in Oregon. It was a great trip. The tourists got to their destination in Portland, and they allowed her to stay with them while she looked for a job.

Candace said that she had always made her own clothes, which let her stretch the small clothing budget her parents gave her. As a result of many years' experience, her sewing had become exceptionally good. She'd never bothered with store-bought patterns once she learned how to make her own, so her clothing was unique and original. One day she was standing in a fabric store in Portland, when a new acquaintance spotted her. The gal told her that some company was casting for a commercial and that Candace, being so young and pretty, ought to go try out. The casting office was only two blocks away.

Candace tried to put the woman off, but the lady was not to be denied. At her insistence, Candace stopped by the office and was ushered in to see the bigwigs. They looked her over and talked to her about her sewing. She thought they were interested in having her make the costumes for the actress who got the part, but instead asked her to make her own costume and do the commercial herself.

"I was so surprised! Here it was, something I wasn't even thinking about doing, but they hired me. I ended up making commercials for about two hundred companies by the time it was said and done."

Christopher smiled and asked, "Then what happened?"

"Oh, that was such a fun story. I had started doing local commercials, and then more and more people saw me and I got more business. I was doing national commercials when I was asked to stand in for the host on Portland This Morning, a local morning program. I ended up co-hosting the show for twelve years."

"But you're a college professor . . ."

"Yes. While I was doing the commercials and television show, I saved my money and went to college part time. I lived in a hovel of a home, but saved and planned and eventually finished my four year degree...in about six years. I went on to get my master's degree in English, and then was offered the chance to get my Ph.D. at Cornell. I'll spare you the details, but I couldn't turn it down. I knew by that time that my days on commercials and television were limited. Back then, a woman over about thirty-five didn't have any chance of getting her contract renewed, so I knew my time on television was coming to an end."

"And the famous people?"

"They were people who were plugging their movies or books or both. They all came through Portland on promotional tours, and I got the chance to interview them. They were always willing to pose for pictures afterwards. Most of them were really nice."

"And the others?" he asked.

"Well, let's just say, Christopher, that some were better behaved than others. Some of the men, men whose names you would still recognize, had difficulty keeping their hands to themselves. Sexual harassment is what it would be called today, but back then it was pretty much understood that you had to put up with a lot if you were pretty and young. I was both."

"Didn't your family see you on television?'

"Nope, except for Johnny. By the way, if you get the chance to meet him, don't."

Christopher said, "Oh, yes, Aunt Candace, we found out about him pretty fast. He's wanted in several states for stealing from people's bank accounts. He got released by mistake. A clerical error."

"If you run into him, tell him I want my $20,000 back. He found his way into my bank account a few years ago. It was a real bother to get that straightened out. Then he broke into my house while I was at a conference. He made a real mess of things and stole some...items that were precious to me. I never did get those back."

"I will pass the message along, should I ever meet him."

"Oh, one thing. When I was on television, I didn't use the name Candace Prescott. I called myself Candace Geraldine, as if Geraldine was my surname. That was a defense mechanism I used to protect myself from people who knew me in Maryland. I also dyed my hair dark brown and used green contact lenses. I don't think anyone ever figured out that it was me, except for

Johnny."

"Good idea." He smiled at her creativity.

"Yes. However, there was one drawback to my being a blonde in real life and having to dye my hair."

"What was that?" he asked.

"As a blonde, my eyelashes were really light, so I had to use false ones. All those years of using glue to hold them on and having to remove them every night made my real eyelashes fall out. I know I'm a bit old for false eyelashes, but I cannot bear to be without them. So here I am, in my seventies, still wearing false eyelashes every day."

"The price of fame . . ." They smiled.

"And I'm a blonde once more, 'by the grace of God and the inventive genius of the people at Clairol.' I think the actual saying went 'and the inventive genius of the people at Wella Balsam' but I'm not sure they're still in business." They laughed.

The rest of the weekend was spent together. He would pick her up for breakfast, and then they would tour Austin, doing both walking and driving tours. She was in great shape and took him all around the campus, on foot. She showed him all the places she loved. By the time he dropped her off on Saturday night, he felt as if he had made a dear, new friend, which he had.

That Sunday afternoon when he was getting ready to leave for the airport after they had one last lunch together, he asked her, "Aunt Candace, would you be willing to visit us in Maryland? The family would love to get to know you like I have."

"My spring break is in mid-March. Would that work for you?"

"Absolutely. I've been texting my mother about the great time we've been having. I know she can't wait to meet you. Neither can anyone else, from what she says."

"Then we have a date, Christopher. I will be there 'with

bells on,' as we used to say."

"My mom says that all the time!" Christopher told her.

Christopher had decided to wait until she came to Maryland to find out about her missing sister Ella, her troubled brother Kurt, and the death of her mother. Why spoil a great visit by dredging up the dark past with the little old lady?

Chapter 30

Christopher felt like he was really growing in his faith. He had finished his counselling with Pastor. He'd begun attending church regularly, sitting with Brooke and Michael and Joshua and his family. He'd made a profession of faith and gotten baptized that very month. Susan and Dan were also involved in the church. They both sang in a senior's choir.

He was getting closer to his beloved Audrey as a result of his newfound faith, seeing her sitting across the sanctuary from him each Sunday. He was at peace with himself and with his family. For the first time in his life, he had joy.

One evening he got home from work a little on the late side, 7 p.m. was unusual but the day had been busy. He grabbed his mail to look at during dinner; there was an envelope from an attorney in Annapolis. Why would this guy be writing to me? He opened the envelope and read:

"December 1, 2018

"Dear Commander Prescott:

"You may recall having a physical relationship with a certain Ms. Shannon Thompson back in February of this year. This union resulted in Ms. Thompson becoming pregnant. On November 18, 2018, she safely delivered identical twin daughters at Anne Arundel Medical Center. The girls were born at 38 weeks of gestation, requiring two weeks in the hospital.

"One result of this pregnancy was that Ms. Thompson's contract to teach at a local Christian school was not renewed. She has incurred the costs of pregnancy, labor and delivery, and supporting the twins. Because we believe that you are the father of the children, we are writing to arrange your financial support of Ms. Thompson and her daughters until such time as she is able to locate gainful employment and the girls achieve the age of eighteen, or twenty-two if they chose to attend college.

"We understand that you may wish to undergo a

paternity test, and have arranged to have the girls' and Ms. Thompson's DNA available for comparison. Please make arrangements to be tested as soon as possible so that financial considerations may be worked out to the mutual satisfaction of Ms. Thompson and you.

"If you do not have legal counsel, I respectfully suggest that you make arrangements to be represented in a timely manner, since the requested support will be an ongoing expense for you for the next eighteen to twenty-two years. I am available to discuss this matter with you and your attorney.

Sincerely,

Darren Smyth, Attorney at Law"

The breath had been knocked out of him. Christopher stumbled into the living room, too numb to even think straight. He threw himself on the couch. He remembered Shannon, barely. He knew that he had gotten her name wrong, that she had left in a huff, and that he hadn't slept with anyone else since then.

If he had passed her on the street this afternoon, he wouldn't have been able to recognize her. It was a one-night stand. How could it have gone so bad? Pregnant? Really? Wasn't she on the pill or something? He had assumed that she was, since she hadn't shown any concern during their sexual encounter. What? Did she assume he was sterile or something, or did she think she was unable to conceive? How could this have happened?

What do I do now? God, please help me! I don't know where to turn. A still small voice told him to call his family. So he did.

"Mom, this is Chris. Can you and Dan come over? I need some advice. Yeah, it's serious. Can you come over now? I know it's kinda late for you but . . . yes, see you soon."

"Joshua- this is Chris. I need some advice. Can you come over? I know Amanda will be busy with the kids right now, but I need your insight on something . . . Thanks. See you in a bit."

"Brooke, Chris here. Can you and Michael please come

257

over to my place? I'm in a bit of a jam, and I need to talk to you all. Mom and Dan and Joshua are headed here . . . Thanks. See you soon."

Christopher started pacing back and forth, unable to sit still. He kept looking at his watch, wondering when everyone would show up. He could feel the sweat pouring down his back. He hoped he wouldn't be a puddle of perspiration by the time everyone came.

He saw headlights in his living room window and headed for the door. He ran outside as his folks pulled into the driveway.

"Mom, Dan, please come in. Joshua and Brooke and Michael are on the way. Thanks for coming so fast."

Susan hugged him to her chest. She said, "Chris, I've never seen you so rattled. What's up, honey?"

"Oh, Mom. I'm going to explain it once everybody gets here. I can't believe this has happened, but it has."

"Sweetie, are you okay? I mean, I hope you aren't sick or something."

Dan spoke up, "Chris you look spooked. What in the world is going on?"

Just then, two more cars pulled up and Joshua, Brooke, and Michael came running.

Joshua and Brooke spoke at the same time, "Chris, what's happened?" "Are you okay?"

"No, I'm not okay. Please, come inside." They hustled into his home. He brought them into his living room. "Everybody, thanks for coming. Please sit down- I have some news to tell you, but I have a confession to make, as well." He remained on his feet.

They exchanged concerned glances and sat as he requested.

"I was not living for the Lord earlier this year, as you all know. I . . . am not proud of myself, but I . . . slept with a young woman who I had just met. I haven't seen her since, but I got a letter from an attorney in Annapolis today. It seems that she got pregnant . . . with twins . . . and she gave birth last month. She wants me to support her new family. Legally, I guess I have to. I just don't know what to do from here."

Silence. Everyone was stunned, he could tell. *What must they think of me? I have royally messed up.*

Clearing of throats. His mom started to speak, then stopped herself. Then she started again.

Susan said, "Well, Chris, I messed up my life in the past, as you all know. I don't think less of you. I know what kind of man you are now, now that the Lord is in your heart, so we just need to look at things from this new perspective." Susan got up and went over to where he was standing by the fireplace and gave him a big hug. "I'm so glad you called us."

Dan got up from the couch and walked over to Chris. Dan told him, "Chris, this must be a huge shock. Believe me, I understand that feeling! I'm not excusing your behavior, but we just need to make a plan of action to get those babies, if they are yours, taken care of." Dan hugged Chris tightly. "We'll get through this, together."

Joshua spoke up. "Okay, Chris, this is not ideal, but we need to get a paternity test done as soon as possible, before you make any financial promises. I'm not an attorney, but I think you need to get one, pronto, to protect your interests."

"Yeah, I was just so . . . I don't know . . . so blown away by this whole thing. I just assumed that any woman willing to sleep with a stranger would have taken care of . . . things. I don't remember even asking her about birth control. I really don't remember her at all." Christopher blushed deeply at having to admit this to his family. At the same time, he thanked God for them.

Brooke came over and hugged him, as well. He didn't remember her ever doing that as a child. Of course, he was a real knucklehead when he was a kid. Shoot, he was a knucklehead as an adult. A few months ago, nonetheless. He had thought Brooke was his enemy. Now he saw her as a dear friend.

"Chris, Michael and I are here for you. You know that, right?" Brooke held him; he returned the hug. Michael and Joshua joined in the group hug.

"Yes, thanks Sis. I do know that." Christopher held her tightly and kissed the top of her head. They all sat back down so they could come up with a game plan.

Michael asked Christopher, "Are you going to ask for partial custody? I know it's kind of soon, but if you are paying for their support you ought to be able to see them, to have some influence in their lives."

"I hadn't thought about that yet, but yeah, I guess so. Something that's really bothering me is- what do I tell Audrey? She's very special to me. This might be a surprise, but I was hoping to marry her someday. This puts a real cloud over that. I mean, here I am with two kids and all. What will she say?'

Susan said, "Honey, it's not a surprise to me. I know you care for her. She cares for you, as well. We have had some chats, Audrey and I."

"You have? When?"

"We talk at church sometimes. I've called her when I thought she might be interested in an event I have heard about, that kind of thing. She's a very special lady." Susan smiled.

"But, what should I tell her?" Christopher was beside himself with worry over the loss of that budding relationship.

Joshua said, "Look, we're putting the cart before the horse here. Let's contact this attorney- what's his name?"

"Darren Smyth."

Joshua said, "Okay, here's the plan. You get an attorney, to find out what your rights are. You and I go to see this Mr. Smyth and see what he has planned. You'll need to take the paternity test. Keep in mind that you might not be the father. When we get things worked out a bit more, you tell Audrey."

Christopher let a deep breath out of his lungs. "You'll go with me, Josh? Thanks so much."

"No problem, brother. You're not in this alone," Joshua

told him.

"I really appreciate this, Josh. You'll never know what this means to me." Christopher put his head in his hands and then looked up at the group. "It would be a relief if I'm not related to these kids. I don't know what kind of father I would make. And who is this Shannon Thompson anyway? I didn't know her last name until about an hour ago." Christopher realized what he had just said. "Mom, I'm sorry. I'm ashamed that I had sex with someone whose last name I didn't even know." He turned to them all. "It wasn't the first time I did that, either. I was pretty messed up there, for a long while." He took a deep breath. "Okay, so nobody says anything to Audrey until we know more, right?"

They all agreed and hugged him good night a little while later, promising to stay actively involved in his catastrophe. They hadn't worked out exactly what to tell Audrey anyway, so they decided that telling her nothing until they had news was probably the best course of action.

The test was taken. Two business days later, he got the results, which were positive. Christopher was the father of identical twin girls that he hadn't even known were expected, having impregnated a woman he'd only been with once.

Christopher made an appointment with a civilian attorney, Nathan Alexander, to go with him to see Mr. Smyth. It wouldn't do to involve the military because the events might end up destroying his career. Joshua went along, just as he had said he would, for moral support. They went into the downtown Annapolis office building, which was an older home converted into office space. It was within the line of sight of Church Circle. The irony was not lost on him.

Once they were seated in the attorney's office, Mr. Smyth began, "Gentlemen, thank you for coming today. I understand that you had the DNA testing done, and that it confirms your fatherhood, Commander Prescott."

Christopher said, "Yes, Mr. Smyth, that's correct, on both counts. Please understand that I was completely unaware

261

of Ms. Thompson's pregnancy until I received your letter."

"Yes, we both know that."

Mr. Alexander spoke up. "Mr. Smyth, we're prepared to make Ms. Thompson an offer of child support, but we would like to see both Ms. Thompson and the girls before those arrangements are finalized. We also wish to have joint custody so that Commander Prescott can have an active role in the upbringing of his daughters."

Mr. Smyth said, "We hadn't planned on a single man wanting joint custody of two infants he has never met by a woman he only knew for one night."

"Nevertheless, my client wishes to be involved with his children by Ms. Thompson."

Mr. Smyth said, "I'll convey those wishes to my client and get back to you. Do you have a proposal for the financial considerations?"

Mr. Alexander said, "We do." He pushed a small stack of papers across the desk at Mr. Smyth. "Please note that our offer clearly states that it's based on Commander Prescott sharing custody with Ms. Thompson, effective on the date of his first payment of monthly support."

"I'll discuss your offer with Ms. Thompson and will be in touch."

Christopher said, "Thank you, Mr. Smyth. I look forward to meeting my children and hope that this can be arranged without delay. Oh, Mr. Smyth, one more thing."

"Yes, Commander Prescott?"

"What are my children's names?" Christopher thought he should know that, in the very least.

"Ms. Thompson named the girls Melanie Grace Thompson and Molly Joy Thompson."

"Thank you. Those names are quite nice."

"You're welcome, Commander Prescott. Good day, gentlemen." Mr. Smyth seemed eager to get them out of his office.

As they walked down the sidewalk, Joshua asked Mr.

Alexander how he thought things had gone.

"As well as could be expected. Mr. Smyth didn't realize that your brother would wish to be involved with the children, Dr. Prescott, so he has to go back to Ms. Thompson and tell her that she has to be open to his involvement if she wants any cash."

Christopher said, "Good question, Josh." To Mr. Alexander: "Is that really such a surprise?"

Mr. Alexander said, "Please understand that she told her attorney you never saw each other after that night. She suddenly reappears with not one but two children, and you say you want to know them. She probably thinks of you as nothing more than a sperm donor who she might be able to get some cash out of. She may be an opportunist, but we really don't know her. We'll just have to wait and see."

They didn't have to wait long. The next day, Mr. Smyth called to say that his client was refusing to let her girls be taken care of, even part time, by a womanizer. They would see him in court.

Christopher's attorney told him that they were probably hoping to scare him away from the joint custody idea. Mr. Alexander said that, in the state of Maryland, the courts were happy to see fathers who wanted to be involved in the lives of their children, and that Ms. Thompson would really not have a choice in the matter, all things considered. To court they would go.

Chapter 31

The legal issues became an ongoing nightmare for Christopher. He was running up quite a bit of expense with Mr. Alexander, even before he paid a dime to Shannon Thompson. Shannon finally agreed to meet with a Master of the Court, rather than take the case before a judge. By this time, Christopher hadn't seen her in almost a year.

Christopher and Mr. Alexander walked down the hallway of the Anne Arundel County courthouse, headed towards the appointed room. There was a young, attractive brunette sitting on a nearby bench. Christopher didn't recognize her, but she spoke up at once.

"Hello, Christopher." Shannon didn't smile or even attempt to do so.

"Hello, Shannon." He didn't smile at her, either.

"At least you have my name right now."

Mr. Alexander spoke up, putting a hand on his arm. "Commander Prescott, I have to advise you not to speak to Ms. Thompson without the presence of her attorney."

"Yes, Mr. Alexander, I understand." To Shannon: "If you will excuse me for the moment." Christopher nodded and moved to the other side of the hall.

While they waited for Mr. Smyth, Christopher looked at Shannon while pretending not to do so. Not bad, but his standards were higher since he met Audrey. Shannon was obviously still recovering from the childbirth and had a few extra pounds to shed. He knew from talking to Dan's daughter-in-law, Lauren, that a twin pregnancy could be hard on the body, and that the weight was difficult to lose post-partum.

So, doing a quick assessment, she was of average height-probably about 5'6" or so. It was hard to tell because she was seated. A little on the chubby side, but that was probably due to the pregnancy. Shoulder length brown hair, unremarkable. Not ugly, but not as pretty as Audrey. Her eye color was hard to see in the hallway lighting, but he guessed that her eyes were most likely brown.

Shannon's attorney came up, hurrying along the corridor. "So, are we ready? Are you sure that you want to fight for custody, Commander Prescott? We could put an end to the matter right here."

"Mr. Smyth, please do not take advantage of my client's lack of knowledge about the law. I have advised him that joint custody is very much an option, and that the state will be happy to see his involvement with the girls." To Chris, Mr. Alexander said under his breath, "He's bluffing."

Christopher nodded and spoke quietly, "I know it. I've been googling about this quite a bit." To Mr. Smyth: "Thank you for your concern, but it's been my plan since I learned about Melanie and Molly to be an active part of their lives."

The Master of the Court was ready for them. Christopher proved that his mother and sister would help care for the girls, and that they would train him in basic childcare. As the youngest son in his family, he had had no opportunity to learn how to care for children, particularly since he had been in California for the early years of Joshua and Amanda's children's lives. Christopher would prepare a nursery. Plans were already underway. And he would convert one of his bedrooms into a room for the girls. When they got older, there were enough bedrooms that each girl could have her own.

At the end of the hearing, the Master determined that Christopher had the right to see and care for his daughters, especially since Shannon expected him to support them. Christopher was willing to do so, and the case was settled. He would have limited visitation until the girls reached six months of age, due to Shannon's breastfeeding, but after that he would have them every other weekend and two days a week. He wouldn't need to pay as much child support this way, very little actually compared to a non-custodial father, because he would be responsible for their care and feeding while they were with him. The Master would reconvene the hearing at that time to determine a satisfactory amount that he would need to pay.

Shannon would bring the girls to his house that weekend, so he could meet them for the first time. Christopher left the courthouse and hurried to Susan and Dan's home to tell them the news that everyone had gathered to hear. They'd been praying for him all afternoon. What he didn't know until he got there was that they were so sure the Master would find in his favor, that they were throwing a baby shower for him.

Christopher pulled up in the driveway and saw a lot of cars, a lot more than just the family vehicles. What gives? He walked in through the kitchen door, as was his custom, then on into the family room.

"Surprise!" There were about fifty people standing there, with huge grins on their faces.

"What in the world? What's going on here?" He was in shock. Pink balloons and pink crepe paper? What was this?

Susan came up and gave him a hug. "Chris, you're going to need everything for the girls, so we decided to help you out a bit. Welcome to your baby shower!"

"What? I . . . I don't know what to say. I've never been to a baby shower before." He looked over at his grinning brother. "Josh, what happens here? What do you say at these things?"

Joshua laughed and said, "You'd better let Mom or Amanda tell you about it. I was at her showers but headed out with the guys pretty fast. Since this is your shower, you're stuck."

Amanda hugged Chris. "Okay, here's the scoop. We're skipping all of the sweet little games we usually play. We'll eat and then you can open all the gifts that folks brought. You can see that the Sunday school class wanted to be involved, so they came along."

Sunday school class? Audrey was in his Sunday school class. Was she here? He scanned the room, looking for her. Yep. There she was, standing by the piano, trying to look unobtrusive. Christopher swallowed. Hard.

Dan said, "Let me pray and then we can all grab a bit to eat before Chris opens the gifts." He bowed his head and others did the same. "Let's pray. Father in heaven, we thank you for this time of fellowship. Lord, we know that Chris didn't expect to be in this situation, and that he lived differently before he came to know You. We pray that You will guide and direct his path and make him into the father You want him to be. We rejoice in the lives of Melanie Grace and Molly Joy, and pray that You will make them into the women You would have them become. May they get saved at a young age and go on to live lives that glorify You. And now bless this food to our bodies. In Jesus' name. Amen."

Christopher felt as if he were in a tunnel and that Audrey was the bright light at the end of it. Time slowed down and the room seemed to collapse in on itself. He was vaguely conscious of asking the others to go ahead and eat. He would join them in a minute. The noise of their laughter and conversation as they headed into the dining room reached his ears, but did not penetrate them. He walked slowly across the room. There she was, in all of her beauty. "Audrey, can we talk?"

Audrey said, "Sure, Chris."

"I was going to tell you about all this, once I had a few things figured out for myself. This has been a huge shock to me. How did you find out?" Christopher stumbled over his words, but they had to be said.

Audrey said, "I noticed your mom looking a bit strained recently. I talked to her a few days ago and asked her what was wrong. She wasn't immediately forthcoming, but I'd heard a few rumors about a difficult situation she was facing and finally got her to tell me about it. We've become good friends since Vacation Bible School last summer. We talk several times a month, and I can tell when she's distracted. She clearly had something going on. I accidentally walked into a conversation she was having with Nancy Ferguson and overheard what the problem was. Susan and I talked about it later, but I asked her not to tell you that I knew. At least, not then."

"Audrey, this relationship with Shannon wasn't serious. I'm not proud of what I did, but it happened. I'm a different man than I was a year ago."

"I know, Chris. I really respect your decision to be involved with your girls and not just turn your back on them. That's why I'm here today, and why I brought you a very nice gift." Audrey smiled. "This isn't an ideal situation, but I'll be praying for you every step along the way. This is probably the Reader's Digest Condensed Version of the conversation we need to have about this, but I don't think we should take any more time from your guests."

Christopher smiled back at her. "Can I give you a hug?"

She smiled at Christopher. "Sure."

He hugged her and said, "Thank you, Audrey. Your support means more to me than I can say." He didn't want to let go, but knew he had to. They walked into the dining room and joined the festivities.

That afternoon, Christopher got deluged with gifts. His mother and Dan had purchased two matching white cribs and a couple of dressers. Joshua, Amanda, and the kids had gotten him a rocking chair. Brooke and Michael gifted him with a changing table. That was great because he didn't have a clue about what he would need once he got to keep the girls with him. The other guests had purchased matching clothing. He got duplicates of onesies, dresses, pants, and shirts. The Fergusons brought him two smocked dresses for the girls' dedication ceremony. He felt helpless, not knowing what he was supposed to do with all these things. Audrey stayed by his side to explain, having been an eldest child. Christopher was greatly relieved by her presence.

As the guests made their departures later, Susan said, "Just leave everything here until the girls' room is painted. We'll come over for a painting party this week."

"Yeah, right." Turning to Audrey, "What color should we paint the nursery? Any ideas?"

Audrey laughed, seemingly surprised by his sudden helplessness. "Sure, Chris. I suggest pale pink with white trim- they are girls, you know."

"Yes, of course." Christopher laughed at his own bungling. Audrey seemed eager to help. "Thanks so much,

Audrey. I don't know what I'd do without you."

As Joshua and Amanda came up to say goodbye, Audrey told him, "I have some news, Chris. I have been given PCS to Annapolis."

Christopher couldn't believe his ears! He wrapped her in a bear hug, and then backed off, not wanting to embarrass her. "What great news, Audrey." He beamed at the news. Praise the Lord! Christopher laughed out loud, unable to restrain his joy.

Joshua asked, "Forgive my ignorance, Audrey, but what does PCS mean? Given Chris' response, I'm guessing it's a good thing."

Audrey said, smiling, "Yes, it's good, if I want to stay in Annapolis." She looked at Chris with a coy expression. "Which I do."

Christopher told Joshua, "Sorry for the jargon, brother. It means 'permanent change of station' – Audrey is permanently assigned to the Naval Academy." He looked at her with all the warmth in his heart. "That means she's not going back to Norfolk." He couldn't stop himself from embracing her in a giant bear hug again.

Audrey hugged him back but then withdrew and said, "Baby steps, Chris. Baby steps." She kissed her fingers and then turned to leave. "See ya."

"Hey, Audrey. You wanna go look at some paint colors after work tomorrow?" He was taking a chance, he knew it, but it felt like the next step.

Audrey glanced back towards him. "Sure, Chris. Why not?" She hesitated, and then turned completely around to face him. She smiled. "Is dinner included in that offer?"

"Absolutely!" Grand slam home run, hit out of the ball

park! He couldn't believe this was happening! Yes!

"Okay then. See you tomorrow. Night."

"Night."

Chapter 32

On Tuesday, Christopher had gone to the Home Depot with Audrey and picked out some great pale pink paint and a can of white trim paint, after which they had eaten dinner at Chevy's Tex-Mex and had chatted for hours. He didn't try to kiss her as he dropped her off at her car back at the Naval Academy. He was willing to wait for her to be ready, and he sensed that the time had not yet come.

Wednesday after work, Christopher met Susan and Dan at his house. The couple had spent the day priming and sanding the nursery, so they could all paint it that night. Joshua and Amanda brought over some sodas and Brooke and Michael stopped by with pizza so they could have a time of fellowship. Christopher was so grateful for his family. He couldn't spend enough time with them.

On Thursday, the men of the family had hauled in the nursery furniture and set it up, under the ladies' direction. The baby clothes had been prewashed by his mom, and folded to be placed in the dressers or hung up in the girls' closet. The room looked ready for its two new occupants.

Before heading out to pick up their kids at choir practice, Joshua and Amanda used a doll to show him how to feed, diaper, and bathe a baby.

Joshua said, "Of course, Chris, you need to keep in mind that the baby will be squirming all over the place, possibly yelling at the top of her lungs, and she may pee while you are in the midst of a diaper change."

Amanda added, "Be glad that your first babies aren't

272

boys. They spray."

Christopher wouldn't be taking care of the girls overnight until they were weaned, but he still had to demonstrate his ability to care for the girls to Shannon. Since she wasn't exactly his biggest fan, that audience would be hard to convince. With God's help, he knew he would manage.

So, here he was. Saturday morning. The weekend had finally come. His mom and Dan would be there when Shannon arrived. The rest of the family and the Fergusons would stop by about lunch time, bringing food, having the desire to meet the girls. Okay, breathe, Chris. He paced the floor. Casual pants, V-necked sweater over a Nordstrom dress T-shirt, loafers. He looked good, but not over-dressed.

He'd paid the housekeeper Mrs. Jennings extra to make the house particularly clean that week. She always did a nice job, but this time the place had to sparkle. All of the spring cleaning chores had been moved to the last couple of days. He didn't need to do anything to the lawn, with it being the beginning of winter, but he'd gone out and checked the outside carefully each morning before work. Spotless.

What time is it? Okay, eight am. Shannon would be here at nine. What did he need to do? Nothing. Should he make some coffee? Nope, not since she's breastfeeding. The caffeine wouldn't be good for the girls. Lauren told him all about that. Mommy drinks the caffeine and breastfeeds. She doesn't have a fun afternoon or night due to a fussy baby. Nope. No coffee.

Mom and Dan should get here about eight-thirty. Christopher had picked at his breakfast, too excited or nervous to eat. My daughters are coming soon! More pacing. He couldn't have sat still to read his email, so pacing was a good thing.

The girls were almost a month and a half old, and he had

never met them. He hadn't seen Shannon since the court date. She had refused to send him any pictures. It appeared that she was going to be hostile. Okay, the old me deserved that. I was a jerk. I'm not a jerk now. Hopefully, I can convince her of that.

A car drove up. Mom and Dan! He rushed out to meet them, with hugs for both. They all came in out of the cold morning, and he offered to make them some coffee. No thanks.

Dan said, "Chris, this is pretty exciting, but let's take a few minutes and pray for the situation, okay? Let's ask for the Lord's guidance here."

Christopher said, "Dan, that's a great idea." He felt calmer after Dan finished. He still paced, mind you, but he felt some inner peace. Mom and Dan sat perched on the couch, also excited, but seeming to be more concerned for him than for the fact that they were going to meet his daughters. Yep, that's pretty typical of Mom. How come I never realized . . . what's that? A car?! He glanced at his watch. Yep, nine o'clock on the dot.

Christopher went outside to greet Shannon and the girls. As he helped her carry the car seats and diaper bag inside, he tried to make small talk with a woman who had no desire to talk to him. They walked into the living room, where Susan and Dan were waiting.

"Shannon, I'd like you to meet my mother Susan and my step-father Dan."

"Shannon, welcome. It's nice to meet you." Susan smiled. She held out her hand, which Shannon took cautiously.

Dan spoke up, "Shannon, it's a pleasure to finally meet you and the girls." He extended his hand, and got a quick touch from Shannon.

"Thank you. It's nice to meet you." To Christopher, she

said, "The Master of the Court says I don't have to leave, so I plan on staying for this whole visit."

"Yes, that's fine, Shannon. How about if I hold the girls for a few minutes, to get to know them a little and then we can show you the nursery?" Christopher was trying to not irritate her any more than necessary. We have to spend the next eighteen years or so in close proximity, so we'd better get off on the right foot. He forced a smile in her direction.

"Oh, yes, that will be fine." Shannon scowled. It didn't seem fine to Chris.

Christopher took the girls up in his arms one at a time, under the close supervision of both his mother and Shannon. He felt like he was getting the hang of things pretty fast. What beautiful children! If only they were his and Audrey's. Later, Shannon approved of the nursery, which was a step in the right direction, though she did complain that it smelled of paint.

"Yes, we just finished painting it this week. I don't plan on having the girls in there on this visit, in case they might have problems with the fumes."

"Oh, I see." Shannon looked at him with a deadpan expression on her face.

Christopher gave her a tour of the house, so she could see how they had worked to baby-proof it.

"When the girls are old enough, I plan on getting them a swing set and I'll put up some fencing in the back yard." He smiled again, hoping to thaw her out a bit.

"Swing sets can be dangerous, you know." He still got no smile from Shannon, though she did step forward to see out into the backyard better.

"Yes, but that'll be several years from now. How about if we pick it out together, so we can make sure you're satisfied that it's safe?"

Shannon agreed, though she was still hostile. Man, what would thaw her dislike? I mean, she doesn't even know me.

Christopher was glad that his mom and Dan were there. Shannon seemed a little bit happier about the whole joint custody thing, especially after his mom told Shannon how nice it would be for her to have a break from the 24/7/365 care of the girls.

Susan said, "You know, my dear, you have a huge responsibility for the girls. Let us help you a bit. You're still their mother, obviously, but we're willing to help you shoulder some of the burden and give you a break."

Thank God for his mother's warm heart. Shannon suddenly seemed relieved, like a huge weight had been lifted from her life. "Yes, that would be nice."

"You're a new mother, dear. Would you like to rest in the spare room until lunch? We'll keep an eye on the girls, if you'd like to nap for a little while."

"That would be lovely. Thank you." Shannon followed his mom into the spare room, and was tucked into bed. His mom was an expert tucker-inner.

"Lunch will be at noon. If the girls have a need, we'll come get you, but I'm sure they'll be fine." His mom closed the door behind herself.

"Thanks for thinking of that, Mom. It never occurred to me that she might be tired."

"Honey, I know that look very well, having had it myself many times. Maybe she'll be happier about this whole business of joint custody if she can see that we care for the girls, and for her."

"I was thinking that maybe someone else should always

be here when she comes, so that we can, you know, 'avoid the appearance of evil.'" Maybe it was a bit late for that, given the circumstances of his girls' birth, but Christopher was trying to be a godly man.

Dan said, "Yes, that's very wise, Chris. We don't know Shannon at all and she doesn't know us, either. I think maybe we can set up a schedule so that someone with a background in childcare who's willing to act as a chaperone will be here each time she visits."

"Great ideas, guys. Now let's go play with the girls!" His mom smiled her most grandmotherly smile. "Got your cameras ready?"

Chapter 33

Susan knew she needed to buckle down and get Kurt's journals finished. The rest of the family was waiting for them since they agreed that everyone would read them, provided she was comfortable with their doing so. She wouldn't have complete closure without knowing the rest of his thoughts, no matter how hurtful they might be to her. She told Dan her plans for that January morning and took a cup of tea into their family room, where Dan had started a fire in the fireplace.

The journal she picked up covered the topic of Kelsey, how he met her, and how their affair began. Like he had told Susan that cold winter night, they met on a flight. He admitted to hanging around outside the cockpit after the flight from BWI landed at the Albuquerque International Airport, wondering what 'talent' was on board. The answer, of course, was the beautiful Kelsey. Mid-to-late 30s he correctly guessed, stunning brunette, gorgeous body. She was striking and, since he was frequently mistaken for a Richard Gere lookalike, they would make a handsome couple.

Kurt was going to be there for a day or so. Kelsey was there to visit friends and see the Albuquerque Balloon Festival. The friends were blown off easily; Kurt and Kelsey went out to dinner at Ruth's Chris Steakhouse and to the festival that night. By the next evening, his wedding vows had been forgotten, and Kurt was Kelsey's married lover.

The journal detailed their trail of rendezvous all over the country. When he had the chance to fly to the Bahamas, he took it and made a vacation of it with Kelsey. He chuckled at Susan's naiveté in believing all of his tall tales. He got into the habit of locking himself into his study when he was at home so that he could spend hours online with Kelsey. He talked to himself in the journal about how he hid money from Susan, saying that she was so dense that she would never notice. He wrote about impregnating Kelsey and being present for Cassie's birth. He was still young and able to father children while his "old, worn out wife was well beyond her years of fertility," he wrote. Susan reflected. Thanks, Kurt. You really know how to make a woman feel elderly. Do you really think that having a younger woman by your side is your key to the fountain of youth? Forget it, buddy, you looked pretty worn out yourself. Having little kids is wonderful, but only for the young who can keep up with them. I wondered why you looked so tired all the time. You couldn't keep up with a young mistress, and you crashed when you got home.

That journal ended. One to go. It was the last one Kurt had written before . . . it happened.

Susan shut the journal, and went for a short walk with Dan. He offered to take her shopping, calling it "retail therapy," but she couldn't think of anything she wanted to buy. She was heartbroken all over again, but she needed to get through this trial so that she could better understand the man she had called her husband for thirty-five years. It wasn't easy. The winter weather drove them inside after thirty minutes or so, where they made a pot of tea and had their lunch before they headed into the family room.

"You know, Dan, I thought I knew him, for better or for worse, but these journals are showing me a brand new side of him that I didn't even imagine. How could someone . . . disguise, for lack of a better word, himself so completely? I just don't understand."

"Suzy-Q, you don't understand because you don't think that way, and you aren't that kind of person. Kurt was difficult, as we all know, but he also had a personality that lent itself to . . . unkindness." Dan leaned across the couch and took her hand to kiss it. "My dearest love, you simply are not wired to think in those terms. For that, I adore you." Another kiss was planted firmly on her hand.

"Thanks, Dan." She shrugged, preparing herself for what was ahead. "Okay, I need to just get this done. Will you sit with me for a while?"

"Yes, I'll sit here all afternoon, if need be. But, yes, let's just have you finish this unpleasantness so you can move on." Dan gave her a quick hug, and then scooted over on the couch a little so that she could have as much privacy as she wished. He picked up a book.

Susan opened the final testimony to Kurt's life. It was less pleasant than she had hoped. He described his wedding to Kelsey on the beach in Hawaii. Their honeymoon was glorious. Kelsey had told him she was expecting again as they prepared to go back home. He was so overjoyed that they almost missed their flight due to their...celebration of the news. Susan skipped some of the particulars.

Kurt detailed the accident she and Kurt had experienced, much of which she had never known simply because of her injuries and hospitalization. And, of course, her six-month coma had kept her out of the loop. Susan learned that he had deliberately placed her in harm's way, so that he could be rid of her without the expense and hassles of a divorce. He had not been looking forward to spending time with her during the vacation he had planned. Having an accident wrecked the car, but it was a faster way of eliminating her. He was happy that the cost of the vacation had been spared, even though the Grand Canyon was a good place to dispose of an unwanted wife, he wrote. When the accident happened in Maryland instead, Kurt had tried to take Susan's life using a shard of glass from their broken windshield, but he had been unsuccessful thanks to the timely intervention of the trucker who hit them. Kurt listed the money he and Kelsey had taken from Susan during the coma. Joint assets became his alone, and then shared with Kelsey. Susan was shocked that he would confess so much. . . mischief, for lack of a better word. That didn't seem like a good idea to her. Pretty bad idea, actually.

Kurt hadn't mentioned his family in a while by then, but wrote about his thankfulness towards his brother Johnny for teaching him how to put himself first. Kurt digressed into talking about his father briefly, wondering if the old man had had as many smarts towards women as he had. As he wrote, Kurt moved towards that of a childlike personality. "If Mommy hadn't died, would he have bankrupted her? What would have happened to her mind if she hadn't died that night? Would she have been a vegetable? Would he have been stuck with her, like I'm stuck with Sue?"

Somehow, his writing those questions seemed to knock some of the bravado out of him. Kurt became like a little boy again, changing his tone completely for the rest of the entry. "Mommy, why did you leave me? Who was that person who threw you to the ground? Why did Daddy stop me? Why did he make me go inside and then grab me out of bed when I did what he told me to? Mommy, what happened to Ella? Why didn't you look for her? Why did you act like you didn't care? I cared enough for both of us. Where is my sister?"

Kurt's handwriting got worse as the journal entry went on. He had written in ink that had become smeared. Susan couldn't make it out. Had he been drinking or crying or had he spilled something on the book? She couldn't read any of the writing for a couple of pages. Then, "Daddy, I've grown up to be just like you. I hope you're happy. Just get rid of someone you don't want any more, is that it? Is it?" Kurt caught himself, matured instantly on paper, and began writing as an adult male who was forced to be married to a woman he didn't love anymore. Susan hesitated, wondering if Kurt had multiple personalities. It sure looked like it, there in the journal, anyway. Wouldn't that be strange? She continued reading, fascinated by this new idea.

Kurt wrote about his anger at not getting rid of his wife at the accident scene. He was mad about Sue's recovery and wrote about his plan to take her to Lookout Mountain in Vancouver. It was true confession time. He detailed how he would get her out of the rehab center, spirit her out of the country with Kelsey's help, and then end her life. He seemed to brag about his ability to carry everything out. Almost everything had gone his way and would continue to go his way. He talked about having Jada, the CNA, in his total control. He paid her to help him, and he knew she would comply with his every wish. He was completely convinced that everything would play out to his advantage and to his wife's detriment. Kurt started a written countdown to what he hoped was Susan's final end.

Susan wondered about several things. Wasn't he worried that someone would find his journals and blackmail him? How could he have been so confident that he would take the chance of documenting everything? Either he was overly self-confident or more than a little nuts. Maybe something had jogged his brain loose. It sure wasn't rational to make such a confession of past sins and future plans where anyone who picked up the journal could read it. What was he thinking? Of course, it could have just been the force of habit from his childhood. He was, of course, a man of strict routines. Maybe this was just part of that, like a huge OCD issue or something. That would explain a lot. He was stuck into writing about everything. It was a cycle he couldn't escape from; a choice to stop wasn't in his power to make. Journaling was his life. There, that thought made sense, and Susan felt a little better. She shook off her bothersome thoughts and kept reading.

The journal finally stopped, dead ended on the day of his kidnapping of Susan from the rehab center. The entries were thankfully over. A tortured man had written about his horrid childhood, his childhood desertion by everyone he loved, the kidnapping of his beloved sister, the mysterious death of his drunken mother, the agonizing passing of his alcoholic father, his troubled marriage to Susan, and then his lustful affair with a woman almost thirty years his junior. Kurt had never returned to the house in Annapolis to write more, having been slammed into by an eighteen-wheeler that took the lives of himself, his mistress, and their two daughters.

The saddest thing of all to Susan was Kurt's lack of a relationship with God. The time he spent in Viet Nam with his friend Joe Barham was the closest he'd ever been to a man of God. Except for Joe, Kurt hadn't written about a single positive male influence that had turned out well.

Susan shut the final journal and turned to Dan. "I can't tell you how sad this has made me. If Kurt had been given the gift of one godly man who didn't go away or die, it might have made so much difference in how he saw life."

"Susan, you are the only person I know who could be almost killed three times by her husband and end up feeling sorry for him."

Susan smiled. "Yes, that's a good point, Dan, but Kurt's life was pretty pitiful. He had it very rough for so many years. He couldn't depend on anyone."

"He could have depended on you. It was his choice not to."

"Yes, but . . ."

"No, 'yes, buts' Susan. We all have choices to make." Dan took her hand. "Yes, Kurt had it incredibly rough as a little kid, but he still chose to make the decisions he did. He chose to have an affair with Kelsey. He chose to harm you. You can't be responsible for that." Dan leaned towards her and kissed her cheek. "It's not your fault, my beloved."

"Do you think he became a Christian, Dan? That would be such a comfort to me."

Dan thought for a moment. "I don't honestly know, Suzy-Q. That's between Kurt and God. I know you'd like to think that everything was rosy at the end, but you told me how he glared at you when you went to visit him. That's not usually a sign of salvation."

"The doctors said he was semi-conscious for a few hours before he started bleeding out. Maybe he made a decision then."

"Perhaps. You'll only know one day when you get to heaven." Dan hugged her close.

Chapter 34

Christopher was really pleased with how things were turning out with Audrey, his daughters, and Shannon. Audrey was willing to go out with him now, and she adored his twins. Shannon had finally calmed down a bit about his fathering and actually seemed to be grateful for her twice-monthly breaks. The girls were a solid four months old and so precious to him. He couldn't imagine life without them.

One March weekend when Shannon stopped by with them, she wanted to chat a bit. Brooke and Michael were running late and had texted to say they would arrive shortly. Because of their tardiness, it was the first time since the twins' conception that he had been alone with Shannon. They were in the kitchen, putting the girls' bottles and food in the refrigerator when she approached him with an idea.

"You know, Chris, we didn't get off to a very good start. I was thinking that, maybe, we could . . . start over." Shannon smiled sweetly at him and moved closer, twisting a strand of hair. She had a certain look in her eyes, one that he had seen from women who found him attractive.

Christopher moved back. He wasn't sure exactly where she was going with this, so he decided to ask. "Shannon, what're you saying?"

"Well, there was a little spark between us the night we met or we wouldn't have ended up with the girls. I was thinking that maybe we could spend more time together, in the best interests of the girls and all . . ." She winked and moved closer still as she ran her fingers through her hair. She looked him up and down, seeming to linger just below his beltline.

Awkward! Good night, I gotta get out of here fast. Just then, the doorbell rang. He excused himself and went to answer, glad that his sister and Michael were on the other side of the door as he opened it.

"Boy, am I glad to see you two!" Christopher whispered as he let them in. "She's coming on to me."

Brooke asked, "Who? Audrey?" She looked shocked.

"No. Shannon. I don't know how to get rid of her without making her angry."

Michael said, "Oh, buddy, are you in trouble now."

Brooke said, "We need to make sure that someone is always here before she gets here or things could get malicious if she wants a relationship and he's turning her down. I mean, things could get really nasty!"

Christopher said, "Yeah. I thought we'd already set that up."

Brooke said, "Yes, we did Chris, but if we're ever late again, we need to give the folks or Josh a call, to get them over here before she shows up. Maybe you could stay outside, in full view of the neighborhood, or something."

Michael said, "I'm sorry we're late, Chris. Really sorry. Traffic was horrible and we got a late start."

Just then, Shannon walked into the living room. "Oh, hi, Brooke. Hi, Michael. I didn't know you two were coming today." She looked disappointed at their presence.

"Oh, yes. We're trying to get in some practice before our own family arrives." Brooke tried to smile at her. Christopher thought the smile wasn't very convincing.

Michael said, "Never hurts to practice, you know. So how are things going, Shannon?"

"Okay. I'm back to work now. Got a job at a private school, though not a Christian one, obviously." Shannon snickered at her own joke.

Christopher said, "Oh, that's great news, Shannon. Congratulations. I'm happy for you."

Shannon said, "Yeah, they have an attached daycare center, so the girls are in the same building. I had some training in December and I started work in January."

Christopher said, "Yeah, well thanks for dropping the

girls off, Shannon. I'll have them back to you later this afternoon. Is 3:00 o'clock good?" He started walking Shannon to the door.

Shannon said, "Sure thing, though, if you want to 'do' dinner, you can stay and I'll fix us a little something." She smiled that come-hither smile again.

Christopher said, "Oh, that's very nice of you, Shannon. I'm going to spend time with my folks tonight. But thanks for the offer."

Shannon looked disappointed. "I should've given you more notice. Let me check my calendar, and maybe we can arrange for something later this month. See ya!" She kissed the girls, smiled seductively at him as her eyes looked him up and down again, and left.

Christopher shut the door behind her, and turned to Brooke and Michael. "What am I gonna do now?"

Michael interrupted, "She's got the hots for you, buddy. Watch out!"

Brooke shushed him and asked, "Are you really spending time with the folks tonight?"

"Yes, and with Audrey. We're going over there for dinner and a movie. I couldn't tell Shannon that or she would have been ticked off."

Just then, Melanie began to cry and Molly joined in out of sympathy. The three of them had their hands full for the rest of the morning as the girls alternated between hunger and diaper needs. The trio finally got them settled down for naps after lunch.

"Thank heaven," Brooke said.

"Michael, do you see what you're in for?" Christopher couldn't help but warn his brother-in-law. "They're a great blessing, don't get me wrong, but some days are better than others." They all laughed.

***

Shannon walked out of the house. Well, that didn't go

too badly for a first try. I can wear him down, if that scrawny little Audrey woman doesn't get in the way. Okay, to be fair, she isn't really scrawny. More like perfectly toned. Compared to me, she looks pretty good, but Audrey didn't have twins four months ago. Shannon sucked in her stomach. And Audrey isn't pregnant.

Boy, I'm gonna have to move fast if I want him to think the new baby is his. Why in the world did I ever get involved with a married man? Shoot, Shannon that was one of the dumbest moves in your whole entire life. It was bad enough to get pregnant on the one night stand with Chris, but at least he was single. Is single. Maybe he's not as serious about Audrey as he seems.

Shannon got in the car and drove to the grocery. At least she wouldn't have to bounce two babies while she tried to restock her baby supplies and groceries. Thank heavens for Chris's visitation rights. And his money. She walked into the store and grabbed a buggy.

Okay, time to take stock here. I'm about five weeks along with the baby. Ray says he's not leaving his wife and losing his family in the process, no matter what, so I better "get rid" of our child. How did that happen so fast? One not-particularly-good-looking, middle-aged guy makes eyes at me during my training at the school, and the next thing you know I'm hopping in bed with him when his wife's out of town. Stupid move, Shannon.

I thought if I was breastfeeding I couldn't get pregnant. Of course, my milk didn't really come in well enough to feed two kids, so maybe the formula I gave them messed me up somehow. I can't manage three kids under two by myself. I have to get married if I want to stay sane.

Shannon thought back to the previous day in the teachers' lounge. I can't believe what the other third grade teacher told me. We were just sitting there on that tacky black leather couch, marking up homework and she started talking. The gal said, "Watch out for Raymond Vincent. He tries to bed every new teacher that comes in the door. He says he has an open marriage, on the rare occasion that he admits being married, but I know his wife. Mrs. Vincent is a lovely person who is clueless about her hubby's activities when she goes to take care of her elderly mother every month."

"Oh?" Shannon had showed enough innocent interest to get additional information about Ray from the woman, who was only too happy to oblige.

"Yeah. Mrs. Vincent gives her three sisters a break from their regular care of their mother, so she drives to Philly every third week of the month. While the cat's away, the mouse plays around. A lot."

"How does he do it? I mean, he's not very attractive. Bald, overweight, old guy. You know." Shannon moved closer to her new confidant on the couch, eager to get information, but not wanting to be overheard.

"Well, first thing, he never wears his wedding band. Did you notice that? He doesn't have a tan line where it would be because he and his wife like to garden, and he makes a point of never wearing it outside. Ray takes it off and puts it on his key ring before he gets to school, and he never wears it to bed. Check out his key ring some time. He keeps it there so he can slip it on if his wife shows up at school, which she only does for special programs. When she does come to a program, he keeps away from her as much as possible, so nobody thinks they're connected."

"How do you know all this?" Shannon was stunned that Ray got away with this kind of stuff.

"By observing, talking to the other female teachers, and...three years ago, I was a new teacher here. Look, I'm not proud of what I did, but I did want to warn you.'

Shannon was shocked. This woman, who seemed so put together, had slept with Ray? "How did he get you . . ."

"In bed? Well, the first thing he did was flirt outrageously when taking me on a tour of the school. He's on the school committee, so he has access to every new teacher.

Everything I said was funny and charming, or so he made me feel. He focused his entire attention on me. It was very flattering. I'd just had a bad break up and was depressed about myself. "

Boy, did that sound familiar. "What then?"

"He sent me flowers, two dozen red roses and a note saying how beautiful I was, and how he was looking forward to working with me. He must have the florist on speed dial. Then he started calling me at odd hours, at weird times of day or night. I figured out later that his wife was either in the shower or had run out to the grocery. And then she left town for a week, to visit her mother. He took me out to dinner on the eastern shore where he wouldn't run into anyone he knew, plied me with wine, and took me home. We slept together for the first time that night."

"Oh. I see." Yep, that's the step-by-step process Shannon had experienced with old lover boy. She was dumping out the roses she had dried as soon as she got home. She noticed that the other woman had kept on talking.

"A few months later, I noticed that I only saw him at night on the third week of the month. All the other weeks, I only saw him in the daytime. I asked around, casually, and found out how he operates. I broke up with him right away. We barely speak now."

"I'm glad you told me. Thanks." Shannon didn't know what else to say.

"Shannon, you're a nice lady, so just watch out for Ray, okay? I wouldn't want you to get involved with him, and he will try. Keep in mind that you wouldn't be the first female he's hit on and you won't be the last."

"Thanks for the warning." Shannon closed up her grade book and left the teachers' lounge soon afterwards. As she walked away, she found herself wishing that warning had come about two and a half months earlier. It was too late now. As soon as Ray had found out she was pregnant, he dumped her. No more flowers, phone calls, or long chats in the teachers' lounge. No contact at all. He avoided her in the hallways, and actually turned and headed in the opposite direction when he saw her.

Where was that gal back then? When will I learn to either control myself or get some really good birth control? Shannon shook her head as she picked up a week's supply of diapers. As she headed down the aisle, she almost collided with a grocery cart going perpendicular to her aisle.

"Shannon." The bald-headed man had stopped just in time to avoid a collision.

"Oh, Ray. Hello." She looked at the older woman accompanying him.

"Shannon, I'd like you to meet my wife, Barbara. Barbara, Shannon is one of our new teachers this term. You teach what, Shannon?'

"Third grade, Ray." He knew full well what she taught. Playing dumb for the wife, I guess. "Mrs. Vincent, it's nice to meet you." They shook hands. Mrs. Vincent had a pretty nice diamond ring, for the wife of a school teacher.

"And you, as well. I hope you enjoy the school as much as my Raymond does. He speaks very highly of the faculty there." Mrs. Vincent smiled sweetly.

Shannon nodded and somehow got away from the happy couple. She noticed that Ray put his hand on his wife's back as they continued on their way, massaging her and showing the world that she was his. His wedding ring was in full view, for once. They were the perfect, happy couple with nothing to hide and their love to show. Shannon almost gagged. Or was that just morning sickness? He "speaks very highly of the faculty" because he has bedded so many of us. Shannon growled and finished her shopping without meeting up with them again.

Shannon headed out to the car, rolling her cart like she was mad. Well, she was mad. This just wasn't fair. Guys got to have all the fun while she was stuck with the results. Moments later, she threw up just outside her car. Calm down, Shannon. Breathe. Good thing she'd parked over a parking lot sewer vent.

The vomit went down there, but she still had to step carefully to get into her car.

So, what was there to do? Plan. Think for a minute. Okay, so she had only a few weeks to get Chris away from Audrey and interested in her. She couldn't take her sweet old time or she would be too far along to pretend the kid was his. Hopefully, she could turn on the charm. She didn't see the point of trying to seduce him any time in the immediate future, or he might insist on another paternity test and this one wouldn't rule in her favor. Still, that was going to have to be her end goal if she was to have any chance of getting him. She would worry about proving Chris' paternity later, if it came to that. Hopefully, he would buy what she was saying.

Shannon would start by wearing more sexy clothing when she was around him. Yep, when he brought the girls back, she would wear her low cut T-shirt and bend over a lot . . . to greet the girls, of course. Okay, home to put this stuff away and straighten the house so she looked like the perfect woman: she has gorgeous children, takes good care of her home, and is beautiful herself.

***

What Shannon couldn't realize was that Christopher was making plans of his own. He called the family together, and they agreed to help protect him from Shannon's apparent plan to derail his relationship with Audrey. He figured it might take a couple of months to let her down, gently he hoped, and without her becoming upset.

"Okay, so here's the visitation schedule. Mom and Dad will take the morning shift, and Josh and Amanda will be here with the kids for the pickup shift. Brooke and Michael will come over at random times. I'll spend as much time away from the house as I can, in case she drops by when I don't have visitation. Good thing I'm so active at church these days. I'm not home much in the evenings any more, what with the men's ministry, Bible study, and Sunday and Wednesday night services. Audrey and I have been busy with finishing up with our classes at the Naval Academy, and the extra work we're doing with the midshipmen takes up some time, as well."

Brooke said, "Chris, you can't avoid your own home forever."

"I know, but she really seemed almost desperate this morning, and I just don't want to take the chance of her trying something. I don't know what's going on with her. She hasn't ever come on to me like this, except maybe the one night when the girls were conceived. Back then, I was into women who were so into me. Now I know it's not the life I want anymore."

Michael asked, "What time do you need to take the girls home?"

"I told her I'd bring them back at 3:00 o'clock. Why?" Christopher looks at his watch as he spoke.

"I think we definitely need to have someone go with you. You shouldn't be alone with her." Michael looked very concerned.

"I agree, Chris. I'll go with you," Joshua said. "You can't have her crying 'rape' or anything."

"Do you really think she would?" Christopher was astounded at the thought.

"Brother, you just called her 'desperate.' That's good enough for me." Joshua looked none too pleased.

Amanda said, "Yes, Chris. You actually need protection, funny as that sounds. Guys, I want to check her out for myself. I'll go along."

Three o'clock came along, with Christopher, Joshua, and Amanda walking up the stairs to Shannon's third floor condo. It was a trip made more difficult because they had the girls in their car seats and the diaper bag with them. Christopher didn't know how Shannon did it, but she somehow managed it every time she wanted to leave her condo. No wonder her figure had come back faster than might be expected with a twin pregnancy. She got a workout just leaving home. He greeted Shannon pleasantly, "You remember Joshua and Amanda, don't you?"

Shannon said, "Certainly." She turned to him. "But Chris, I expected to see you alone. I thought you had plans for the evening." Shannon was wearing a low cut black T-shirt and hipster tight jeans. She had reapplied her makeup and shampooed her hair. She looked just this side of a tramp, Christopher decided, when comparing her to Audrey. Shannon couldn't have been more obvious, to his mind.

Shannon bent over to greet the girls, exposing a great deal of breast tissue. Wow, at one time, that might have been effective. Not now. She picked each girl up in turn, lifting the child above her head, and exposing her belly as she made motherly noises in each one's direction. She was so happy to see them. It was a bit much, he told himself.

They left a few minutes later, with Amanda looking like she was ready to burst at the seams. Amanda practically ran down the stairs. They got into Christopher's car, preparing to drive away and head to Susan and Dan's house.

"She's pregnant!" Amanda looked like she was ready to come out of her skin.

"What? It's not mine, you guys." Christopher couldn't say that fast enough.

Joshua said, "Honey, slow down. How do you know that?"

"She has a linea nigra. She didn't have that before, when we first met the girls." Amanda was practically shouting.

Christopher was completely dumbfounded. "What in the world is that?"

Amanda said, "It's that brownish line that sometimes appears on the belly of a pregnant woman. It goes from her navel to her . . . private parts or thereabouts. She has it now, but I know she didn't have it before, because her shirt pulled up when she was breastfeeding the girls at your house that first day. She and I talked about it. I had one with all my kids and she didn't. She has it now. I'm willing to bet that she is expecting, and she's trying to blame it on you."

Joshua said, "Good catch, honey." To Chris, he commented, ""Amanda's exactly right."

"Oh, dear Lord, preserve me." Christopher bowed his head in prayer. He couldn't believe it. What in the world was going to happen next?

Chapter 35

Candace arrived in Maryland, settling in at the Hampton Inn and Suites. She unpacked her belongings for her one-week visit. She'd been invited to stay with Susan and Dan, but she preferred the solitude she was used to at the end of each day. She rented a car, feeling more independent that way. She could come and go as she pleased and visit the sights she loved but had not seen for many years, in between her meetings with her new family. She was a loner and fine with it.

Candace knew that the lovely story of her rise in the world was not the real reason that the Prescott family wanted to meet her. She was certain that Christopher had shared her background with his family as soon as he got back home, and rightfully so. She did not expect anything less.

If they knew about her, then she knew they had found out about Kurt's other siblings. They had probably located the journals that Kurt had been writing since he was a little boy, the journals his coach had encouraged him to write about their horribly dysfunctional family. She had read all of his journals on the sly, from the first one he had written to the journal he had written about Ella, right before she had fled her father's house, once their mother died. She didn't think that Kurt ever suspected that she knew what he was writing, until the very end of their time together. He must have seen that she had torn some pages out of the journal, and realized they were the entries he had written about their mother's death. Still, he hadn't mentioned it to her. Maybe something inside Kurt made him want to know she cared enough to be concerned. Candace would never know for sure. Not now that he was dead.

"Oh, Kurt, you poor, troubled little boy." Candace hadn't meant to speak the words out loud, but was thankful there was no one in her hotel room to hear her pining for her lost brother. "From what I hear, you were pretty messed up as an adult, as a result of our terrible upbringing. Why do you think I never married? I wanted to avoid bringing more pain into the world and destroying the lives of some innocent children. I couldn't get away from what Mom and Dad did to you, to us." She had to stop this verbal reminiscing or someone might overhear and think she was nuts.

Candace thought back to the journal pages she'd lost when her brother John ransacked her house a few years back. He'd gotten in touch with her right before she left for a conference, and had broken into her house while she was out of town. When she returned, she discovered her home office had been burgled. John had gone through her books, apparently believing she had money hidden inside, only to discover the torn journal pages inside an empty book shell. I wonder what he did with them. You could barely read the writing, but it might be enough for John to blackmail Kurt. John had gotten many of her collectibles and taken them to the nearest pawn shop. She estimated their worth at about $20,000. She got a few of them back, but the journal pages were never recovered.

She'd torn the pages out of Kurt's journal, not to be mean, but to protect Kurt from their father and from himself. If someone had gotten ahold of them at the time, Kurt's life might have been completely different. She shrugged those feelings off, preferring not to second-guess what his fate might have been.

Candace remembered the days immediately following Ella's kidnapping as if they were yesterday. She and Kurt had gone off to their respective schools after breakfast that morning. It was still summer vacation, but they both had activities to keep them busy during their time off. She was on the swim team and was preparing for the fall swim season of her senior year in high school. Kurt was involved in a reading camp which prepared children for the next grade. They were gone all day, arriving at home in late afternoon. Candace had given him a ride to and from school, as was her habit in the summer.

Kurt had looked for Ella to come running out as she always did, but there was no Ella. Instead, the house was surrounded by police cars, and the neighbors were standing by the side of the road, wringing their hands and whispering to one another.

Kurt jumped out of her car before Candace had even come to a complete stop. He ran inside, calling for his sister. They found their mother, seated at the kitchen table, crying.

Tears streamed down Candace's face even now as she remembered hearing that her sister was missing. The little girl was so special to them all and to Kurt particularly. Candace had turned to see how Kurt was taking the news. He screamed, "No!" and began hitting their mother. Their mother accepted the blows without moving. Mom didn't try to protect herself from his fists. Their mother met Kurt's anger with silence and tears.

Kurt became hysterical. He ran outside, tearing at his clothes and beating himself as he ran screaming. Candace followed him to the creek, where he threw himself on the bank and pummeled the ground until he was too exhausted to move. Candace gathered him in her arms and cried with him. It began to rain very hard, as if the world itself was crying with them.

How long had they sat there? An hour? Two hours?

Three? Lightning and thunder crashed about them, and still they sat. Evening came upon them. Candace saw their father stumbling towards them in the twilight.

"Go away! Don't come near us," Candace screamed. She hated the man in that moment.

Her father might have been grieving, that was probably the case now that she thought of it, but the idea of having to be in his drunken presence at such a time gave her unusual boldness in forbidding him to come near. He turned back to the house, brightly lit in the presence of many people.

Candace combed Kurt's hair with her fingers, sodden mess that it was. She made motherly noises to calm him, and his sobs had grown quieter. Her own heart was breaking for that precious little girl Ella, but even more so for the grief-stricken little boy who could not be comforted. She kissed his forehead as the rain finally petered out. She held him closely as he fell into the exhausted sleep of the bereaved. She picked him up and took him into the house, slipping in the sodden grass. She passed through the white picket fence gate, which her father had left open in his trek back to the house. She carried him on, finding strength she hadn't known she possessed.

Candace entered the house and walked in silence through the kitchen, dining, and living rooms filled with neighbors. They moved aside to let her pass with her human burden. They could not begin to know how she felt in those moments. She could not trust herself to speak.

Wordlessly, she climbed the stairs to his room, and got Kurt ready for bed. He barely acknowledged her presence. It was as if he had fallen into a coma and could not be roused. She changed her rain-soaked clothing, and then brought a blanket and pillow into his room, to be ready if he should call out. The din of voices downstairs finally ended, as people left the house. She laid down to unpleasant dreams.

Kurt had a fitful night, crying out for Ella. Candace hadn't slept well either, wondering where Ella was and what was happening to her. How could God, if there was a God, have let this happen to their precious sister? Candace awoke with the morning light, stiff from a night on the floor. At some point in time, Kurt had snuggled up with her.

They headed downstairs together, finding their mother asleep over the kitchen table, their father passed out on the living room sofa, a bottle of whiskey next to him. Typical. Peter had come home at some point in time, though Candace did not remember seeing him come into their house of anguish. Peter was sitting on a chair in the living room, staring blankly into the fireplace.

Peter looked up at them and asked, "Where's our sister?" It was all he could say before bursting out in tears again.

Candace could only shake her head. The lump in her throat prevented any words. Kurt threw himself on the threadbare couch and began to sob once more.

One of the neighbors knocked on the door. Mrs. Whatshername who owned the big black dog was standing there, a breakfast casserole in her hands. "You have to keep your strength up, for Ella." The woman started to cry as she handed the dish over to Candy. "Such a precious child. I'm so sorry." The woman squeezed Candace's arm.

Candace thanked the woman and then closed the door. She carried the foodstuff offering into the kitchen, dropping it hard upon the table, near her now-conscious mother. "For us."

Her mother spoke, barely audible. "We have to go to the police station this morning. I need to make a statement, they said."

Kurt entered the kitchen just as their mother spoke. He moved menacingly towards the woman who had given birth to him. Candace grabbed Kurt before he could begin pounding their mother with his fists once again.

"What will you say?" Candace held Kurt in her arms as she spoke to the mother she hardly recognized because the woman's face was so swollen from crying.

"I went into a store for a few minutes." Her mother hesitated. "I came out, thinking Ella was asleep in the back seat. I drove home. I left her to sleep while I came inside. When I came back out, she was gone."

"What you mean is that you went into a bar. God knows how long you were there, drinking yourself silly. You came out and did not bother to check on your little girl. You came home to drink some more. You finally missed her, who knows how long you were in here, and then you couldn't find her. You screamed bloody murder and here we are." Candace had never spoken to her mother like that, confronting her with her drinking, but there it was. Good thing Dad was still passed out, or he would have beaten her for being insolent. He did not tolerate that kind of talk, no matter how accurate.

"I suppose so." Her mother slumped over the table again. "My little Ella. Where are you?" The tears started up again. She howled, bereft beyond belief.

"Spare me." Candace slopped some of the casserole into bowls and shoved one towards her mother. "Eat this. Then go take a shower and fix yourself up. I will take you to the police station where you will make your pathetic statement." Candace shoveled some of the food into her own mouth after making sure Kurt ate a little. She turned to him again, noticing that he

301

had eaten hardly anything. "Kurt, honey, we need to be strong for Ella. Eat something, and then we will go see if the police have found her yet." Candace turned back at her mother, scowling. "You make me ill."

Peter came into the kitchen. "I'm going to go look for her."

Their mother spoke up. "They said something about a search party. I didn't get it all."

Candace spoke to her mother. "No, you were too drunk." Candace turned to Peter. "I understand. Eat a little something, Peter, and you can ride down to the station with us, if you want."

"I don't want. I'll take my own car. See you around." Peter left the house, slamming the front door, and screeching his tires as he left the driveway.

They went to the station later, as promised, where her mother made her statement. Mary went on television, begging for the life of her daughter. It was to no avail.

Days folded into more days. Searches went on and then finally stopped. No trace of the child had been found. No witnesses could remember seeing Ella taken out of the car, though several people stated that they remembered Mrs. Prescott drinking at the saloon. No one saw her check the backseat before driving away. It was impossible to say where Ella had been taken, at the saloon or at home in her own driveway. There were no suspects.

The family closed in upon its unhappy self. The neighbors whispered behind their hands whenever Mr. and Mrs. Prescott, Peter, Candace, or Kurt stepped outside. The family avoided going out as much as possible, running to the car whenever it was absolutely necessary to go somewhere. Their father went to work and then came home. Their mother went to the store and on errands, returning to her nest as quickly as possible. The drinking reached new heights, as the couple dealt with a disappearance that was their own fault.

Peter's search had been as futile as the police's attempts to find Ella. When Peter couldn't take the pressure of the home, he moved out. They never saw him again.

Candace worked to get Kurt ready for the new school year. Their mother was totally worthless, as she spent her days nursing yet another drink. Candace didn't know how Kurt would cope with school, but she bullied her mother into giving her enough money for some new clothes for him. Candace saw his anger whenever he went outside, throwing rocks into the creek behind their house and pelting small animals with stones. Candace grieved as well, for her brother, her sister, and herself.

Chapter 36

Candace drove over to Susan and Dan's home. It was lovely to meet her extended family. What delightful people they were. They broke bread together, after Dan offered a prayer of thanksgiving to God for bringing them together. Candace didn't believe in God. She hadn't been anything remotely like a Christian since the night Ella disappeared, but if these people found their religion a comfort, that was fine with her. After the meal, they all settled into the family room couches and chairs while the smaller children were occupied outdoors, with Joshua's daughters Madison and Abby keeping a close eye on them.

Candace knew the story she had to tell would not be a fun one, but they wanted to know, so she would tell the whole sad tale. "I think we better start with the disappearance of Ella, since that played into Kurt's story so much." With tears in her eyes, she revealed the past that she remembered as if it had been days ago, not years. She told them about her mother's sojourn into the bar for who knew how long, followed by the drive home. She shared that her mother had driven home and gone into the house, leaving Ella in the car, asleep, or so Mrs. Prescott thought. Candace wept a little at the memory of her mother's discovery of the missing child, and what that night had been like. The days had collapsed into weeks, and the weeks into a single, horrible, tear-drenched month.

Candace continued, "And then came the night when our mother died. It had been one month to the day when Ella disappeared. My parents had been fighting, as always. I could never figure out why they stayed together so long when all they did was fight. Why would anyone want a life like that?"

The family made sympathetic noises, which Candace shrugged off.

"We had just finished dinner. Mom pulled a note out of

her purse. I didn't stop to see what it was. Peter, Kurt, and I went upstairs to our rooms, figuring that the fireworks were going to start as soon as the liquor started flowing more freely." She looked around the room. "It was best to get out of the way before that happened." She thought for a moment. "It had been raining all afternoon, heavy, soaking rain, but it had stopped by the time evening came. My parents' voices were subdued at first, and then escalated into shouts."

Candace's eyes focused on the fireplace, as if it would help her memory. She couldn't bear to look at the sympathetic eyes of this normal family. "I couldn't make out what they said, something about the note. I knew that my mother had been writing to Maggie." She glanced over at Susan. "I assume you know about Sister Margaret Frances?"

Susan nodded. "Yes. We found her before we found you."

"Yes, my sister the nun. Trust me, she was no saint when I knew her!"

Everyone laughed. Candace smiled, and laughed a bit herself. They were all glad to have this small break in the tension that surrounded them, she realized.

Candace resumed her story. "I figured that maybe Dad found out about the letters between Maggie and Mom, but no, this correspondence seemed to be from someone else. Dad was shouting that Mom shouldn't get roped into this . . . whatever this was. Mom insisted that she was going down to the creek, to see what it was all about. So she went. I heard the kitchen door slam and looked out my window. Sure enough, she was headed for the creek."

Christopher asked, "Could you see her very well?"

"Yes and no. The moon was coming out from behind the clouds. It wasn't a full moon, so I could see a little, but not a lot. I knew it was Mom walking out back because I knew her walk. Her right foot had been broken as a teenager and she limped a bit whenever it rained."

Joshua commented, "She was a little young for arthritis, but if she had broken her foot that would've caused a limp that would've been exacerbated by the rain and humidity."

"Yes. I noticed that had been the case for several years. I saw someone come up to her. She didn't appear very happy with him or her. She didn't hug the person or anything, and she didn't seem to know the individual. She stood apart from the person and made no attempt to get closer than, say, five feet."

Dan asked, "What happened then?"

"They talked for a few minutes. Mom seemed to be getting very upset. I'm guessing it was a man because the person was so big and tall. Mom shook the note at the person. He grabbed at it, but I didn't see what happened next because I headed downstairs to go out and help her. I stopped into Kurt's bedroom really quickly on my way past, to check on him. His room was a mess because he'd been fighting with his possessions, as if that would bring Ella back. I quickly straightened things up, so that he wouldn't get into trouble with Dad and then headed downstairs. As I came through the kitchen, my father walked out of his study and gave me a hard time about leaving the house. I told him I thought Mom was in danger, and that I was going down to the creek. I ran out the kitchen door."

"How much time do you think went by between when you looked out the window and when you got to the creek?" Susan was curious.

"Quite a few minutes. Maybe nine or ten. I'd gone into Kurt's room, like I said, and then tried to get past my father. He could be very demanding, and he gave me a hard time about going out."

Brooke asked, "Was Kurt in his room?"

"No. I didn't know where he was, but I assumed he was in the bathroom or with Peter. He wouldn't have gone downstairs. We all tried to avoid the kitchen and living room at night. They were not happy places."

Christopher asked, "Was anyone else out there at the creek?"

"Yes, actually, Peter and Kurt were both there by the

time I arrived. While Dad was giving me grief in the kitchen, I'm guessing they ran outside, probably through the front door. It was a longer trek to the creek if they went that way, but they got there before I did."

"How much longer?" Dan asked.

"Well, they had to go out the front door, circle around the house, and then run to the back of the yard where the creek was. They knew the area well. We had lived there our whole lives. But they couldn't run too fast or they would slip on the grass. The grass was long and it was hard to keep your traction when it'd been soggy out." She stopped to think. "It had been raining a lot over a couple of days. I'm guessing that they got to the creek in, what, five or six minutes? Maybe longer. I wasn't keeping track of them. I just noticed that they were there when I got there."

Brooke asked, "Did they go through the gate?"

"No, they would've gone around it. The yard was set up so that you could avoid going through the fenced in area and get right to the creek, if you came out of the front of the house. That was good because the rain had swollen the latch on the gate, which made it take longer for me to get to the creek. Mom had shut the gate when she went through, to avoid making my Dad angry, most likely. Peter and Kurt would have gone around the fenced-in area, not through the gate like I did."

"Were they breathing hard when you got there?" Joshua asked.

Candace thought for a moment. "Now that you mention it, I think maybe Peter was, but not Kurt."

Joshua said, "If Peter was still breathing fast, he either just got there or his adrenalin was still pumped up. Given the circumstances, that wouldn't be surprising."

Susan said, "That's weird that Peter would be out of breath, but not Kurt. His legs were shorter so I would think it would have been harder for Kurt to run as fast."

Christopher asked, "Is it possible that they might not have run out together? Was there any other way out of the house?" He had drawn a picture of the house set up on the white board, based on what Aunt Candace said, as they talked.

"You know, I never thought about that before until this minute." Candace took the marker from Chris and drew in the details. "Kurt could have come out of his bedroom window. Our bedrooms were on the second floor, but there was a wraparound porch for the whole house. There was a big tree next to the roof of the porch near the front door. The older boys used to climb out and go into town whenever they wanted to get away for a while."

Candace paused as she stood and faced the white board. She walked over to the drawing of the house and pointed some things out to the family. "Oh, my! I just remembered. Kurt's window was open and the screen was missing when I went in to straighten his room." She turned to them and explained. "We always kept the screens in, to avoid the mosquitos. When the older boys returned from their outings, they always had to replace the screens so the folks wouldn't know they'd been gone. I remember now that Kurt's screen was on the porch roof that night. I had to reach out and put it back into the window frame so he wouldn't get into trouble. It was the end of summer and the mosquitos had been really bad. He could've climbed out the window, gone down the tree, and gotten to the creek several minutes before Peter and I got there."

Susan said, "So they might not have gone out together. Kurt might have been there for a while. How did he seem to you? Can you remember?"

"He was upset. He hated Mom after Ella disappeared and never made any secret of it. He was yelling about some man who was with Mom at the creek. I don't know if he thought the man knew where Ella was. Kurt was yelling a lot. He really wasn't making much sense."

"What happened next?" Brooke asked.

"By the time I arrived, the person had left. Peter was standing there, looking shocked. Kurt, like I said, was unhinged.

Our mother had fallen into the creek and was dead."

Susan was amazed. "How could it all have happened so fast? I thought she died from drowning."

Joshua said, "Mom, someone can drown in less than one minute. We need air to live. We don't do so well if we're breathing water!"

Susan said, "Good point, Dr. Josh."

Candace told them, "I think what probably happened was that someone pushed her down and she fell on the rocks, which knocked her out. Somehow, she ended face-down in the creek, where she drowned. The tide was high just then, and the water was rushing by pretty fast. Because she was unconscious, she couldn't pull herself up to get away from it. By the time the boys and I arrived, she was already dead." Candace drew in the details of the creek and rocks on the white board as she spoke.

Dan asked, "But didn't anyone try to pull her out?"

"Yes, we tried. We all tried but, like I said, she was dead. My father came up like a roaring lion. When he figured out she was dead, he put her back into the creek and told us to let the police find her like that or we would all be arrested and thrown in jail. He actually moved her a bit, as I remember, so that the variances in the tide would still keep her face under water. He made us go back into the house. He lectured us on the importance of having the same story to tell the police the next day, and he kept at us until we all said the same thing. He wouldn't let us go to bed until we told exactly the same story."

"And the note?" Amanda asked.

"We got part of it. I took it out of her hand before Dad put her back in the creek. Whoever she met had ripped it out of her hand before he left. I have part of it here." Candace showed them the torn note. Candace had kept the yellowed note in a Ziploc bag for all those years. She handed it over to Susan. The family looked at the note through the baggie.

The note read:

"Mrs. Prescott:

I know about Ella. If you want

Meet me at the creek behind

She is doing"

That was it. The note was torn in a jagged half and the writing was a bit blurry. Most of the message was lost. The only thing they knew was that someone was telling Ella's mother that her daughter was still alive, though that information could have been tainted by the person who had taken the little girl.

At the time of her mother's death, Candace had taken the note inside the house and put it with the journal pages she had taken from Kurt's journal. She had kept them through the years, until John got a hold of her possessions. It seemed that John had not seen the partial note when he took the notebook pages as he ransacked Candace's house. She was glad for that; this little note was all she had left of that night.

"What happened then?" Michael asked.

"Dad called us together for a family meeting. His meetings were always punctuated with lots of liquor. He hounded us until we all told the same story. Mom had apparently gone out to meet someone after we were all in bed. We never saw her again until the next morning when the police arrived." Candace paused. Oh, my! How had she forgotten this detail? She hadn't thought of it in years. "I just remembered. When we came into the house, my father insisted we change our damp clothes, and he put them into the washer while he talked to us. He did a load of laundry, washed and dried it, while he yelled at us and told us what had happened." Her speech slowed as she recalled that night. "I had not remembered that until this very minute."

Susan asked, "But by then it was pretty late, wasn't it? Your mother had gone outside at, what, eight o'clock?"

"Yes. I think it was around eight. Why?"

Susan said, "Because it was probably eight-thirty or

almost nine when you got back inside, is that right?"

'Yes. That sounds reasonable. What are you thinking?" Candace asked.

Brooke joined in, "Did your father ever do the laundry?"

"Never." Candace replied with some annoyance at the memory of her late father.

Amanda asked, "Why would he suddenly do it that night? At that time of night? Wasn't your washer pretty loud?"

'Yes. It was very loud. Nobody could sleep when that thing was turned on," Candace said.

Susan asked, "Where was your laundry room located?"

"Just off the kitchen next to Dad's study. Why do you ask?" Candace wondered.

Susan asked, "Did you ever do the laundry?"

"Yes, I helped my mother on Saturdays and on school holidays. She insisted I learn how to run a household and laundry was part of it." Candace added, "Women's work, you know."

Brooke asked, "How long did it take to do a load?"

"About forty-five minutes to wash and at least forty-five minutes to dry a load, depending on what was in it. If the weather was nice, Mom used to hang the laundry outside to dry," Candace replied.

Amanda said, "But the weather hadn't been nice. And it was night, so no sunshine would have dried the clothes. If you did the laundry at that hour, you would have had to run the dryer."

Joshua asked, "Girls, what are you getting at?"

Susan turned to him. "Mr. Prescott, who never did the laundry, was suddenly doing it the night his wife died. In the late evening. Well after she was dead. The load wouldn't have gotten finished until, what ten o'clock or so? No one could have slept through the washer and dryer noise. The kids should have been in bed by then. Why was a man who never did laundry so eager to do it that night?"

Christopher said, "He was hiding their wet clothes. He

311

couldn't tell the police that they had been inside if the cops found wet clothes in the house when they came over the next day."

Joshua said, "An alibi made complete by totally clean, dry clothes. Makes sense. Aunt Candace, what happened next?"

"We went to bed and tried to sleep, knowing that our mother was outside, dead and wet. The next morning, the police came knocking on our door. The neighbor's dogs had found her when they let their animals outside first thing in the morning." Candace sighed. "It wasn't a night I would chose to relive."

Joshua asked, "What happened after that?"

Candace said, "We told the story that our father told us to tell, that we were a happy family who had spent the evening watching television together. We had all gone to bed, but Mom must have gotten out of bed and gone outside in the night, slipping on the rocks by the creek and falling in."

Brooke asked, "Did the police buy that story? Surely they knew the family history." She hesitated. "No offense."

"None taken. They noised around a bit. It looked like a drunken woman had slipped on the rocks, hit her head, couldn't get out of the water because she was unconscious, and died. Her face had taken quite a beating by morning, what with the creek water banging her into the rocks, so she looked a lot worse by the time the police got to her." Candace hesitated. "They seemed to feel it was pretty cut and dried. The autopsy showed her blood alcohol level was .08. She had been drinking most of the afternoon, if she was staying true to form that day, so there was no argument that she was intoxicated. No charges were pressed and no suspects were ever found."

"And Kurt?" Susan asked.

"He was devastated because he had mistreated our mother so much when Ella disappeared. He had never made up to Mom, no matter what she said. He didn't forgive her, and he wasn't about to let her forget it. He never hugged her from that day forward, and only answered her when our father was around. Dad would have beaten him if he ignored her in his presence, so he did talk to her then. Of course, he couldn't talk to her now that she was gone."

"And then?" Joshua asked.

"We had her funeral three days later. The whole neighborhood showed up . . . family cursed, that kind of talk." Candace paused. "Dad went out of his way to blame us for the accident that killed her, though only in private. He eventually settled on it being Kurt's fault. I don't think Kurt ever forgot that his father blamed him."

"Did you see Sister Margaret Frances during that time?" Brooke asked.

"I didn't know to look for her, but I seem to remember seeing a couple of nuns hanging around on the edge of things. I thought that was strange because we didn't have any convents near my parents' house. They didn't say anything, and I didn't go up to them. I thought they might be at the cemetery for someone else. We weren't Catholic, so I never thought they were there for Mom. I focused on Kurt; he was a mess," Candace shook her head. "Very sad situation, I'm afraid."

"How did you cope? You were still a young woman...this must have been very difficult for you," Susan said.

"Yes, it was. I had Kurt to deal with. He was really doing very poorly. He had a disastrous beginning of school that fall, as you might imagine. He did manage to get through the school year. I worked with him a lot, took time with him. He wrote in his journals every day. I confess that I tore some of the pages out." Candace looked at the family. "He could've gotten into a lot of trouble if anyone had found them. He ranted and raved about his mother and her part in Ella's disappearance. He cried a great deal as he wrote them. The pages were smudged and warped by his tears. He had whole paragraphs scribbled over in his anger. It was heartbreaking for me to read them, but I felt I had to, so that I could keep track of his progress getting through the whole sordid mess. He seemed to be getting his life back together with sports and all, when the time came that I knew I had to leave."

Brooke said, "We know you stayed around longer than most of your siblings. What triggered your need to get away?"

Candace hesitated for several minutes. Should she tell them? It's not good to speak ill of the dead...she really didn't want to share this, but they were such open people. Okay, here goes nothing, as they say.

Candace told them, "My father was a difficult man. He felt that women had a special place in the home, and it was not a good place. The year after my mother died, he felt that he had the . . . right . . . to be 'serviced,' as he called it, on a regular basis. He told me a few weeks after the anniversary of Mom's death that he wanted me to . . ."

Candace hesitated. Could she even speak this horror? It had driven her away so many years before. She could not remain even one more night in the home she had grown up in because the thought of this was so unbelievable.

"He expected me to move into his bedroom that night. I would become his new wife. He left for an afternoon at the bar, and I left home that same day. I never went back," Candace wept as she spoke these truths.

The family sat in stunned silence. Candace could not continue. She had never told anyone this part of her story before. She had put it out of her mind so completely that it had not been in her conscious thoughts for years, but here it was. Candace sat in her comfortable chair, breathing deeply and trying to calm her unsteady nerves. This had taken more out of her than she had expected. She felt the world spinning around. She slumped over in her chair.

Chapter 37

Christopher gave Candace a drink of cool water and a moment to collect herself. She assured the family that her emotions had overwhelmed her, but that there was no need to go to the hospital. Joshua checked her out informally but found no evidence of anything wrong with her heart or anything else that was concerning. Joshua had wanted to transport her, "just to be on the safe side," but she turned him down, saying that she just needed a moment to rest. They turned the conversation to other subjects, once Aunt Candace felt like herself again.

Aunt Candace returned to Austin a few days later, none the worse for wear and promising to keep in contact with her new-found family.

Christopher had been happy to have had Aunt Candace in town, but was sorry that her revelations had caused her such personal distress. Aunt Candace's presence had been a nice change of pace from the campaign that Shannon started in earnest about that time.

Shannon tried everything to get him alone, but Christopher made a point of always having someone with him. She started showing up at odd hours, as seen on his home security camera, so he started doing sleepovers at his mother's house as well as spending the occasional night with Joshua or Brooke and their spouses. It was getting very old.

One day, Christopher had finally had enough. He told his family, "What can I do? I have to do something. She's driving me nuts."

Susan told him, "Invite her over for a family bar-be-que. We'll confront her. We'll be nice so that she won't give you a hard time about seeing the girls. Chris, you can't keep being driven from your own home."

Joshua said, "She's probably about two or two and a half months pregnant now, so she'll be making a move soon, or she'll be stuck. There's no way she can say that the baby is premature, that the child is yours. She's just too far along."

***

Shannon had plans of her own. She made the appointment, not happy about it, but feeling trapped. There was no way Chris was going to believe the baby was his. She couldn't get him alone for even a minute. She couldn't afford to lose this job. She didn't have a family to rely on, with her folks out of state and angry at her first pregnancy. "You made your bed," they told her.

Shannon didn't have any real friends since she had given birth to the twins. Her so-called friends at the Christian school didn't want to lose their contracts by hanging out with a sinner like her, so they dumped her as soon as she left her employment with them. Well, maybe that was her fault. She felt like such a sinner whenever they got together, before she left the school. She couldn't stand the looks of pity she saw in their eyes. She had lost her job, so there was no daily contact with her former colleagues. Her contract hadn't been renewed due to her 'moral failure.' She understood, though she didn't like it.

The added cost of childcare for another newborn would sink her carefully crafted but precarious financial ship. Ray might be sued for child support, but he was already approaching retirement age and would only be good for a couple of years' worth of money, if that. If, no make that when, his wife got word of his infidelity, then she might sue for divorce, making his financial resources even more limited than they were now. Private school teachers didn't make much money and having to split it so many ways would give Shannon very little added income. It wouldn't be enough to raise another child, much less get ahead of the financial curve that was already threatening to destroy her.

Shannon knew what her pro-life former friends at the Christian school would say. They would be horrified at what she was doing. "Why not give the baby up for adoption?" "How could you destroy a life on purpose?" They might even offer to pay for her pregnancy expenses, if she gave up the baby. No, I am not giving up my child. No other person is going to raise this kid if I can't. The fetus . . . It feels better calling it that than 'baby'. . . would go to heaven early. It would be saved from a life like hers, from the mother she would be to it. It's hardly more than a lump of cells right now. It's a mistake.

Shannon told Chris she had an appointment and needed him to take the girls an extra Saturday that month. He was surprised and asked if everything was okay. She skirted the issue pretty well, if she said so herself, and got out of his house before he could ask her where she was going. He looked at her kinda funny, but was happy to see Molly and Melanie. He invited her to come back for a family dinner that evening. She hedged and did not commit. She left as he was singing "The Itsy Bitsy Spider" in his baritone voice. Silly man.

Shannon drove back home, then took an Uber to the clinic. She asked the driver to return for her later that afternoon. She was shepherded by clinic escorts past the protestors who were begging for the life of her . . . fetus. This is best for my fetus. There is no other way. She entered the clinic, filled out the appropriate forms, and handed over the money Ray had given her for the procedure. She was glad that he had at least paid for her...procedure. He was nowhere in sight, of course, since this was not the third week of the month. He probably wouldn't have come, anyway. Fine with her . . . Good riddance.

She had the procedure done. It didn't take long, once they got started. They removed the 'pregnancy tissue,' as they called it, and moved her into the recovery room. She stayed in the recovery area with all the other sobbing women for about an hour and then was escorted out the door with a discharge paper that warned of side effects. It was not a happy place. She was glad to leave.

Glad, if you can be happy after one of those . . . procedures. She couldn't bring herself to call it what it was. She went back home, numbed by her experience. She climbed the two sets of stairs, exhausted. She took a shower, hot as she could stand it. Done. Over. Problem solved. She rested in bed for about an hour and then realized she had to go get the girls from Chris. Would this day never end?

She dragged herself out of her comfortable bed, put on a loose sweatpants outfit, and headed over to Chris's house. She knew she shouldn't be driving, but there was no choice. The whole family was there. Bother! Oh, that's right. The family gathering he had invited her to attend was tonight. This big happy family stuff was really getting on her nerves. Christopher answered the door, one daughter on each hip.

"Hey, Shannon, come on in. Say, you don't look too good. Are you okay?" He stepped aside as she brushed past him.

Shannon felt a pull in her abdomen. What was happening? She slumped to the floor.

*****

Christopher called for help. Everyone had gathered in his downstairs family room, where the stone fireplace was providing a welcome respite from the winter chill. They heard his cries and came running.

"She came in and collapsed. I don't know what's wrong but look at all the blood."

Joshua did a quick exam as he ordered, "Somebody call 911." He rolled her onto her back. "Did she have an abortion, does anyone know?"

Amanda said, "Let me look through her purse." She riffled through the huge bag. "Here's an appointment card for the Women's Health Center. Her appointment was this morning at eleven. I guess she kept it."

The EMTs arrived. Joshua told them, "I suspect Disseminated Intravascular Coagulation. She had an abortion this morning. Transport her to the hospital STAT."

Susan asked Joshua, "How serious is this, honey?"

Joshua answered, "This isn't my realm of doctoring,

318

Mom, unless she goes septic. But it is very serious, given the amount of blood she's lost. She'll need immediate surgery to stop the bleeding. She may lose her ability to have children. She could lose her life."

Brooke asked, "What are you going to do, Chris?"

Christopher said, "Amanda, please check and see if she has an address book in her purse. We need to get in touch with her folks. I think they live in South Carolina, but I'm not sure. She never talked about them." He turned to Brooke. "I think I need to go to the hospital. She is the mother of my children, after all."

Brooke said, "Sure thing, Chris. You go. Michael and I will watch the girls. Stay as long as you need to. We'll be praying for Shannon. Keep us posted, okay?"

"Absolutely, Brooke. Thanks." Christopher hugged her as he handed the girls over.

Joshua said, "I'll go with you, Chris. Amanda, can you take the kids home after you all get finished helping with the twins? I'll hitch a ride with Chris when we leave the hospital, okay?"

"No problem, honey." More hugs, quick ones at that.

Dan said, "Susan and I will follow you over. We want to be there, in case you need a break."

"Thanks Dan." Christopher grabbed a few things, hugged everyone again, and ran out the door with Joshua.

Things did not go well for Shannon. Blood transfusions were given. She was rushed to surgery, but it was difficult to stem the flow of blood. Her reproductive organs were removed. Then all of her major organs began shutting down due to blood loss. She died of sepsis later that afternoon, having never regained consciousness.

***

Shannon looked at herself lying on the foyer of Christopher's house. Sure is a lot of blood. "Things don't look good for me right now." Oh, she had spoken out loud. No one seemed to notice.

"No, Shannon, they don't."

A large black-haired man dressed entirely in white stood at her right, slightly behind her. Shannon felt his presence, loving and strong. She turned and looked over her shoulder at him.

"Who might you be?" She wasn't feeling threatened by him but wondered how he had gotten past Chris and all his family. The family didn't seem to notice either one of them. Shannon felt self-conscious about her casual attire, especially since the man looked so nicely dressed. Maybe I should have put on better clothes before I left home.

"My name is Robert. I'm a friend, Shannon."

"Well, I don't have too many of them right now." Shannon looked back at her body. "What's happening here, Robert?"

"You're bleeding out as a result of your abortion this morning," Robert told her.

Well, that's getting right to the point. "How do you know about that? I didn't tell anyone." Shannon looked at him with a tinge of distain.

"You didn't have to tell anyone. I just know," Robert said.

"Oh, I get it. I've read enough fiction. Angels visit people who are dying and there is a fight between the good angel and a demon-type being for the person's soul. Am I right?" Shannon scowled a bit in Robert's direction.

"You're on the right track. The difference is that you made a profession of faith when you were a small child in Vacation Bible School. Do you remember that?" Robert smiled.

"Yes. You mean that actually held?" Shannon continued to stare at her body as the team of EMTs arrived and began working on her inert form.

"'Once saved, always saved,' as we like to say, Shannon. You actually did 'keep the faith' for most of your childhood and into your young adult years. It's only been in the last couple of years that you got interested in what the world had to offer," Robert told her.

"I screwed up." Shannon shook her head. "Big time." They were loading her into the ambulance. Shannon followed the EMTs. Robert followed her.

"You listened to popular culture and believed it." Robert's words were not unkind.

They got into the ambulance with her body and the paramedics. It surprised her that there was enough room for all of them.

"We don't take up much space, you and I, Shannon." Robert smiled at her fondly.

"So, there's not going to be some big celestial argument for my soul?" Shannon asked Robert, with a hint of melodrama.

"Nope. The bad guys can't touch you. The Bible says that no one can snatch you out of His hand." Robert patted her hand.

"Well, that's a relief. So what happens now?" Shannon watched the EMTs taking her into the hospital. The hospital personnel were scrambling, running in an orchestrated panic, or so it seemed to her. She followed them into the exam room, with Robert close behind.

"They'll fight for your life. You're so young that they will try especially hard. It won't work, but they're hoping for the best." Robert stood nearby.

"How long?" Shannon knelt down and hunched over, her head in her hands. She hated to know the end result before it happened, but decided the truth was important. It was like someone telling you how a movie was going to end before you saw it. Major spoiler alert.

"A couple of hours. You'll be rushed into surgery which, if it had succeeded, would have left you sterile. It isn't going to work, Shannon, just to give you some advance notice. Christopher's sister Brooke is trying to get in contact with your parents to let them know what's happening." Robert tried to comfort her, putting his hand on her shoulder.

"Will they make it here in time?" Shannon asked, not looking away from her inert body.

"No. They'll call Chris, and he'll hold the phone to your ear. They'll say goodbye that way. Of course, you'll be able to hear everything they say because you're with me," Robert said.

"Chris is here?" Shannon stood straighter and began looking around wildly. "Where is he? I don't see him."

Robert put his left arm around her and patted her right arm. "In the waiting room. Joshua is with him. Dan and Susan will arrive soon. Brooke and Michael are with Amanda, caring for the girls back at Christopher's house. They'll be there for hours."

"So Chris does care?" That was a surprise. I thought he only had eyes for little Miss Audrey. "That's nice to know, I suppose."

"Yes. You're the mother of his children." Robert hesitated. "You're in very bad shape, Shannon. He's a Christian who cares about others. He will stay until...there is no more reason to stay."

"You mean until I'm dead." Bluntness seemed to be the order of the day. So be it.

"Yes." Robert spoke quietly. "Until you're dead, Shannon."

"What will happen to Melanie and Molly? My girls! What will happen?" Shannon looked at Robert, shrinking at the thought of something bad happening to her precious babies. She twirled around, looking for some respite. "What have I done? I got rid of an unwanted baby, and now I can't have my little girls?" She began to weep hysterically.

Robert let her cry it out. Then, "Shannon, Christopher will raise the girls. He and Audrey adore them. They will marry and Audrey will adopt Melanie and Molly. She'll treat them as her own flesh and blood. This is a devout Christian couple, who will lead both girls to the Lord at a young age as a result of their own lifestyle and testimony."

"How can you know that?" Shannon mopped at her face and tried to straighten her messy hair. He handed her a tissue.

"I've been told, so that you can have comfort now."

"Someone in high authority?" Shannon asked.

Robert smiled. "Yes, Shannon, the Highest."

Shannon watched as the medical team rushed her into the operating room. She and Robert looked down at the doctors and nurses as they tried everything that could be done for her. She didn't understand most of their conversation, but the pressure in the room was obvious. Finally, the lead doctor threw down his instrument and called Time of Death. Her surgery was over, having failed at keeping her alive. She was placed on a respirator so that her organs could be harvested. Shannon followed as they wheeled her back to the cubicle where she would be prepared for the morgue. She noticed that Chris and Joshua were entering the cubicle where she lay. The doctors stepped aside, shaking their heads.

Christopher walked over to her body and put his hand on her shoulder. He leaned close. "Shannon, I'm so sorry. Why did you have to do this? We didn't even talk about it. It wasn't my child, but I would've tried to help. Your actions of the past couple of months were out of desperation. I understand that . . . I forgive you for trying to deceive me. I don't know you well enough to know if you're a Christian, but I pray that you are and that you can find peace. Your parents are calling soon, and I'll be back to let you, hopefully, hear what they have to say."

Joshua put his hand on Christopher's shoulder as he talked with Shannon then added, "Shannon, we'll all take part in raising Melanie and Molly. They will not want. Our family loves the girls. We might have loved you, if you'd let us get to know you. I'm so sorry that this has happened. Take care." Joshua squeezed her lifeless hand.

Chris and Joshua took a few minutes to pray for her, asking the Lord to save her if she wasn't a Christian. The two men walked out, talking to the doctors on the way. Shannon heard them talking about organ transplants: corneas, kidney, liver, heart, lungs, and skin.

"Hey, I'm not done with my organs yet! Hands off for now!" What if a miracle happened? She didn't want to be killed by someone else's generosity. Shannon thought she saw that her chest was rising and falling. Yes, it most definitely was. "I'm still alive, you jerks!"

Robert took her arm. "You feel alive because we're talking, but Shannon, you're dead. You're not going to get a miracle. I'm so sorry."

She whirled around and stood directly in front of Robert. "But I can see my chest going up and down. I'm not dead, Robert!" Why won't these doctor dudes listen to me? What's wrong with them? "I'm alive!"

"Shannon, they have you on a ventilator to keep your organs working, while they see if they can be transplanted. You are dead. I promise." Robert tried to comfort her, but she pushed him away, angry at his efforts.

Shannon heard Chris say, "I think we'd better let Mr. and Mrs. Thompson decide about any organ transplants. Shannon and I never talked about that, and I have no idea what she would have wanted. We weren't married. Can you wait a bit?"

"Thanks, Chris! Good call!" Shannon forgot he couldn't hear her. Whew! I dodged a bullet there. Let me keep my stuff till I don't need it anymore. No premature donations, thank you very much.

"Yes, Mr. Prescott. We can give it some time, but we'll need to decide in the next few hours so that the organs can be...removed while they are still usable." The doctors walked to the nurses' station. They told the nurses to contact the transplant teams as soon as the decision was made. They told the nurses Time of Death had been called about 15 minutes before.

Shannon started yelling. "Leave my stuff alone! I'm still here!"

Robert said, "Shannon. Shannon. Try to calm down a bit.

They can't hear you." He hugged her from the side and reminded her of the facts. "The surgery didn't work. You died on the table. Your parents are going to call in a few minutes. You'll hear them talking because we're still here, but your body has shut down." He tried to calm her. "Let me tell you what will happen next. The doctors will do a brain scan to see if you have any brain activity. You don't. You see that you're still breathing now, but that is because of the respirator being used to keep your organs viable. The doctor has already called Time of Death. You died about fifteen minutes ago, in the world's time. It won't be long before you are wheeled away to the operating room for the organ transplant, and then you'll be taken to the morgue. An autopsy will be performed to determine why you died. This is the way things are going to play out." He pulled her around and looked directly into her eyes. "Do you understand?"

Shannon shook him off once more. "Leave me alone. I'm still alive, I know I am." She continued to watch herself lying there. "No!"

Sure enough, Chris came back in a short while later and held the phone to her ear. She heard her parents say how much they loved her. They spent a few minutes telling her they would miss her and that she had been a good daughter, at least 'until she messed up,' her father said. Her mother got upset with her father for saying that, and he said that he was sorry but he was right. Shannon saw her body lying there, completely unresponsive, except for the ventilator's forced breathing. Chris hung up the phone and then leaned over and kissed her forehead. "Goodbye, Shannon." He left.

"But I'm still here! Can't anybody hear me?" Shannon began swinging at Robert. "Can't you tell them I'm alive? Help me!" She started beating on his chest. "Make them understand!"

"No, Shannon. You took a chance. You lost. I'm sorry, but you aren't going back. You have a different future now. Try to calm down." He hugged her again. Her body was wracked with huge sobs . . . finally, she felt herself go limp. She was done. There was nothing anyone could do. She faced it and pulled away from her visitor.

Shannon dried her eyes, thanks to yet another tissue from Robert's stock. She looked at him, resigned. "So what now?"

"The medical professionals will take care of your body. Your next stop is back to the operating room. Your parents, who did approve of the organ donations by the way, will arrive in a couple of days. Your burial service will be private. Chris will come, and he will bring the girls out of respect. His family will be there to support him, like they always do." Robert waited.

"I see. Well, what about me? Now? What do I do next?" She faced him. "Give me the scoop, for good or bad." She squared her shoulders.

"We're going to a much better place. And there's someone you need to meet." Robert smiled.

"Who's that?" This was all new and curious.

"Your son." Robert smiled.

"My . . . son? I don't have . . . it was . . . a boy? The baby, I mean?" Shannon shook her head in confusion.

"Yes. You need to name him, of course. You hadn't done that." Robert waited

"I didn't name him on purpose." Shannon hung her head. "He would've been a person then, not just some 'pregnancy tissue,' like they said."

Robert held out his arm. "Any ideas? Better think fast."

Shannon took his proffered arm. "Hum . . . maybe Ethan would be nice."

"Yes. His name means 'strong' and 'firm.' Good choice." They left the room, headed, like Robert said, to a much better place.

Chapter 38

Christopher answered the door that April Saturday morning, a couple of weeks after Shannon passed, expecting to see his mother and sister. They were dropping by to offer some planning ahead tips on fathering twins while the Thompsons had the girls for the day. The couple would be returning home in the morning, and wanted one last chance to spend time with their granddaughters.

It was a surprise, then, when Christopher opened the door to a middle-aged, 60ish woman he had never seen before. There was something vaguely familiar about her, but he couldn't place how he might know her. Dressed kinda plain but not homeless, he guessed. She smelled of old lady perfume. Maybe a little too much perfume for his taste, but not bad.

"Yes, Ma'am. Can I help you?" He thought maybe she was the grandmother of one of the neighborhood kids. He looked past her, straining to see if there were children nearby. Nope.

"Hi there. Are you Christopher Prescott?" she asked, showing him a sweet smile.

"Yes, I am. What can I do for you?" He smiled back.

"I, uh, think that we might be related." She smiled again, but said nothing more.

Christopher ran through the missing relatives in his life. They hadn't found the children of Maggie, maybe that's who she was. Nope. She's probably older than they would be. Peter's children would be a bit older than the woman standing in front of him. As he was contemplating who she might be, his mother and sister drove up. "Excuse me just a minute, please."

"Certainly. No problem." The woman seemed perfectly happy to wait.

He side-stepped the woman on his front step and walked up to Brooke's car as the two women got out. "Chris, what's happening?" Susan looked at the woman standing by his front door. "Who's that?" she whispered.

He spoke very quietly "She came knocking on the door, and said she might be related to me. I haven't even had the chance to ask her name yet, but I'm really glad you're both here."

"What, Chris, you want me to protect you?" Brooke smiled.

"Nope, I'm just glad to have some witnesses, that's all. I never saw her before in my life but she looked kinda, I don't know, familiar. Come take a look." Christopher turned and walked back towards his house. He smiled at the woman on his front step.

The trio headed up the walk to where the woman was standing. "Let me introduce my mother Susan Prescott Walsh and my sister Brooke Prescott Bench. And you are?"

"My name is Jennifer Lynette Peterson Douglas. At least, that's what I thought my name was. I just found out that my name is different. Are you folks related to Kurt Prescott?" She smiled through her comments but seemed a little on edge.

Susan spoke up, "Yes, he was my husband for thirty-five years. Why do you ask?"

"I am a relative of his." Jennifer looked unsure of exactly how to proceed.

Christopher asked, "Ladies, why don't we step around to the back of the house, rather than chatting out here on the front step? We might be more comfortable on the patio." He wasn't sure he wanted this woman, whoever she was, to step foot inside his house, but the backyard might be safe. They walked around the side of the house and sat on his patio chairs.

Brooke said, "Well, you're about the right age for Kurt Prescott's wife, but my mother is the only legitimate wife my father ever had."

"Yes, yes, of course. I'm sorry. I'm approaching this the wrong way. It's just that I'm not sure how to tell you this, but my real name, my given name, is Ella Cassandra Prescott. Have you ever heard of me?" The woman looked a bit unsure of herself.

They looked at her in stunned silence. Ella? "Would you excuse us for a minute?" Christopher asked. "Mom? Brooke?" He grabbed his mother's arm and hurried them inside, shutting the back door behind them. He quietly said, "What do you make of her?"

Susan whispered, "First things first. We call the whole family over and talk to her as a group. We need to find out if she has any proof or if she's just someone trying to profit from pretending she's Ella."

Brooke nodded, "Yes. Good idea. I'll call Michael. Mom, you call Dan. Chris, you call Josh and see how fast they can all get here. Too bad Aunt Candace went back to Texas last week. She's the only one of us who had actually met Ella."

Christopher said, "So let's call Aunt Candace. We can Skype, show her this woman, and see what she thinks."

Susan said, "Good idea Chris. Let's do it."

He went back outside. "Mrs. Douglas? The rest of the family will be here soon. Would you like to have a glass of sweet tea while we wait?"

She smiled. Again, something was so familiar, yet he knew he didn't recognize her. "That would be lovely, thank you. I know my showing up must be quite a shock."

The additional family members arrived a few minutes later, having dropped everything to come right over. They got Aunt Candace on Skype, even though it was only about 9:00 am in Maryland and 8:00 am in Austin; she was an early riser.

"Hello, everyone. It's good to see you again. What's new? I'm surprised to hear from you so early on a Saturday morning," Aunt Candace said.

Christopher said, "Aunt Candace, I have someone to introduce you to, but you'd better sit down." He spoke in a whisper, "Aunt Candace, a woman showed up this morning and said she's Ella. She's out on the patio. I'm going to invite her in,

329

but I wanted to tell you first."

"What?" Aunt Candace looked shocked. "I'm not sure what to say." Her eyes filled with tears. "After all this time?"

Christopher told her, "We don't know if she's a weird fake or if it's really her, but we wanted to include you." He looked at his aunt with care. "Are you okay?"

"Yes. Thank you, Christopher. Yes, I'm fine. A little shaken, but let me see her. It's been so many years. She was just a little girl. I can't imagine that I'll recognize her, but you never know." Candace seemed frail for a moment; they could see she was overcome with emotion.

"Aunt Candace, when I first saw her I thought that I knew her, but I didn't know how. See what you think." Christopher tried to reassure her.

"Yes, of course, Christopher. Bring her in." Candace smiled weakly.

Christopher invited Jennifer in and introduced her to everyone, including Aunt Candace. They shook hands and sat in his downstairs family room. After getting settled comfortably, Christopher said, "Well, Mrs. Douglas, please tell us your story."

***

Ella/Jennifer took a deep breath and began to talk.

"I don't have many memories of my early childhood, just occasional flashbacks to a big house and a creek. There was a white picket fence in the side and back yards where I was allowed to play. I remember looking out the front window. I was excited to see someone who was coming, but I can't remember who I was waiting for. I think it might have been my brother Kurt." She paused to see if anyone had any questions. Nope.

"I also remember being in the back seat of a car. There were some blankets there, and I was asleep. A lady woke me up, and she said she was going to take me to my Mommy. I went with her. We got in a car and drove away. I yelled and yelled when my Mommy didn't come, but the lady kept driving." She paused again, waiting to see if anyone had questions. Still none. Ella/Jennifer continued.

"I fell asleep again and, when we got to this big house, a man came out to see me. He got all upset when he saw me. He asked the woman if she was out of her mind. He asked if it was her grief talking. Their daughter had died of leukemia, I found out many years later from my father's confession notes. The woman who took me from my mother's car was substituting the real Jennifer with me."

"She took me into a beautiful room. There were dolls and all sorts of toys. She said they were all mine. The man and the lady talked in the other room, but I couldn't hear what they said. I remember crying a lot at first, but they were both so nice. They kept calling me Jennifer, not Ella. I told them, 'my name is Ella my Bella,' but they wouldn't listen." At that last comment, everyone had sucked in air. Ella/Jennifer waited.

Joshua asked, "Ella my Bella seems like a weird name for a child."

"It's what my brother Kurt called me. We were very close. Nobody else in the family called me that, just him."

Susan asked, "How old were you at the time?"

"The nearest I can figure is that I was about four. Maybe a few months over four. Not four and a half yet."

Aunt Candace asked, "How did your new 'parents,' for lack of a better word, avoid awkward questions from the neighbors?"

"I found out from my father's notes that they told the neighbors I had undergone chemo and couldn't be near anyone for a while. As soon as he could, he took a job in another state and we moved." Ella/Jennifer waited while they processed this news.

Brooke asked, "How did you find this information?"

"I learned this story while my 'adoptive' father was dying of cancer a little while ago. He told me to go to the lockbox in the family safe. I learned the whole story of my kidnapping from papers he had in the box. My parents had struggled over whether to ever let me know that I was raised with another person's name and identity. His full confession of his part in my hidden life was written out in his own handwriting, including the story of Mrs. Prescott's death the night he visited her." Ella/Jennifer paused to wipe away a tear. "He died of pancreatic cancer a few months after he confessed what had happened, in 2018 at the age of eighty."

Brooke asked, "Didn't your father realize that it was wrong to kidnap a child?"

"Yes, of course. He said that he found out where my parents lived and went to see them after he and his wife Norma had had me with them for about a month. He said that the family was known for drunkenness." She hesitated. "I'm sorry. I mean no offense. I'm just repeating what he said. He had tried to see my birth mother." Ella/Jennifer looked around apologetically.

Joshua spoke up quickly, "And how did that go?"

"He wrote that he had sent her a note and did see her, but that some kid came running out of the house. He ran away before the kid could yell and attract attention. He hid behind a big tree, hoping that the kid would leave and he could talk to Mrs. Prescott."

Susan asked, "How big was the kid? Did his notes say?"

"Pretty small. Elementary age, he said." Ella/Jennifer looked embarrassed at her father's lack of knowledge. "Sorry, he wasn't good with ages."

Brooke asked, "So the kid came up and your dad ran away. What happened after that?"

"He told me that the kid tackled Mrs. Prescott, which made her fall on the rocks by the creek. She didn't move, so I guess she was unconscious. The kid kept raising her head and dropping it on the rocks. He didn't seem to be trying to save her. In fact, Dad said that he seemed to be holding her head under water," Ella/Jennifer told them. "Since Mrs. Prescott was unconscious, she didn't fight back. He heard a door open on the house and a taller boy came running. About that same time, the back door opened and a young woman came out. The boy arrived at the creek just before the girl did. By the time they arrived, Mrs. Prescott was dead. My dad took off, never to return. My father realized just what a horrid family the Prescotts were and never made another attempt to reunite me with them." Jennifer/Ella looked at the floor. She sighed.

Susan gasped, "What? Are you saying that my husband murdered his mother?"

Ella/Jennifer looked up quickly. "I'm sorry. I don't mean to upset you, Ma'am. I'm just repeating what my father said."

Susan slumped against Dan. "I never would have thought that he would do that, not from the journals we've read." She began to cry.

Christopher spoke up. "Mrs. Douglas, my mother has had quite a shock. I think we had better call it a day for now. Please leave us your contact information, and we'll be in touch."

"Yes, of course." Ella/Jennifer turned to Susan. "I'm really sorry to have upset you, Ma'am."

Christopher repeated his request. "Please Mrs. Douglas, you need to leave. Now."

"Certainly. Here's my cellphone number and my hotel information. Goodbye." The woman walked out of the house, got into her car, and left.

***

Christopher turned back to the family, all of whom were silent as they processed this new information.

"Well, that was a surprise." Christopher gave Susan a hug. "Mom, are you okay? I'm sorry she upset you." The rest of the family gathered around and offered a hug or a squeeze.

Aunt Candace said, "Folks, we need to be a bit skeptical here. I don't know how someone would get this kind of information, but she certainly knows her stuff. Do you know any police officers who could run a background check on her? Oh, what about Patrick Ferguson? Could he help?"

Susan wiped her tears and said, "Sure. Patrick is a great

cop. I'll call my friend Nancy Beth right now."

Joshua said, "Yes, please do, Mom. See if the Fergusons can come over right away. We'll tell Patrick what we know and go from there."

Susan straightened up a bit. "Good idea, guys. I mean, here I am getting all upset over a woman I have never met telling me bad things about my late husband. I know Kurt was a difficult person, but would he have deliberately killed his mother? Would he have done it when he was a little boy? I'm not sure, but I can't imagine that he did."

Amanda spoke up. "Mom, I'm sorry to remind you, but he did try to kill you three times. Her story might be accurate. We need to be prepared for that possibility." She hugged Susan. "I might add that I'm VERY glad Kurt didn't succeed."

Christopher turned to the screen and asked Aunt Candace, "How are you holding up, Aunt Candace? I don't want to tire you."

Aunt Candace said, "Thank you for your concern, Christopher, but I'm just fine. Actually, there is something I wanted to discuss with all of you, while we're all here. This might not be the right time, but I've been considering it and want to know what you think. Do you have a moment?"

Christopher said, "Sure thing. Let Mom call the Fergusons real quickly, and then we can chat while we wait for them to get here."

The call was made, and the Fergusons assured Susan that they were on their way.

Christopher said, "Aunt Candace, we're ready to chat. What's up?"

Aunt Candace said, "You know how much I enjoyed getting acquainted with you all on my visit. I'm here in Austin where I've had a nice, but somewhat solitary life." She hesitated. "I was thinking I might retire and move to Maryland."

The family reacted immediately and with joy. "That's a great idea, Aunt Candace!" "We would love to have you nearby!" "Yes, the sooner the better!"

Aunt Candace smiled the prettiest smile they had ever seen on her. "Okay. Well, that's good news. Let me see what I can work out and when that might happen. You've given me great joy. Thank you all for your kindness." Candace started to cry. She dabbed her eyes, then straightened up. "All right. Now that that's settled, let's see what Patrick has to say about our little Mrs. Ella/Jennifer Douglas."

Right on cue, Patrick and Nancy walked in.

***

Patrick said, "Hi everybody. Is there something wrong? How can I help?"

They filled him in as best they could, which was a bit difficult as they all started talking at once.

"Hold on folks. One at a time. Give me the details you can remember," Patrick said. "Did she show any identification?"

Susan said, "Identification? No, she didn't."

Christopher said, "I guess we were so shocked by her showing up that we didn't think of it. I kept thinking that she looked vaguely familiar, but I couldn't place her."

"Okay, then. You all give me the basic information you have on her, based on what she said and let me run it through my computer." Patrick pulled out his police computer and got it up and running.

They did so, as best they could remember. They showed him her contact information. He ran that through his computer and learned that the phone was registered to one Ms. Karen Judith Lamont. He ran a background check on her, only to learn that she was wanted in connection for her part in an embezzlement scheme. Her accomplice was . . . John Kenneth Prescott.

"Oh, my goodness! She's a crook!" Susan said in amazement. She put her hand to her chest. "I didn't think that Kurt was so bad he would kill his own mother. Thank God for that!"

Patrick said, "Let me call one of our detectives. She hasn't asked for any money yet, but you never know what she and John have in mind for you all. Let's stop them in their tracks, shall we?"

Christopher said, "Absolutely. Let's get them before they get us."

Everyone agreed that was the way to go.

Joshua said, "Aunt Candace, you had better lay low where you are for now. Go ahead and start getting things in place, but we don't want you to run into John."

Aunt Candace agreed at once. "He stole $20,000 worth of my possessions the last time I met up with him. That's more than enough for me. I'll wait to hear from you." She said "goodbye for now" and got off line.

***

It took some time but, after meeting with the detective that afternoon, they decided to help the police catch Mrs. Douglas aka Ella/Jennifer aka Ms. Karen Judith Lamont. Christopher invited the woman to return Sunday afternoon. The entire family was once again at his house, but this time they added a police detective who specialized in DNA testing. They called him "Cousin Charlie who is really into genealogy." Fortunately, the man looked something like them.

Christopher let Ella/Jennifer into his house and said, "I think you know everyone, except for our Cousin Charlie. Please tell us more of your life story."

Ella/Jennifer greeted Charlie and said, "Well, like I told you last time, I was raised as Jennifer Lynette Peterson. My adoptive mother died only two years after I was with my father and her. I was coming down a flight of stairs when I tripped. She saw me and ran up as I fell down. She saved my life but..." Here, she hesitated and wiped away a tear, "she lost her own balance and fell, breaking her neck. She was killed instantly."

They all made sympathetic noises, having already

checked out the story online, where they found out that a Norma Turner Peterson of Cincinnati, Ohio had fallen to her death saving the life of her 6-year-old daughter Jennifer. In fact, they knew quite a bit about the Petersons, since it was a pretty simple google search to turn up Theodore Russell Peterson's life history, as well. They had figured that their imposter would mention the Peterson's sad story at their next meeting and didn't want any surprises.

"My father remarried two years later. Peggy White became my step-mother. She was a wonderful woman who had no children of her own. My father told me that he never told Peggy that I wasn't his daughter. She never knew that I wasn't related to Teddy. She raised me as her own child and I adored her. She told me one day when I was a teenager that she had had two abortions, which had made her sterile because of complications. She died of breast cancer in 2015. She was seventy-three."

Yes, Christopher thought, this gal has done her homework. She's telling us exactly the story that we found on my computer search last night, sans the abortion information. Smooth operator! I wondered if she and Johnny just picked the rest of this story out of thin air or if there might have actually been some truth to it. Wouldn't it be funny if they really did find Ella? They are crooks, after all. Maybe they're crooks with great internet search abilities.

Joshua asked, "Mrs. Douglas, do you have your father's confession notes? I'd love to see them."

Mrs. Douglas answered, "No, I'm sorry, I don't. At my father's request, I destroyed them shortly before he died. He didn't want any letters to besmirch his reputation after he died, so I burned them out of respect for him."

Joshua asked, "So there's nothing left of them?"

"No, nothing at all. He was a proud man who had done his job by me and now that I knew the truth, he wanted the notes destroyed." Ella/Jennifer paused to wipe away a tear.

"Cousin Charlie" spoke up, "Hey, Chris, I wonder if we

might do that little experiment we were talking about before Mrs. Douglas arrived?"

Christopher said, "Great idea, Charlie. Thanks for bringing it up!"

Ella/Jennifer asked, "What experiment?" She looked ill at ease.

Susan said, "Oh, it'll be fun!" Susan clapped her hands in false glee. "Wait till you see what Charlie can do, Mrs. Douglas. It's so interesting." She turned to Charlie. "Tell her about it."

Meanwhile, the others agreed that it was a superb idea. Ella/Jennifer looked confused and asked, "What's going on?"

Charlie spoke, "Well, I am a genealogy buff, and I've gotten into DNA testing. Did you know that, because you and Aunt Candace are full siblings, there should be a one hundred percent match between the two of you? As it turns out, Aunt Candace had some genetic testing done a short while ago to determine if she was likely to suffer from chronic, fatal illnesses, and she sent the results to me. We thought it would be fun to see if you are a match. You don't mind giving us a quick rub of the inside of your cheek, do you?" Charlie turned to Christopher and then to Brooke, in turn. "Actually, as nephew and niece, you will both have a twenty-five percent match with Mrs. Douglas."

Ella/Jennifer said, "Oh, I don't think so. I don't like tests."

Charlie assured her, "It doesn't hurt, and it only takes a few seconds."

"No, I don't want to do that. No, it sounds like a bad idea." She appeared ready to bolt.

***

Patrick stepped out of Christopher's den, "Mrs. Douglas? Or should I say Ms. Lamont? I'm police officer Patrick Ferguson." He flashed his badge at the woman. "I'd like to ask you some questions down at the station, if you don't mind."

"What? I'm Jennifer Peterson Douglas, also known as

338

Ella Prescott. I don't know who this Lamont person is." She stood up, moving towards the door.

Patrick stopped her. He knew his size could be intimidating. He stepped in front of her. She looked intimidated. Good. "Whoever you are claiming to be, there is an arrest warrant out for your work with John Kenneth Prescott, so there're a few questions we'd like to ask you." He moved to her side and slapped handcuffs on her. "You have the right to remain silent . . ." the Miranda Rights were some of his favorite sayings. He recited them to her, glad that he had gotten her without a struggle and before she harmed his second family.

Christopher held the door for Patrick and his captive. "Thanks for coming, Patrick."

"Sure thing, Chris. See you Wednesday night at Bible study."

"Stay in touch, my brother."

"Will do." He placed Ella/Jennifer in the back of his car and headed to the station.

Chapter 39

Ella/Jennifer/Karen, now known by her real name of Karen Lamont, made some choice comments to Patrick on the way to the station. The long shot of the police officer's conversation, along with a consultation with her court-appointed lawyer, was that she would turn state's evidence against John Kenneth Prescott, in return for a more lenient sentence. Patrick told the family later, "Now all we have to do is reel him in."

Patrick got the confession pretty quickly, as they sat in the interrogation room at the police station. It turned out that Karen Lamont, a nurse in the hospital where Mr. Ferguson had died, had met John Prescott at a local bar. She talked about this man whose background she had overheard from his daughter, a woman who looked a lot like her. She was tired of working, spending long hours on her feet and getting vomited on by cancer patients. She had a bit of a gambling problem that set her back financially some years ago, and she had many more years of hard work before she could even consider retiring. Like never.

John Prescott knew exactly how to push the right buttons, she told the police, and before she was aware of what had happened, she had moved in with him and had agreed to conspire with him to bilk his Maryland family out of some funds. If things worked out really well, John had told her, they would go back to the Petersons and blackmail the real Ella into a nice payday, to protect the reputation of her adoptive parents. Karen and John would spend the sunset of their days in the Bahamas or some other warm climate. No more work for either of them, if they played their cards right.

"I was supposed to make contact with the family using information that I overheard and what John told me about their home and parents. I would get the trust of Christopher and then get ahold of his banking information so we could clean out his accounts. If I got really lucky and was invited to Susan and Dan's house, I could fake a stomach problem and then use the time I was supposed to be in bed to look for their financial information. They have such a nice house. John drove me by the other day. We figured they might have some jewelry and other stuff we could fence."

Patrick asked, "Any other plans?"

"Joshua might have had some cash stashed, but he has four kids so we figured it would be harder to find anything quickly at his house. He's probably saving for college for the kids and it might be too hard to get to his money. Brooke's too young and newly-married to have much. She bought an expensive house a few months ago, so John and I figured she's probably broke right now and not worth the bother. Nope, our best shot was with the parents and Christopher."

Patrick said, "This family has been through so much in the past couple of years. How could you do something like this to such nice people? Pretending to be a long-lost daughter is pretty awful, but then to steal from them . . ."

"Not all of them are nice and I really don't care. I've had it pretty tough and this was the way for me to live well for the rest of my life." Karen, the former Ella/Jennifer, shrugged at Patrick. "You snooze, you lose."

Patrick said, "Well, when you're convicted, you won't have to worry about where to live. Well, at least a few years." He turned to the officer standing near the door, and nodded

341

towards Karen. "Lock her up."

***

Christopher reported to the family later that month, after an online search, that John Kenneth Prescott had been extradited to Tennessee, where charges were pending. Following that, John would be sent to Virginia and then back to Maryland. The court systems were in the process of deciding who would get him next, after Karen Judith Lamont's testimony was presented to the court. She had plea bargained to get her charges reduced like they thought she would, but Christopher learned that she would still be spending time behind bars. Good riddance! They could get on with their lives without worrying about whether or not John would show up again. John would be spending many years in prison. Aunt Candace was still out her $20,000 worth of collectibles, but the family was all safe for now. Funny thing, no one in the family expressed any desire to meet with Uncle John before he was sent away.

Chapter 40

Joshua and Amanda invited everyone over for Madison's high school graduation party. They were so proud of her, graduating with honors and getting a partial scholarship to college. The Saturday afternoon party was held in their backyard. The pool was opened a little earlier than usual so that folks who wanted to take a dip could do so. Joshua was glad they'd had the pool heated when they built it; the early May temperatures could still be a little chilly.

While the graduate was busy swimming with her friends and guests, Joshua and Amanda went over to his mom and Dan who were standing with Brooke, Michael, Christopher, and his twins, to suggest a family vacation.

"Hey everybody, I was just thinking. With Uncle John locked up for the foreseeable future and since we know that we'll be busy helping Aunt Candace move later this summer, what would you think of our taking a trip to see if we can actually meet the real Ella?" Joshua asked.

Susan said, "You know, Josh, I was just thinking that same thing. With the graduation ceremony over and the crooks on their way to the big house, that would be really nice."

Brooke said, "She lives in Cincinnati, from what the fake Ella said. That's not too far from the convent where Sister Margaret Frances lived. Could we maybe go see the Sisters again? They're really nice folks, and I'd like you to see where she lived . . . and died."

Joshua said, "Maybe Aunt Candace would like to fly in and meet us in Cincinnati. She could fly right out of Austin, though it would be a long flight."

Christopher said, "I'll give her a call tomorrow after church and see what she thinks. Are we still getting together tomorrow afternoon? I'll have the girls with me, of course. Audrey's coming over and giving me a hand. She'll be back from

Florida tonight." Joshua noticed that Christopher couldn't wipe the smile off his face at the mention of her name.

Susan said, "Yes. I think five or so would be good. Will that work for everyone?"

"Sure thing." "Absolutely." "Are the Fergusons coming, Mom?"

Susan said, "Yes. I talked to Nancy Beth today. They just got back from their cruise, so they'll be able to make it."

***

The clan was at Susan and Dan's house promptly the next afternoon. Susan smiled as she met them outside on the front lawn. Brooke and Michael showed up just as Christopher and Audrey were taking Melanie and Molly out of their car seats, so Brooke helped get Christopher's latest culinary wonder into the house for him. Nancy and Patrick trailed in behind them.

Brooke asked, "What kind of cake is this, Chris?"

"It's a chocolate cake with boiled frosting topped with a chocolate drizzle. I think it's a great recipe. It's from Audrey's grandmother," Christopher told them.

Audrey spoke up, "Chris is such an amazing cook that I think his cake is actually better than Grandma's was."

"It looks yummy!" Susan said. "How are my grandbabies this afternoon?" She smiled at the girls and held out her arms to them.

"Mom, they're getting pretty heavy. Better take them one at a time."

Susan took Christopher's advice. "Six months old now. It won't be long before they're walking!"

After their family meal, everyone settled into the family room for a planning meeting for their trip. They would take a flight into Cincinnati, and then rent two large vans for the trek to Ella's house. Joshua had been in touch with Ella/Jennifer, the real one, explaining what had happened and telling her that they believed her to be their long-lost relative. They would finish off the trip by driving to Sylvania, Ohio, to see the Reverend Mother and the Sisters of St. Francis. Brooke and Michael had emailed the nun to let her know about their plans.

Susan said, "Okay, let's count heads now. Who all is going?"

Joshua chimed in, "Mom, Amanda and I will go, but the kids will be at Awana camp."

Brooke said, "Michael and I are in."

Christopher told her, "Count me in, Mom. The girls will be staying with Shannon's parents."

Nancy spoke up. "Patrick and I would love to join you, if that's okay."

Susan smiled. "Absolutely. It would be great to have you along. You two are our 'sister and brother by other mothers' as they say." She turned to Audrey. "If you want to come along, dear, that would be lovely."

Audrey said, "Thanks for the invitation, Susan. Yes, I think a trip to Ohio with you all would be great."

Christopher's happiness was obvious. Of course, there would be separate sleeping accommodations for her, but just having her want to come along made this trip an event to anticipate with joy. "That's terrific, Audrey."

Susan said, "With Aunt Candace confirmed and Dan and me, we'll have ten on the trip. We need to make all the reservations pretty quickly, to keep the cost down."

***

The group arrived at the airport in Cincinnati, eager to meet their long-lost sister/aunt Ella. Candace's flight arrived, like theirs, right on time. Because they didn't want to wear her out, they planned on spending the night locally before heading to Ella's house the next morning. Candace was thrilled to be meeting her sister again. It was all she could do to lay down that night, but she knew the family was right. She would do much better over the long haul if she rested this evening. The DNA tests that Ella had willingly taken did indeed confirm that she was "Ella my Bella." Tomorrow was the big day. Candace rested but was too excited for much sleep.

They pulled up outside the tasteful rancher in the southwestern part of Cincinnati about ten the next morning. Candace climbed out of the van and walked towards the front door of Ella's home. Her heart was racing as she took each careful step. It would not do to fall flat on her face; the flagstone sidewalk would be unforgiving if she landed on it. A grey-haired, slender woman came out of the house, walking slowly at first and then broke into an all-out run. "Candy! My dear Candy! How great to see you!"

The women met halfway up the sidewalk and immediately embraced as tears flowed freely and without embarrassment. "Ella, my dearest Ella. I thought I would never see you again!" Their hug lasted several minutes before they were able to tear themselves apart. Tissues came out and noses were blown as the sisters were reunited and their families met.

Ella greeted them each, one at a time. "Susan. Brooke. Joshua. Christopher." She went to each person there, looking them over and embracing them with unspeakable joy. Even Dan, Michael, Amanda, Audrey, Nancy, and Patrick were hugged and loved on. "Come in. Please, please come in. You must meet my husband Jimmy and our four children. Well, they aren't children anymore, having made me a grandmother sixteen times." Ella held Candace's hand as they walked.

Candace wasn't used to having her hand held, but she got over her embarrassment and entered into the spirit of pure joy. She sat in the Lazy Boy rocker that Ella indicated was the place of honor in her living room, as they shared their life stories. The fake Ella had gotten the story very accurately, which did save some time in the telling. Ella told them that the entire Douglas clan was keen to meet them and would be joining them for lunch at noon.

Candace said, "That gives us two hours to catch up on fifty-five years of living."

Ella pulled out her photo albums from when she was a

small child, plopped down on the floor next to the Lazy Boy, and shared her life in pictures. There were pictures of Jennifer as a baby, then a toddler. She grew painfully thin at about the age of three, and then became obviously ill at age four. If she had been healthy, though, she would have been the spitting image of Ella. There was Ella the first year she was with the Petersons. Her room was, like the fake Ella had told them, a lovely pink bedroom filled with toys and dolls. It was much nicer than her home had been with her biological parents.

Her 'adoptive' mother did look a bit particular, which was to be expected since the woman kidnapped Ella. They all agreed to call the Petersons her 'adoptive' parents, rather than continuing to call them "the people who kidnapped you." It seemed harsh to tag the couple that way, since Mrs. Peterson had been reacting with grief and had been very kind to Ella during the short time they had together, before Mrs. Peterson had died saving Ella's life.

Ella told them, "How can I explain what she did? I can't really. She died when I was only six years old, so I don't remember her that much, but the lady who married Dad next, Peggy White, was the very heart of loving. She did die a few years ago, but she didn't know that I was anything but the real Jennifer. I know Dad never told her and she never acted like she was suspicious."

Candace looked at her sister, who was now firmly into middle age. "You've gone your whole life, almost anyway, as Jennifer. What do you want us to call you?"

Ella said, "I've lived the life that Jennifer would have had, possibly, if she hadn't died. I missed out on the life that I would have had as Ella, though from what you have said, it wouldn't have been a happy childhood. I would've had scars from it. To you, I am and always will be Ella, so why don't you call me that? My family calls me 'Mom' except for Jimmy, who knows me as 'Jennifer.' He can call me that and I'm happy for him to do it. How does that sound?" They all agreed that would work just fine.

Ella showed them the evidence her adoptive father had left behind, including the scrap of paper from that night at the creek. He had torn it from Mrs. Prescott's hand but had been unsuccessful in getting the whole letter. When added to the note fragment they already had, the missive read:

"Mrs. Prescott:

I know about Ella. She lives with my wife and me and is safe.

Meet me at the creek behind your house at 8 pm tomorrow.

She is doing fine but I am not bringing her back to your home.

A stranger who knows what kind of mother you are

Susan said, "That must have been heart-wrenching for her. To know that a stranger knew what a miserable life her daughter would have with her, but wanting the woman to know her daughter was safe. Or so he said."

Candace looked down at her sister and said, "My parents were not good parents. Ella, you have lived a better life than you could have if you had stayed home. I'm glad you escaped before their poison changed your life. As it is, you probably don't remember much of your early life, except with the Petersons."

Ella said, "No, I don't. I guess that's a blessing of sorts. I mean, you don't usually look at being kidnapped in a positive light, but I guess it worked out well in this case. I'm sorry you had to live through such...difficulties, Candy."

Ella reached up to her sister and they embraced.

The noon hour arrived, as did Ella's four children and sixteen grandchildren, all of whom were eager to meet these unknown family members. Ella had broken the news of her true identity to her husband as soon as she had learned her parents' secret and had sat down with her children and grandchildren a short time later, so everyone had been given the chance to adapt to the news.

Ella said, "How about some lunch? Since we have so many folks, I decided to have our luncheon made by a friend who's a caterer. It's almost 12:30, and I imagine everyone's hungry." The crowd agreed and moved into the sun room, where tables and chairs had been set up. The tables were decorated with floral arrangements and Victorian place settings.

Susan said, "Ella, this is lovely. You shouldn't have gone to such trouble."

Ella's oldest daughter spoke up. Jenna told them, "My mom is the original 'Hostess with the Mostest.' She loves to do this kind of thing, luncheons and teas and such. This was fun for her. My sister Jess and I helped, but she did most of it. She lives for this kind of thing. Oh, Dad, Justin, and Jonathan set up the tables and chairs. 'Credit where credit is due' and all that. "

Ella smiled at her hubby. "Dear, would you ask the blessing, please? We don't want this wonderful food to get cold."

After Jimmy thanked the Lord for reuniting the family, he asked for God's watched care over their upcoming trip, and for the food. They all went through the buffet line, settling into the long tables for a time of food and fellowship. The brown stacked stone fireplace along one wall was similar in style to the one in Christopher's home, so they all felt right at home. They enjoyed looking out the picture windows that graced two sides of the room, noticing that small animals roamed outside in the trees.

As they ate, they learned about Ella's family. Her hubby Jimmy was sixty-four and had retired from his work as an engineer just the previous year. He'd taken early retirement when the company he had worked for had been bought out. The retirement package was too good to turn down, so he took it. He enjoyed teaching project management as an adjunct faculty member at the local community college.

Ella had raised her family of four children, working part

time as a teacher's helper when the kids were still in school. When they graduated, she went back to college and got a degree in interior design. She worked for a local decorating company, staging houses that were on the market. She confessed to being in great demand and that she loved her work.

Candace turned to her sister and said, "Ella, you need to work on my house in Austin. I'm getting ready to put it on the market and move to Maryland. I could use your touch to get it sold quickly."

"Sure thing, Candy." Ella smiled at her.

"Sadly, I inherited our mother's decorating taste, which isn't saying much."

Christopher spoke up, "No, Aunt Candace, your home is really nice. You don't have any reason to 'hang your head in shame,' like Mom says."

"Well, our mother might have had taste that just reflected the time in which she lived then." Candace glanced at Ella. "Avocado green and indescribable harvest gold dominated our home. She had plastic flowers in various planters throughout the house. She couldn't be bothered with the real thing, so she settled for something that couldn't even qualify as second-best. Maybe third or fourth best, if we're being charitable."

They all laughed. Ella said, "Well, tastes and styles change, I imagine."

"You're too kind, dear sister. But do tell us about your family. What are your children doing these days?" Candace's curiosity had finally gotten the better of her.

Ella explained that their oldest son Justin was in television. He and his wife had four children. Next in line, Jenna was a real estate agent. She also had four children. Their second daughter Jess was a fulltime mother of six children and part time event planner. Their youngest, Jonathan, was a Ph.D. student and father of two. He was studying communication with the hopes of teaching on the university level.

"Oh, a fellow educator, I see. Excellent. We can always

use fresh talent in the world of academia." Candace looked at Jonathan. "What is your field of study?"

Jonathan said, "Aunt Candace, I'm focusing on the use of indirect communication in television and film as a means of conveying the message behind the message. You know, the directors and producers have a definite message they want to get across to the audience, so I'm studying how they use various literary tropes such as irony/sarcasm, metaphors, and deception to share their ideas with the audience." He paused, embarrassed. "I'm sorry. I have a tendency to really go off on my dissertation topic. I don't mean to bore anyone."

"No, no problem, Jonathan. You weren't boring in the least. Though, perhaps we ought to discuss this later." Candace smiled at the thought of her nephew being an academic.

"Yes, Ma'am." Candace thought he still looked self-conscious.

Ella shared that their oldest son, Justin, was actually a local television celebrity. He was a nightly news anchor on the local Fox affiliate, WXIX, and the newsman in him thought their story would be a great "puppy dog" story on the evening news. He talked it over with the family.

Justin said, "You know how Fox loves to have heartwarming stories at some point during their broadcasts. Well, I think the story of how two sisters reunited after fifty-five years apart would be a great lead-in for the news Monday night. This is an even better story because I'm related to both of you. How about it? Mom? Aunt Candace? Would you let me interview the two of you?"

Candace said, "Humm . . . I appreciate your enthusiasm for the project, Justin, but I'm not sure what the legal ramifications would be for Ella, since she lived her whole life as Jennifer. Have you checked into it?"

Justin told her, "Yes, ma'am, I checked with our legal department. Mom didn't intentionally steal Jennifer's identity, she was forced into it. Jennifer is dead and, since she died at such a young age, there was no income or property owned by her. My grandparents left everything to Ella as Jennifer, knowing who she really was, so they weren't being tricked into anything."

Ella said, "Correction, honey. Peggy didn't know I was really Ella, just Dad and my mother Norma. Still in all, I did live the bulk of my life honestly thinking I was Jennifer. There were no other relatives to come forward and say otherwise, except for the Prescotts and they didn't know where I was." Ella turned to her, "Candy, there's 'no harm, no foul' as they say. If you're willing to do this, I'm comfortable with the idea."

Candace asked, "Christopher, what do you think of this idea?"

Christopher thought for a few minutes. "I'm not the person in the family with legal connections. Brooke, what do you think?"

Brooke explained, "Aunt Ella, I'm a paralegal. I don't know the laws in Ohio at all, but I'm thinking that it would probably be okay. You weren't acting out of a desire to harm the Petersons. The reverse could be argued, except that they gave you a wonderful life that's actually better than the one you would have had with William Prescott Sr. and Mary Taylor Prescott. If you want to do the interview, I would say you should go ahead and do it. You're the only person alive that's related to your branch of the Petersons, right?"

Ella said, "Yes, that's right, Brooke. My adoptive parents had one sibling apiece, but they never married and died without children. My parents only had Jennifer, who died at age four, when my adoptive mother kidnapped me. No one came forward when they died, to claim any of their estate. They weren't wealthy by any means, but we were always comfortable. The only problem we ran into was with John Prescott and his nurse friend, Karen Lamont, who claimed to be me."

Brooke said, "Then I think you can move ahead with the interview, if Aunt Candace would like to do it."

Candace said, "Certainly, Ella. If you would like, I could be involved in the interview. I used to do television. I was the anchor of a popular morning show. I am very comfortable in front of a camera, though it has been a long time." She looked at Justin. "Yes, young man, I think you have an interview!"

**

Susan stood in the corner of Ella's living room and watched as Justin set things up for the interview. She took mental stock of her family and was pleasantly surprised at how her life was working out. Her children were settled into their own lives now. They were reconciled and safe in the knowledge that they would go to heaven when they died. The siblings she had never known about were "all present and accounted for" as Kurt would have said. She was out of harm's way, no longer married to a man who wanted her dead. She was married happily to her high school sweetheart, who was Joshua's father. She and Dan would be meeting Peter's widow Glenda Jo in the next few months when they drove down to Florida. After their visit with Ella and her family, the whole family would be on the way to touch base with the convent where Kurt's sister Maggie had lived and died. Ella and her husband Jimmy had been unaware of her sister Maggie's religious life and had asked to go along. Yes, life was good.

A few minutes later, Susan settled into the sofa, surrounded by her family and friends, to watch Justin do the interview between Ella and her sister Candace. Justin's camera, lighting, and sound people had come right over when he called. Susan noticed that Justin had hoped for the best and had already prepared a list of questions to ask the women as they talked. Apparently, Justin was an important man at WXIX, judging from how the personnel treated him. How nice.

The ladies talked with Justin for about thirty minutes, knowing that their interview would be cut and manicured back at the station. They shared the story of their childhoods, so different from one another and how the treachery of their brother had actually led them to each other. Justin commented, "so what your brother John had meant for evil actually turned

353

out for your good." Susan's head swung around at those words. Her ...what was he to her? She would have to think about it . . . ummm, he was her nephew by marriage . . . Justin was obviously a Christian! Susan recognized his words from the story of Joseph in the book of Genesis.

"Yes," Candace was saying, "My brother John was trying to hoodwink the family into giving him money but, instead, Ella and I found each other."

Ella said, "Yes, and I praise God for bringing us back together."

At those words, Susan thought Candace looked a bit uncomfortable, but the woman's television professionalism kicked in. Susan didn't notice any squirming on her sister-in-law Ella's part. Susan would try to find the opportunity to share more of her own testimony with Candace sometime in the future. She would begin praying toward that end immediately.

Justin closed the interview saying, "thank you ladies." He turned to the camera and said, "This story is especially precious to me because Ella is my mother, and Dr. Prescott is my Aunt Candace." He looked back at the two and smiled. "What a blessing this is!"

***

The next day, the family, including Ella and Jimmy, packed up and headed to Sylvania. The Reverend Mother was expecting them because Brooke and Michael had been in email contact with her since their honeymoon. They arrived at the convent in mid-afternoon. Susan was looking forward to meeting the elderly woman, since Brooke had told her so much about the Reverend Mother.

The nun greeted the family as they got out of the van saying, "I may have found something you will be interested in, folks. I was going through some of Sister Mary Catherine's belongings. She didn't have any relatives to give her few possessions to, so we kept them for safekeeping. I found a note from Sister Margaret Frances. I haven't opened it because I believe that it belongs to you, as her next of kin." The Reverend Mother invited them into her study, where she withdrew the note from her desk drawer and handed it over.

Brooke took the note from the Reverend Mother and then handed it off to Susan.

"Mom, I think you should be the one to open this, since you were married to Dad and he was a suspect in the murder of his mother."

"Oh, Brooke, I don't know. Two of Kurt's sisters are here, one of whom was there that night. Candace, would you like to see this first?" Susan asked.

Candace said, "Susan, you've been the first to look at all of the journals, except for the first one that Brooke and Michael read. I have no objection to your seeing this note first. I was there the night it happened, but my mother was dead by the time I got there. I didn't see what actually occurred. Go ahead and read it."

Ella said, "By all means, you read it first, Susan. That's fine and dandy."

The Reverent Mother spoke up. "Mrs. Walsh, we have a small courtyard where you could read the note in private, if you would prefer, or you may stay here and I'll withdraw for a few moments."

Susan said, "May I stay here, if you don't mind? Your office is so comfortable."

"Certainly. Ring the bell on my desk when you want me to return." The nun departed.

"Mom, are you ready to see what Maggie has to say? You might not like it." Brooke's concern was evident.

Susan said, "I think it may clear a lot of things up, Brooke, so let's see what she wrote. I'll read it out loud, so that everyone can hear it at the same time."

Susan opened the note and began to read the note to

them all.

"March 15, 2012

Dear family members:

"You may notice that this letter is not with my personal possessions. I did that purposefully so that I could take time gathering my own thoughts, and to not overwhelm you with family issues. Sister Mary Catherine was with me in Maryland and she died a short time after our return, so I felt safe in putting this note in with her belongings.

"You may have noticed by now that the dates for my trip to Maryland are different from the dates entered into the convent's log. You may have figured out that I was mistaken or perhaps you think that I deliberately misled you on when I was home. I did it on purpose, to draw attention away from the fact that I witnessed my mother's murder. I have asked God to forgive me for this sin and I ask for your forgiveness now, as well." The family gasped at this new information.

"Sister Mary Catherine and I were in town when my mother passed. I left the Sister in our hotel room, having waited until she slept to leave. She was an early riser and was, likewise, someone who was used to the early bedtime at the convent. She was a heavy sleeper, as well, and did not wake up when I left or came back, from what I could tell. She never confronted me on my absence, and I was never punished for it by my Mother Superior so I believe she did not know I had left her alone in the room.

"I slipped out the door, got into the convent car that we were using for the trip, and headed to my family's home. I sat outside the house for a while, debating about going inside because I figured my parents would be three sheets to the wind by that time of night. I wasn't right in front of the house. I was just at the edge of the property, so people might think I was visiting the neighbors. The car windows were rolled down because it was a warm September night. My habit protected me from the mosquitos pretty well.

"The house windows were open, though there were

screens that protected the family from bugs getting inside. I had left home in May of 1960 and so my sister Ella, who was born in February, was still a newborn. My mother had told me about the child's disappearance in her last letter to me. I overheard some yelling about Ella and figured that they hadn't found her yet.

"It was very sad to realize that the child I had known so briefly was probably dead or worse, so I began to pray for her soul, as I had been doing since learning about her disappearance. While I was sitting there, I saw a man walk into the yard. I hunched down in my seat, hoping he wouldn't notice me. Someone had driven down the street slowly a few minutes before but had not parked at the house. He didn't seem familiar with the area, so I figured he was up to no good. I waited. The man hid behind a tree, apparently hearing a car approach.

"I was surprised to see my brother Will drive up. I hadn't seen him in years, but I realized he was just home for a visit when I saw his Pennsylvania tags. It was a very short visit. He parked and went into the house for a little while, but didn't stay long. He was escorted from the house by my very drunk father who yelled something about "taking his Christian butt out of my house and never coming back." Will drove away and I didn't see him again. I wish I had followed him, to get some contact information, but I didn't think of it fast enough. Dad didn't see me. He would have come over to my car, if he had.

"I realized that my own new-found faith wouldn't be welcome in my father's house either, so I stayed where I was, wondering about the stranger. A few minutes later, the man came from behind the tree and walked around the back of the house. I heard the back door slam and heard the sound of my mother's voice. I couldn't see the back of the house from where I was, so I got out of my car and walked around back, hiding behind trees as I went. I got to a big tree that was about ten or fifteen feet from the creek and stayed there. I didn't want to be seen.

"They had a pretty quick conversation. He said

something about Ella being better off with him. Mom had a piece of paper in her hand, but he tore it away from her as he turned around and left. I think he had gotten spooked by some noise that he heard. It was my brother Kurt showing up. I had heard someone coming off the roof of the porch and guessed by his size that it was Kurt. I had left when he was about six and he'd grown a lot, but I was pretty sure it was he. It was.

"Kurt was yelling at Mom. He was angry, I guess about Ella being gone. Peter came up just then, and they both yelled at her. Kurt got even madder and shoved Mom. She fell on some rocks next to the creek and didn't move. The boys were fighting with each other by then, pushing and shoving like kids do. I'm not sure why they were fighting, but they had turned their anger on one another. It went on for a few minutes when they realized, I guess, that Mom hadn't gotten up. They stopped fighting and just looked at each other, then back at Mom.

"Candy came running over. She tried to help Mom. She pushed past the boys, but she had trouble trying to get Mom out of the water on her own. She kept dropping Mom back into the water. I guess Mom was pretty much a dead weight by then. The water was rushing pretty hard. It can be very unforgiving in that creek at high tide. Candy couldn't get a good handle on Mom. I noticed that she found the slip of paper that Mom was holding. I saw Candy put it in her pocket, in between times of trying to lift Mom up. She yelled for the boys to help, but they just stood and stared at her.

"My father came barreling out of the house about then. He was mad, as usual, and screamed at Candy, asking her what she thought she was doing. He grabbed Mom's arm and yanked her out of the creek. I heard a crack and guessed that he either broke her arm or dislocated her shoulder. He threw her down on the ground and felt for a pulse. Nothing. He screamed at the boys and Candy, asking "what happened here?" None of them answered. They were probably too scared to move, knowing my father's temper. It's a good thing the house is so far from the neighbors or they might have heard what was going on and called the police.

"Dad carefully put Mom back in the creek, with her face completely under water. He smoothed out the grass where he had thrown her at first and then ordered the kids back into the house. No one was saying anything. They just walked in silence. Mom was lying in the creek, face down. I hurried away, running down the street a short distance before the police could arrive, but then I realized pretty quickly that Dad, being drunk, wasn't going to call them. I waited behind a neighbor's shrubs for a few minutes, but the police didn't come. I realized that Dad was going to leave Mom lying there in the creek until someone else found her. I came back and got in my car when everyone was inside the house. I drove back to the hotel. I sneaked into the room that Sister Mary Catherine and I were sharing and climbed into bed after a quick trip to the bathroom to change my clothes.

"Sure enough, the next day I overheard people in town talking about "poor Mrs. Prescott" being found in the creek behind her house, dead. Drunk, as usual. No one seemed particularly surprised or saddened by my mother's passing. Sister Mary Catherine asked me about it, but I just hushed her and said that was the way things were.

"You might wonder why I stood so close by but did nothing. I've asked myself that question a hundred times over the past few years. I don't have an answer. I was frozen behind the tree. No one saw me, as far as I can tell. No one has ever come forth to say they knew I watched the whole thing. Was it because I knew my mother lived a life of constant ridicule, punishment, and abuse? Was it because I knew it was only going to get worse as the years went by? Did I see this as a way out for her? That her death was perhaps a blessing in disguise? Was this my mother's only way out?

"I just don't know the answer to that question. I know from the letters we exchanged that she was hungry for a better life. I know that she felt incredible remorse over the loss of Ella. I know the family blamed her, and rightfully so. I believe that

Kurt was the person that pushed her into the creek, but did he kill her or did we all kill her? Did my father kill her with his abuse? Did her drinking so much contribute to the accident? Did Peter kill her by fighting with Kurt instead of saving her?

"Candy tried to save Mom, but she wasn't strong enough in those circumstances. My father didn't even try mouth-to-mouth resuscitation, even though he had taken training in how to do it. He made no effort to save her life. He just covered up her death. Made it look like an accident. Did I kill her by standing by, watching it happen, and doing absolutely nothing?

"I truly believe it was an accident that went terribly wrong. If she hadn't been drinking so much...if she hadn't agreed to meet a total stranger at night at the creek...if Kurt hadn't been so unforgiving and angry . . . if Peter hadn't used that exact moment to push a little boy who was in such pain . . . if Candy hadn't been too weak to pull her out while there was still a chance . . . if Dad had made some effort . . . if I hadn't stood silently by. In the end, we all failed her. May God forgive us.

"I'm sorry you had to learn about the weaknesses of your deceased family members through this letter. Well, some of us are dead, but perhaps some are still among the living. I wonder if Peter is still living, how he reads what happened that night . . . or Kurt . . . or Candy . . . or my father.

"I hope that Kurt doesn't carry the burden of guilt by himself. He was a little boy who was grieving for his kidnapped sister. He didn't have a normal family life. Yes, he was the one who pushed our mother, at least from what I saw, but he couldn't have foreseen what would happen next. I don't think that his ten-year-old mind could have conceived that his action would lead to her death. Children aren't wired that way, from what I understand. Once she fell, Kurt couldn't have pulled her out because of his size. Peter could have helped, but didn't. Candy was the only person there that night who tried to save our mother. My father tried to save his own neck and he did, but our mother died so he could cover his own backside.

"I often wonder how my siblings have gotten through life, knowing what happened. Did our father blame Kurt? I understand my father's nature well enough to realize that he probably heaped blame on Kurt at every opportunity, even though my father wasn't there to watch our mother fall. He couldn't have known that Kurt was the one to push her down, unless Peter told him. Peter was many things, but I don't believe he would have tattled.

"Candy hadn't gotten there in time to watch the accident unfold, so I hope she bears no false guilt. She tried her best to save Mom. I . . . I carry the guilt of not helping. I've tried my best to help others my entire life as a nun, but I failed my own mother. I pray that God will forgive me. I pray that you will find it in your heart to forgive us all.

"I find my strength is waning these days. I haven't got the stamina I once had, and I suspect the end of my life is near. I'll place this document with Sister Mary Catherine's things so that perhaps it can be found when the time is right. I pray that you will love and serve the Lord, as I have tried to do these 40+ years. I'm sorry for the weakness I demonstrated so many years ago. Perhaps my mother would have lived, had I taken action. Please, forgive me.

Love,

Your Relative, Sister Margaret Frances"

Brooke looked at her mother after she read the note to them all. "So, I guess we know what happened."

Aunt Candace was crying, but she wiped her tears away and said, "That's close, but not really how I remember it. We need to keep in mind that everyone has his or her own point of view. Though Maggie, Sister Margaret Frances that is, was no doubt sincere in her remembrances, she might have been too far back to hear everything clearly."

Dan said, "That's true. Everyone sees things in his or her own way. Maggie's line of sight might have been bad. Maybe she didn't see the stranger push her mother down first. Kurt's actions might have been to block her from rising, or maybe the boys were so busy fighting that neither one of them was near enough to contribute to her death."

They decided to table the discussion for the time being, until they could get home and map things out on their white board. They spent the rest of the day touring the church, convent, and grounds, and placing flowers on Maggie's grave. Everyone was lost in his or her own thoughts about the most recent development. Brooke spent a lot of time hugging Michael, trying to make sense of such an unhappy family and the death of its matriarch. Susan took Dan's arm and silently thanked God for her new husband as they walked around the ground, wondering what the family would learn next.

Chapter 41

Christopher was glad that Audrey had decided to become involved in the family mystery. It gave them something to talk about besides classes and his daughters. While the former was something she was involved in, the latter was still a source of embarrassment for him, though he adored his girls. Christopher invited her to the next family meeting at his mother's and Dan's house, interested in what she had to say about his grandmother's death from the viewpoint of an outsider. Of course, he hoped that she wouldn't be an outsider forever.

It was a lovely but hot Saturday in late afternoon the week following their trip to Ohio. They all settled into the couches and chairs with their sweet iced tea after an early family dinner, while Joshua's kids entertained Melanie and Molly. Madison and Abby, Joshua's two oldest children, were in charge of the younger kids and loved the thought of taking care of two identical little girls. They were playing in the family room just off the great room, where the adults were gathered to piece the puzzle together. Dan, as always, was wielding the white board marker as Brooke took charge of the meeting itself.

Brooke said, "Okay folks. Let's talk things through. First, we have Dad, aka, Kurt. He was mad at his mother and blamed her for Ella's disappearance."

Christopher said, "Yes. Dad was very upset about his mother's role in the kidnapping, but does that mean that, as a ten year old boy, he killed his mother?"

Michael answered, "No, I don't think it does."

Susan said, "I just can't accept that my husband was a murderer." She looked around. "Okay, I know what you're thinking. He tried to kill me three times. He probably had a distorted sense of right and wrong. I understand. But something tells me that he didn't do it. I don't know why, but that's what I think."

Brooke looked over at her elder brother. "Josh, what do you think?"

Joshua answered, "Kurt was a complicated man. I'd like to think that he didn't do it, but I don't know that we can rule him out. Let's look at the other suspects."

Brooke said, "Okay. Let's take Will. The only report we have of his being there is from Maggie, who said that he came and then left when his father got mad about his being a Christian."

Michael said, "But what if he came back? Maggie says he didn't, but we already know that Maggie lies." He hesitated, and then corrected himself. "Lied. Would she have protected him for some reason, or did she not see him return?"

Joshua said, "When Amanda and the kids and I went to pay our respects in Philly, there was nothing left of Will except a grave stone. We didn't get any special letters. There were no confessional messages from beyond the grave that we found. His house had been sold years before he died, since his wife was already dead. They had no children, and he knew he would be hospitalized until he died. The folks at the veterans' home said that he left any money he had to some veteran's organization. He literally died with nothing. I suppose he might have done it, but I really don't know."

Christopher asked, "What about Peter?"

Dan said, "We know he was there. We know that he came down and had a fight with Kurt. Every witness says they fought, while ignoring their dying mother."

Susan said, "Peter wasn't a Christian yet and was only a couple of weeks away from moving out. After they got married, Glenda Jo said he had an anger problem and that he went through therapy with some men from church. He might've done it, I suppose."

Brooke asked, "What about John? He isn't a nice person to this day, and he's a crook. Maybe he came back and did the deed when, oh, I don't know, he couldn't extort any money from his mother?"

Christopher argued, "We don't have any evidence that he was in the area, but we don't know that he wasn't either."

Susan said, "Well, I don't trust him for a minute. Look what he did to Aunt Candace."

Christopher interjected, "Actually, Mom, as much as we love Aunt Candace, we do have to consider her as a suspect, as well."

Brooke objected, "Aunt Candace was a buffer between her mother and Kurt, after Ella was gone. She took care of Kurt, acting as a surrogate mother when their mother died. I can't imagine a young girl killing her mother so she would have a boatload of new responsibilities. Maggie said Candace was the only person who tried to help her mother, remember? And then there's the deal with her father wanting her 'services.' I just don't think Aunt Candace did it."

Joshua asked, "What about Mr. Prescott? He was a drunk and adulterer. Maybe he wanted to get rid of his wife to make room for someone new."

Brooke asked, "Why would he have needed Aunt Candace to "take care of him,' so to speak, if there was a lady waiting in the wings?"

Susan said, "Maybe the prospective Mrs. Prescott took off when she realized that he was a man whose little girl was kidnapped and his wife died, all inside a month. Maybe she wanted no part of a man like that."

Dan warned, "Hold on here. Let's slow things down a bit. Brooke, you want to review what we know?"

Brooke summed things up, "Sure thing. Okay, so Mr. Prescott might have had a reason to kill his wife. Will might not have been the nice Christian boy everyone thought he was. He had just gotten back from Viet Nam a couple of years before that, so he might have had PTSD or something. Maggie was a nun who lied, at least before she took her vows. Johnny was, and still is, a crook. We don't know if he was there or not, but he might've been. We don't know where he was at the time, just that he had left in 1962. Peter was there and had anger issues. He left soon after his mother died. Candace was also there, but she says that the area was crowded by the time she arrived at the creek. Candace was cleared by Maggie's letter, if we can trust it. Kurt, meaning, Dad, was there and everyone says he was upset, and they all say he did it. The man who had Ella also had a reason to kill Mrs. Prescott, and we know that he was there."

Audrey asked, "But what if she was dead before either boy got there, before Candace got there?"

Christopher asked, "What are you thinking, Honey?"

Audrey answered, "We know she met someone at the creek, and that it was probably the husband of the woman who kidnapped Ella. What if he drowned her and then propped her up so that the first person who touched her would knock her into the creek? I mean, I know it's a stretch but, in the dark of the night and the heat of the moment, I think it's at least plausible."

Joshua said, "You know, you might have a point there, Audrey. It only takes a few seconds to drown someone. If Kurt came running at her, he might not have noticed that she was dead before he touched her. It was dark, like you said, and he was a very angry little boy."

Susan said, "Audrey and Josh, I think you both might be onto something. Let's think a little further outside the box, okay? We know that the three kids still at home were upstairs when they heard their parents fighting. They knew it was best to not get into the middle of things with their parents, so they probably avoided going downstairs. They heard the backdoor slam, but no one knows if Mrs. Prescott went outside alone. We've just assumed she did. Her husband was a jealous man, from what folks have said. What if he went out with her, but lagged behind while she met with Teddy Peterson, the man who had Ella?"

Brooke said, "Or maybe Mr. Prescott came out while she was talking to Mr. Peterson, but he came out very quietly. He was a sneak, so he came out of the house with no one the wiser. Mr. Prescott comes up and starts pushing and shoving Mr. Peterson and Mrs. Prescott accidentally falls into the creek. The men are so busy hitting each other and rolling around on the wet ground that they don't notice Mrs. Prescott is dying. Mr. Peterson takes off. Mr. Prescott sees what happened to his wife and goes back inside to protect himself from suspicion. He changes his wet clothes quickly so that it appears he's been inside all along and then he runs into Candace when she comes into the kitchen."

Susan explained further, "Yes, Brooke, they argue because Candace wants to go to her mother and he wants her to stay inside. Candace leaves anyway. Meanwhile, Kurt has, by now, climbed out his window to get down to the creek, without his father knowing it. He sees his mother by the creek and holds her head under water or, at least knocks her over, not knowing that she's already dead. Peter runs outside and around the side of the house. He sees what Kurt is doing to their mother. Mom is in the creek, and Peter starts a fight with Kurt. Candace shows up a few minutes later and tries to save her mother while the boys fight. Mistaken identity about who actually killed her?"

Dan declared, "Susan and Brooke, I'd need a flow chart to explain that, but you might be on the right track. We've always assumed that Mr. Prescott didn't do it because we weren't expecting that he did. What do we know about him and his behavior that night?"

Michael said, "Mr. Prescott was an angry man who showed his sons how to disrespect their mother. He was also a drunk who might have had one wife too many, right then."

Brooke argued, "He was known to be ill-tempered. Look at what he did to Mrs. Prescott's Bible. That's not the sign of a nice person."

Christopher added, "When someone is an adulterer, they tend to see it in others. We know he abused Mrs. Prescott. He probably accused her of some pretty bad things that he was already doing himself."

Susan said, "Okay, so we know that Kurt wanted to get rid of me so he could marry Kelsey. What if my life was so expendable to his way of thinking because he saw his father kill his mother to make room for an affair he was having?' She turned to Audrey. "Sorry to air the family's dirty linen here, but this is simply the way it was with my marriage to Christopher's father."

Audrey said, "No, no problem, Susan. Chris has told me all about it. I think you have a good point. That would explain a lot of Kurt's attitudes towards you." Audrey nodded.

Joshua said, "Okay. I'm thinking really far outside the box time now. What if Mr. Prescott did follow Mrs. Prescott to the creek and overheard her talking to Mr. Peterson? Mr. Prescott exchanges some fisticuffs with Mr. Peterson, who got mad and left. He then turned to his wife and started yelling at her. He claimed she was having an affair, maybe even with Mr. Peterson, but the reality was that he was having an affair and wanted to be rid of her. He pushed her down and then held her face under the water to kill her."

Christopher broke in. "Then he set her up to look like she was sitting at the creek. He high tailed it back into the house before anyone could see him there. Whoever reached her first, like an angry Kurt, pushed her over, thinking that he was killing her. But she was already dead and had been for several minutes. Peter came running up; Kurt defended himself. Or maybe he prevented Peter from saving her by starting a punching match with him. Then Candace ran up."

Susan told them, "Candace only saw part of what happened. Because of the timing, she wouldn't have seen that her father killed her mother. She's thought all along that Kurt did it, which was added to in her mind because Mr. Prescott heaped guilt on Kurt his whole life and she probably overheard a lot of it."

Dan asked, "What about Maggie? She thinks that Kurt

did it, too."

Brooke said, "We don't know exactly when Maggie got there. She might have arrived after Mr. Prescott and Mr. Peterson had already fought."

Michael said, "But she saw Will . . . unless Will arrived in between the fight that the men had and killing of Mrs. Prescott and the second fight that Peter and Kurt had. Maggie said that Mr. Prescott was yelling at Will for being there, but we don't know if Mrs. Prescott was alive or dead by then."

Christopher argued, "Maybe Mr. Prescott was yelling at Will to keep him out of the house and away from his mother. The best way to do that was to accuse him of being a bad Christian. It had to be strong enough to drive Will away permanently."

Joshua said, "It would be so helpful if someone was alive that could tell us what happened for sure."

Audrey said, "Your Aunt Candace is alive but might have not seen everything. Timing is everything. Johnny's alive, but I doubt he'd want to talk to the family, since he's back in jail because of us."

Christopher told them, "These are some really good ideas. I wonder if we could play it all out, to see if the story hangs together."

Brooke asked, "You mean role play it? That would be very interesting."

Joshua said, "We know the address where Kurt grew up because it's in his journals that 'if lost, please return this journal to Kurt Prescott at . . .' So we can google the address and maybe find a google map of the house itself. Even if the new owners have changed things around, we have the description of the house and where it was in relation to the creek. We know about the white picket fence in the side and back yards and the difficult latch. The creek is probably still in the same place, so why don't we see what we can find?"

Amanda said, "Great idea, Josh. Of course, Aunt Candace knows the address as well, and she could fill in any blanks we have on the actual location of things like the fence, the trees, and the porch roof. Chris, can you call Aunt Candace and ask?"

Christopher looked at his watch, "Sure thing, but it's getting kinda late for now. I need to get the girls home and to bed or they will be bears to wake up in the morning for church. I'll email Aunt Candace in the next few days and ask her about the logistics of the house. How about if we get together next Saturday afternoon, when the girls are with the Thompsons, and see if we can hash this out?"

Everyone agreed that it was a plan. Joshua would do the google map search and let Brooke know what he'd found so she could set up the yard with the appropriate landmarks. Christopher would contact Aunt Candace. He was especially close to her, so everyone was happy to let him be the go-between on things Aunt Candace-related.

Christopher scooped up his exhausted daughters and then decided to bathe them there before taking them home. That way, he could get them in their jammies before leaving and put them straight into bed when they got to their house. Audrey lent a hand and things went pretty quickly. He loved how they worked together. It would be great if it was permanent.

Chapter 42

Christopher took Audrey out for an early lunch at Reynold's Tavern in Annapolis on Saturday, reminding her about the family meeting later that June afternoon. He had smiled at her attire when he picked her up. They were both wearing crisp white slacks and navy blue polo shirts. "We must have gotten the same memo."

Audrey said, "Either that, or you have exquisite taste."

He bowed and thanked her. He did, in his opinion, at least where it applied directly to Audrey Johns.

"Where are Melanie and Molly?"

"Mr. and Mrs. Thompson have them for the day."

"Oh, that's right. I remember you told me they were in town for the weekend." Audrey said.

Christopher told her, "You can't really do too much with kids who are only eight months old, but they wanted to take them over to Shannon's condo and hang out. She had all of the necessary nursery stuff, of course, and the Thompsons stay in her condo when they're in town. They inherited it. I think it's very sad, but they haven't touched a thing since Shannon died."

Audrey shook her head. "That was such a waste of a human life. Lives, actually."

Christopher agreed, in spite of the subterfuge Shannon had tried on him in her closing days. "If only . . ." he shook his head.

The twins spending some time with their maternal grandparents gave him a little bit of a break in the now-normal routine of weekend lunch and naps and dinner and early bedtimes. His former nightly trips to the local bars had been replaced by trips to the daycare center and pediatrician's office. Boy, his crazy, swinging bachelor life had evaporated. For that, he was very thankful. He didn't miss it one iota. His girls, all three of them, were a such a blessing in his life: Audrey,

Melanie, and Molly.

They had what Audrey called "a delightful luncheon," with the high tea served at the Tavern. He could tell that Audrey was really 'into' that kind of thing. He wanted to please her more than anything. The food itself was good, though not very filling in his book. But, what was it that Robert Frost said about a man having to give up part of himself for the woman in his life? Christopher could accept that, even though he would have preferred a steak. They finished up and headed out the door. He stopped and bought her a small bouquet of colorful flowers at the vendor right outside the Tavern. He bowed as he presented it to her, "My Lady."

Audrey thanked him and smelled the fragrance the blooms presented. She dropped a curtsy.

Christopher looked at the sidewalks crowded with tourists and locals alike and said, "It's such a nice afternoon. How about if we take a little walk around downtown before we head over to Mom's and Dan's house?"

"Sounds great, Chris. What time do we need to be at your folks' house?"

"We're getting together at three. We have plenty of time to walk around and enjoy the day." Tourists were taking photos of the nearby church; he was eager to get away from them. The crowds were jostling the two of them, and he knew they needed to make a decision quickly to either move on or stop blocking the way.

"What time will the girls be back?" Audrey asked.

"Probably about seven. The Thompsons are only in town for the weekend. They'll be coming up about every three months or so from now on, but I know they have to head out early tomorrow morning." He pulled Audrey over to one side, lest she be run over by the enthusiastic passersby. The sidewalk wasn't particularly narrow, but people were everywhere today.

Audrey said, "They seem very nice. Do the girls know who they are yet?"

"We spend some time every visit with the girls eying

them suspiciously. After about ten minutes, they warm up to them. I think actually knowing them will come much later. Mr. and Mrs. Thompson are talking about moving up here when he retires, so they can spend more time with Melanie and Molly. I'm encouraging them to do it. They have a place to stay, what with Shannon's place being available to them, so they could sell their house and have a small but nice condo."

Audrey seemed suddenly conscious of the need to move on. "Not to change the subject, but I would love to take a walk. Let's go!"

Christopher took Audrey's hand and began swinging it as they walked. They visited the grounds of St. John's College, since that was the road less traveled that afternoon, enjoying the respite from the summer heat under the huge trees that dotted the campus.

"Fatherhood becomes you, Chris." Audrey laughed and said, "I can't imagine the Christopher Prescott I met last fall swinging hands and being content to walk around Annapolis after just eating high tea."

"I think it's more like 'Christianity becomes me.' Fatherhood is great, but the Lord is the One who changed me." He smiled at his beloved Audrey. "You've helped, as well."

Audrey curtsied slightly, "Thank you for the compliment. I'm in heady company."

Christopher hoped the time was right. He thought it was. Perhaps, well, he knew he didn't deserve her. He had lived a pretty raunchy life there for several years. Make that many years. She seemed to realize that he was a changed man. He prayed that his timing was good.

"My lovely Audrey, shall we sit for a moment?" He waved at the one bench in the shade. They sat. She giggled. She was not a giggler, so he guessed that she probably knew what was coming. He cleared his throat. Man, I'm a wreck. I've never done this before. Sweaty palms, trickle of perspiration making its way down the middle of my back. It itched, but he didn't want to scratch it. How unseemly that would be at a time like this. He definitely didn't want to cross the lines between acceptable and unacceptable behavior. Not now.

"Audrey . . . umm . . . Audrey?" Why wasn't his voice cooperating? He sounded like a preadolescent boy. He got down on one knee. More giggles from the feminine side of the bench. "I'm not the man I once was. I'm not the man I'm going to be, but I have loved you from the first day we met. I know that I come with some baggage. Cute baggage in some cases, but baggage nonetheless." A huge smile. "Will you be my wife? Will you marry me?" With those words, he took a black box out of his pocket, where he had carried it for weeks, and presented her with a 1.5 carat Radiant cut diamond. His forehead was a mess of sweat.

"Chris, the day I saw you at your mother's and Dan's house after the VBS party, God told me that you are the man He had prepared for me. Yes, I'll marry you and I'll be the mother of your children." She beamed at him. It was the most beautiful sight he had ever seen.

For the first time, they kissed. They hugged as he tried very hard not to present his terribly wet back to his new wife-to-be.

At precisely the same time, they said, "Let's go tell the family."

They headed for his mother's home, knowing that they were arriving an hour early for the three o'clock meeting, but he couldn't wait to share their news. Audrey is mine! Praise the Lord! He looked over at her and got chills to think that she had agreed to marry a sinner like he was. He couldn't stop smiling, though he had to admit she looked pretty happy herself. The ring was stunning on her finger.

They pulled into the drive and his mother and step-father came out.

Susan asked, "Is everything okay?" She looked the part of the concerned mother which, given his background, was completely understandable. Then she saw his face. "Yes, I'd say everything is more than okay, Chris."

Dan looked at the couple and then back at his wife, "Yes, Suzy-Q, that is a 'more than okay' look if you ask me. Confess, old man."

Before either he or Audrey could say a word, they were engulfed by an embrace from the older couple. You know, this happy family stuff is really a lot of fun. I don't know what I found so appealing about my old life, but this beats it by a country mile. And I have the most beautiful woman in the world who has agreed to be my wife. It simply can't get any better than that. Audrey showed Susan and Dan her ring, which was greatly admired.

Audrey turned to Christopher and said, "We really need to phone my folks." The happy couple excused themselves from Susan and Dan for a few minutes, walking over to the Bay, and called Audrey's parents.

Christopher asked Mr. Johns, "Sir, may I marry your daughter?"

Mr. Johns replied, "Christopher, I've heard so much about you. Yes, you may. And it's "Dad," from here on out."

"Yes, sir, I mean "Dad.'"

Audrey giggled with her mother for a few minutes, agreeing that they needed to come to Florida to visit very soon. They would check their schedules for a brief trip and get back to her folks right away. How excited they all were. Christopher and Audrey went back to visit with Susan and Dan.

They chatted with Susan and Dan about their engagement and possible plans while they waited for the minutes to tick by until the family gathering. Sure enough, Josh and his family, Brooke and Michael, and Nancy and Patrick rolled in right on the dot of three.

Christopher couldn't wait to tell them, but Brooke caught him red-handed the minute she saw his face. "You're engaged, aren't you, Chris? Audrey?"

Audrey asked, "Now, Brooke, how could you tell?" She held out her left hand and showed one and all the ring Chris had presented her with.

Everyone shared hugs and their well-wishes. What a great way to spend the afternoon! There's nothing I would rather be doing. Christopher laughed for the sheer joy of life. Audrey looked at him sweetly and laughed, as well.

Everyone went inside the house and gathered in the family room. Susan grabbed some sodas from the kitchen, and Dan immediately proposed a toast.

Dan said, "To Chris and Audrey. May the Lord bless your family with many years of happiness as you strive to serve Him. Yours is truly a match made by God." The family raised their glasses and drank to the health, happiness, and long lives of Chris and Audrey. What a day of rejoicing!

Christopher said, "Thanks everyone. We really appreciate your well-wishes." He took a deep breath. He still couldn't believe this was happening. "I don't know how we can top our engagement for today," he breathed a sigh of joy, "but let's get back to the mystery that we're trying to figure out." Even in his great happiness, Christopher didn't want it to dominate the family's afternoon since they had planned to spend time with the family mystery before the announcement. He had spent enough of his life being self-centered and selfish.

Susan said, "Yes, if we can calm things down a bit, how about if Josh and Chris share their findings and then Nancy, Audrey, and I will get dinner on the table. We can grab a quick bite and then get to work trying to figure things out."

Joshua got out his laptop and put it on the kitchen island where everyone could see it. He pulled up the google map aerial view of the house he'd found after Chris verified the address and basic landmarks that Aunt Candace had confirmed with him. Joshua said, "Okay, here's the street they lived on. You can see that the road comes up almost all the way to the front porch. This house was built right on the street, so it's a good thing the street wasn't a busy one. The driveway is on the right side of the house, but it's not a very long one, given the placement of the house on the land. You can see the trees are pretty close, as well."

Christopher broke in, "Yes, Aunt Candace looked at the map and said that some of the trees had been cut down and smaller ones planted in their places. I guess the old ones rotted or something. But she told me that the map was pretty accurate, except that the white fence had been taken out."

Brooke asked, "Chris, did Aunt Candace say where the fence was in relationship to the yard?"

Christopher answered, "Yes, she did. She said it went out about five feet from the side of the house here." He pointed to a place about halfway back on the right hand side of the house as you faced it. "And then it went completely around back." He traced it with his finger. "Until it came back to about the same spot as it was on the right, but on the left hand side of the house as you faced it."

Susan asked, "Where was the gate that they fiddled with so much?"

Christopher told the family, "Aunt Candace said that there were three gates, one on each side of the house and one at the back, in the middle. They usually avoided the ones at the sides of the house because they just ran around it when they were already outside, but the one nearest the creek was the one whose latch was swollen most of the time." He looked around. "The side gates were just there so that someone inside the fence could get access to the front yard without having to go to the back of the property and then walk around. Mr. Prescott was one for saving steps as much as he could. The fence doesn't go all the way to the back of the property. It just went back about halfway through the yard and then stopped."

Brooke said, "Josh, I can't see the creek at all. There're too many trees."

Joshua replied, "Let me back out of the screen shot a little." He ran his fingers along the screen, pointing where the creek was. "The trees are really grown up, but you can see where the creek enters the property on the right side. See there? And it exits the property on the left hand side. Can you see it?"

"Oh, yeah. There it is. Thanks." Brooke nodded.

Nancy shivered, "I can see why everyone says it was so dark that night. It's really overgrown. That'd be really spooky."

Susan agreed, "Especially for a young boy like Kurt, who had a vivid imagination and anger issues."

Brooke added, "I can't imagine living in that eerie old place. I mean, I realize that it's a lot older now than when Dad was there, but it's really kinda creepy, don't you think?"

Josh said, "It's an old wooden house. I did a little bit of a property search on the history of the house. It's about a hundred years old."

"So the Prescotts weren't the original owners, then?" Patrick asked.

Josh answered, "Oh, no. It was passed through the Henderson family before the Prescotts. The Hendersons were a family of four girls and two boys. Their parents died under, let's say, unusual circumstances. The house passed from them to their children to their grandchildren by one of the boys, and then it was sold to William and Mary Prescott. Here's a newspaper picture of them." The photo showed a large woman in long skirts and a much smaller man in typical turn-of-the-century clothing. They were surrounded by their unsmiling children.

Susan asked, "What kind of 'unusual circumstances,' Josh?"

Joshua said, "They drowned in the creek. According to the newspaper reports, she fell in and he apparently died trying to save her. The kids were older and had already moved out, but one of the boys was local and came over for a visit. He heard the shouts of his father. The mother was mentally ill and quite strong. She was a big woman and she pulled her husband under when she fell into the creek. He probably couldn't get her out because of the weight of the water in her skirts. She had floor-length skirts and petticoats on. The boy couldn't save either one of his parents."

Nancy asked, "So, do you think Mrs. Henderson was demented?"

Joshua answered, "Yes, but they didn't call it that back then. Everybody they interviewed for the newspaper accounts said she was 'off her rocker' or something along those lines."

Nancy said, "They didn't understand the medical condition back then, so 'off her rocker' was one of the nicer things that they called demented patients. Too bad she took her hubby with her when she died." Nancy looked more closely at the computer screen's picture of Mrs. Henderson. "Patients can be very strong, and her picture shows she was quite large by the time she passed."

Susan shared, "It's my understanding that demented patients lose their ability to realize when they're in danger. Maybe she didn't know what she was doing when she went out into the creek."

Nancy answered, "Yes, that's right, Susan. She might have been completely unaware that she and her husband were drowning. It's very sad. It's good that the children were grown."

Christopher added, "This is a creek with a dark past, that's for sure." The thought of three people dying there gave him the willies. He glanced at Audrey, whose expression indicated that she agreed. He gave her a quick hug. He could tell by the looks the others had on their faces that 'creepy old creek' was the general consensus.

Susan said, "Okay, no more crime solving before dinner. Let's eat and then we'll try to sort this whole thing out with Brooke once and for all."

***

Brooke loved this kind of thing. She was glad Michael supported her in her endeavors to solve the mystery of her family. They gathered back in the family room and took seats on the couches. "Okay, everyone, let's get started. Dan, will you do the honors with the whiteboard and marker?"

Dan said, "Sure, Brooke." He looked at the others. "Feel free to jump up and add whatever you want while we're talking."

Brooke said, "Thanks, Dan. Okay, so we know the layout of the land, so to speak. Anyone have any thoughts on this, overall?"

Susan said, "Well, we know Mary didn't kill herself, so she's innocent."

Dan laughed and noted on the white board that Mary was not a suspect.

Brooke said, "Mom, you're right about that! Signs point to her being murdered, not being a suicide. So, what else do we have here?"

Joshua said, "We know that Maggie was nearby. But she was behind a tree." He got up and drew one on the whiteboard. "Maybe here, do you think?" The consensus was that the tree was probably one of the trees located on the right hand side of the house as one faced it, so that she would have had a view of the backyard and the creek where the body was found.

Amanda said, "But we have to remember that Maggie lies, so she might have been somewhere else."

Christopher said, "Good point. We don't know if Johnny was there or not, so I guess we should just put a big question mark by his name." Dan wrote the name and question mark as Chris had instructed. "He's a crook and he might very well have been there, but I guess we'll never know."

Michael asked, "What about Peter? He was in the house but came out at some point in time."

Brooke answered, "Yes, Dan why don't you put Peter up by the front of the house with a line showing him walking around the fence and into the backyard? I think that would work."

Dan said, "Sure, Brooke. This reminds me of a football scrimmage or something." He drew the line, and added Peter's name to it. "We need to keep these folks straight. I think naming the lines with the kids' names might help." Everyone agreed it was the thing to do.

Susan asked, "What about Candace? She says she was talking to her father and then came out the back of the house."

Dan drew a straight line from the back door to the creek, with Candace's name on it. "What about Kurt?"

Susan suggested that he draw a line showing Kurt climbing down the tree next to the porch roof, after climbing out the window. Dan did so.

Nancy said, "What about William Prescott, Senior? We know he was inside, but we aren't totally sure exactly when he came outside."

Dan drew a William Prescott line from the back door to the creek, but added the word "time" and a question mark. "I think that does it."

Patrick said, "Yep, I think we have all of the main players there. Oh, wait a second. What about William Junior? I think we forgot about him."

The group groaned. Brooke asked, "What do we do about Will? He was there that night, but it seems that he never got further than the front door." They agreed to keep him in a circle at the front of the house.

Susan asked, "What about Mr. Peterson? He could have done it- we know he was with her." Dan added Mr. Peterson's name, drawing the man's line from the left hand side of the house as one faced it.

Then Dan asked, "What if he came in on the right and passed Maggie?" Everyone agreed that it was a possibility, so Dan drew two lines for Mr. Peterson.

Brooke said, "Okay, now let's walk through this. In one scenario, we could have Mary coming down to the creek where she has a brief chat and then a fight which ends in Mary's being thrown into the creek, where she drowns. Mr. Peterson leaves as Peter and Kurt join her, followed by Candace. Mr. Prescott comes barreling down to the creek after throwing Will out of the house. Maggie watches from behind her tree."

Amanda said, "Okay, so that's scenario one, where Mr. Peterson kills her. What about another scenario where Kurt kills her?" She turned to Susan. "Sorry, Mom." Then, "Mr. Peterson leaves with Mary's life still intact. Oh, you know, Mr. Peterson might have passed within a few feet of Maggie. We need to think about that in a minute. Kurt comes running, knocks his mother into the creek, and holds her head down as he yells about her losing Ella. Peter arrives, followed by Candace, who tries to get her mother's head out of the water. Mr. Prescott comes running, having thrown Will out of the house by the front door."

Patrick said, "You know, Mr. Peterson might have come within a foot of Maggie. I wonder if Mr. Peterson saw her and realized there was a witness to his visit. It must have bothered him if he did notice, knowing that it was described in the headlines the next morning."

Nancy said, "Mr. Peterson never made contact with the family again, from what you all've said. I wonder if that's why he waited to tell Ella about her real life. He was afraid of getting arrested for Mary's murder."

Brooke said, "Great ideas, you guys. That's something we need to consider."

Susan asked, "What about Mr. Prescott Senior? Mr. Prescott might have snuck down to the creek behind his wife and killed her after Mr. Peterson left. He set things up to frame Kurt, returning to the scene of his crime at the very end."

Dan said, "That's very possible, honey."

Nancy said, "We realized how close Mr. Peterson could have been to Maggie in that first scenario, but how could she have not mentioned it in her letters unless she killed her mother somehow?"

Josh said, "I wonder if she did kill her mother. But how could she have gotten into the creek to do that without getting her habit wet?"

Christopher said, "I heard once that nuns wear shorts

under their habits in the summer time. It would have still been warm out in September in Maryland, so maybe she took off her habit and wore her shorts down to the creek."

Brooke asked her brother, "Chris, are you serious? Shorts? On a nun?"

Christopher answered, "Yes, shorts. And keep in mind that she hadn't made her final vows yet. She was an immoral woman before she became a nun, so she probably wouldn't have been too concerned about showing her legs, not that there was anyone to show them to that hadn't already seen them. They were all family, remember."

Susan said, "Okay, so how would Maggie have done it? We didn't consider that situation."

Amanda said, "She watched Mr. Peterson leave, having overheard enough of their conversation to realize her mother was a bad person or something. He leaves, she drops the habit, and runs down to the creek to her mother. She knocks her mother into the creek, knowing that no one knows she's there. She holds her head under water, and then props her up to look like she's still alive, when she's certain her mother is dead."

Brooke said, "Thanks Amanda. So I guess that's one vote for Maggie to be the killer. Who's next?"

Dan said, "How about Will? Could he have done it?"

Christopher answered, "We don't have any proof that he got closer to the creek than the front door. I think that would be a bit of a stretch to blame him."

Everyone pretty much agreed that Will probably didn't do it. He was called out by his father for being a Christian, and he hadn't been around for long enough to know the family dynamics since Ella disappeared.

Susan added, "He may have gone there to comfort the family. He might have read about it in the paper and wanted to help. He'd left home six years before Ella was born, so he never knew her but, if he lived in Philly, he might have read about her disappearance in the newspaper or heard about it on television."

Dan updated the white board, writing that Maggie was a suspect, but Will was not. "What about Johnny?" Dan asked.

Patrick asked, "Do we have anything that says he was in the area? He's the one sibling that no one has said was there, but he is the one who was, and still is, a crook."

They all thought about it, but no one was aware of anyone saying Johnny was around. Dan put a question mark by his name. They moved on to Peter.

Brooke said, "Peter was upstairs in his room. No one was with him, from what we can tell. Candy says that she checked on Kurt and straightened his room before she headed downstairs to help her mother, but Peter was older and she didn't check on him."

Michael argued, "He could've come out of his room earlier than we thought, gone and done the deed, and then come into his room through the front of the house, returning to the creek after he saw Kurt go outside."

Susan shared, "That does sound plausible, Michael, and Candy did say he was out of breath." She turned to Brooke, "Put a 'maybe' on his name."

Brooke said, "Okay, this is gonna be unpopular. Did Candy do it?" Her question was greeted with groans. "Oh, I sure hope not." "Please tell me no." "Anybody but her."

Dan said, "She was with Kurt, then with her Dad, then with her mother. She says her mother was dead before she got there, and Maggie says that Candy was the only person who tried to save her mother. I vote 'no' for Aunt Candace."

The general consensus was that Candy had not done it, so Dan put a big "no" next to her name. Everyone breathed a sigh of relief. Dan asked, "Kurt?' Again with the groans.

Brooke said, "As much as he wanted our Mom dead later in life, was he strong enough to have held his mother's head under water? More importantly, would a ten-year-old kid back in those days even be thinking about murder?"

Joshua answered, "It wouldn't have been the normal way

a kid thinks, but he was very angry at his mother. Still in all, I think there were too many adults around who could've done it, so it would be a stretch to blame him. What do you all think?"

Susan said, "I just don't think he did it. I know, I know, he tried to kill me, but I believe that his father or Mr. Peterson did the deed. His father, from what he has written, spent a lot of time trying to convince Kurt that he was responsible."

Michael asked, "Yeah, what about Mr. Peterson? He refused to return Ella, and we know he thought very little of the Prescotts. Could he have killed her? Whether it was an accident or not, do you think he did it?"

Audrey said, "I think that's a real possibility, if Mr. Prescott wasn't on the scene."

Chris asked, "Why is that honey?"

Audrey answered, "I don't think Mr. Prescott would've let him leave if he'd just killed Mrs. Prescott. The evidence would have fallen on him. It's a long shot, but maybe Mr. Peterson knocked her down, whether by accident or on purpose, and she drowned."

Susan said, "I'm still leaning towards Mr. Prescott as being the guilty party. Maybe it's because he was such a mean drunk, I don't know, but look at his relationship with Kurt afterwards."

Dan said, "Yes, Susan, that in itself is enough to convince me that Mr. Prescott did it. Look at all the guilt he heaped on Kurt for his entire childhood. I think Mr. Prescott is the guilty one."

Brooke agreed, "And there's the laundry done in the late evening by a man who cared nothing for doing laundry. I vote that Mr. Prescott did it, as well."

The general consensus was that Mr. Prescott had done the deed and then covered up the fact, blaming an innocent boy with anger issues for an act he had committed himself. They still weren't completely sure, since Maggie the Lying Nun and

Johnny the Family Crook were still on the hot seat of guilt.

Brooke said, "I guess we'll never know for sure."

On that note, the meeting moved on to happier things, like planning for Chris and Audrey's wedding.

Chapter 43

William Charles Prescott Senior knew he was a man on his way out, as he sat by the creek behind his white house. He was currently between wives that May day in 1976, though he was not convinced that there would ever be a third Mrs. Prescott. Marriage was getting tiring. Instead, he had this pain-in-the-butt caregiver who came over every weekday to do annoying things to him. The good news was that she was a good cook and made him fresh dinners, leaving enough behind for lunch the next day and to cover the weekend.

William wasn't hungry that much, though. His belly was swollen all the time and he had trouble getting around. His children hadn't visited him in years. He didn't know if they were alive or dead. He didn't really care, all things considered. When the kids moved out, they moved completely out, except for Kurt, that is. At least the kid was still around, more or less.

The hired woman had brought in a wheelchair, but that just ticked him off. Who did she think she was, making him feel like a blasted invalid? He could get around just fine, most of the time. Well, it was helpful sometimes, like when he wanted to go down to the creek. He had to admit that. But he would never tell her. That woman was a real bother.

The creek was one of his only joys in life. Kurt had come back from Viet Nam safely, but he wasn't home much. Out cruising, picking up girls was William's guess. More power to the kid. Don't commit to anybody and enjoy whatever you can get from a woman. Kurt was the only one of his kids who stuck around longer than necessary. With Kurt's mother long since dead and his second wife history thanks to the divorce court, Kurt was all he had left. Kurt and this bothersome helper woman, that is. He was paying her good money, for what?

Well, she could jolly well take him to the creek if he wanted to go, when he wanted to go there. And he had wanted to go out there that afternoon. So here he was. The woman complained that pushing his two hundred twenty-pound body was hard on her back, but that's why she made the big bucks. Earn your keep, woman.

When they got to the creek, it was so peaceful. The helper woman had sat down on his left. She'd brought a stool to the creek a few days earlier when he wanted to come here and she hadn't bothered to take it back into the house. Lazy woman! You gotta take furniture in or it'll get moldy. Didn't she realize that? He gave her his best scowl, but she only smiled at him, infuriating woman that she was. Bother!

Ah, the peace and quiet. The trees surrounding the water were mature now, not scrawny like when he planted them through the years. There were rocks even in the middle of the creek, with water flowing swiftly over them. That's what killed his Mary: the fast water flow and the sharp rocks on the shoreline. He reminisced that she had slipped on the grass because had been raining a lot that night, and hit her head on the rocks. The kids were nearby, but they were so busy fighting that they didn't notice their mother's face was in the water until it was too late.

He came running and tried to save her, but all he succeeded in doing was dislocating her arm when he yanked her up out of the water. It wasn't the first time he'd done that dislocation thing. Women like her were just too scrawny to hold together well. He'd jerked her arm back in the socket and put her back in the creek. He warned the kids not to say anything when the police came or they'd all be in big trouble. He couldn't have talked his way out of that one.

But back to the peacefulness, the breeze on his worn face. Yes, he could sit out here all day and not get tired of it. He seemed a little sleepy this afternoon. He felt like all he did was sleep these days, come to think of it. That helper woman wasn't going to earn her pay if he kept dozing off. Boy, this was irksome. Stay awake, William! Make her miserable so she has to work for her money. She's too expensive, anyway. Waste of his hard-earned money.

So William sat there, sleeping in the sunlight. He jerked awake, certain that someone was watching him. You know that feeling you get when someone is present when he or she wasn't there a minute ago? That's exactly how he felt. And rightfully so. There was a guy sitting over on the biggest rock in the middle of the creek. How'd he get there? The creek wasn't very wide, maybe ten, twelve feet at its widest part, and this fellow was sitting right in the middle, pretty as you please. The man looked very happy with himself.

William peered at the fellow. The man wasn't wet. But that was impossible. He would have had to wade or swim out to where he was. The creek ran about three to five feet deep in places. But his clothes looked completely dry. No way, what with the swift current and high tide. William rubbed the sleep from his eyes. Come on, William, wake up. Nope, the dry guy was still there.

"Hey there, what are you doing on my property?" he asked the man. The nerve of some people, trespassing and all. The guy looked like a Pat Boone wannabe, with all of his white clothes and neat appearance. Come on, man! Shoes in the middle of the creek? White ones at that. The man looked like a holier-than-thou type, judging from the pretty little smile on the fella's face. "What do you want?"

"Hi, William. I'm Seth. How're you doing today?"

Okay, guy. You know my name, you're sitting in the middle of my creek in my backyard, and you want to know how I'm doing? I'm gonna knock that smile off your face, pronto. "Get off my land, buster."

"Technically, I'm not on land right now, William." The white-attired guy smiled at him again. Annoying.

William glanced over to the left at his caregiver, to see if she would take him back inside, but she seemed to be moving in slow motion. Then she froze. Okay, this is really weird. "What's going on here?"

"We need to chat, William. This seemed like a pleasant

place to talk, so I waited until Mrs. Jones brought you out for the afternoon."

"Mrs. Who?" William was getting angrier by the moment. This whitey-tighty guy had moved from bothersome to downright exasperating.

"Mrs. Jones, your caregiver." Whitey looked over in her direction.

"Oh. Her. I didn't know her name. The agency sent her." He grumbled under his breath, why should I take the time to learn her name? She won't last a week; the others didn't.

"She's a hard worker who cares for you all day and then goes home to take care of her elderly father and sickly husband in the evenings. She works about sixteen hour days, every day. You're only a small part of her world, and not a very pleasant one, at that."

William hooted at the news. "So what're you here for?" Then, "What did you say your name was?"

"I'm Seth, William. I'm here to talk with you for a while." Seth got up and started to walk towards him, then apparently decided against walking and took a huge leap that brought him to the shore.

"Hey, how'd you do that? That's a good five or six feet distance and you didn't have a running start."

"Let's just say that I'm good at long jumps."

Seth came nearer and pulled up a chair on the right hand side of the wheelchair. William was sure that chair wasn't there a minute ago. William didn't have any lawn furniture this close to the creek, except for that stool his caregiver brought out and left. She was sitting on it this very minute. Where'd that chair come from? It didn't look like anything he had around the property. It was pure white. Oh, no, not more white. Maybe the guy brought it with him. Great. Looks like he means to stay a while. Gotta get rid of him, fast.

"Hope you don't mind my making myself at home. So, William, we need to talk about some things. Your life would be a good place to start." Seth relaxed into the chair; he was a tall man with blond hair and green eyes.

"What about it?" William begrudged the man, giving Seth his attention.

"You've had an interesting past. How about if you tell me about it?" Seth asked.

As long as the caregiver was off the job, William probably didn't have any choice. He was a captive audience, as they say. He reached over to shake her, but there was no response.

"That won't work, William. She isn't aware of us right now."

William looked at Seth. "I was born. I grew up. I got a job that was okay, but my bosses were all idiots. I got married to Mary Taylor. I had seven kids, six of whom left home, one way or the other. My wife died somewhere in the middle of all that leaving home. I got married again. She left me. I don't see any of my kids any more except for Kurt, who lives with me off and on. The end."

"Well, that's certainly a condensed version of a life. You're in the process of dying from cirrhosis of the liver, so I imagine there was a lot of drinking going on there."

"Hey, don't count me out yet. I've come back from illness before. It's only a matter of time before I beat this, too." William straightened up. Blasted chair! It was hard to look authoritative when he was sitting in a wheelchair.

"I'm sorry, William, not this time." Seth picked up a small stone and threw it into the creek. Plop!

"What? What makes you so sure of that?" William shifted in the chair, starting to sweat profusely on his forehead. The nerve of some people, telling him what was ahead. How could this clown possibly know?

"Let's just say I'm good at guessing outcomes. Your general condition right now is a dead giveaway, no pun intended." Another stone hit the water. Seth considered William's appearance as he spoke. "William, I want to talk to you about where you are, spiritually speaking."

"Oh, I get it. You're one of those door-to-door religious

nuts. Well, let me tell you right now that I've never had any interest in what you people are selling. You might as well give up."

"William, I'm not selling anything. I'm giving something away."

"Oh, yeah? What's that, altar boy?" William's sneer was one that always sent his kids running for the hills when he used it on them. No effect, this time around.

Seth appeared completely unbothered. "New life in Jesus Christ."

William would've gotten up and slugged the guy, if he'd had the strength. What nerve that man had. Coming onto his property, making his caregiver go frozen like a mannequin, and then spouting off about some religious stuff.

"Like I said, Seth, I'm not interested in anything you're trying to push off on me." William gestured with his hand for the man to go away.

"Oh, Seth, looks like you have a bit of a hard sell here!" Another man stood nearby.

William jumped. He hadn't noticed till then, but another man had come up right alongside of him from behind and to the right while he was talking to Seth. William was clumsy as he turned in his wheelchair and looked the man over. Dark clothes, greasy hair, smelly, ugly as sin. Whew! That guy 'had been beaten with the ugly stick,' as his Mary used to say.

"And who might you be?" William had never seen such an odd person before, but he wanted to get rid of him, for sure. "Step over in front of me so I can see you better."

"Devin. Pleased to make your acquaintance." The man moved directly in front of him and made a bit of a bow.

William felt immediately repulsed by the man. He shivered at the sight of the guy. He turned to his first visitor, angry at being disturbed. "Seth, do you know this fella?"

"Yes. I guess you'd say that Devin and I have been working opposite sides of the same street for a very long time."

Seth nodded at the new companion. "Devin."

Devin nodded back, "Seth."

"Get him off my property, will you? I don't like the looks of him." William shifted in his chair. He couldn't get far enough fast enough from this human turd. Or inhuman, more like it.

"I don't blame you for wanting him gone, William. Unfortunately, you have a choice to make, and I can't make it for you." Seth was sitting up straight in the chair he had been comfortably lounging in a moment ago.

Devin said, "Oh, no, not that Jesus stuff, Seth. You know how I hate to hear you trying to convince the unconvinceable that God loves them, Jesus died for them, and all that. You might as well give up now. William's been on my side for most of his life, even to the point of having s secret wife and four more kids that nobody ever knew about, till now."

William sputtered, "What the heck? How did you know?"

"About Billie June? Oh, I know. Whose idea do you think that was?" Devin turned to Seth. "He's not coming over with you. He's my boy." Devin patted William on the shoulder. Then he leaned closer to him and said, "He'll give up eventually, William. You're all mine, and have been for years. Decades, even."

William swallowed hard. Nobody ever knew about Billie June, he was sure, but this guy seemed to know. He wanted this guy gone. Get him away from me! William shuddered. Just then, Devin smiled at him. Oh, yuck. His teeth were yellowed and some of his front teeth were missing. Devin's breath reminded him of the time his septic tank backed up into the bathtub. How disgusting. Whatever Devin was selling, William definitely didn't want any of it. He looked over at Mr. Whitey Tighty. "Okay, Seth, whatcha got?"

Seth smiled and started telling him about Jesus' sacrifice and how God loved him and always had. The more Seth talked, the madder Devin got, but too bad. William knew he didn't want to have anything to do with Devin, so Seth seemed like a good alternative. Funny thing, the longer Seth talked, the more peaceful William felt. He didn't recall ever having such a warm feeling. Kindness and love flowed through him. Even though he was weak, he felt stronger than he had ever felt in his entire life.

William shook himself, trying to free his mind of the thoughts he was having. Unconditional love sounded like the theme song here. He wasn't any holy roller Christian-type. It had never been "his thing," as his kids used to say. He'd hooted at Mary when their daughter Maggie had tried to reach her with this same kind of talk. He'd thrown Mary's Bible in the fireplace that night so many years ago. It was probably the only comfort she had in her life and he destroyed it. For the first time, he felt badly about having done that.

His son Will had come back safely from Viet Nam and, when Will tried to tell him about Jesus, William had told the boy to "get your dirty Christian butt out of my house." Not exactly a ringing endorsement for William's support of the Christian faith. He was ashamed. His head felt too heavy for his neck and he drooped in the chair. What would God want with a guy like him?

Seth looked at him with love and said, "William, what will you chose? New life in Christ or a future with Devin?"

"I'm not worthy of Christ, Seth. I'm not proud of how I mistreated Christians . . ." William hesitated. "How I've treated everyone, actually. I've been a bad person."

Devin spoke quickly, moving more closely to the wheelchair, "Right on, William, You aren't worthy. They aren't going to let you into heaven with a deathbed confession, so you might as well not even try."

"Stifle yourself, Devin." Seth looked a bit put out, but acted as if he was used to Devin's comments.

"No, no, I won't be silent." Devin looked deeply into William's eyes. "They're all lies, William. You know you can't qualify for heaven, not at this late date. You're a bad boy, William. You haven't been good a day of your life, except maybe when you were a little kid. That's a lot of water under the bridge. You can't win. You're a sinner. You're a drunk. God doesn't love you. You mistreated your wives and your children hate you. Give up. You are a killer and an adulterer. You can't go to heaven, you can't!" Devin's voice reached a fevered pitch.

William looked over at Seth, glad to turn away from Devin. "Seth, I'm sorry for what I've done. If God can forgive me, then I want Him to."

"A very wise choice, William. Let's pray." Seth took his hand. "Repeat after me, William. Dear Father in heaven, please forgive my sins. I pray that you will come into my heart and mind and life and save me. I believe that Jesus Christ is Lord and want Him to be my Savior. In Jesus' name. Amen." Devin responded by screeching and crumbling in on himself.

William prayed earnestly and added in several more sentences, apologizing for everything he had ever done. He confessed before God what had happened the night his Mary had died. "Lord, I didn't mean to do it. The liquor made me mad. Her trust in the man who had our Ella made me livid. I accused her of many things that I knew she'd never done. Saying she had slept with other men, when I was the guilty one who broke our marriage vows with Billie June and other women, too. I was the one who held Mary's head under the water that night, set her up to look like she was still alive, and then snuck back inside and changed my clothes so no one would know. I framed my children, Kurt especially, for what I had done. I screamed at them until they were too scared to tell the police the truth. I kept them up half the night yelling and changing things around so much until they weren't sure what had happened. I was threatened by Candy's knowledge of the truth and frightened her away by telling her she had to sleep in my bed. God, I never planned to do that, I just needed her to move away and stay away so I could change Kurt's memories of that night permanently, without her interference. I'm an evil man. Lord, please forgive me." William broke into sobs that shook his body so much he almost fell out of his wheelchair. He caught himself as he started to tip over.

William felt a hand on his shoulder. He opened his eyes. Devin was gone, vanished. William saw a light streaming down from the heavens, casting a brilliant light on the creek. Seth looked at him.

"Stand up, William."

William got up easily and realized that all his pain, all his discomfort had vanished. "What in the world?" He had never felt so light, so happy, so loved.

"You're a child of God now, William. Come on, there's someone you need to meet."

"Who?" William stood to his full height.

"Jesus. Your time really was running out, but you made a wise decision in the end." Seth smiled. "Great choice, William."

"But what about Mrs. Jones?" William turned to look at his caregiver.

"We'll leave and she'll come back to herself. She'll call the police, having discovered that you passed quietly while dozing. Time has been standing still for her, so what seemed like a long time to you was actually only a few seconds to her. She blinked, basically, and you died."

"I'm dead then?" William asked.

"You are raised to new life in Christ. You're more alive than you ever were on earth."

"Will Mrs. Jones be okay?" William was very concerned about someone, for the first time in his life. It was a new, unique emotion. It felt wonderful, somehow. Cleansing.

"Yes. She's a devout Christian. You'll one day see her again in heaven. She's had a hard life, but her rewards will be great." Seth told him.

"I'm sorry I was so mean to her. I wish I could apologize." William looked at Seth.

"When she sees the look on your dead face, she'll know that you're a changed man and it will comfort her. She's been praying for you the whole time she's been with you. All five days of it." Seth smiled.

"She has? Why?" William was flummoxed.

"She prays for everyone she works with. Many people have come to faith as a result of her prayers. She's a good and faithful servant. And you're living proof . . . or maybe I should say, dying proof. Why do you think I'm here? By her invitation." Seth held out his hand to William.

"I wish I could thank her," William told him.

"You will, one day. Come on, William, let's go look at your new home."

William took Seth's hand and the two men walked towards the creek, and then seemed to rise up on the light beams that came from the heavens. Forgiven and forever at home with God.

The Beginning

Sequel to From the Valley to the Mountaintop
On the Winds of Change

Thanh William Prescott was a man on borrowed time. The Vietnamese boat child had immigrated to Harris County, Texas with his mother and two sisters, shortly before their village in Vietnam was destroyed. When he, his sisters, and his mother finally made it to America, they learned that their father and their mother's husband had remarried and was living in Pennsylvania. Rather than upset the proverbial apple cart by intruding on William Prescott Jr.'s established life, his mother decided to raise her family in Texas, far away from her husband. But now there was a problem: Thanh had developed hereditary hemochromatosis and needed a partial or full liver transplant. His mother was too old to donate, and his sisters were already showing signs of the disease themselves. Thanh learned via the Internet that William Jr. was long-since dead and buried, but what about potential donors from the rest of William's extended family? They were his only hope.

www.ingramcontent.com/pod-product-compliance
Lightning Source LLC
Chambersburg PA
CBHW072338020726

47506CB00004B/920